COLD RIVER

To Elizabeth Raper,
brave and beautiful daughter of one of my
former students at Concrete High

Walnut Springs Press, LLC
110 South 800 West
Brigham City, Utah 84302
http://walnutspringspress.blogspot.com

Text copyright © 2011 by Liz Adair
Coverdesign copyright © 2011 by Walnut Springs Press
Interior design copyright © 2011 by Walnut Springs Press

ISBN: 978-1-59992-803-6

This is a work of fiction. The characters, names, incidents, and dialogue are products of the author's imagination and are not to be construed as real, and any resemblance to real people and events is not intentional.

COLD RIVER

Liz Adair

WALNUT SPRINGS PRESS

ACKNOWLEDGEMENTS

This book is a valentine to the town of Concrete, Washington. I taught school there over three decades ago for just a year, and I've based the town of Limestone on wispy memory fragments—tenuous stuff. That's why I write fiction. I don't have to get it right.

A second valentine goes to the school system in Chilliwack, B.C. They have a marvelous tradition of teaching jazz in the schools. My husband, Derrill, and I always look for the Big Bang Jazz Band when we go to jazz festivals—they're all Chilliwack High School alumni, and they're terrific musicians. In addition, the school has a huge steel band that charms audiences wherever it performs.

Thanks to Bill John, a member of the Lummi Nation, who is dedicated to reviving the Lummi language among his people. He gave me the words *hiesel* and *stallo,* which I have used as names in this book.

And thanks to Katy Melom, my hairdresser. Her family came to Sedro Woolley from North Carolina in 1940, and she's the one that gave me the phrase, "I love you like a mule a-kickin'."

A big thank you goes to beta readers, Melisse Lee, Mark Chatt, Andy Gifford, and my daughter and son-in-law, Ruth and Rich Lavine. Thanks to my critique group, Terry Deighton, Ann Acton, Tanya Mills, and Christine Thackeray, for great feedback. I've learned so much about the craft from those ladies.

Thanks to Ron Davis for permission for my fictional character, Mandy, to use the Davis Symbol Mastery that he describes in his real book, *The Gift of Dyslexia.*

And to Walnut Springs Press, thank you for the warm reception.

1

Mandy Steenburg gripped the steering wheel tighter as a blast of March wind buffeted her tiny Miata. The log truck up ahead turned off the highway, giving her the first glimpse of the town that was to be her new home. Her heart sank, and she felt as bleak as the weather.

Limestone, Washington, squatted a block off the highway, and she craned her neck as she drove by. In the waning light of a rainy afternoon, she got an impression of tired buildings, vacant streets, no stoplights, and huge fir trees marching en masse down the mountainside to invade the town.

Mandy stayed on the highway as she had been instructed. As she crossed a short bridge, she started looking for Shingle Mill Road. Slowing, she squinted at the first sign she came to. "Harvey's Still Road." Nope. *Harvey's Still Road? What kind of name is that?* Tarheel Road. Nope. Finally, there it was—Shingle Mill Road.

She turned right and passed a large building with rusty, corrugated-metal siding and a faded sign that said "Anderson's Cedar Shakes." Driving down the road, Mandy began to wonder if she had written down the directions correctly. There were no houses or businesses, and the forest grew right up to the road on both sides. Finally she came to a clearing, and after the oppressive tunnel of green, it was like the world opened up. Her eyes grew wide, and she hit the brakes. There before her on a small, landscaped rise stood an imposing house that looked like something out of a fairy tale.

Painted a pale yellow, with gingerbread on gables and porch, the large house had a circular room at one corner that went up both stories and ended with a shingled cupola. Shiny-leaved shrubbery accented the manicured grounds, but it was the flowers that made it seem as if the house was sitting in a pool of sunshine. Daffodils, hundreds of them, bent in the breeze and brightened the end of Mandy's very trying day.

A huge wooden sign with painted letters declared that she had reached the end of her journey: District Offices, North Cascade School District. Heartened, she turned into the parking lot and spied a space marked "Reserved for Superintendent." She hesitated only a moment before pulling into it, unable to resist a small smile.

When she opened the car door, a gust almost tore it from her hand. Leaning into the horizontal raindrops, she made her way down the walk and up the porch stairs. Saying "Dr. Steenburg" under her breath for practice, she pushed open the door and stepped into the grand entryway. On her left, a beautifully crafted wooden staircase swept up to a mezzanine that circled around three sides, leaving the entry open to the ornate second-story ceiling.

A mirror hung on the wall just inside the door. Mandy glanced at it and took a moment to run her fingers though her short, dark, springy curls to undo some of the wind damage. After brushing the moisture off her navy suit, she surveyed her reflection, aware she was about to make a first impression. Certainly she had nice eyes, brown and fringed with thick lashes. Her straight nose and high cheekbones were fine, too, but not for the first time, she wished she were taller.

A semicircular reception desk backed up to the staircase, but there was no receptionist, and no bell to summon one. Wondering if she should call out, Mandy looked around and spied four grim-faced people framed by the window in the door leading to the corner room. Four pairs of hostile eyes stared at her through the glass.

Mandy blinked. This certainly wasn't the welcome she had envisioned. She raised her brows in inquiry as she studied the visages. The one in front belonged to a plump, gray-haired, grandmotherly looking lady. On the right stood a younger woman, tall and horse-faced, with stringy hair. To Grandma's left was a smallish man, balding on top, with a thin pencil moustache making a dirty mark above his upper lip. Behind them all, head and shoulders above even the tall woman, was a dark-haired, square-jawed man with piercing blue eyes and a strange look on his face. One brow was lowered, and one corner of his mouth was compressed, but the other side of his face was expressionless. It made an otherwise handsome face odd-looking, almost menacing.

The tall man said something to the others. Grandma turned the doorknob, and they stepped out in single file. Silently, they walked to stand in a group in front of Mandy.

After waiting for one of the four to speak, Mandy finally said, "I'm the new superintendent. I spoke to Mrs. Berman?" She looked questioningly from one of the women to the other.

"I'm Mrs. Berman," the older lady said.

Mandy forced a smile. "Your directions were very good. Thank you very much."

Mrs. Berman didn't reply until the tall man placed his hand on her shoulder. "You're welcome," she said crisply. Her eyes didn't offer any welcome at all.

The tall man stepped forward. "I'm Grange Timberlain, assistant superintendent." Half of his face formed a wooden smile, but the other half was vacant of expression. He held out his hand, almost as an afterthought, it seemed, and Mandy, determined to be civil in the face of such rudeness, shook it briefly.

Grange Timberlain continued, "This is Midge Cooley. She's in charge of records, and this is our accountant, Elmo Smith. We call him Mo."

Neither Midge nor Mo offered to shake hands. Mandy nodded to each, and an uncomfortable silence ensued.

Grange looked at his watch. "Shall I show you your office? It's too late in the day to take care of any business, so we won't keep the staff any longer."

"I was delayed in Oregon. Car trouble."

"No problem," Grange said. "If you'll follow me . . ."

As Grange headed to the stairs, Mandy turned to the other three. "Glad to have met you," she said, but they had already turned away, and no one responded.

"Whew! What a reception," she muttered. As she followed Grange up to the second-floor landing, she had a good view of his blue flannel shirt, Levi's, and boots, and she wondered if he dressed that way every day.

He waited for her in the middle of the mezzanine. "Your office is the corner one." He pointed. "Mrs. Berman's is next to you, between your office and mine. Mo is across the way on the other side of the stairs. Midge is downstairs with records."

Grange winked at her. Then he walked to her office, opened the door, and stepped aside so she could enter.

Taken aback, Mandy hesitated a moment, watching with narrowed eyes for a follow-up to that obvious come-on. When there was none, she walked through the door and found herself in a pleasant, circular space. Even on this gray, blustery day, the room seemed suffused with light. Warm-grained wood trimmed the surrounding bank of windows, and a matching crown molding curved gracefully around the ceiling.

The expansive desk, though obviously old, had a high polish that made it a handsome piece of furniture. A bank of wooden filing cabinets stood along the one straight wall where the circle joined the house. "This is very nice," Mandy said. "I wasn't expecting anything quite so grand."

"This was the Anderson's home—you probably noticed Anderson's Shingle Mill when you turned off the highway. They were fairly well to do, but childless. When old Widow Anderson died, she left the house to the school district. This was Mr. Anderson's desk."

Mandy noticed that Grange talked out of one side of his mouth. *Like Harry the Horse in* Guys and Dolls, she thought.

"Edith—Mrs. Berman—has your keys laid out for you." Grange pointed to the key ring on the top of the desk.

"She has us all color coded," he went on. "The blue one lets you in the front door. Green one is your office. Red is for cupboards. Yellow opens filing cabinets." He looked around. "I guess that's all. Oh—the restroom is downstairs. There's a kitchen down there, too. Midge keeps the coffee pot going, and there's a fridge and microwave. Oscar, the IT guy, will be in tomorrow to set up your computer and passwords." Grange winked again.

"Thank you." Realizing suddenly that what she thought was a wink was simply his inability to close one eye, Mandy couldn't think of anything else to say. She looked away, afraid she might be staring at the frozen left side of his face.

"I guess that's all," he said again. "Look around. Settle in. Stay as long as you want tonight, and come as early as you want tomorrow."

"Thank you for your . . . uh . . . introduction. And for the keys. Do we consider this the changing of the guard?"

A rosy tinge crept up Grange's neck and settled on his cheeks. He looked first at his feet, then at the door, and finally at Mandy.

"Yes, the guard has been changed." He cleared his throat. "Edith usually locks the front door when she leaves, but if you'll check it on your way out, that would be great. Leave the lights on in the entryway."

He turned to go, but paused with his hand on the doorknob. "Um, I know your name is Amanda. Is that what you would like to be called?"

She picked up the keys and held them in one hand, remembering the cold reception downstairs, so different from the camaraderie she had left behind in Albuquerque, where everyone called her Mandy. Everyone except one special person who called her "chérie" when they were working late and alone.

All of a sudden, she felt her lip quiver. She dropped the keys on the desk, turned away for a moment, and willed the trembling to cease. Then she faced Grange, and with her chin up, she met his eyes squarely. "I'd prefer that you call me Dr. Steenburg. Good night, Mr. Timberlain."

Mandy stood for a moment looking around her office as snatches of conversation drifted up from downstairs. Humming to show she didn't care that she was left alone and ignored, she examined her desk.

A skillfully crafted computer station that matched the antique look of the desk sat at a right angle to it, and a burgundy leather chair swiveled between the two. Trying the chair, Mandy opened the pencil drawer and discovered an ample supply of mechanical pencils, pens, notepads and sticky notes. Exploring further, she found the top right-hand drawer held stationery with North Cascade School District letterhead. Her brows went up when she saw her name listed as superintendent of schools. Grange Timberlain's name was just below hers as assistant superintendent.

The middle right-hand drawer held a district phone list printed on crisp, yellow card stock, a dog-eared pamphlet that seemed to be a more complete district directory, and a slender North Cascades phone directory. Mandy glanced at the yellow phone card and saw that her name was again listed as superintendent. After noting that her extension number was 2292, she picked up the receiver. The dial tone was somehow reassuring.

She closed the middle drawer and opened the bottom one. It was full of hanging files, all empty. She swiveled around and eyed the filing cabinets along the wall. The vacant brass label holders gave no clue as to what the cabinets contained. She stood and went to the first and pulled out the top drawer. Just like the desk, this one was full of empty hanging files. So was the next. And the next. "Welcome to North Cascade, Dr. Steenburg," she said acidly, then opened and closed each of the next nine drawers. "I wonder what they're trying to hide."

Suddenly aware that her voice was loud in the stillness, she listened, but no more conversation drifted up from below. Just then the entry door slammed, and she heard footsteps outside. She moved to the window and saw Grange Timberlain descend the porch stairs. She continued to watch his tall figure as he walked to a pickup parked at the far corner of the lot. He had his collar turned up and the brim of his baseball cap pulled low against the rain. As he opened the door to climb in the truck, he looked up at her window. Mandy pulled away, wishing he hadn't caught her watching him.

She stayed at the window, though, until his taillights disappeared into the darkness of the conifer tunnel. She turned away and surveyed the empty room. "What to do?" she asked aloud. After a moment's thought, she answered her own question. "Make a list." She smiled as she remembered her stepfather's comment that people who talked to themselves weren't crazy, just the ones who answered.

"I guess I was crazy to leave Albuquerque." With a long sigh, she sat again at the desk and pulled out a notepad. She adjusted the lead on a pencil, thought a moment, and wrote—

1. *Place to stay*
2. *Supper*
3. *Meet staff (tomorrow a.m.)*
4. *Ask for district handbooks, curricula, etc.*

> 5. *Meet school board (read minutes of school board meetings?)*
> 6. *Staff meeting to set goals*
> 7. *Look at next year's budget*

Mandy put arrows from number 6 to number 7, thinking that before goals were set she needed to know what the district had to work with. The grumbling in her stomach reminded her that she hadn't eaten since the bag of Fritos she grabbed as they were fixing her tire in Corvallis. She had skipped lunch, since she had a seven-hour drive and wanted to make up for lost time. Number 2 on the list suddenly became top priority.

She fished the phone directory out of the drawer and opened it to the skimpy yellow-page section. There were three listings under "Restaurant," and she dialed the first number, intending to ask for directions. On the second ring a recorded message announced the number was no longer in service. Mandy disconnected and punched the number for the second restaurant on the list, only to get the same recording. Feeling a little desperate, she dialed the last number. When the familiar mechanical voice spoke the third time, Mandy dropped the receiver in the cradle and groaned, "What now?"

Her stomach growled again as she paged through the listings, hoping for a miracle. It appeared in the guise of a Qwik-E Market located on Highway 20.

"I think I can find that!" She joyfully gathered up her purse and the rainbow ring of keys and headed for the door. As she hurried downstairs, she made sure to turn off all the lights, but dutifully left the reception area lit.

The wind had lessened, but she hunched her shoulders against the drizzle that dampened her well-cut jacket. After folding herself into the sports car, she switched on the ignition, turned on the lights, and with high hopes set out for the Qwik-E Market.

It wasn't hard to find. She turned right when she reached the highway, and there it was. The market consisted of a small, rustic building with two gas pumps in front. It was well lit, and one of the large windows had OPEN written in welcoming red neon. Mandy pulled up next to a mid-size pickup, the only other car in the lot, and made a dash through the rain for the door. Just inside, she paused to brush herself off.

"Can I help you?" The girl at the counter, who looked about seventeen, had a smile as cheery as daffodils. She had dark hair, dark eyes, a sprinkling of freckles across her nose, and a name tag that said Elizabeth.

"I hope so," Mandy said. "I'm starving, and I can't seem to find a restaurant."

"Oh, they're all closed for the winter," Elizabeth said. "They'll open when the pass does."

"So what do you do if you need to buy a meal?"

There was that smile again. "You come to Qwik-E Market, home of Lorenzo's Polish Hot Dogs." She indicated a small appliance where four fat wieners rotated on a spit.

"Polish hot dogs?" Mandy found herself salivating. A hot dog had never looked so good.

"My dad calls them depth charges," the teenager admitted, "but I think they're good."

"They look heavenly."

"The fixings are on the counter. There's pop in the cooler. If you want beer, I'll have Fran ring it up because I'm not old enough."

"I'll have a root beer." Mandy got a bun out of the warming drawer and put a wiener on it, leaning down to savor the smell. She added mustard, ketchup, and relish and then thought, *What the heck?* and added onions.

As she stood at the counter to pay, the door burst open and a petulant beauty, dressed to the nines and exquisitely made up, strode into the room, followed by an anxious-looking young man in a dark suit with a white carnation pinned to the lapel.

"All you had to do," the beauty said, anger showing in the fists she clenched and in the ugly downturn of her mouth, "was to find a place to stay. Was that too much to ask? I took care of the ceremony, the caterer, and the flowers. All you had to do was find a place to stay."

"I found it! I keep telling you, Kathy. Winthrop is a marvelous little town—all western style and old-fashioned. I got the honeymoon suite at this great hotel."

"Only we can't get to it," Kathy almost screamed. "The road is closed. It's always closed in the winter, didn't you hear them say? How could you not know that?"

"I'm sorry, honey." He pulled her over to the automotive-supply aisle, away from the unwitting audience. Only partially shielded by the display table, he tried to put his arms around her.

She pulled away. "I'm hungry and I'm tired, and I want to know where I'm going to stay tonight."

"We'll find a place," he said, succeeding at last in pulling her into an embrace. "Don't worry. Just think of the great story we'll have to tell about our honeymoon."

Her lower lip trembled. "I don't want a story. I just want something to eat."

As Mandy picked up her purchase, the young man stepped forward and asked the question that she was just about to frame: "Where is the nearest motel?"

"Back downriver at Stallo," Elizabeth said. "Twenty-five miles."

"You're kidding!" The young man's face mirrored Mandy's feelings exactly.

"But my Grandma runs a bed and breakfast," Elizabeth added. "She doesn't advertise when the pass is closed, but she'll take you in if you need a place to stay. You'll love it. It's a log cabin that overlooks the river." She held out a business card from a holder on the counter. "There's a map on the back. It's easy to find."

"Will she feed us supper, too?" The beauty followed her new husband as he came to get the card.

Elizabeth shook her head and pointed to the rotating spit. "You'll have to have Polish hot dogs."

"Come on," he urged, pulling his bride over to the food counter. "It'll make a great story for the grandkids."

"There may not be any grandkids if we don't find a place to stay." Kathy laughed as she said it, and he laughed too, giving her another hug.

As they began fixing their wedding supper, Mandy approached the checkout counter again, the words "bed and breakfast" carrying the same emotional charge as "blessing" and "boon." "Uh, excuse me . . ." Her heart beat faster as she picked up one of the cards.

The clerk turned her attention from the couple to Mandy. "I'm sorry. What can I do for you?"

Just then a woman came out of the back room with a deposit bag in her hand. "All right, Elizabeth," she said, "I'm off to drop this in the night deposit, and then I'll come back and let you go on home."

Elizabeth glanced briefly at her boss. "Thank you, Fran. I've got a ton of homework." Then she turned her attention back to Mandy and waited expectantly.

"Your grandmother," Mandy began. "Does she have any more rooms for tonight?"

"Oh, I'm so sorry! She only has two, and someone else came in earlier. Do you need a place to stay?"

"I was hoping to find a place. The nearest hotel is how far?"

"Twenty-five miles."

"But the Yellow Pages lists three right here in town. I looked it up before I left New Mexico."

Elizabeth's brow furrowed with concern. "They're closed for the winter. Are you here on business? How long are you staying?"

"I'm moving here," Mandy said. "I'm the new school superintendent."

The teenager's smile faded. "Oh," she said in a colorless voice. "I'm sorry, but I can't help you."

Fran, who had listened to the conversation from the door, broke in. "You'll need a house to rent, then. Do you have one lined up?"

As Mandy turned to this new entrant in the conversation, the woman approached and introduced herself. "I'm Fran Porter. I manage the Qwik-E Markets, but I also have a house to rent. I've been renovating it, and it's almost ready. I have a couple more things to do, but it's livable. Would you be interested in seeing it?"

Mandy took only a moment to balance the marginal term "livable" with the well-kept order of the store and nodded.

"Meet me here tomorrow morning, say eleven o'clock. We can go look at it."

"Thank you very much," Mandy said.

Fran waved a reply and was out the door. The newlyweds came back to the checkout register with their supper wrapped in foil and the bride's humor restored. Mandy carried her own depth charge out into the rain and contemplated her options as she got into her car.

Twenty-five miles. That's thirty-five or forty minutes on that two-lane road. Forty minutes down and another forty minutes back tomorrow morning. She leaned against the headrest and watched the raindrops as she considered. Sighing because she had no other option, she wearily turned the key. Just as the engine sprang to life, she remembered the couch in the reception area at the district office. Grange had said there was a bathroom—and a kitchen, too.

Without hesitation, she backed out and retraced the dark passage down Shingle Mill Road, thinking as she emerged from the conifer canopy into the clearing that the house definitely looked spooky in the dark. The one light she had left on was swallowed up in the high entryway and only served to cast eerie shadows on the ground. The golden daffodils no longer bobbed their artificial sunshine dance. Instead, they were undulating patches of gray, a ghostly, writhing force surrounding the empty house.

Mandy pulled into the lot and parked in her spot at the back of the house. Her spirits rose to see her headlights turn the daffodils back to gold, and she laughed to think that she had thought the house looked sinister. Even so, she grabbed her Qwik-E Market sack and her suitcase and hurried to the door, where she fumbled with the keys in the darkness, trying first one and then another until finally the lock clicked. She realized that she had been holding her breath, and she exhaled as the door swung open.

She carried her suitcase in and set it by the couch and then made her way in the dim entryway light to the back of the house. Looking for the kitchen, she opened a closet door first. The next door revealed a bathroom, complete with tub and shower. The third door was, finally, the kitchen.

"Aha!" She smiled triumphantly as she clicked on the lights and looked around the cheery space. The walls were pale yellow and the cabinets were white, as were the appliances: stove, refrigerator, microwave, dishwasher. A round oak table with six chairs sat in front of a bank of tall windows topped by a yellow and white gingham valance.

Mandy sat at the table and took out her supper. Unwrapping the hot dog, she savored the spicy aroma. She took a bite and chewed for a long time, staring at her reflection in the windows. The only sound was the hum of the refrigerator, but in a moment that stopped, and the house was completely silent. When she finished eating and got up to throw away the wrapping, the scraping of chair on wooden floor seemed unnaturally loud.

She spent a moment looking for the garbage can, finally locating it under the sink. As she closed the cupboard door, she straightened up and listened. The wind seemed to have picked back up, but that wasn't what got her attention. Someone was tapping on the kitchen window.

Mandy stared at the window, but all she could see was her mirrored image staring back. The hair on the back of her neck stood on end, and goosebumps rose on her arms. She felt exposed and vulnerable, standing in the light for whoever was tapping to see.

She looked at the window and called, "Who is it?"

No answer. But there it was again. *Tap tap tap.*

With a trembling hand, she opened the drawer by the sink and looked inside. A dozen table settings of silverware were neatly stored in dividers.

Tap tap tap.

Mandy opened the next drawer and found several knives. Picking a wooden-handled butcher knife, she felt wise and foolish, brave and cowardly at the same time as she forced herself to walk to the back door. Thankful to find a porch light switch, she flipped it on. Light flooded the back deck and she opened the door and stepped out, wondering at the last moment if she shouldn't have called 9-1-1 instead.

When she saw that her "intruder" was a branch of a climbing rose bush blown against the window, her first thought was gratitude that she hadn't called the police. The second thought was chagrin that she had let her fancy get away from her.

She turned off the porch light and went back in the kitchen, shivering from the cold night air as she returned her weapon to the knife drawer. Her heart was still pounding, and she didn't like the fact that people could see in and she couldn't see out. After checking to make sure there wasn't a blind she could pull down, she muttered that she'd do something about that. She turned off the kitchen lights, but that didn't help. There was no moon, and it was as dark outside as it was inside, so she still couldn't see beyond the windows. In fact, she couldn't even see the windows.

Feeling her way, Mandy made sure the back door was locked and then went in to the dimly lit reception area. She pushed the light on her watch and saw that it was eight thirty. That was far earlier than her usual bedtime, but she'd had a long day, and she wanted to be up in the morning in time to shower and get dressed before the first person arrived.

She dug a pair of sweats out of her suitcase and found an empty hanger in the closet for her suit. She also found a heavy overcoat, which she appropriated for bedcovers. As she spread it on the couch, a *Sunset* magazine on the coffee table caught her eye, and she carried it into the brightly lit, windowless bathroom. She sat on the floor, then leaned against the tub and read for half an hour until the adrenaline ebbed and she began to yawn.

Before she put out the bathroom light, she set the alarm on her cell phone and discovered there was no service in Limestone. "You're kidding," she muttered. She padded barefoot to the couch, lay down, and covered up with the overcoat.

Everything was fine as long as she lay curled up on her side, but when she turned on her back and stretched out, the coat didn't cover her feet. Sighing, she turned back on her side and tried to get comfortable. The entryway light that had seemed so dim now glared in her eyes. The tapping on the window continued erratically, and the old house creaked and groaned as the wind gusted around the eaves. "It's going to be a long night," she muttered, but before another thought could come on the heels of that one, she fell asleep.

She thought at first it was her cold feet that woke her. The clock on the wall said a few minutes to midnight as she pulled her frigid toes under the overcoat and rubbed them together. Finally, she sat up and clasped her feet with her hands.

It was then that she heard the sound of someone at the front door.

Reminding herself that this might be akin to the rosebush, Mandy tried to stay calm, but her heart started pounding, and she found she was holding her breath. She forced herself to inhale but froze again at the sound of a key scraping in the front-door lock. In the silent darkness, she heard a tumbler click.

There was an opening squeak, and a shadowy figure entered and turned to close the door. Mandy threw back her cover, rose, and stood in indecision as the lights came on in the room and the figure at the door turned to face her. She was relieved to see it was the district accountant, but he apparently didn't see her until he had taken a step in her direction and she spoke.

"Hello, Mr. Smith."

Mo Smith's eyes and mouth opened wide, and his arms flailed in the air as he uttered a high-pitched shriek of surprise.

On edge and startled by his reaction, Mandy screamed too, and they stood silently facing one another for a moment.

Mo was the first to speak. "What are you doing here?" The brown line of his moustache stood out against the pallor of his skin.

"I might ask you the same question."

He smoothed the thin hair that was combed over his bald spot. "I forgot my—I left something behind that I need tonight. I came back to get it."

"Be my guest." Mandy stepped back.

She watched him mount the stairs and disappear into his office. He emerged only moments later with a briefcase, which he showed to her as he came down the stairs. "I just came to get this," he repeated. "I need it tonight."

"At midnight?"

"It's just that I . . . well, you see, I have this . . . Vince wanted me to . . ." By the time he reached the bottom of the stairs, Mo had run out of sentence beginnings and simply said, "Yeah."

"Well, good night, then," Mandy said calmly, though her eyes were twinkling. "I'll lock up after you." She followed him and saw him out the door, but just as she was about to close it, Mo stuck his hand in and held the door.

"Don't tell Grange I came in tonight. Don't tell him I got this."

"Uh, I don't even know what you've got, Mr. Smith."

"Right, right." He nodded, paused a moment, and then scuttled away, clutching the briefcase to his chest.

Mandy closed the door and turned off the lights. On her way back to the couch, she opened the closet and felt inside. She found a fleecy jacket, which she pulled out and spread over the bottom of the couch where the overcoat didn't reach. Then she lay down. When her feet didn't warm up quickly enough, she sat up and stuck them into the fuzzy sleeves, then lay back and snuggled in.

Turning on her side so the dim, overhead light wasn't in her eyes, she remembered how Mo looked with his arms in the air and his Adam's apple sticking out under his frightened face as he screamed. But her smile faded as she began to wonder about the contents of the briefcase and the reason Grange shouldn't know about it. As her feet warmed she grew drowsy, and she drifted back to sleep with the thought that she'd work it out tomorrow.

It was still dark when Mandy surfaced again, sure she must be dreaming because of the whirling lights. Around and around the room they raced in quick succession, bands of light that painted the walls red, blue, white, red, blue, white. She watched from under the covers and blinked to make sure her eyes were open. *I'm dreaming,* she thought. *I'm dreaming that I think I'm awake, but this has to be a dream.* She sat up and craned her neck to see out the window. Suddenly, the glare of a spotlight caught her full in the eyes, and she cried out as she squinted and turned away.

Rap rap rap! The sound of metal against window glass reverberated through the stillness. *Rap rap rap!*

"I seen you!" someone shouted, the "you" sounding more like "yew."

Mandy shrank back against the couch, trying to stay out of the powerful beam of light.

"I seen you! Come on over here. I seen you!"

Still trying to work out if this was a nightmare or reality, Mandy stayed put.

The light moved over to the doorway, and Mandy saw it shining through the leaded glass as she heard the doorknob rattle.

"You open this door, you hear? I'm the deputy sheriff, and if I have to get Grange Timberlain down here to open this door, I'm going to be madder'n a wasp on the wrong end of a fly swatter. Now, git on over here and open this door!"

As the three-tone kaleidoscope continued to whirl, Mandy decided to take advantage of the time when the would-be intruder was at the door to get up without being seen. Heart racing, she swung her legs off the couch and stood, intending to head for the kitchen. Hobbled as she was by the fleece, she only took one step before she pitched headlong. As she put her arms out to break her fall, she felt such a sharp pain in her left wrist that it brought tears to her eyes.

She cradled her left arm in her right. "Ow, ow, ow!"

There was the spotlight again, casting her shadow in stark relief against the back wall of the reception area. "I seen you! Now you come open this here door."

After tearing the fleece away from her feet, Mandy scrambled up and fled to the kitchen. The light from the open kitchen door was enough to let her find her way to the bank of drawers by the sink. Holding the throbbing wrist to her breast, she opened the second one, and as she reached into the interior, she felt the comfort of a wooden handle against her palm. Pulling it out, she felt a little less vulnerable as she stepped back out into the glare.

"Who are you?" she called.

"Doc MacDonald, deputy sheriff of Cascade County. Open this here door!"

"Come over to the window. Show me your badge."

"I'll show it to you when you open this here door."

"I'm not opening anything until I know you are who you say you are," Mandy shouted. "Show me your badge."

There was a moment's hesitation, and then a bulky figure moved across the porch in front of the window and lifted the light to shine on himself as he held his jacket open. A brass shield gleamed on his uniformed chest, and Mandy moved closer to get a better look.

She saw a middle-aged man, about five foot ten with a stocky build, bulldog jowls, and bushy eyebrows under his Smokey Bear hat. "All right. I'll open the door."

Mandy went to the door and turned the bolt. As she swung it open, the glare of the officer's light caught her full in the face, and she raised her hand to shield her eyes.

"Why, you're no bigger than a minute! Who are you?" His voice was gruff.

"I'm Dr. Steenburg."

"You planning on pancakes for breakfast?"

"What?" Unease prickled the skin on Mandy's arms as she realized how vulnerable she'd become the minute she unlocked the door. What if this was some escaped lunatic who had managed to steal a policeman's uniform and car?

Deputy McDonald pointed to the spatula in Mandy's right hand. For the first time, she realized she hadn't grabbed a butcher knife when she reached in the drawer.

"I'm the new superintendent of schools." She hid her weapon behind her back. "Go on home, Deputy MacDonald. There was no place for me to stay tonight, so I'm bunking here. Grange Timberlain knows I'm here. Call him if you like."

"The new superintendent, huh?" The deputy scowled, but said nothing more. He snapped off the spotlight, turned abruptly, and marched off the porch to his waiting cruiser. The whirling lights went out, and Mandy found herself standing in the open door, watching him drive out of the parking lot.

"Well, that was strange," she said aloud as she turned to lock up. On her way back to the kitchen, she held the utensil up threateningly. "Don't come any closer—I have a spatula!"

She giggled as she turned on the kitchen lights, but the laugh became a gasp when she used her left hand to pull open the drawer.

"Ow, ow, ow." She clutched her wrist and remembered the fall that caused the pain. "It's like being in a Chevy Chase movie," she said as she began opening and closing cupboard doors, careful to use only her right hand. "I wonder where they keep the first-aid kit."

Mandy went through every storage place in the kitchen before realizing the bathroom might be a more logical place to look. In that room she found plenty of cupboards, but they were stacked with copy paper and office supplies. There was no first-aid kit, but she did find a bottle of Tylenol in the medicine cabinet. She took two tablets and wondered how long it would take for the throbbing to ease.

"An Ace bandage would really help," she said to herself. "Surely they have a first-aid kit." She stepped into the reception area and looked around. Certain that the curving counter must hold lots of storage space below, she turned on the light and went to investigate. Behind the counter, she found forms, manuals, and district pamphlets on the upper shelf. Down on her knees, she opened the lower cupboards to discover Tarheel T-shirts, sweatshirts, and an afghan in progress. No first-aid kit.

"Rats."

She pulled herself to her feet with her right hand and thought for a moment before opening the suitcase that sat on the floor. She unzipped a side pocket and pulled out a pair of pantyhose, then wound them around her injured wrist. Next, she went to the kitchen, checked in the freezer, and was delighted to find a commercial ice pack.

Mandy carried the pack with her, and after making sure all the lights were out, she wrapped her feet in the fleece and pulled the topcoat over her as she lay down on the couch. The throbbing in her arm and the thoughts racing around in her head vied for top wakefulness honors, but the pain relief must have started kicking in, because she finally threw back the covers and dug around until she found a pencil and paper. With the ice pack atop her left hand, she wrote a list with her right:

1. *Find out WHERE THE FIRST-AID KIT IS!*
2. *Talk to Mo about what papers left office in his briefcase and why.*
3. *Why doesn't Mo want Grange to know about #2? Probe.*

*4. Establish rapport with Deputy MacDonald. Express
thanks for his watchfulness over district property.*

Mandy yawned. She checked her watch and discovered it
was four o'clock. Feeling suddenly very tired, she set the list and
pencil on her suitcase and went back to bed. She couldn't seem to
find a position that would keep the light out of her eyes and at the
same time allow her to keep the ice pack on her wrist, so she gave
up, let the ice drop to the floor, and turned on her side. The next
thing she knew, a tinny *beep beep beep* sounded in her ear.

She sat up. A simple night's sleep was turning into an ordeal.
She checked her watch to find out the time and discovered that it
was five o'clock. The insistent noise that had wakened her was
her cell phone. It was time to get up. She moaned and entertained
the idea of sleeping for one more hour, but the thought of
someone coming early to work and finding her disheveled and
sleeping under a borrowed overcoat was enough to pry her out of
her warm nest.

Stretching and yawning, she winced as she extended her left
arm too far. Then she hung the coat and the fleece in the closet
and put the ice pack back in the freezer. Knowing there were
no linens in the bathroom, she took two terry dish towels from
the kitchen cupboard. She moved her suitcase to the bathroom,
retrieved her suit from the closet, and set about making herself
presentable.

By six o'clock Mandy had not only showered, dressed, put
on makeup, and cleaned the bathroom, but she had also eaten a
breakfast of Ramen noodles she found in the kitchen cupboard.
The only evidences of her night in the district office were the
dark circles under her eyes and the two wet towels that sat on
top of her suitcase in a corner of her office. That left her an hour
before the office would open.

She prowled around the premises for a few minutes, but, unwilling to invade other people's territory, she did no more than peer through the glass door of each office. All seemed to be neat and orderly, with the exception of the one just down from hers, which was piled with boxes and books. She passed by and entered her own office.

The sun was obviously up, since the sky had turned from black to woolly gray. Standing at one of the windows, she leaned her forehead against the pane and felt the leaden weight of the gloom pulling her mood down with the unrelenting force of gravity. She sighed, but just then a bit of sparkling movement caught her eye. A daffodil, stirred by a breeze, was nodding its yellow head. Though dripping with moisture, others followed suit, agreeing with that first positive, radiant flower. *Yes, yes, yes. We carry our own sunshine within us.* The corners of Mandy's mouth lifted, and she looked at her lime green sports car. It too seemed a bright spot in the gray day. She checked her watch. She had half an hour before people would be arriving. After grabbing her purse and her keys, she hurried downstairs and out the door, then locked it behind her. As she walked along the flower beds, she sang a snatch of a song she learned as a child,

"How do you do?" they say.
"How do you do today?"
In my pretty garden, the flowers are nodding.

By the time Mandy pulled out of the driveway, the daffodils had acted as an anti-gravity device, and her mood was considerably lighter.

At the highway, she turned left and drove the few blocks to where downtown Limestone hunkered off the highway to her right. Taking the first street that led in to town, she examined the odd assortment of buildings. Square, cinder block shops butted against gangly, wooden-shingled buildings. Several were boarded up, and nowhere was there a look of prosperity. Even the red brick post office looked worn around the edges.

As she drove by, a man in a white postal-service jeep with the steering wheel on the right pulled out in front of her. His longish hair curled like a honey-colored halo, and his face was sculptured and hollow-cheeked. He seemed to be singing, and his head nodded in rhythm to a beat she couldn't hear.

Mandy could see a school on her left, sitting on a rise in the next block, but she didn't go by it. Instead she followed the road she was on past a white clapboard church that had a steep roof, a bell tower, and a reader board announcing morning worship at ten every Sunday.

Beyond the church, the street ran alongside the rushing torrent of Lemon Creek, then crossed it on a graceful arch made of concrete. She pulled over to the side of the road and watched the water tumbling down the mountainside in a foaming cascade just beyond the bridge. The creek beside her ran swiftly, and as she watched, an arching flash of silver glinted against the gray water. So fleeting was the glimpse that she blinked and examined the stretch of river again, hoping to see it repeated.

There it was! But in that instant, quicker than her brain could process, a huge bird swooped down, caught the fish as it jumped, and carried it away clutched in talons that looked like steel traps. As strong wings beat the air and the bird ascended with its prey, Mandy was conscious of a white head and a wicked-looking, hooked beak.

"A bald eagle," she whispered. "Wow."

She sat a while longer, hoping to see another eagle, but nothing happened. The water continued to cascade down in a roiling, whirling mass only to straighten out at the bottom and rush headlong. She pulled onto the roadway again. As she drove over the bridge, she glanced at her watch and realized she had been gone twenty minutes. Hoping she could find her way back to the district offices, she followed the street as it wound past four aging and abandoned concrete silos before intersecting with Highway 20 again. When she looked to her left and spied Shingle Mill Road, she smiled in satisfaction. A quick jog across the highway and soon she was speeding through the green tunnel toward the daffodil-lighted end.

As she turned into the parking lot, Mandy counted five cars in the lot. Mentally pairing cars with known workers, she realized there was one extra and figured the sleek, new Escalade probably didn't belong to someone who worked for the public schools.

Pulling into the space marked "Superintendent," she hoped her second entrance would be more welcome than her first.

There was no one in sight when Mandy walked in. She could hear voices from the kitchen and supposed everyone had gathered there for coffee. It was exactly seven o'clock.

"Hello." A voice spoke behind her.

Startled, Mandy whirled. A stranger stood in the doorway. Handsome in an angular way, he was of medium height, with black hair, dark eyes, high cheekbones, and an aquiline nose. He was dressed casually in khakis and a long-sleeved shirt open at the neck, but both the pants and shirt were pressed to perfection. As he extended his hand, he smiled, and his teeth flashed against his olive complexion.

"I'm sorry to have startled you," he said. "I'm Vince Lafitte. School board. Are you Dr. Steenburg? I've come to say welcome."

She liked his handshake. It was firm and reassuring and the first real warmth she had felt in Limestone. She smiled back. "Thank you, Mr. Lafitte."

"Vince."

"Vince," she repeated. "Would you come to my office?"

Without waiting for a reply, she led the way up the stairs. As she gained the landing and turned to walk around to her office, she glanced down and saw Grange Timberlain watching from below with a scowl on the working half of his face.

Her eyes slid away. "Good morning, Mr. Timberlain." She forced a pleasant note into her voice.

"Good morning." His tone was as dark as his look had been.

As she walked on, Mandy heard Vince say, "Grange," in a neutral tone.

From below came the equally neutral answer. "Vince."

Feeling Grange's eyes as she walked along the landing, she was glad to reach her office. She opened the door and stood aside for Vince to enter, then stepped in and closed the door behind her.

"Won't you sit down?" She sat in the burgundy chair, grateful for the solid expanse of the desk between her and this man, for he had a surprisingly cosmopolitan presence, and she suddenly felt a little shy.

"Lafitte," she said, seizing upon the first conversational gambit that came to mind. "That's an uncommon name."

"But you recognized it. I saw it in your eyes." He sat in one of the side chairs and leaned back.

"When I was in college, I wrote a paper on Jean Lafitte for an American History course."

"Then you know he was not a pirate." Vince's teeth were white and even, and his eyes crinkled at the corners.

"Not technically." Mandy returned his smile. "He had letters of marque from an upstart South American country, giving him the right to plunder Spanish and English ships, but I've never heard the name Lafitte without the word 'pirate' preceding it."

"I think it is unfortunate. The man was a patriot who very possibly turned the tide at the Battle of New Orleans. He deserves better than to be known as a pirate."

"You certainly are a partisan. Is he an ancestor of yours?"

Vince spread his hands. She noticed his nails were clean and trimmed. There was no ring on his left hand.

"My line gets lost in the bayous of East Texas in the mid 1800s," he said. "We were in the right place at the right time. Could be that I connect with him somewhere. But tell me about yourself. How was your trip?"

"Other than a flat tire in Corvallis, it was great. I just followed the map."

Vince looked out the window at her car. "How could you bring enough with you to last more than a day?"

She laughed. "You have to plan ahead if you drive a sports car. The trunk will hold an overnight bag, and I managed to fit a suitcase in the front seat. I'm expecting some packages today that I mailed before I left."

"I've never seen a lime green Miata. Aren't they usually British racing green?"

"I wouldn't have any idea. I didn't choose the shade. Someone ordered that color and then decided they didn't like it—no, don't look like that! I can tell you don't like it either."

Again, the even, white teeth flashed as he laughed. "No, no. You've got me all wrong. The color is . . . exotic."

"Well, it is what it is. I got a good deal on the car, and it's really heaven to drive with the top down on a warm desert night."

"That's right. You're from Albuquerque. The headhunter told me, but I had forgotten. We're very lucky to have a person of your caliber and education sign on with us." He paused. "Though . . ."

Mandy raised her eyebrows. "You have some reservations?"

There was that smile again. "I didn't expect anyone so young. You can't be—" Vince held up his hand. "Forget it. I know I'm getting into forbidden territory here."

"I'm thirty," she said. "I guess that is young to be superintendent, but I grew up fast. My mother was a single mom until I was ten, and she's always been a bit of a scatterbrain. We kind of raised each other."

He paused for a moment, obviously studying her. "I was raised by a single mom, too. It's . . . yeah, you do grow up fast."

There was an awkward pause. He had finished speaking, but he continued to regard Mandy with those dark eyes.

To bridge the gap, she said the first thing that came to mind. "Your agent did a good job of speaking for the district." She was relieved when Vince smiled.

"What lures did he cast to get you to sign on?" he asked. "What were the strong points that made you decide in favor of a tiny district so far upriver there's not even cell phone service, where there are no—"

"—restaurants and motels," Mandy broke in, grinning.

"Oh, no! I see the agent didn't prepare you. But didn't Mrs. Berman?"

"Well, she gave me very good directions about how to find the district office." Mandy rubbed her arm. The Tylenol she had taken early in the morning was wearing off.

"But that's all. I see. Where did you stay? Where did you eat?"

"Um." The corners of Mandy's lips twitched. "I found a marginally comfortable couch for the night. And I had a delicious hot dog at the Qwik-E Market."

"There you go! I'll bet the agent didn't describe those plusses."

"He didn't."

"I'm sorry I couldn't be at the job fair to expound on the wonders of Limestone, but I had an explosive situation I had to deal with." When she raised her brows in question, Vince went on to explain, "I have a company that does demolition. We were taking down an old factory in Chicago."

"One of those where it comes down in two seconds in a cloud of dust?"

"Exactly."

Mandy picked up a pen and turned it in her hands. "The agent who hired me didn't know anything about district circumstances, so he couldn't tell me why you needed a replacement at the end of the year. I looked online, but the district doesn't seem to have a website, and the places where the district is mentioned just give statistics. I'd be interested to know the lay of the land. There seems to be some . . . resistance to my being here, and it would help if I understood what was behind it."

Vince looked at his watch and stood. "That's going to take longer to answer than I've got right now."

Her brows drew together. "Whoa! That sounds a little ominous."

He shook his head. "Not at all. It's small-town stuff, but I want to have time to answer all your questions, and right now I have an appointment downriver. Can we discuss it when we talk about other district matters? I just came by to say welcome."

"Mrs. Berman will have my schedule. I'd be happy to meet with you. I just hope it's soon." Mandy rose and walked around her desk. "I had contacting school board members on my to-do list for tomorrow. You're helping me be very efficient." She offered her hand. "Thank you for coming by."

Vince took her hand in his. "My pleasure. How are you doing with the dreariness and rain?"

"It's a little daunting, but the daffodils are a good antidote."

His eyes crinkled at the corners again. "You like the daffodils?"

"I love them! They're like the New Mexico sun to my soul." Suddenly, she realized he still held her hand, so she withdrew it. "In addition to that other matter, as soon as I get a little more up to speed," she said as she stepped away to open the door, "I'd very much appreciate getting together and talking about the school board's vision for the district."

"We'll make sure it happens." He nodded—whether for emphasis or as a hint of a bow, Mandy wasn't sure—and then he left.

She stood at the door and watched as he walked around the mezzanine and descended the stairs, and she waved and smiled as he paused at the corner of the reception desk and looked up at her.

She continued to smile as she returned to her desk, though she cradled her aching left arm in her right hand. After glancing at her notes from the night before, Mandy first consulted the yellow phone card and then picked up the phone. She dialed a number and spoke in a pleasant voice: "Mrs. Berman? Could you bring a notepad and step into my office? Thank you very much."

She leaned back in the chair and swiveled around to face the window. As she visualized the conversation she would have with her secretary, her attention was caught by Vince Lafitte standing by his car, talking to a man. Mandy could see the sheen of the man's scalp showing beneath a meager fringe of dark, combed-over hair. Vince seemed to be listening intently, frowning as he nodded. Finally, he said something and held out his hands. Just before the man handed over the briefcase he was holding, he turned to scan the parking lot, and Mandy recognized Mo Smith. As Vince put the valise in his trunk, she looked around the parking lot too, and noticed Grange's pickup was gone.

"You wanted to see me?" Ice crystals hung from each syllable. Mrs. Berman stood in the doorway, and her manner could not have been more frigid.

"Yes. Thank you. Won't you sit down?" Mandy was determined not to be deterred by a difficult staff. She had won over tougher customers than Mrs. Berman, including several older women in the district office in Albuquerque who had resented a younger woman in a position of authority.

After Mrs. Berman settled her ample rear into a chair, Mandy leaned back and considered her for a moment, taking in the silvery hair piled on top of her head in a neat bun, the large bosom, the nondescript print dress, and the sensible shoes. Trying to keep her voice even and pleasant, she glanced at her list and asked, "Mrs. Berman, where is the first-aid kit?"

The older lady's eyes widened imperceptibly and she paused for a moment. "Why?"

"Beg pardon?"

"Why do you want to know?"

Against her will, a steely edge crept into Mandy's voice. "There may be any number of reasons why I ask the question. Is there a reason why you won't give me an answer?"

"Not at all. The first-aid kit is in my office in the cupboard."

"Thank you." Mandy allowed her glance to stray to the window. Vince Lafitte was just pulling out of the parking lot. "Will you please make a note to get it hung in the bathroom on the wall so that anyone unfamiliar with the district office can have access to it?"

"I don't think that's a good idea."

Mandy's gaze shifted to her secretary, and one eyebrow lifted slightly. She made no comment, but simply waited.

There was a long silence. Mrs. Berman's mouth compressed into a straight line while Mandy maintained a pleasant, inquisitive presence.

Mrs. Berman spoke first. "There are things in the first-aid kit that I wouldn't want the wrong people to get hold of."

"All first-aid kits have things that, if taken by the wrong people, might cause discomfort. Ipecac, hydrogen peroxide, ammonia salts. But the benefits of having someone able to get to those supplies in an emergency outweigh the dangers, I think."

"It's not that I'm thinking of. It's the yarbs."

"Yarbs?"

"Yes. I've got some of my best yarbs in the first-aid kit, but if they're not used right, some can cause harm."

Mandy's mind searched, trying to place this foreign word. "Would you show me these 'yarbs'? I'd like to see what you've got in the first-aid kit that worries you."

"I don't like other people messing with my yarbs," Mrs. Berman muttered as she stood and marched out. She disappeared into her own office next door and reappeared carrying a suitcase-shaped basket, which she deposited on Mandy's desk. She undid the latch, then opened the kit wide, revealing the usual assortment of bandages, gauze, antibiotic ointment, and first-aid cream, along with several zip-top bags filled with dried plants, and four small, brown bottles.

"Oh, I see. Herbs." Mandy picked up one of the bottles. It had a handwritten label with a crude skull and crossbones drawn on it.

"That's my tincture of arnica," Mrs. Berman explained. "That's what I wouldn't want someone to get hold of. It should never be taken internally."

"What would happen?"

"It's poisonous. Causes vomiting, raises the blood pressure, makes your heart race, makes you weak and trembly. Sometimes it causes delirium. That's why I don't like having the first-aid kit out of my sight."

Mandy stood. "Mrs. Berman, you cannot be treating people with these things. That's practicing medicine without a license. There are strict rules about what we can do as far as first aid."

The older woman grabbed the bottle out of Mandy's hand. "I'm *not* practicing medicine without a license. I don't ever do anything beyond put on a band-aid. But people know I have things that can cure, and they come to me. I tell them what to take, and they get it themselves. I don't dispense any of my yarbs. They take them themselves." She put the bottle back in the suitcase and began to close the lid.

"Wait. Was there an Ace bandage in there?"

Mrs. Berman stopped in mid-slam and looked questioningly at Mandy.

"Um, I thought I might wrap my wrist." After pushing the lid back, Mandy looked inside and found an elasticized bandage.

"Your wrist is swollen." It was almost an accusation. "What did you do?"

"I tripped and fell. It's nothing."

"It doesn't look like nothing." Mrs. Berman snapped the lid closed and picked up the case. "Follow me."

Thinking the interview with her secretary wasn't going as she had visualized, Mandy did as she was bid, tagging behind as Mrs. Berman descended the stairs and went into the kitchen. She sat on a stool and allowed her secretary to apply a warm chickweed poultice to the swollen wrist, but she baulked at the brown, bitter-smelling tincture offered for pain, opting instead for Tylenol from the medicine cabinet in the bathroom.

Half an hour later, the first-aid kit, complete with yarbs, was back in the locked cupboard in Mrs. Berman's office, and Mandy was again seated behind her desk. The poultice made a lump under the Ace bandage that swathed her wrist, but the throbbing had stopped. She smiled at her secretary, again seated in the side chair, and picked up her list. "Now, about a first-aid kit in the bathroom—" Mandy began, but she was interrupted by Mrs. Berman.

"Before we go any further, I need to remind you that you have an appointment with Nettie Maypole at eight, and one with Tom Fellows at eight thirty."

Mandy frowned. "How can I have appointments with these people? What do you mean 'remind'?"

"I mean that they have each made an appointment to see the superintendent. You're the superintendent, so they're coming to see you."

"What about?"

Mrs. Berman rose. "Nettie works at the high school cafeteria. That's her pulling in right now. She's a bit of a bulldozer, so don't let her run over you."

Nettie turned out to be more barnacle than bulldozer. No matter how many discussion-ending ploys Mandy tried, the other woman couldn't be pried off the chair until she had an assurance of redress, for Arvella Shonefeld, chief cook at the cafeteria, had hijacked Nettie's recipe for Yum Yum Potatoes and was calling them Tarheel Spuds in the weekly school menu.

"It's the principle of the thing," Nettie said. She was a large barnacle, with rimless glasses sitting on a bulbous nose. "That was my mama's recipe that I let her use. She had no business changing the name. Why, Doc McDonald said to me the other day, 'Wasn't that your mama's recipe they was serving at the school?' Taste don't lie, Dr. Steamburger. Taste don't lie."

To Mandy's relief, her secretary opened the door. "Excuse me, Dr. Steenburg, but your next appointment is here."

"Thank you, Mrs. Berman." She stood and walked around her desk, holding out her hand to Nettie. "What is it you wish me to do, Mrs. Maypole?"

"I just want her to call the potatoes by the right name. No more Tarheel Spuds. I want to see Yum Yum Potatoes on the menu from now on."

"Well, I'm sure that can be accomplished," Mandy said briskly. "Thank you for coming in. You people in the cafeteria do a great service to the school."

Nettie shook Mandy's hand but didn't rise. "She serves them every two weeks. They'll be on the menu for next week."

"I'll see what I can do. I'll get back to you."

"The menu is printed on Friday so it's ready to be posted on Monday."

"Well, that gives me a couple of days." Mandy opened the door.

Nettie didn't stir. "I'm headed in to work right now. Do you want me to tell Arvella you want to talk to her?"

Mandy's smile turned brittle. "Thank you, no. Mrs. Berman will arrange an appointment for me. I know you don't want to infringe on someone else's time. It was nice to meet you, and we will be in touch." She said no more, but stood expectantly, waiting for Nettie to rise.

When she didn't, Mandy called, "Mrs. Berman?"

Her secretary came out of her office.

"Would you tell my next appointment that I can see him now? Mr. Fellows, was it?"

Nettie snorted. "Good luck with him!"

Mandy was beginning to think she was going to have to forcibly remove Nettie. Considering she was about a third the size of the cafeteria worker, she had her doubts about being able to do so and wondered if Mrs. Berman's job description included such things.

It wasn't until Tom Fellows appeared on the landing that Nettie finally gave up her chair. "All right, then," she said, stomping out with hunched shoulders and a scowl on her round face.

Mandy judged Tom to be about her own age. He was short and stocky and sat uneasily in the side chair, glancing now and then through the door as if checking that the coast was clear for his retreat. His complaint, which he had a hard time voicing, was that he was never assigned to drive the bus on athletic or band trips. It was always Harvey or Les who got those assignments, and though Tom and the other drivers had asked to be given a turn for the extra work and money, it had not happened. Tom had been elected to come and talk to the superintendent.

"Who makes the assignments?" Mandy asked.

"Harvey," Tom said bitterly, clenching the baseball cap he held in his lap.

"I see. Tell me what you expect of me."

"Talk to him. He needs to make it fair for all concerned. We all have families. Some of us are just getting by, and he goes out and buys a boat. It doesn't need to be that way."

"I see." Mandy pulled her notepad over and found a pen. "What is Harvey's last name?"

"Berman."

Mandy looked up. "Is he related to—"

"Her son."

Mandy wrote the name and put down her pen. "I will definitely look into this. It's in the district's best interest to have our transportation people work together in harmony, since you get the students safely to and from school. I want you to know your work is appreciated." She stood. "I'll get back to you as soon as I can."

Tom stood as well. "That's it? 'I'll get back to you?'"

"You asked me to talk to Harvey. I have said I will do that."

"What's wrong with hauling his sorry . . . Pardon, what's wrong with calling him in right now?"

"Well, I would imagine he's driving the bus right now, picking up students. Or am I wrong about that?"

"School starts at eight."

"Nevertheless, I would rather speak to him at another time. I assure you, I will get back to you before the end of the week."

"There's a band competition the end of April. Four buses will be going. I'd like to be one of the drivers."

"Before the end of the week. I promise you." Mandy held out her hand.

Tom hesitated a moment and then briefly took it in his.

"I'll hold you to that." His exit was similar to Nettie Maypole's—shoulders hunched, brows down, almost stomping.

Mandy shut the door behind him, reflecting that her people skills seemed to be slipping. She returned to her desk, sat, and turned to face the windows, watching as Tom stalked out to a yellow bus and got in. As he exited the parking area, she saw him wave to Grange Timberlain, just entering. She grabbed her notepad and wrote next to Tom's name, "Talk to Grange about this."

A knock at the door made her turn her head, and a tall young man waved through the glass at her. "Come in," she called.

He did so and introduced himself with a lopsided smile. He was very dark, with brown eyes behind rectangular glasses, and a five o'clock shadow. "I'm Oscar, computer tech for the district."

"Hello, Oscar. You're very young to be a computer tech." She got up to give him room to work.

"I'm a senior," he said as he turned on her computer.

"Where? Is there a school nearby?"

Oscar laughed. "Right down the road. North Cascade High School."

"You're still in high school?"

"Yep. Dear old Inches."

At Mandy's quizzical look, he explained, "North Cascade High School. NCHS. We call it Inches for short." Turning his attention to the computer screen, he clicked on an icon and worked intently for a minute at the keyboard, then gave the chair back to her. "If you'll enter your password, you'll be in business."

She sat and followed his instructions. "Okay. Now I want to make sure that the calendaring program is up and running."

"Calendaring program?"

"I want Mrs. Berman to have access to everyone's schedules so she can arrange appointments and meetings. Is that already set up?"

"Nope. That will take me a little while to work out. Do you have something else to do so I can have your desk for ten minutes or so?"

Mandy hesitated, but the note she'd written by Tom's name caught her eye, and she said, "Yes. I'll be next door at Mr. Timberlain's."

She picked up the notepad, then walked past Mrs. Berman's small office to Grange's slightly larger one. It had a multi-paned door similar to her own, and she noticed again the room's untidiness. Three filing cabinets, piled high with books and arranged along the wall, encroached on the door's ability to open all the way. Boxes covered every other available surface. Seated at his desk with his back to the door and his forearms resting on the desk, Grange studied a document spread out in front of him. His shirt pulled tightly over his broad shoulders, and Mandy could see the muscular definition of his back. His dark hair curled a bit over his collar.

There was no response to her first, hesitant knock, so she tried again. As he straightened and turned, she saw the good side of his face first, and she had the impression—more a physical reaction than a thought process—that he was an extremely handsome man. But when he faced her full on, the expressionless half was so jarring that the feeling fled, and Mandy had to force herself not to look away.

He stood and opened the door but said nothing.

"Oscar is working at my desk. I thought, if you had time, I could confer with you about some district business. Do you mind?"

Still not speaking, Grange shook his head and looked around his untidy office for a place for her to sit.

As he moved boxes to free up the side chair, she examined the room. Two objects hanging on the wall next to the door caught her eye. One was a framed diploma from Central Washington University, with "Frederic Granger Timberlain" written in gothic script. The other was a picture of a young woman with sable curls and brown eyes, dressed in walking shorts and hiking boots. She stood on a rock with the sky as a background, and she laughed as she looked down at the picture taker. Mandy touched the corner of the frame to straighten it.

"Who is that in the picture?" As Mandy spoke, Grange invited her to sit, but before she could repeat her question, Mrs. Berman sailed in, crowding the area with her girth.

"Tea time," she announced, a steaming cup in each hand.

Mandy put up her hand in refusal. "I'm really not a tea drinker."

"You'll drink this," Mrs. Berman insisted. "It's comfrey. Also called knitbone. I don't think you've broken anything, but it couldn't hurt." She turned to Grange. "And here is yours. Do I have to stand here and make sure you drink it?"

One side of his mouth curled into a smile. "No, Edith. I'll drink it. Or, at least, if Dr. Steenburg will drink hers, I'll drink mine."

Mandy took a tentative sip. "It's really quite nice. It even sounds nice. Comfrey. Mmm."

Mrs. Berman nodded her approval and slipped out, then closed the door behind her.

Grange raised his mug. "Mine, on the other hand, is called skullcap and tastes like it."

"But you did promise."

In answer, Grange took a sip. He grimaced, and the sight of his face was so comical that Mandy laughed.

"Excuse me," she said. "I didn't mean to be rude."

"No, that's all right. What happened to your arm?"

She tried to ignore the surreal, periodic wink on that half-frozen face. "I fell. It was a stupid thing to do. It may be a bit of a sprain. I was looking for an Ace bandage, and the next thing I knew Mrs. Berman had me in the kitchen and was putting this mass of wet weeds on my arm, all the while assuring me she never treated anyone with her 'yarbs' unless they asked."

"Does it feel better?"

"That's just the thing—it does! How do you account for that?"

"She knows her stuff." Grange took another sip and set his cup down. "Now, what can I do for you?"

"I need to talk to you about the people who came to see me this morning."

"I saw Tom. Who was the other?"

When Mandy told him it was Nettie Maypole, Grange turned away. She couldn't see his expression, but she thought she heard a chuckle.

"I'm unfamiliar with district policies," she said, "and I don't want to blunder into an area where I have no authority, so I'd like you to advise me." She went on to outline the problem that each presented.

Grange listened intently, head tilted toward her and eyes on her face as she spoke. He nodded as she finished and leaned back in his chair. "The simple answer is that you can do nothing for Tom and the other drivers. You were right about not wanting to blunder into an area where you have no authority. The classified staff has a strong union that favors seniority, and the fact is that Harvey is the most senior of bus drivers and therefore gets to assign the other drivers. Les, having almost as much seniority as Harvey, gets to drive the extra hours if he wants them. Tom is on the bottom of the heap and is out of luck. The only way the situation can be changed is for the drivers to talk to their union reps and change it from within, and that can't happen for two more years. That's how long this contract has to run. Tom is talking to the wrong person. You couldn't do anything about it if you wanted to."

"I see. I think I'd like to read the contract we have with the classified people. Where would I find that?"

"Midge has it. Downstairs, in records. Just ask her and she'll get it to you."

"Thank you. Now, about the other matter."

"The Yum Yum Potatoes? I can't advise you there. You're on your own."

The way Grange's lips lifted on one side irritated Mandy. "Thanks a lot," she said dryly.

He took a moment to sip on his skullcap brew. "You've got another personnel situation you need to address."

"Oh?"

With one long arm, Grange reached up and grabbed a thick folder from the top of a filing cabinet and handed it to Mandy. "This is next year's budget in the current rendition. We were just under by the skin of our teeth, and then we got hit with something that threw it out of whack. The only way we can balance the budget is to let two teachers go."

"You're kidding!"

"I am not. You may have noticed that this is a depressed area. We don't have the tax base that we used to when the cement plant and the lumber mills were operating, and we have to manage what money we have very carefully. Take some time to go over the budget. Then read this." He handed her another folder. "That's the contract we have with the teachers, who also have a powerful union where seniority rules. The teachers that will go are obviously the last two hired."

"There must be another way," she said.

"If you can find another way, let me know. I'll be the first to cheer you on."

Oscar tapped on the door. Mandy stood, cradling the files in her bandaged left arm as she opened the door to speak to the young man. "All done?"

"I'll need to take a moment at each of the district office's computers, but I can do that in a minute. Do I need to walk you through the procedure?"

Mandy shook her head. "I'll study these files," she promised Grange over her shoulder as she stepped into the hall. She closed the door and spoke to Oscar. "It's the same program we had in Albuquerque. I know my way around it. Thanks so much."

"No problemo. Call me any time. It gets me out of World Lit."

As she walked back to her office, she heard Oscar asking Mrs. Berman if he could borrow her computer for a moment. Checking her watch, Mandy saw she had an hour before she needed to meet Fran at the rental house. She dropped the files on her desk and sat, eyeing them. Dull reading, and she needed to get some others, equally dull, from Midge.

Mandy noticed that Mrs. Berman's poultice had leaked out onto the Ace bandage, so she decided to take it off. When it was unwrapped, she put the soggy green mass in the trash can and set the bandage on her suitcase to wash, then wiped her arm with one of the towels she had used that morning. She compared both wrists and decided the swelling had certainly gone down.

She was about to turn back to her reading assignment when she remembered she wanted to make some appointments for the next morning. The names she wanted weren't on the yellow phone sheet, so she got out the older, well-thumbed directory. As she set it on the desk, it fell open to the district office page, and something caught her eye. Her name was not listed as superintendent of schools. The name of the man she replaced was there, and all of a sudden Mandy understood the lack of welcome, the frigid tones, the icy stares. She even understood the cramped, untidy office two doors down. There, staring back at her like that unblinking eye, was the name Grange Timberlain.

Mandy's mind whirled with questions as she made her way downstairs. Why was Grange demoted to assistant superintendent? Did it have anything to do with his frozen face? What sort of dynamics would that cause for the long term?

At the foot of the stairs, she saw the teenage clerk from the Qwik-E Market manning the reception desk. "Good morning, Elizabeth." All she got in return was a muttered reply and lowered eyes.

Mandy persisted. "It's nice to see a familiar face. You're a busy lady, it seems. Could you tell me where Ms. Cooley's office is?"

"Back there." Without looking up, Elizabeth indicated a door behind the desk under the stairway. A faint, rosy tinge suffused her cheeks.

"Thank you." Mandy stepped around and knocked on the door.

"Go on in," Elizabeth said.

Mandy did. The door opened onto a large room with windows along one wall. The other three walls were lined with banks of five-drawer, oak file cabinets. In the middle stood a businesslike arrangement of two copy machines, a supply cabinet, and a work table. Two students, a boy and a girl, bent over the task of folding and stapling booklets together.

"Excuse me. I'm looking for Ms. Cooley." When the teens looked up, Mandy introduced herself, feeling once more the disadvantage of being barely five feet tall.

The young man said, "Hey," and smiled. "Mrs. Cooley is over there, behind the file cabinets."

His coworker, slender, raven-haired, and sullen, wore black pants, a black T-shirt with a Maltese cross on it, and black boots. She simply stared.

Mandy said thanks and walked to where a cozy nook had been carved out of the room by a notch in the arrangement of the filing cabinets. Midge Cooley, sitting behind a stack of papers, looked up as Mandy walked through the keyway. She didn't answer Mandy's smile, but looked apprehensively past her as she brushed a limp tendril of hair away from her face.

"Hello, Ms. Cooley. May I sit down?"

Midge didn't meet her eyes. "Yeah. Sit."

"Mr. Timberlain said I could get some things from you. Would you tell me the protocol for your department? How you control who has access to the records, and how one goes about requesting files?"

Midge obliged, explaining the way the files were set up and how they were maintained, Every now and then, she glanced nervously over her shoulder as if she were afraid of being caught consorting with the enemy. She made a list of the files Mandy wanted and produced them quickly, handing them silently over with her long jaw clenched.

Mandy said thanks and carried the stack back to her office, glancing through open office doors on her way. Grange was hunched over his desk again. Mrs. Berman was busy at her computer, but she frowned over her reading glasses, and her eyes slid to Mandy's bare left arm. Without a change of expression, the secretary turned back to her work.

Mandy walked on to her own office, thinking for the first time that maybe she should have taken that job offer in the Alaskan bush, the one made on the same day as the one for North Cascade. The money had been better, but the remoteness and climate had weighed against it. As she set the files down on her desk, she looked out at the rain wrinkling the puddles in the parking lot and wondered if Chevak, Alaska, could have been much worse.

"Ahem."

She turned and instantly recognized the postman from earlier that morning. Standing in her open doorway, he was dressed casually in Levi's and a Carhartt jacket, and as he met her gaze, she could tell by the tiny muscle movement around his clear blue eyes that he remembered her, too.

"Dr. Steenburg? I have three boxes for you. Where shall I put them?"

"Right next to the last filing cabinet, if you please. I'm so glad to see them. You do good work!"

"U.S. Postal Service. Neither rain nor snow, and all that jazz. We aim to please." He stacked the cartons against the wall and leaned on his hand truck. "I saw your license plates. You're a long way from New Mexico."

"It would seem so." It came out a little more wistful than she intended, so to cover, Mandy asked, "Do I have to sign anything?"

"No." He regarded her for a moment and then offered his hand. "I'm Israel Timberlain. They call me Rael."

"Rael. Glad to meet you. I'm Mandy."

"Hello, Mandy. Have you found a place to stay yet?"

"Maybe. A lady I met last night at the Qwik-E Market has a rental. I'm going to look at it" —she checked her watch— "in just a minute."

"That's Fran. I was going to tell you about her place. It's just down the road from mine."

"Well, thanks. Maybe we'll be neighbors."

"Maybe." Rael wheeled his hand truck ahead of him to the door. "Nice to meet you, Mandy."

"Wait. You said your name was Timberlain? Are you and Grange—"

"Identical twins," he deadpanned. Then, grinning at the look on Mandy's face, he confessed, "First cousins. See you around."

She watched as Rael sauntered down the hall and stopped to lean a shoulder against the doorframe as he talked to Grange. The difference in the cousins was stark. Grange was tall, dark, and broad shouldered, well kempt in a rugged, backwoods sort of way. Rael was slight and angular, about five foot six, with high cheekbones and unruly hair.

"Identical twins." She chuckled as she gathered up her purse and keys.

She let Mrs. Berman know she would be out for a couple of hours and drove to the Qwik-E Market, where Fran was waiting. Of medium height, trim and fit, Fran looked to be about forty. Though her face was too round and flat to be attractive, she played up her dark eyes and shiny, shoulder-length hair.

Mandy got in Fran's pickup, and they headed east on Highway 20 for several miles before angling off on a secondary road. Mandy read the sign out loud. "Timberlain Road? There sure are lots of Timberlains around here."

"They've been here a long time. Rael Timberlain lives on the original property. It's on this road."

A huge wooden bear stood upright by a gravel driveway where a double-wide mobile home and a large, metal-sided pole building occupied a clearing. Other, smaller wooden statues were scattered around the front yard.

"That's quite a carving!" Mandy kept her eyes on the bear as they drove past.

"That's where Wesley Gallant lives. Have you heard of him?"

"No. Should I have?"

"He sells his stuff all over the U.S. He's on the school board, too. I thought, one way or the other, you might know the name."

Mandy shook her head. The woods closed around them again. Bright green leaves burst out of low-growing bushes, relieving the darkness of the forest wall. "It's good of you to take me out to see the house," she said.

"Glad to do it. If you want the house, it'll be good for you and good for me. Finding responsible renters isn't easy, especially in a place this small."

"Do you have other rentals?"

"One. It's a tiny house in town. I buy fixer-uppers."

"Who does the work for you? Fixing them up, I mean?"

"I do it myself." Fran explained how she had taken some manual arts classes a few years before. Her first project was a bookcase, but before the year was out, she had remodeled a house. As they rounded a bend, the river appeared below them, a metallic gash in the valley floor.

"That's quite a river," Mandy said. "What we call rivers in New Mexico are a lot smaller than that."

"Whereabouts in New Mexico are you from?"

"Albuquerque."

"I've been there. Nice town." Fran pointed to a small story-and-a-half farmhouse sitting beside a gravel road that veered off the asphalt. "That's where I live."

Mandy noted the white siding, the green shutters, the well-kept grass with daffodils blooming in random patches along a low fence. "Was it a fixer-upper?"

"Yes, you should have seen it!" Fran took the gravel road that dropped down below her house and ran closer to the river's edge. "I had to rewire it and put in all new plumbing. The house is eighty years old."

"And you did it all yourself?" Mandy never got an answer, because they rounded a bend, and she exclaimed, "Oh!"

Before her, a rustic A-frame nestled in the woods, facing the road that ran alongside the river. The front wall was completely made of windows, and a deck ran the length of it.

"I'll take it," said Mandy as they parked in front.

Fran laughed. "You haven't seen inside yet."

"It's charming. I love it already."

"Let me show it to you first."

They got out, and Fran let them into the living room, a space that opened to the roof and had a wrought-iron, circular stairway leading to the master loft. Mandy looked around. Watery winter light flooded into the room, taking away some of March's chill. A faint musty scent hung in the air.

Fran went to a green porcelain gas fireplace and lit it. Immediately, orange flames danced against the dark wood of the wall.

"I'll take it," Mandy said.

"Let me show it all to you first," Fran said again. "This fireplace heats the downstairs. It has a blower that forces air through heat exchangers in the back, so it's very efficient."

Mandy followed Fran to the open kitchen area, enchanted to discover she could work in the kitchen and still see the cheery flames in the fireplace. A door to the right opened to the laundry room, and a sliding glass door opened to the back deck. Mandy noted the stainless-steel appliances. "I'm serious. I'll take it."

Fran smiled and shook her head. "Let's look at the upstairs."

They climbed the metal corkscrew to a master bedroom that was separated from the downstairs living area only by a balustrade.

To the left, a walk-through closet led to a three-quarter bathroom. On the back wall, French doors opened onto a balcony, inviting the outside in. Skylights in the bedroom, closet, and bath made everything light and airy.

"I'll take it," Mandy said for the fourth time. "When can I move in?"

"I've still got a few things to do. If you don't mind me working while you're living here, you can move in today. Do you need help?"

Mandy laughed. "I've got a suitcase and three boxes. I can manage."

"What are you going to sleep on?"

"I shipped up an air mattress. I can survive until my things come. My furniture is sitting in a warehouse in Seattle. They can have it here day after tomorrow."

"I'll need you to sign a year's lease."

Mandy hesitated. The few hours she had spent at North Cascade School District didn't recommend it as a dream job. She thought of Grange, with his half-dead face and his reason to bear a grudge. She thought of the district staff, all clearly demonstrating they felt Mandy didn't belong here. Could she stay a year? Did she want to?

She walked to the loft railing and looked through the living-room windows out to the river. Most of the clouds had lifted, and she could see the tops of the mountains on the other side, but cottony, low-lying stragglers lay in the vertical ravines gouged into the mountain's rugged flanks. A blue hole opened in the sky downriver, and just for a moment, the sun shot rays through the wispy vapors and made silvery shafts that spread like an angel's fan.

Mandy stood transfixed. "I'll sign the lease."

"Great. Let's go back to my office and get the paperwork done."

As they turned around in the A-frame's driveway, Mandy asked, "Where does this road go?"

"It continues on about a mile to where a sawmill used to sit. The clearing has grown back in cottonwoods, and we get a few mushroomers coming by each spring to hunt morels. But I guarantee you won't be bothered by traffic."

When they reached Fran's house, they went in the back door and climbed a steep flight of stairs to an attic office. As Fran filled out the papers, Mandy examined the room, appreciating the paint and wallpaper and the inventively designed cupboard space.

Fran finished filling in the blanks on the lease and turned it around for Mandy to read.

Taking a big breath, she signed her name. "First and last, is that what you said?" She pulled her checkbook out of her purse.

"And damage deposit. It's there in the lease." Fran laid a set of keys on the desk. "Utilities are already on. Just call to get them put in your name. I've written the numbers on the bottom. If you've got a phone card, you can call downriver on the phone, but until you get it set up, no one can call you."

Mandy wrote the check and gave it to Fran. "Thank you very much," she said. "It's lucky I met you last night, though Rael Timberlain told me about your place this morning."

"Rael lives down Timberlain Road about a mile. He's as near to the river as you are, but he's on a high bank." Fran looked at her watch. "Would you like to have lunch with me?"

"That sounds great." Mandy stood and followed her down the narrow stairs. They turned right at the bottom to enter a small kitchen with white cupboards and a table painted to match.

"I hope you don't mind a low-carb lunch. I don't keep bread in the house."

"I'm grateful for anything. I had Top Ramen for breakfast."

Fran opened the fridge. "I try to stay below fifty carbs. One piece of bread has thirty-five. We'll need knives and forks. In that drawer over there."

By the time Mandy had the table set, Fran brought plates with ham, cheese, celery, cauliflower and snap peas.

"That looks good." Mandy pulled out her chair. "I'm glad for the chance to visit with you, too. I haven't met with a lot of openness, and I'd like to ask a couple of questions."

Fran set ranch dressing on the table and sat down. "Limestone is your typical small town. People are cliquish. Well, maybe it's not typical. Most folks here are descendants of settlers who came from the backwoods of North Carolina during the Depression. They came to work in the lumber industry."

"Is that where the 'Tarheel' comes from?"

Fran nodded. "They brought a lot of their culture and customs with them, coon dogs and whisky stills included. In fact, just last year the police arrested someone for operating a still about five miles upriver."

"They didn't include that in the fact sheet about the district," Mandy said.

"Don't get me wrong," Fran said. "They're proud of who they are, but it's a little hard to get to know them, get them to trust you. I've been here three years, and I'm just now feeling at home."

Fran dipped a cauliflower floret in the dressing. "You mentioned a lack of openness. I have an idea it's more like hostility."

Mandy looked up quickly. "How did you know?"

"Grange is well liked, and people don't like the fact that he's been kicked down to assistant superintendent. It's natural that they would resent your appearance, even though you had nothing to do with what happened to Grange."

"What did happen to Grange?"

"Vince happened to him."

"Vince Lafitte? I just met him this morning. He's on the school board."

"Yes, I know. He was elected last fall, and the first thing on his agenda was to make sure the district hired a new superintendent."

Mandy blinked. "I still don't understand."

Fran shook her head. "Neither do I. Folks don't talk about it, but there's bad blood between Vince and Grange. Something that happened a long time ago."

Mandy wrinkled her brow. "You're kidding. How could that be? You don't just demote a superintendent of schools."

"It had something to do with state guidelines about qualifications. Several years ago, Grange took over when the superintendent had a heart attack and died. He was doing a great job, and the board kept him on, even though he doesn't have the right degree."

Mandy frowned. "Is it guidelines or requirements? If it's something that the state mandates, it looks to me like Vince is getting a bad rap for bringing the district into compliance."

"Don't get me wrong. Vince is a great guy. I work for him, you know."

"Really?"

"Yes. He owns the Qwik-E Markets—one here and one up in Trillium. Grange is a great guy, too. I've worked with him on the Opening Festival committee."

Mandy took a bite of cheese and chewed while her mind assimilated the information. "How did you come to work for Vince?"

"I was managing a convenience store down in Arizona across from a building he was taking down. He'd come in for coffee as they were working on the setup, and we'd visit. That was about the time he bought the Qwik-E Market here, and he asked me to come work for him. That was three years ago."

"How did you make the transition from the Southwest?"

Fran laughed as she got up and began clearing the table. "I wore a coat and wool socks for the first year, summer and winter, but I've acclimated. I don't think I'll ever go back. In fact, I don't think I'll ever leave Limestone."

As they cleaned the kitchen, Mandy listened to Fran recount the story of the first little rental she bought and how she had lived in it as she renovated around herself. Buoyed by Fran's good-natured and down-to-earth manner, Mandy felt less alone by the time they drove back to the Qwik-E Market. She thanked Fran again, got in her own car, and headed back to the district office with a determination to prove her worth.

She walked in to find the reception desk empty. As she climbed the stairs, she made a mental list of what she wanted to accomplish that afternoon. Grange wasn't in his office, and Mrs. Berman frowned as she passed, but Mandy's mood was too light to be daunted. She smiled at the secretary and stepped to her own door.

She stopped with her hand on the doorknob, for the room was alight with yellow. A dozen plastic buckets of daffodils were scattered around the office: on the desk, atop the filing cabinets, on the deep windowsills, even on the floor. Mandy laughed aloud in delight.

She stepped in, closed the door, and looked around. An envelope stuck in the bouquet on her desk caught her eye, and she opened it, knowing the author before she saw the bold signature. It read, *A little artificial sunshine for your day,* and was signed simply, *Vince.*

Mandy could have danced. She clasped the card in both hands and held it to her heart, smiling as she closed her eyes and twirled on her toes. She was still smiling as she opened her eyes and was confronted by the contorted face of Grange Temberlain, who stood in her doorway.

The sight of that one expressionless, staring eye disturbed her more than his lowering brow and turned-down mouth, and it lingered in her memory, fighting with the daffodils for precedence, long after he had turned on his heel and stalked into his office.

Mandy woke the next morning after the first night in her new house. She stretched and sat on her knees by the balustrade above the living room. Resting her arms on the railing, she looked through the tall windows at the vista spread out beyond. The river looked like a steel-gray ribbon winding around a spreading bouquet of Douglas fir and rosy-brown alder. Above the river, fog lay in a fluffy white stratum, like an eiderdown that had been shaken out and was floating down to cover the bed again.

Mandy got up, wrapped a blanket around her shoulders, and opened the sliding glass door that let onto the back balcony. Stepping out into the chilly air, she looked around. She had worked late the previous afternoon, reading files, meeting with Mo Smith, and planning strategy, and it had been dark by the time she headed downriver for groceries. When she had returned to the unlit house, she couldn't see anything except the dim outline of the mountains across the way.

Now, in the morning light, she saw that the forest began about fifty feet behind her cabin. Looking to the right, she could see how the land sloped away in a gentle grade down to where the river, visible through the trees, curved around. Someone had recently done some work with a trackhoe, pushing up a ridge of gravel that made a gray scar on the green landscape. Mandy took a deep breath and turned back inside.

As she knelt by one of her boxes to find a towel, she noticed the phone sitting on the floor. Recalling that Fran had said she could call out, she lifted the receiver to try it. The dial tone buzzing in her ear suddenly reminded her how far she was from home, and she grabbed her purse and fumbled in a zipper pocket for her phone card. Holding it in a trembling hand, she whispered the string of numbers under her breath, punched in the sequence, and waited while it rang once, twice, three times. Disappointed, she was just about to hang up when she heard a breathless voice.

"Hello?"

"Mother?" Mandy's voice had a catch in it.

"Who's this? Mandy?"

"Oh, hi, Leesie. Where's Mother?" Mandy sniffed and wiped her eye with the corner of the blanket.

"Are you all right?"

"I think I was a bit homesick for a moment. Silly. Is Mother there?"

"She's in Chicago, remember? Some sort of conference for reading teachers."

"Oh, yeah. I remember." Mandy slumped against the wall.

"Is anything wrong? How is Washington? What's the district like? Have you got an apartment yet?"

"What are you doing home, Leesie? I thought you were staying at the Millers' while Mother was gone."

Leesie was Mandy's half-sister. Younger by twelve years, she had been born a year after Mandy's mother married Conroy Wheeler.

Mandy's life had changed dramatically with that marriage. Her mother, Clara, had been a single mom at sixteen, and Mandy had learned early about hard work and strict economy. Mandy had been pretty much on her own as her mother finished high school and put herself through college. Clara had just finished her degree when she met and married Conroy.

Conroy brought more to the union than economic freedom. He brought color to a world that Mandy only remembered in black and white. Although a successful CEO of a large grocery chain, he loved music and drama and was head of the Albuquerque Allied Arts. Under his aegis, a new performing arts center was built, and he actively promoted the support of young artists in the community. He made sure that Mandy studied piano, and when she wanted to play jazz instead of classical music, he cheered her on. His sudden death last year had drained the color out of the world again. It had come back, or she thought it had, with the person who used to call her "chérie."

"I forgot my history notes and had to come back for them," Leesie said. "I was just going out the door when the phone rang. You didn't answer me. Have you got an apartment yet?"

"Yes. I moved in last night."

"What's it like?"

"Well, it's a small district. Um, I really can't tell more than that. I just got here."

"No, not your school district. Your apartment. What's it like? How many bedrooms?"

Mandy could picture her sister on the other end of the line. Tall, blonde, vivacious, a natural leader—everything Mandy was not. Leesie had her father's exuberance for life and his single-mindedness. Mandy sighed and figured she'd better tell her what she wanted to know. "My house is something out of *Sunset* magazine."

"Are you being sarcastic?"

"No, I'm not. It's an A-frame, about a stone's throw from the river. The front is all glass, and I'm sitting in the upstairs bedroom right now, looking out at mountains and forest, with a river running through it. Belongs on a calendar." *But on a calendar the sky would be blue,* she thought.

"How many bedrooms?"

"Two. And two baths."

"Sounds wonderful. Do you have a phone number yet? I'll give it to Mom."

"Not yet. I'll email her. You'd better go. You'll be late for school."

"Yikes—I already am. But that's okay. It was great to talk to you."

"You too. Bye." Mandy heard the click as her sister rang off, but she sat for a moment, still holding the receiver. When an ugly *beep beep beep* sounded in her ear, she hung up. She shrugged, then picked up her underwear and towel and padded into the bathroom.

She felt better after a hot shower. After dressing quickly, she went downstairs to fix breakfast. She boiled oatmeal in the saucepan she had sent in one of the parcels and ate it out of the pot with the stirring spoon. She sat on a folding chair that Fran had loaned her, using two empty boxes stacked atop one another for a table. Both counter and cardboard table were graced by buckets of daffodils.

As she ate, Mandy stared at the river flowing in the distance and reflected on the staff meeting the day before. There had been resistance to her suggestion that Mrs. Berman handle all calendars and that issues important to the district be tracked by email for documentation. It irked Mandy that everyone looked to Grange for permission. It wasn't until he said in a noncommittal voice that they could give it a try that everyone had agreed. Next, by her invitation, each reluctantly and sketchily described his or her responsibility in the district. Mandy closed the meeting, saying she had noticed that, though math scores were strong, reading was woefully deficient. She announced that at their next staff meeting, set for the following week, they would be strategizing on ways to remedy this, and she asked Mrs. Berman to make sure that meeting was on everyone's calendar.

As Mandy scraped the last of the oatmeal out of the bottom of the pot, she realized that, save for the short recital each staff member had made about areas of responsibility, she was the only one who spoke during the meeting. She sighed, remembering Albuquerque's district staff meetings full of give and take, overflowing with ideas and enthusiasm.

She set the pot to soak in the sink and ran upstairs to get her jacket and purse. Then she locked the door behind her and drove through the morning mist back up to where Wesley Gallant's metal-clad carving studio sat behind his house. This was her morning to visit the school board.

Mandy could hear proof of Wesley's industry the moment she got out of the car, but instead of the throaty roar of a chain saw, a high-pitched whine scraped the air.

The large metal building had two garage-style roll-up doors on the long side, but it was to a smaller door on the end that Mandy headed. She knocked twice, and when no one answered, she turned the knob and pushed the door open. Immediately, the whine became louder, and Mandy could see why there was no response.

A tall, lean man with safety glasses and ear protectors worked intently with a small rotary tool that sent clouds of powder into the air, making a rusty, aromatic fog inside the building. Under his skillful hands, the scene Mandy had seen the previous morning emerged, captured in cedar. An eagle, wings stretched up, legs extended, held a writhing fish in its talons.

As Mandy stepped through the door, a suspended particle lodged in her eye, and she paused for a moment, staring at the ground and blinking furiously to try to float it out on tears. Clenching her hands to keep from rubbing the eye, she finally was able to see without discomfort. That was about the time she realized the whining of the air tool had stopped, and she looked up to meet the stern gaze of Wesley Gallant.

He took off his earmuffs and safety glasses. "Dr. Steenburg, I presume?"

Mandy smiled and extended her right hand as she rubbed tears away with the back of her left. "Yes. Thank you for taking the time to talk to me."

After setting down his tool, Wesley took her hand briefly, but he did not return the smile. Instead, he strode to the corner and turned off the compressor. "For what it's worth," he called over his shoulder.

Wesley must have been six foot six. Dressed in Levi's and a brown flannel shirt, he looked to be about forty. His sandy, shoulder-length hair was cut in a casually careless way, and his short beard, mustache, and dark eyes lent him a rustic air. *A Los Angelino trying to look like a Tarheel,* Mandy thought. She had read his bio online and found he had a degree in marketing from UCLA. He was a major player in the chainsaw sculpturing subculture, and his pieces could be found in galleries from Alaska to Mexico.

"Pull up a stool," Wesley said. It sounded more like an order than an invitation.

Feeling her hackles rise, Mandy paused a moment to count inwardly to ten before she sat.

"What can I do for you?" Wesley's tone was curt, but his mouth curled into a small smile as his eyes met hers, and that softened the question somewhat. Mandy noticed he had a dusting of sawdust on his face and in his beard.

"I didn't come by to ask you to do anything," Mandy said. "You're a member of the school board. You hired me. I've come to—to pay my respects, you might say. To report for duty."

"Whoa, there, Nellie! I didn't hire you. You're not going to pin that on me."

Taken aback by the vehemence of his denial, Mandy stared. "I was assured that the board unanimously approved my contract."

"The board was unanimously railroaded by Vince Lafitte. That's the only unanimous thing about the whole sorry mess."

Mandy frowned. "I'm sorry. I don't think I understand."

"It doesn't matter. The only thing you need to understand is that, no matter who has the title, Grange Timberlain is superintendent. You may have the office and the salary, but nothing has changed. Grange is still in charge."

"And he has the files," Mandy murmured.

"I'm sorry. I didn't catch what you said."

"Nothing." Mandy stood. "Thank you for being so frank, Mr. Gallant. I'll be equally frank. I came here to do a job, and I intend to do it to the best of my ability."

Wesley's voice softened. "Does that mean you want to do what's best for the students?"

"Yes, certainly."

"Then throw your lot in with Grange. There's not a person in the district better qualified to lead."

"Oh? And what makes him so qualified?"

Wesley counted the points on the fingers of one hand. "He's a Tarheel. He understands the people of this area. He's dealt with adversity in his life and risen above it—way above it. And in doing so, he's found the key to involving students in something bigger than they are. They look up to him, and—"

"—and he doesn't have the degree. Period. Paragraph. I didn't make the rules, Mr. Gallant. I didn't depose Mr. Timberlain, and neither did Mr. Lafitte. He deposed himself when he made no move to comply with the state code."

"That attitude will win you no friends."

Mandy's chin came up. "I didn't come here to make friends."

"It's a lonely place without them."

"I don't wish to quarrel with you. Any quarrel that we have can only hurt the district and the students. Can we continue this discussion another day, after I have found my feet?"

"There is no point. You won't change my mind, and I don't imagine I can change yours. You were brought here under false pretenses, and I'm sorry for it. You can blame Vince for that, since he made arrangements for the hire."

"It looks to me as if the people of Limestone are blaming Vince for bringing the district into compliance with state mandates. They're there for a reason, and it has to do with excellence in education." She took her keys out of her purse. "I think Vince Lafitte is very forward-thinking, and I'm surprised that you, as an educated man, aren't more supportive." Mandy headed toward the door but paused as she passed the eagle sculpture. Turning back, she asked, "Could it be a calculated business decision to side with the old-timers? I realize you sell your sculptures elsewhere, but who supplies your raw material?"

To Mandy's surprise, Wesley threw back his head and laughed. "Touché. I'll tell you what, Dr. Steenburg. I'll take you up on that talk when you've 'found your feet.' It shouldn't take long as you don't have to look as far as most. I'll be anxious to hear what you've got to say when you know more of what's going on." He stood and followed her to the door.

She consciously took three steps after she was outside before she turned to take her leave. It was a trick she learned years before when she realized she wasn't going to grow any more. Those three extra steps made it so she didn't have to crane her neck to look people in the eye. "Thank you again, Mr. Gallant. I'll be in touch."

"Any time." He raised his hand in farewell and then reached to pull the door closed.

A light rain had begun to fall, and Mandy hurried to her car. She got in and brushed the droplets off her jacket before starting the engine and turning the heater on high. As she waited for the car to warm up, she glanced in the mirror and was dismayed to see a black streak where her mascara had run and been smeared across her cheek. She took a tissue from her purse and did her best to rub it off, trying to remember how long she had been talking with a dirty face.

She took out her planner and read again the directions to the home of the third school board member. She repeated them aloud as she backed out of Wesley's driveway, and then she headed toward Highway 20.

Gertrude Foley's house was not easy to find, as it sat at the end of the road on a bench above town. Mandy found the retired schoolteacher out back of her house. On the cusp of eighty, big-boned and ruddy, Mrs. Foley wore bib overalls over a gray sweatshirt and slowly followed a rototiller as it churned a textured path through her garden spot. Five ducks waddled behind her, nuzzling their bills into the coffee-colored soil as they searched for grubs. At the far end of the garden, peas twined their way up a hog-wire lattice.

Mandy had to call Mrs. Foley's name twice before she got her attention. The old lady turned, and Mandy noted the generous mouth and hazel eyes that looked like they wouldn't miss much. Though the old lady had agreed to meet Mandy this morning, there was no smile of welcome. She turned off the tiller and waited.

"I'm Dr. Steenburg," Mandy said. "Thank you for saying I could come by."

Mrs. Foley stood her ground, so Mandy stepped into the newly plowed garden. When her stylish high heels sank in and tipped her backward, she overcompensated and lurched forward. Had it not been for Mrs. Foley's steadying hand, she might have gone down.

"Excuse me," Mandy said, color rising to her cheeks. "I didn't mean to fall on you."

"That's all right. You're not wearing gardening shoes."

"No, I'm not. I think I'll go back to where the footing is better." She made the return trip with more grace, trying not to think what the rain and dirt were doing to her shoes. When she gained solid ground, she said, "I wanted to come and meet you. Report in, you might say."

"I suppose you've already talked to Vince Lafitte."

"Yes. Mr. Lafitte came to see me yesterday."

"I'll wager he did. I taught that boy in fifth grade. Taught him and Grange both." Mrs. Foley leaned down and began tugging on a hank of grass from around the tiller axel. "Poor Vince. He always wanted to be somebody."

Mandy frowned. "He seems like somebody to me. How long must someone wear a childhood label?"

Mrs. Foley's head was still down as she yanked at the snarl of grass. "I don't know, people being what they are. It's a different world now, but back when he was in grade school, there was a stigma attached to being born out of wedlock."

Stunned at the old lady's revelation, Mandy stood with her mouth gaping.

Mrs. Foley straightened up and threw the grass on a compost pile, and the ducks ran to investigate, quacking interrogatives. The old lady wiped her hand on her pant leg. "I think it still haunts him. He didn't have time to be somebody in high school. No time to play football, like Grange. He had to work to help support his mother. As soon as he finished high school, he left to go to work for someone, setting off dynamite. Now he owns the company. And quite a few things around here, too."

Mandy shivered. The rain was growing heavier, and she hadn't brought anything that would shed water. "Mrs. Foley, perhaps you're telling me things that shouldn't be told. Mr. Lafitte's parentage is no concern of mine. What is my concern is the future of our schools. I'd like to sit down with the school board and talk about your vision for the district, maybe write a mission statement."

"Is that the way you talk in the big city?" Mrs. Foley stomped through the tilled earth to get a hoe that leaned against the fence. "What you're implying is that we have no vision. We're not capable of looking to our children's future because not having a mission statement means we have no focus."

Mandy blinked. "No, no. I didn't mean that."

The older woman began cultivating between the rows of peas with the corner of the hoe. "Well then," she said without looking up, "what did you mean?"

"I meant that I wanted you to tell me what the district's vision is. I'm new. I don't know where you're going and what you've already done to get there."

Mrs. Foley straightened and put a hand on one hip. "For that you need to talk to me? Grange can tell you. Talk to him."

Mandy flapped her arms against her side in frustration. "I'm not getting a lot of help there."

"Have you asked for help?"

"Not from Grange. I'm asking you."

"And I'm giving it. Talk to Grange."

Mandy felt her throat tighten. The cold drizzle had made her hands numb and plastered her hair against her head. Water dripped down her neck and nose. She was miserable and fighting a lonely, losing battle. *You are NOT going to cry,* she told herself sternly and waited to speak until she could do so in some semblance of a normal tone.

"Thank you so much for seeing me, Mrs. Foley." She cleared her throat and went on. "I will talk to Grange, as you suggest. But I hope you'll give Vince Lafitte credit for wanting to help prepare North Cascade students for life in the twenty-first century. Maybe he's remembering the preparation he got and what it was like when he left Limestone. Maybe he wants better for the children of this community. They obviously have to go away for jobs.

Let's prepare them to be on an equal footing with graduates of other schools."

Mrs. Foley watched her through narrowed eyes. Then she nodded and took hoe in hand. "I'll see you at the next board meeting, then?" She began loosening the dirt along the back of the trellis, and the ducks flocked around her feet.

Feeling she had been dismissed, Mandy turned to go back to the car. She had taken only two steps when she heard Mrs. Foley call, "Dr. Steenburg."

Mandy turned and wiped the hair out of her eyes. "Yes?"

There was a smile on that generous old mouth as Mrs. Foley said, "You're very young. Welcome to Limestone."

"Thank you," Mandy said woodenly. She turned and slogged back to her car, noticing too late the little mounds of duck droppings along her way.

"Fits," she muttered. "A perfect end to a lovely morning."

She wiped her shoes as best she could on the grass before she got in the Miata. Then she retraced the route back to the highway, making only one wrong turn on the way, and headed home to dry out before the next stop on her list.

An hour later, Mandy pulled up at the bus garage, dressed in the only other suit she had packed. In her briefcase she carried the classified workers' contract, a set of charts and graphs Mo had put together for her, a job description she had written after networking with colleagues superintending small school districts, and two affidavits. She'd had the foresight to ask Mo to draw a diagram of the garage facility, located next to the high school.

Harvey Berman sat waiting for her in the driver's lunchroom. Fortyish, a small, wiry man with a thin face and wary eyes, he wore jeans, a black T-shirt, a Levi jacket, and a black baseball cap. He stood when Mandy entered, though he didn't speak.

"Mr. Berman? How do you do?" Mandy shook his hand. "Thank you for making time to see me."

Harvey murmured something inaudible.

"Before we sit down and talk, would you please show me around?"

Harvey ducked his head in assent but didn't move.

There was an awkward silence, which Mandy broke by asking, "Is this the break room?"

Harvey nodded.

"And through that door?"

"Garage."

"May I see it?" Mandy moved in the direction of the door, and Harvey scooted by her to open it. The cords in his neck stood out as he plastered himself against the doorjamb and held the door open with his extended arm as she passed through into the cavernous bus barn.

At a nearby workbench, a man in greasy coveralls bent over a vise and plied a file. He looked up at Mandy's approach.

"Are you Del? I thought you must be. How do you do? I'm Dr. Steenburg."

"Mechanic," Harvey offered in strangled syllables.

"Yes, I know. Where are the other—oh, I see."

A dozen faces of different ages and both genders looked down on Mandy from the windows of a bus parked in the garage. Thinking she was growing accustomed to grim visages, she walked to the open door and climbed up the yellow stairs. Harvey followed.

"Hello," she greeted. "I'm Dr. Steenburg, the new superintendent. I know some of your names, but I'd like to meet you all." She went down the aisle shaking hands and saying each name after it was given her. Then she turned and asked, "Did you abandon your break room so Harvey and I could talk?"

One of the women drivers nodded, and Mandy looked at Harvey, who stood on the bottom step. "Don't you have an office, Harvey?"

Tom Fellows offered, "He don't want you to see his mess."

"Well, we can't keep these good people out of their break room. Let's go into your office, mess or no mess." She walked down the aisle and paused at the exit, smiling. "It was nice to meet you all." Then she turned to Harvey, "I'll follow you."

He led her to a room that was more cell than office. Thinking that the word "mess" was the understatement of the century, Mandy surveyed the grimy paperwork stacked on the olive drab metal desk, the gray steel filing cabinet, and the floor.

"I'm a bit behind in my bookwork," the man mumbled.

Mandy tried to suppress a smile. "Can you get another chair?"

Harvey disappeared for a moment and returned with a folding chair. He opened it, set it beside the desk, and then stood awkwardly, waiting.

"Thank you. Now, if you will close the door? Good. I appreciate you letting me come by here so I could see the bus facility. It helps me to get acquainted with the district. Please sit down." Mandy sat in the swivel chair and gestured for Harvey to take the folding chair, which he did, sitting on the edge with his hands clenched in his lap.

They stayed in the office for an hour, at the end of which Mandy emerged with her briefcase in her hand. Turning to Harvey, she smiled and said, "I'll see you in my office next week, then?"

Harvey didn't return the smile. "I'll be there."

"All right, then. Now, can you point me to the cafeteria? I have to see Arvella Shonefeld."

For the first time, Harvey lost his hangdog look. The corners of his mouth lifted. "It's right across the way," he said. "Come, I'll show you."

Mandy checked the next-to-the-last item off her list, arched her back to stretch out some of the kinks, and swiveled around to look out her office window. The parking lot was empty except for Grange's pickup, and she realized it had been a while since she had heard any of the normal noises of the district office in motion. She looked at her watch, saw that it was five minutes to five, and fingered the list, considering as she read the last item: *Contract notes in Hawes and Cally files.* She sighed and muttered, "Come on, Mandy. Finish it up!"

Mrs. Hawes, a second-grade teacher, and Mr. Cally, high school math, were the last to be hired by the district, and therefore would be first to be let go because of budget constraints. The standard teacher's contract was quite clear that today was the deadline for notices of non-renewal to be mailed. Mandy had dictated the letters to Mrs. Berman as soon as she got back at noon, and two hours later they were on their way to the post office.

Mandy printed out two copies of the abstract she had made of pertinent contract sections, along with her comments. She opened the first file, and before inserting the notes, she scanned Vonda Hawes's profile information. A native of Limestone, she had graduated from Western Washington University three years ago. She married a local fellow and worked summers at a restaurant in town until a position opened up in the district.

Mandy next opened Sumner Cally's folder. He was from the Midwest, and as she flipped through his transcripts and application information, she was interested to find he had graduated at the top of his class from a small private college. His cover letter mentioned his love of math, his talent for making it relevant to students, and his desire to make a difference. He had included a picture, and Mandy, expecting a studious, shirt-and-tie fellow, was surprised at the tattoo of π on Sumner's neck above the ribbing on his T-shirt.

Mandy punched two holes in the top of her notes. As she was undoing the metal fasteners on the files, she glanced at the copy of her letter and froze. The latch stayed half undone in her fingers as she read a note scrawled under her signature. She grabbed the other file and examined the copy of Vonda Hawes's letter.

"Count to ten," she admonished herself between gritted teeth, but she didn't get past five before she sprang from her chair, scooped up the folders, and stormed through her door and down the hall to Grange Timberlain's office.

His door was open, but she rapped on the frame before entering. The sound echoed through the quiet office, and he turned to face her with one eyebrow raised. His good eye widened when he saw her face, and when she tossed the files on his desk, he jerked his pencil out of the way.

"How dare you?" She was so angry that her voice quivered, and that made her even madder.

"I beg your pardon?"

"You added a post script to my letters before they went out."

"Yes?"

"You don't do that! It isn't done! If something goes out with my signature on it, I need to okay it first."

Grange leaned back in his chair. "If you had come and discussed this with me first, there would have been no need to add anything."

"What was there to discuss? You said yourself that two teachers had to go so we could balance the budget. I read the contract. Those letters had to go out today."

Grange opened Sumner's file and tapped the letter with the pencil he still held. "Today is the day, but whether these particular letters had to go out is debatable."

"And just what's wrong with them?"

"They'll ensure that in next week's mail, Sumner Cally will be sending out applications to other districts."

"Hello? That's the intent of the contract. It's meant to protect teachers from a district waiting until there are no openings left before telling them their positions have been cut."

"Yes. I understand that. But Mr. Cally is too good a teacher to let go. I've got five students signed up for AP math next year. That's a first."

Mandy leaned over and put her finger on the note Grange had written. "Come and talk to me about this," she read. "What do you intend to say to Sumner Cally when you have this little talk?"

"I'm going to ask him to give us a little time. If I had written the letter, or had some input in its writing, I would have softened it, told him this was official notice, but we were trying to work something out."

"And you would have laid the district open to a suit from the union when there wasn't a job for him." Mandy picked up the files and turned to go. "By contract, the letter cannot be ambiguous."

"Well, as to laying the district open to a suit from the union, what about your little trick today?"

She paused at the doorway and turned to face Grange. "What little trick?"

"Your sleight of hand over at the bus garage."

Mandy frowned. "What are you talking about?"

"Did you or did you not get Harvey Berman to sign something saying he would spread the extracurricular duties among all the drivers, when I expressly told you that went by seniority?"

"I don't know how well you read the contract, but there was certainly a provision there to have a supervisor with assignment duties in his job description. It seems to me that things have been allowed to continue because of tradition when all that was needed was for someone to care enough to do a little reorganizing."

"And how are we going to pay for this reorganizing?" Grange drummed the pencil on his desk. "I can't believe that Harvey went for this just because of a title."

"Certainly he's getting a raise. However, when you spread the overtime hours over all the men, the difference in what they make as opposed to what Harvey would have made will pay for his raise."

Grange's good eye narrowed and one corner of his mouth curled down. Mandy took it to be a look of disdain, and she felt the anger rising again. She concentrated on speaking slowly, as if explaining to a child. "I worked it out with Mo. We'll have the same outlay, only we'll have peace in the bus barn. And I'm going to get him some clerical help."

"And where is that going to come from?"

"The same place we get the clerical help for the district offices—from student aides. What he needs are routines set up and someone to stay on top of it."

"Who is going to set up these routines?"

Mandy had a fleeting thought about delegating that to Grange, and though she didn't voice it, the idea was so delicious she had to smile. Instead, she said, "Maybe I'll do it."

"Oh, that makes sense." Grange stabbed the pencil into a mug and threw up his hands. "What a great use for the mega salary they're paying you! Have you tumbled to the fact yet that the reason we have to let Vonda and Sumner go is so we can pay you? Two teachers! The best math teacher we've ever had, and we have to let him go."

Mandy was so surprised by Grange's words that she couldn't reply. Feeling as if she had been kicked in the stomach, she hugged the files to her and stood with her mouth open.

Grange apparently didn't notice, because he went on without a pause. "By the time the classified union gets done with us, we'll have to let another teacher go."

That accusation helped Mandy find her voice, and she didn't even try to keep the edge out of it. "Don't be absurd! Two things are operative here. First, I didn't act without legal advice. I knew I was on pretty solid ground, but I called the State Superintendent's office and talked to their guru. Secondly, I would most forcibly remind the union that they represent all the drivers, not just the ones with most seniority." Mandy's voice rose as she warmed to her subject. "And by the way, do you know why Harvey and Les have all that wretched seniority? Because no one will stay in the job. They can't afford to. There is no equity. Have you seen the figures on the turnover rate? How can you hope to retain good people if you don't treat them like they have value?"

"Interesting," Grange said through gritted teeth. "I wish you could hear yourself."

"What do you mean?"

"You're lecturing me about the district as if you're not a part of it. You said, 'How can *you* hope to retain good people.' You didn't use 'we.'"

"Well, I'll tell you, pretty much everyone has been doing everything they can to convince me that I'm not a part of any 'we' and I never will be." Mandy slapped the files against her hand. "But I'm not yet convinced. Now, Mr. Timberlain, do you understand that I need to see anything that goes out of this office on a document with my signature?"

"And do you understand that the district will be better served by collaboration?"

"The two do not equate. I am asking you to adhere to standard protocol. You are asking to be included in making policy."

Grange stood. "The policy is made, Dr. Steenburg. Your job—your extremely well-paying job—is to not get in the way."

She had no chance to step her usual three paces away, though his office was so small she would have been hard pressed to do so. She found herself looking up at him like a child, and her anger boiled over. "What I saw at the bus garage wasn't policy, Mr. Timberlain. It was laissez faire that bordered on neglect because you're afraid of the driver's union." She turned on her heel, then stalked out of the room and down the hall to her own office, where she closed the door with more force than she meant to. She set the files on her desk, and then, with trembling hands, she put on her jacket and gathered her keys. As she turned out her light, she hoped mightily that she could get past Grange's office and downstairs before he decided to leave.

She glanced through his door as she hurried past, but he was hunched over his desk with his back to her. She exhaled a great sigh, then fled down the stairs, through the reception area, and out the front door.

Not wanting to stand in the rain looking for the Miata key on her ring, she stopped at the edge of the porch to find it. Intent on her task, she didn't see the black Escalade until it had pulled up in front of her.

The driver's tinted window rolled smoothly down, revealing Vince Laffitte's angular face. "You're frowning," he said.

Mandy looked up and smiled. "My keys seem to have multiplied in the darkness of my purse. I was trying to find the one to my car."

"I see you're just leaving. Do you have time to talk for a moment?"

She hesitated, looking back at the door to the district offices.

"Why don't you sit in here with me for a minute? It's warm and dry. We can talk briefly, and then I'll give you a lift to your car."

She laughed. "Clear across the parking lot?"

"As far as you want." He leaned over and opened the passenger door.

She hurried down the steps, around the sleek front end of the car, and climbed in. The interior smelled of new leather and aftershave, and as she set her purse down on the floor, she was aware of her nearness to Vince and the intimacy of the moment. Before she could find something light to say, he spoke. "I was going to ask why you were frowning, but I see now."

She followed his gaze and saw that Grange had just come out and was locking the front door. Looking like a storm cloud, he descended the stairs and walked in front of the Escalade, nodding curtly to Vince as he did so.

"Yes," Mandy said. "We've been crossing swords."

Vince held her eyes for a moment, and then his teeth flashed in that attractive smile. "I believe you could hold your own in any fencing match."

"Thank you for that vote of confidence." She watched as Grange stalked toward his truck, head down, hands shoved in the pockets of his jacket.

"I hear you've been cutting a wide swath."

She looked back at Vince and raised a brow.

"Mutt Maypole works for me. Nettie's husband."

They both turned their heads at the sound of spraying gravel and watched Grange roar out of the parking lot.

Vince murmured, "Mature."

Mandy looked down at her hands and compressed her lips to keep the corners from turning up, unwilling to join him in making fun of Grange. She said instead, "Nettie thought she ought to have a copyright on a potato recipe."

"Did you convince her otherwise?"

Mandy shook her head. "I didn't try. I left that with Arvella Shonefeld. She's the head of the food services department now, and along with the title comes responsibility for harmony in the ranks. She says she's going to give Nettie credit. She says she'll do it with an ostrick."

Vince looked puzzled. "A what?"

"An ostrick." Mandy's eyes twinkled. "As she says, 'You know, one of them little star thangs.' I think she means she's going to footnote on the next menu—with an asterisk—that the inspiration comes from Nettie Maypole." Mandy chuckled. "I shouldn't make fun. Arvella is doing a great job. She was making cream puffs for the students. Cream puffs! She gave me one, and I told her she had won my heart. I'm a sucker for anything cream filled."

"I'll remember that. But they're still going to be called Tarheel Spuds?" He shook his head. "You haven't made a friend there, you know."

Mandy looked down at the keys she still held in her hand and nodded, an almost imperceptible movement. "Not the first, either. I seem to be *not* making friends all over the district." Her eyes grew shiny, and she set the keys on the console beside her, careful not to look at Vince. "It's all really different from what I expected." She cleared her throat and forced a lighter note. "I meant to thank you for the daffodils."

"I got your message. You already thanked me."

"But not sufficiently. I was going to write a note as soon as I unpacked my stationery. Wherever did you get so many?"

"That's what I wanted to talk to you about, why I asked you to sit with me a moment. I'd like to show you. Would you come with me tomorrow?"

Mandy cocked her head and regarded him. "Are you asking me out?"

He didn't answer but held her gaze.

"Is that a good idea? Profession-wise, I mean, for me?"

Vince shrugged. "Call it a lunch appointment. You wanted to talk about school board business. We can do that while I show you around the district. Can I pick you up around eleven tomorrow?"

"Yes . . . no." She touched her forehead with her fingers. "I forgot. I can't. The van is coming tomorrow with my things. I'm moving in."

"Oh? Where?"

"I'm renting from Fran Porter."

"Oh, really? The house down by the river?"

"Yes. It's really lovely. I feel so lucky to have found it."

A crease appeared between his black brows. "Let's hope your luck, and the levee, holds."

Now it was Mandy's turn to frown. "What do you mean?"

"During a high, high flood, the ground floor of that house gets two, three feet of water in it."

She stared. "What is a high, high flood? How often do those come?"

"I guess you could consider those ten-year floods. I can remember five or six of them."

"Which would make you sixty if they happen every ten years."

Vince smiled. "Yeah. I guess they happen more frequently than that."

"How frequently? When was the last one?"

"Year before last, I think. Fran bought the house after it had been flooded." He leaned forward and turned the heater fan to low.

"I thought there was a bit of a musty smell when I went in the house the first time," Mandy mused. "Fran didn't say anything about it."

"Of course not. She needs a renter right away. It cost her more than she had planned to fix it up, and she had to pay more for financing and insurance, too, because it's in a flood zone."

Mandy sighed. "Life is never simple, is it? Sometimes the most attractive things turn out to be disasters."

"Don't let me scare you. This isn't a disaster. We're not due for another flood that high for a few more years. You'll have time to find another place. One on higher ground." He picked up her keys and rubbed his thumb absently around the ring. "So, if you can't go with me tomorrow, how about Sunday?"

"Sunday? Um, I thought I'd go to church. Can we do it in the afternoon?"

Vince shook his head. "I've got to be downriver in the afternoon. Come on. I'll show you a whole field of daffodils."

Mandy looked at the rain streaming down on the windshield. "I don't have an umbrella or a raincoat."

"You won't need one. We're going to have sun."

"Really?"

"Cross my heart. Will you come?"

"If you promise it will shine, I'll come."

"Done." His white teeth flashed. "I'll pick you up at eleven." He selected the Miata key from her ring and held it out to her. "I'll take you to your car."

He put the Escalade in gear and pulled over to her car. As she picked up her purse, Vince held out his hand. She gave him hers, and he said, "Till Sunday, then."

He had a strong, confident handshake. Mandy returned the pressure and said, "I'll be ready."

She jumped down from the high SUV and quickly unlocked the door of her Miata, noticing that he waited until she had started the engine before he pulled away. She waved to him and drove out of the parking lot, smiling at the thought of daffodils and sunshine.

11

Mandy opened her eyes Saturday morning to sun streaming in from the skylight in the bedroom of her new home. She sat up and looked out the front window through the posts of the balustrade. Blue sky blazed above the mountains on the other side of the river. "Wow!" she breathed. "Vince was right."

She picked up her watch from the floor beside the air mattress to check the time and saw that it was five minutes to eight. The movers had promised they would arrive by nine. She scrambled up and hastened to shower and dress, but she found herself more than once gravitating toward the window to stare at the vibrant scenery. The conifers' hunter green stood out against the lacy blush of bare-limbed alders, and the cloudless sky arched over all like lapis lazuli—the most intense electric blue she had ever seen.

At eight thirty she was at an east-facing window, letting the sunlight stream in on her face, when the moving van came lumbering down the road. She hurried out on the deck to wave them in, and soon she excitedly directed the crew of three where to place each piece of furniture and how to stack the boxes. Even with putting together the bed and bookcases and manhandling the old upright piano over the doorsill, the crew and van were on their way back up the hill by ten thirty. As they left, Mandy stood in the doorway of the spare bedroom and looked at the boxes filling every available inch of floor space, stacked as high as her chin.

Courage flowed in with the warm spring air as she threw open doors and windows, and she dug in with a will. Salvation came at noon in the form of her landlady. Mandy was in the kitchen, awash in a sea of crumpled newspaper, unwrapping dishes and putting them in a cupboard, when she heard Fran hallooing at the door.

"It's open," Mandy called.

"I've brought lunch, and I can stay for three hours," Fran announced. "I brought string cheese, cold cuts and veggies. We can munch as we work. Give me a job."

Mandy directed her to the book boxes and after that to the linens. By that time, she had finished the kitchen, and they tackled the upstairs together. They made the bed in tandem, and as Fran squared a corner to tuck in the top sheet, she said, "I heard you've stirred things up at the school cafeteria."

In the act of smoothing out a wrinkle, Mandy looked up. "Who told you that?"

"Nettie Maypole came by to see Mutt, and she told me. Something about Arvella bribing you with a cream puff? Sounds far-fetched to me."

Mandy grinned. "I take it you've never had one of Arvella's cream puffs."

Fran shook her head. "Too many carbs. So, what was the deal?"

Mandy took a comforter out of a box and shook it to loft the down filling. "It was a tempest in a tea pot—something that should blow over soon."

Frowning, Fran shook her head. "The Maypoles have long memories where grudges are concerned."

"Well, I'm not going to lie awake nights worrying about it. I've got other things that have lots more precedence." She looked at her watch. "Your three hours are up. Thanks so much, Fran. You're a good friend."

"No problem. I love a project. You've just got one layer of boxes left. If you don't get done today, I'll come help you tomorrow."

Mandy dropped the empty box over the balcony railing and watched its descent. "I'm going to finish today if it kills me."

"I have to close tonight, but I'll look for your light when I get home. I'm right above you, did you know? I can see your upstairs light through a break in the trees."

"Oh?" Mandy went to the balcony. "I can't see your house."

"No. If I cut some trees, you could, but we'd both lose privacy. There's a trail down through the woods. Sometimes I come down to walk along the river." She looked around. "Where's my purse? Oh, there it is. Good luck on the rest of the boxes."

"Thanks again." Mandy watched her friend disappear down the circular stairway. Then she turned to open a box marked "Bathroom" in Leesie's distinctive handwriting.

Things went slower without Fran, and it was way past dark by the time Mandy hung the last picture and flattened the last box. She stacked it atop the rest out on the back deck. Then she came in, locked the back door, and walked through her house, turning on familiar lamps, looking at the furniture grouping with a critical eye. With a sigh, she sat down at the piano and played "In My Adobe Hacienda," a slow, sweet number that Poppy, her stepfather, used to ask her to play.

"It doesn't fit," she murmured and sat for a minute with her hands lax on the keys. "What's a Pacific Northwest song? I don't think there are any." But her fingers found a sad song about leftover dreams saved for a rainy day. She chuckled. "It fits." Then she played an arpeggio to segue into another song about stormy weather. It was a breakup song, and the refrain about rain all the time made Mandy suddenly feel empty, like she was hollow. Tears sprang to her eyes, and she blinked them away. "I must be hungry," she muttered. "Either that, or I need to stop playing songs about love gone awry."

She closed the piano and went to the kitchen to open a can of soup. When it was hot, she poured it in a mug, turned out the lights, and drifted out to sit on the front deck. The stars twinkled overhead, and in the distance she heard a pulsing, chirruping sound, like a thousand crickets, but not so shrill. A cool breeze sprang up, and above her, the eerie *hoo hoo hoooo* of an owl made goosebumps rise on her arms. She shivered but stayed to finish her soup, waiting for the hollowness to disappear.

A full moon rose and cast a shimmering, silvery reflection on the river. She stared, entranced, until her attention was drawn to a stealthy sound to her right. Her heart began to pound in her chest as she searched in the shadowy bushes, and she held her breath so she could listen better. Suddenly, into the moonlit clearing of the road stepped a deer—a doe with dainty feet and an elegant muzzle. The creature took two steps then stood like a statue, and tears welled up in Mandy's eyes once more. She sighed, and at the sound, the deer bounded away into the darkness of the woods on the other side of the road.

Mandy rubbed her arms and shivered, then stood to go inside. As she closed and locked the door, it felt as if she were shutting beauty out of her life. She put her cup in the sink and climbed the stairs to her bedroom, and long after she lay down in her familiar bed, as she listened to the night sounds and contemplated the shadows cast by the shaft of moonlight coming in the skylight, she wondered why she should feel so sad.

Sunday morning Mandy again woke to sunshine. She lay with the covers up around her ears and smiled as she thought about her planned excursion with Vince Lafitte. *I'll go to church next Sunday,* she promised herself as she flung off the covers and sat up. Looking across the river at the sunlight on the mountain, she began to sing "It's a Lovely Day Today."

The song stayed with her all morning. She hummed the tune, sang the words, or scatted nonsense syllables as she showered, as she put on her makeup, as she ate breakfast and did the dishes. She even sat down at the piano in her sweats and played a bouncy rendition, stopping in mid phrase as she realized that some of the bass notes were not completely in tune. She frowned, played a scale, and muttered, "Now, why didn't I hear that last night? I must have been slightly out of tune myself."

She left the piano and went upstairs to dress. As she considered the contents of the shoe rack against the closet wall, she murmured, "He said fields of daffodils." Remembering the debacle in Mrs. Foley's garden, she chose a pair of lightweight hiking boots. She put them on and looked at herself critically in the mirror. "I don't suppose you're going to grow any more," she told her reflection. "But you look sufficiently Pacific Northwest in those shoes."

She checked her watch. Ten o'clock. Vince wouldn't be here until eleven. Mandy walked to the balustrade and looked down at the living area. Everything was neat and tidy—nothing to do there. A stack of district procedure notebooks sat on her desk in the corner, but she couldn't muster any enthusiasm for an hour spent amid state-mandated regulations.

She raised her eyes to the river. Sunshine glinted off ripples like newly minted coins scattered on the water. Without even a conscious decision to do so, she descended the stairs, went out the door, and crossed the road. She spied a trail in front of her house and followed it through ankle-high grass until it dropped down into a sterile, stony expanse that bordered the river's flow.

She walked upstream, keeping her eyes on the ground because of the difficult footing. She was conscious of the warmth of the sun on her face, the songbirds in the trees alongside the river, the freshness of the air, and the soft sound of the river lapping against the rocks littering the shallows. She had gone perhaps a couple hundred feet when she came to an immense pile of tree trunks all jumbled together like a game of giant Pickup Sticks. The snarl of logs rested mostly on dry riverbed, reaching only about a third of the way across this wide, inexorably flowing river.

Mandy stood with her hands on her hips and surveyed the logjam. After picking her way among the cobbles, she walked alongside a huge, horizontal trunk that lay on the ground until she reached the grassy bank where the upended roots of a huge tree were still anchored into the soil. She grabbed hold of one of the roots, pulled herself up onto the trunk, and walked out toward the flowing river. When she reached the water, she sat on one of the logs that had piled up behind at bench height. Leaning back against another that had been thrown up diagonally by the forces of the flood, she looked out over the scene before her: mountains rising steep and forested to her left, and the river stretching before her, reflecting the blue of the sky.

She breathed deeply and compared the peace of this moment to the anger she had felt toward Grange Timberlain on Friday afternoon. She closed her eyes and saw again that one brow pulled down and heard him saying, "Have you tumbled to the fact yet that the reason we have to let Vonda and Sumner go is so we can pay you?" She had been too angry to consider his words, but she considered them now.

No, she hadn't realized that her salary had put the district budget out of whack. That information had rocked her more than she let show. But, she told herself, she wasn't the one who caused the problem. If Grange had stepped up to the responsibility he had to the district, taken the classes he needed, he would still be superintendent and she would be . . . where? Chevak, Alaska? Still in Albuquerque? Still involved with . . . She shook her curls and forced her thoughts back to her surroundings.

The sun climbed in the sky, and she looked at her watch. Vince would be here in twenty minutes. She stood, dusted off her pants, and retraced her steps along the log. She jumped down onto the grassy bank and spied a path that took off into the woods. Following it, she discovered that it paralleled the river for a while and then angled up to the road just before the A-frame. As she stepped into the sunshine, she saw the black Escalade parked in front of the house. Vince stood on the deck.

"Hello!" she called, waving when he turned to look her way.

A broad smile replaced the frown on his face, and he hurried down the steps and came to meet her. He was dressed casually in chinos and a shirt of muted brown plaid, pressed to perfection as before.

"You're a bit early," Mandy called. "I've been down by the river."

He met her halfway to the house and walked the rest of the way beside her with his hands in his pockets, looking down with warm eyes as he spoke. "I hope you don't mind. I couldn't wait."

"No. I've been ready for an hour, too. I wonder . . ."

He stopped. "What?"

She stopped as well. "Would you mind taking the Miata? It's such a lovely day. We could put the top down."

He nodded. "You got it. The Miata it is." They continued on and he didn't speak again, but as they walked, his elbow lightly brushed her upper arm every now and then.

When they got to the house, Mandy put the car's top down, and Vince took a small cardboard box out of the back of the Escalade.

"Is there room in the trunk for this?" he asked.

"I think we can manage that. What do you have there?"

He opened the box and she peered inside. "What are they?"

"Morel mushrooms."

"Is that right? They look like brains."

He threw back his head and laughed. "Brains? I've never heard anyone describe them like that. Most people say they look like little Christmas trees."

"Yes, but look at all those wrinkles and folds. And the color is very brain-like."

"Mutt Maypole brought these to me. It's early for morels, but he knows a place up on the mountain where you can find them early. Must be some geothermal activity that makes the ground warmer than usual."

"You've got hot springs around?"

"Yes. That and other activity. Mount Stevens is a dormant volcano, you know." Vince put the mushrooms in the trunk.

Mandy's eyes widened. "How dormant? Wait, don't answer yet. Let me get my driver's license." She ran into the house, grabbed her purse and car keys, locked the door, and rejoined

Vince, who was holding the driver's door open for her. She got in and smiled up at him. "Thank you very much."

"Quite dormant," he said as he shut the door, "though Mt. Stevens is a cousin to Mt. St. Helens, and ever so often she blows steam through a vent at the top."

Backing out of the driveway, Mandy chuckled. "That's another thing your agent neglected to mention when he hired me."

Vince gave her directions that took them back to the highway and farther upriver. As they drove, he leaned back and turned slightly so his shoulder was against the door and his view of the driver was unobstructed.

She glanced over at him. "What are you smiling at?"

The wind ruffled his hair. "You. Me. The day. What's not to smile at?" He pointed. "See where that truck is turning? Turn there, only go left instead of right."

She did as she was told, downshifting to make the turn. The road climbed through trees for about a mile and then suddenly opened out into a huge, flat, open field of yellow daffodils.

"Oooooh!" Mandy slowed, looking from right to left. "Oh, Vince! I've never seen anything like this." She glanced at him and found his eyes on her.

"Drive on," he said. "We'll turn at that sign. Do you see it?"

"The one set in those rocks? What does it say?"

"Bratararia," he said, still watching her. "I see you recognize the name."

Her brow wrinkled. "Well, yes. I recognize—winery? This is a winery? Where?"

"You'll see. Keep going."

They had passed the daffodils, and now they were in a vineyard, trellised and pruned, row upon row of grapevines marching in formation at eye level as far as they could see.

"You're full of surprises," Mandy observed. "Since Bratararia was the name of Jean Lafitte's colony off the Gulf Coast, I'm assuming this is yours?"

"Yes. The winery is just ahead. There's a more direct way to get to it, but I wanted to show you the flowers."

They approached a quaint stone building, with Roman arches along the front and a red tile roof. Mandy pulled into the yard, where topiary trees and daffodils grew out of half casks lining the parking lot.

"Let's go in." Vince opened his door. "I'm going to cook you lunch, but I want to show you around first."

Mandy got out and preceded him through the heavy, rounded front door into a shadowy interior. She looked around at the massive beams and leaded glass, rough stone walls, and slate floor of the empty room. "It has a medieval feel to it."

"By design. This will be the wine-tasting room. It's still a work in progress. Step through this way." He led through an archway into a long, narrow, windowless room with sets of empty wine racks perpendicular to the wall all the way down. "These lights are temporary. We'll have better lighting after next week."

Mandy folded her arms for warmth. "Reminds me of the stacks in the library on campus," she said. "It was cold there, too."

"This will be climate controlled. They're coming next week to get it installed."

From that room they stepped into another that was large, open, and windowless. "Temporary lighting here, too," Vince said. "This is for the casks. They're over at the other place right now. We've been operating for ten years in a pole building in the fields down closer to Limestone."

She looked around dutifully but could find no apt comment, so she just nodded and followed him to the last room, a clone of the previous one. "This is where the vats will be, the actual making of the wines. We'll move our stock of wine this spring and the machinery this summer in time for the harvest in the fall."

He stood uncertainly in the middle of the room, obviously waiting for some comment.

"This is something completely out of my world, Vince," she said, "but I can tell that it's something you're excited about. I'm glad for you." She touched his arm as she said it. He looked down at the floor and then up at her, and exhaled.

"I don't know why I was so nervous about bringing you out here," he said. "Come out on the patio. I'm going to cook for you."

Mandy followed him willingly out into the sunshine. A green resin table with a red-and-white-checkered tablecloth, set for two with china and crystal goblets, sat on the flagstone patio under a grape arbor that did no more than filter the sunshine. It was pleasant after the dim chilliness of the winery.

Vince drew up a chair and seated her. Then he lit a propane barbeque and took two steaks out of an ice chest. As he cooked, he explained about the grapes he grew, pinot noir, and how he hoped this area, with its east-facing slopes and soil high in calcium carbonate, would be good for growing consistently good grapes. They were difficult to grow, he said, and difficult to ferment. "But when you get it right," he said, "it creates a lasting impression on the palate, and it sticks in your memory."

He looked at his watch. "It won't be long, now. Oh! The mushrooms. May I borrow your keys?"

She handed them over. He walked quickly around the building and returned momentarily with the box. He put a sheet of aluminum foil on the grate, poured the mushrooms out, dusted them with salt and pepper, and closed the lid.

Ten minutes later he set a steak smothered in mushrooms in front of Mandy and then produced a crisp green salad and vinaigrette dressing to go with it. "Mmm," she said. "You are full of surprises today."

"Here's the last one." He produced a bottle of red wine and a corkscrew. "This is the product of my winery."

She sat still as a statue as she watched Vince ply the corkscrew, then pour the dark red liquid into her glass.

"What's the matter?" He paused with the mouth of the bottle suspended above the goblet.

She had a stricken look on her face. "Oh, Vince," she whispered.

His black brows drew together. "What's the matter?"

She pressed her hands over her face as she felt the color rising to her cheeks. "You've made such a lovely lunch, and you've brought your wine to share with me . . ."

"Yes?"

There was nothing to do but say it. "I don't drink."

"What do you mean?"

It was easier now that she had said it once. "I mean, I don't drink alcohol."

He leaned back in his chair. "You're kidding!"

Mandy took her hands from her face. "Why would you say that?"

"You're intelligent, educated, sophisticated."

She shook her head. "I don't know about that. Maybe that's the way you see me, but I'm a lot of other things that you know nothing about."

"Ouch!" He set the bottle down on the table. "I'm not doing very well here, am I?"

She looked at her hands, clenched in her lap. "That came out wrong."

"No, you're right. I know very little about you. I suppose it's a religious thing? I shouldn't have pushed." Vince put down the bottle. "Try the steak." His white teeth flashed. "You do eat meat, don't you? Or do I have that wrong, too?"

She picked up her fork and knife. "Not at all. My grandfather is a rancher. I grew up on beef."

Hoping to take the sting out of her refusal to drink his wine, she kept up a flow of light conversation during lunch. She talked about her house and about her morning amble. She told him about walking out on the great trunk to sit in the sunshine above the river.

Vince frowned and told her that logjams like that were deathtraps. Mandy lifted her brows, and he went on to explain. "The current is flowing so fast when the river is high that it creates suction as it goes under. If your boat comes up against the logjam, first it's going to turn broadside and then it's going to capsize because of the forces pulling on it." His mouth was set in grim lines. "'Hiesel' is a local Indian word that translates as 'dangerous.' Only it's more than that. It carries the meaning that death can be sudden and you've been forewarned. 'Stallo' means 'river,'" and before white men came, they called the river 'Hiesel Stallo' to let strangers know a person in the water didn't have a chance. I hope you'll be careful." He paused and looked away.

He didn't speak again, and she searched for a way to break the silence. She picked up the wine bottle and studied the label. A picture of a square-rigger, flying a black flag, rode the crest of a wave that melded cleverly into the word 'Bratararia.'

"I like your label," she said. "Did you design it?"

"Yes. Thank you."

Mandy smoothed the label with her thumb where it had come unstuck from the bottle. "So, why wine? What made you, a building demolisher, decide to become a maker of wine?"

"It must be in the blood. My father made moonshine."

Involuntarily, her eyes flew to Vince's face.

"Ah," he said. "You have heard that I'm a—that I'm illegitimate."

She felt her cheeks getting hot and looked away.

"Don't be embarrassed. It's the truth, but I know who my father was."

"Who was he?"

"Buck Timberlain."

Mandy blinked. "Timberlain? Then, you're Rael's—"

"I'm Rael's cousin." Vince took the wine bottle from her, as she was in danger of tipping the contents into her lap. "Grange is also my cousin." He set the bottle on the table. "Israel Timberlain—my grandfather—was a baby when his family moved from North Carolina in the twenties. Rael lives in the house he built."

Mandy nodded. "That's just up the road from me."

"Old Israel had three sons." Vince lined up his knife, fork, and spoon. Touching each in turn, he said, "Rael's father's name was Jacob. Grange's father's name was Frederick, and my father's name was Benjamin, but everyone called him Buck."

Vince raised his brows for permission and she nodded, so he picked up her spoon. He put the spoon down with the others. "There was a sister, Lucinda," he said. "She married Ben Hawes and had two children, Tammy and Stevie Joe. Anyway, Buck had a still in the woods on his father's property." He moved the wine bottle to the edge of the table. "It sat on a bluff by the river, and he did a tidy bit of business around the county."

"You speak of him in the past tense. Is he dead?"

Vince took a sip of wine before he answered. "Yes, he is. He was found in the woods near his still, shot to death. I was eighteen at the time, and I remember my mother wept when she read about it in the newspaper. It was the only time I ever saw her cry."

"Did she tell you why?"

Vince shook his head. "I didn't find out who my father was until just before she died."

"When was that?"

"Thirteen years ago. I was twenty-two."

Mandy carefully folded the checkered napkin on her lap. "I never knew who my father was," she said without looking up.

"But your name—Steenburg. Is that your father's name?"

She smoothed the edges of the folded napkin. "No. It's my mother's maiden name. It's funny how society's views have changed in the last thirty years. People don't think anything about it anymore. Back then it was called 'out of wedlock.' I came to hate that phrase."

Vince leaned back in his chair and fingered the stem of his wineglass as he regarded her.

Mandy didn't look at him. "I made the decision not to drink when I was ten. I asked my mother why I didn't have a father, and she told me how she had been drinking one night at a teenage party, and that's when I was conceived. I decided right then that I was never going to let alcohol influence my life in any way. Too many people carry the scars."

She laid the napkin on the table and met Vince's eyes. "But it turned out all right. When I was eleven my mother married a man I called Poppy. He wanted to adopt me, but I wouldn't change my name, because I wanted my real father, though that's silly because Poppy was a real father to me. But in my childish fantasy, I wanted the man who . . . who . . . you know. I wanted him to be able to find me, and I was afraid if I took Poppy's name, he wouldn't be able to."

Vince reached over and laid his hand briefly over hers, curling his fingers under her palm and giving just the slightest pressure. "It's tough, isn't it, waiting for your father to recognize your existence?"

"Yours never did?"

He shook his head. They sat in silence for a moment.

"I don't know," he went on, "maybe the wine business is to do what he did, only better. Legitimate, you know? Make a name for myself and my label in the world. Invite the world in to see my operation instead of skulking around trying to elude the revenue agents."

Mandy nodded. "I bet you'll succeed."

He smiled ruefully. "Well, I haven't gotten very far with you. I tell you what. You may not drink, but you don't have anything against smelling, do you?"

"What?"

Vince picked up her glass. "Here. I want you to smell this."

"Are you serious?"

"Yes. I want you to smell it and tell me what it reminds you of."

She took the goblet and held it under her nose.

"Close your eyes," he prompted.

She did as he asked, then sniffed.

"Take your time."

She inhaled again.

"Say the first thing that pops into your head."

"Cherries."

"Good girl. Anything else?"

"Cinnamon? Is that possible?"

"Yes. What else?"

"It was a more of a remembrance of how the morels smelled when you showed them to me. Just a fleeting memory, really. I can't explain it."

"You don't need to. I know. It does the same for me. Open your eyes."

Mandy did as he bid and found him facing her, leaning forward, with elbows on his knees. He held one hand out to take the glass from her and set it on the table. Then he took her hand and brought it to his lips. "Thank you."

He didn't prolong the moment but stood and began to gather up dishes and place them in the cooler, tossing Mandy's leftover wine into the ground by the arbor.

She stared for a moment at the wet patch on the sod. Then she folded up the linens and handed them to Vince. "I can't tell you what a lovely day this has been."

"My pleasure."

"Truly? I'm glad." She eyed the cooler. "I don't think we can get that in the trunk."

"That's all right. I have to come back out this afternoon. There are some things I need to get done before the crew shows up on Monday." He stood aside to let her walk in front of him on the narrow path around the building.

They got in the Miata and drove home at a leisurely pace on back roads, and as they went, Mandy asked about the demolition business. Vince explained the basic laws of physics that govern how they set the charges and then went on to tell a couple of stories about disasters when those laws weren't fully taken into account.

They were descending the gravel road to her house as he recounted the tale of his first demolition job when, as a young man, he worked for someone who contracted to get rid of a beached whale by disintegrating it with dynamite. Mandy laughed so hard at his description of the resulting blubber bombs and fatty shrapnel and how all the spectators had to dive for cover that she could hardly see to stay on the road.

It was only as she pulled into the driveway by the A-frame that she noticed Rael Timberlain's Jeep parked by Vince's Escalade.

"It looks like you've got company," Vince said.

Still giggling from his story, Mandy nodded, but she frowned when she saw her open front door. "Rael doesn't seem like the kind of person to go into someone's house . . ."

The sentence never made it the rest of the way from her brain to her mouth. Rael was indeed standing in the doorway of her house. On one side of him slouched the sullen, raven-haired girl who worked for Midge Cooley at the district office, but it was neither of them that made Mandy stare openmouthed. It was the tall, blonde girl standing on the other side with a tentative smile, her hand half raised in greeting.

Mandy finally found her voice. "Leesie? What on earth are you doing here?"

Half an hour later, Vince, Rael, and his daughter were gone, and Leesie sat at the kitchen table munching a peanut butter sandwich as Mandy set a mug of tomato soup in front of her.

"Thanks, Sis," Leesie said. "It's been a long time since the Twinkies I had for breakfast."

Mandy sat down across from her and tucked one foot up. "Let me get this straight. You got on a bus right after you talked to me Friday morning? Why didn't you tell me you were coming up here?"

"Because you would have told me not to."

"Well, yes, I would have. This doesn't make sense! And riding all the way up here from Stallo with a complete stranger!"

"Who's a complete stranger?"

"Rael."

"He's not a complete stranger. The agent at the bus station introduced me to him, and he had his kids with him, anyway."

"Kids? Do you mean there's another gothic sibling?"

"No, the sibling isn't gothic. But never mind that. Where were you today? Or maybe I should ask who you were with. Who's Heathcliff?"

"Heathcliff?"

"The guy you were with—the one with the big, black Cadillac SUV, which, if you want to be judgmental, could really tell you a lot about the guy."

"Why are you calling him Heathcliff?"

"Because he looks like someone out of *Wuthering Heights*— all dark and brooding and more than a little sinister. Rael, on the other hand, looks like the Angel Gabriel." Leesie laughed. "No, don't look cross-eyed at me. Don't you think his hair looks like a halo, the way it curls around his head?"

"I'm looking cross-eyed because you shouldn't call him by this first name. He's an adult."

"He told me to call him that." Leesie took a drink of soup and regarded her sister over the rim of the cup. "You haven't told me who he is."

"Rael is the mailman."

"Not him. Heathcliff."

Mandy stood and went to the kitchen. "His name is Vince Lafitte," she said as she began to wash the soup pot. "He's a member of the school board."

"Oh, and I'm sure all you talked about today was school board business. You looked very chummy when you drove up. Where had you been?"

Mandy rinsed the pot, dried it, and put it away. Then she stood with her hands on her hips and said severely, "We've strayed from the original point, which was what are you doing here? And does Mother know?"

"Who's that?"

Mandy frowned. "Leesie, what's the matter with you? Mother. Your mother. My mother. Does she know?"

"No. I meant who's that?" Leesie pointed. "You're very popular. Big frog in a little puddle, I guess."

Mandy turned and looked out the window at the white-haired lady getting out of a blue sedan. "I have no idea."

Mandy took off her apron and went to answer the doorbell, steeling herself to be gracious.

It turned out to be easier than she expected. Her visitor swept in with a smile as wide as the Hiesel Valley, and resist as she might, Mandy smiled back.

Millie Barlow, wife of the local pastor, brushed aside Mandy's declaration that she would attend church the following Sunday, saying that was her husband's affair. Taking the chair Leesie offered her and declining refreshments, Millie Barlow stated she had two reasons for visiting and launched in. When she left half an hour later, Mandy had not only agreed to visit Granny Timberlain each month, but had also said she would work in literacy outreach. Mrs. Barlow explained that Tammy Wilcox couldn't read, and she asked Mandy to spend three hours a week coaching her.

"Wow," Leesie said as Mandy closed the door after her visitor. "She really is a powerhouse!"

"I'll say. I need to study her technique. Did you see how she got me to say I'd teach this lady?"

"Yeah. Usually the pastor's wife just brings a plate of cookies and an invitation to come to worship service. How did she even know you were here?"

Mandy curled up on the couch. "News travels fast in a small town, I guess."

"Well, I think the cookies would have been a good idea." Leesie went to the kitchen table and looked in the empty soup mug. She put it in the sink, then opened a cupboard door and began scanning the contents.

"Me too. I don't know how to teach a grown person to read."

"Can it be different than teaching a child? I've heard Mother say that you just need to give a child a safe place and the tools to teach himself to read."

"Mother said that? Which reminds me, I was just asking you if she knows you're here."

Leesie closed the cupboard and looked at her watch. "Actually, yes. Do we have an hour's difference? We're earlier? Let's see. Her plane landed at four." She cast her eyes to the roof and did the math. "I expect to get a call from her on my cell phone any time."

"Well, you'll be waiting quite a while. There's no service upriver." Mandy rubbed her arms and, looking outside, noticed the house was sitting in shadows. She walked over and closed the front windows. "Did you leave Mother a note?"

"Matter of fact, I did."

Mandy dug in her purse and pulled out her phone card. She handed it to Leesie. "You'd better go call her. Use the phone upstairs in my bedroom. Tell her I'll put you on a plane tomorrow. We can run down to the district office tonight and use the internet there to get reservations."

Leesie took the card and bounced up the stairs, calling out, "Hey, you should see the view from up here! The river looks like it has pink lights in it. Where's the phone? Oh, I found it."

Mandy heard a door close and figured Leesie must have carried the telephone into the bathroom for privacy. She rinsed the mug and put it in the dishwasher. Then she stood quietly, leaning against the counter, listening for some clue as to what was going on upstairs. Finally she gave up and sat on the couch in the living room. Her eye fell on the cello case standing in the corner. There was apparently no other luggage. *Just like Leesie to take off on a thousand-mile journey with nothing but her instrument,* she thought.

A few minutes later Leesie came down. She was teary-eyed but smiling. "I'm to stay," she announced.

"Whoa." Mandy frowned. "Don't I have a say in this?"

Leesie stopped in mid stride. Her eyes welled up and her chin began to quiver. "Are you saying you don't want me?"

Mandy patted the cushion beside her. "I'm not saying that. It's just that this—this running away is totally out of character. What's going on?"

Leesie sat down, tucked up her feet, and hugged her arms against herself. "Is it chilly in here? Can you turn on some heat?"

Mandy lit the stove and sat back with her sister.

"That's nice," Leesie said. She drew a deep breath. "All right, I'll tell you why I'm here. I've been dating a boy, Rob Greer. He's bright and funny and an athlete. Popular. Macho. Drop-dead gorgeous. Dozens of girls would give anything to be his steady girl."

"And are you his steady girl?"

"I guess I am. He's, like, the only person I want to date. I think about him all the time." She covered her face with her hand. "I hate it, but I even sit in class and write his name on my notebook." She looked out at her sister from between her fingers. "How lame is that?"

"Sounds normal to me. So why did you bolt?"

Leesie sat back and picked up a throw pillow. "Rob was ready to take the relationship to the next level. He was pressuring me to—to—well, you know."

"All you had to do was say no," Mandy said gently.

Leesie hugged the throw pillow and leaned her cheek against it, staring into the fire. "That's easy to say when you're not there with his arms around you, and he's whispering in your ear, and your whole body is voting yes. Do you know, I get weak in the knees just thinking about him?"

They sat in silence for a moment, and then Leesie picked up the thread again. "I signed up for a class this semester called The Bible in the Arts."

Mandy nodded. "I was on the committee that okayed that class. It was real controversial. What did you think of it?"

"Oh, it was great. The first thing we did was watch the video about Joseph and his amazing Technicolor dream coat. It was all music and lots of fun. Then we had to read the story."

"The script?"

Leesie shook her head. "No, the story from the Bible. In the play, and in the Bible, too, Joseph is a servant, and his boss's wife keeps hitting on him. In the play, his boss comes in and catches them together, but in the Bible, he runs away and leaves her holding on to his coat." Leesie closed her eyes as if replaying it in memory. "It says 'he fled and got him out.'"

She opened her eyes and turned to look at her older sister. "The moment I read that, it hit me: that's what I had to do. I had to flee and get me out. So I did."

The room grew gradually darker as they sat without speaking, each lost in her own thoughts.

Leesie was the first to break the silence. "It felt right, Mandy. I told Mother why I came, and she agrees with me. You know how paranoid she is about us not falling into the same trap she did." She giggled. "When I started dating Rob, she started dropping heavy hints about making a visit to Planned Parenthood."

Mandy smiled, remembering her own discussions with her mother. "Of course you can stay."

Leesie leaned over and hugged her sister. "Thank you." Resting her head against Mandy's shoulder, she chuckled. "Oh, Mandy! The trip was such an adventure! First, I sat by a girl my age. She and her baby were going to her parents' house because her husband was on his way to Iraq. Then, this guy from Bosnia got on. All his family was killed in the ethnic cleansing there, and he was here in the U.S. as a student. He was on his way to visit an aunt in Spokane, the only member of his whole family that was still alive, and he was so excited to see her. They both had stories that made my problem pale into insignificance. Like, someone was saying to me, 'Hello? Get a clue, Leesie!'"

Mandy squeezed her sister's shoulder. "Well, we need to arrange a place for you to sleep, I guess. I have an air mattress."

"It's all taken care of." Leesie jumped up. "Come and see."

Mystified, Mandy followed her sister to the downstairs bedroom. Leesie opened the door and turned on the light. "Ta-da!"

"When did you do this?" Mandy asked. "Where did the bed come from? I recognize the blankets, but where did you get the pillows?"

"Fran helped me. It's your air mattress, see?" Leesie lifted the blanket to reveal a piece of plywood sitting on plastic buckets and supporting the mattress. "She said this is what she did when she first moved here, before she bought any furniture. She knew where the linens were, and she loaned me the pillows. She's the one that let us in the house. Rael knew she was your landlady, so when you weren't home, we went up to see her."

Leesie opened the closet door. "There's more. See what she brought, too?"

Mandy peeked in the closet, and up against the wall stood a rack of wire bins that held Leesie's underwear, socks, T-shirts and sweaters.

"She had those in her garage. Isn't that cool? I love it."

"Well, we certainly will have to tell Fran thank you," Mandy said.

"Yes. I like her. Did you know her sister used to work for Poppy?"

"How did you find that out? She didn't tell me."

Leesie climbed onto the bed and sat cross-legged on the pillows. "Well, she had no way of knowing you're related to Poppy. When I told her my name was Leesie Wheeler, she said her sister used to work for Conroy Wheeler, and I said that's my dad. She said her sister thought he was a real good man, and she asked how he was doing."

"And you said . . .?"

"I said he's fine."

"Leesie, you can't keep doing that."

"Why not? I know he's in a better place, and there's no more pain. Just because I can't see him anymore doesn't mean he's not near." Leesie sat on the bed. "You know, that's why I like Jake Timberlain so much. When he talks about his mother, he says 'is' instead of 'was,' too."

Mandy frowned. "Who's Jake Timberlain?" Leesie patted the place beside her, and Mandy sat on the edge. "Who's Jake Timberlain?" she repeated.

"He's Rael's son. Willow's brother."

"Rael has a son? Where was he this afternoon?"

"He was here for a while, but before you came, he left to take his great aunt Clara to see her friends. She lives in a rest home in Stallo, and they bring her up once a month to visit. That's how I got the ride up. The bus depot man's wife works at the rest home, and he knew Rael would be coming down today. Aren't small towns great?"

"Maybe Jake's mother isn't dead. Maybe they're divorced."

"No. When it was obvious there were just the three of them in the family, I asked Willow if her mom and dad were divorced. She said her mother was dead."

"Is that why she always wears black? Does Jake look anything like Willow?"

Leesie laughed. "No. He looks more like his dad, though he's taller. But he has the same mop of curls. He's going to come by and pick me up for school tomorrow."

"That's not necessary. I can drop you off."

"I know. But we're going to Granny Timberlain's before school. It's kind of a family tradition."

"If it's family, maybe you should wait."

"Nope. Rael says it's okay." Leesie put a pillow behind her back, leaned against it, and sighed. "I'm starting to hit the wall. I didn't sleep very well on the bus. I think I've been running on adrenaline all day. I was excited to get here, but at the same time I was afraid you might not let me stay."

"Well, you'd probably better go to bed, though if the piano wasn't out of tune, I'd make you come play with me first. I've got to find someone to tune it."

"Rael can do it."

"I need a professional. I don't want to trust my piano to someone who doesn't know what he's doing."

"He tunes the school pianos."

"Leesie, how do you know all this?"

"While we were getting the bedroom set up, Willow was messing around on the piano—everything she played was in a minor key. Jake mentioned that it needed tuning and asked his dad, but I knew you didn't want just anyone doing it. You know, he delivers mail in that funny old Jeep. That doesn't add up to a piano tuner, does it? But Jake says he does the school pianos, and Rael said he would come by tomorrow and tune ours. He says he doesn't want you to pay him. You can fix dinner instead."

"Dinner? But I'm not ready to have people over for dinner."

"It's not 'people.' It's just the Timberlains. I like them, Mandy. Willow is a bit strange. But Jake and his dad are super."

Mandy laughed. "All right. We'll have them over." She stood. "I guess you found out that the bedroom shares the bathroom with guests, so you'll probably want to make a habit of locking the other door when you're in there. Towels are in the cupboard. I'll fix oatmeal for breakfast, and you will eat it. That's a condition of staying here."

Leesie climbed off the bed. "Are you going to make up conditions as we go along?"

"Probably. What time will Jake be by to get you?"

"Six thirty."

"Six thirty! That's some family tradition." Mandy stood and smoothed the blanket. "I'll leave shortly after you do, as I like to get to my office well before seven." She hugged her sister. "I think I'm going to enjoy having you here."

Leesie yawned. "Mother said she'd come up for my graduation, if not before. She said she'd bring Aunt Mary and Uncle Ron and whoever else she can convince to be part of her entourage."

"She does love an excursion. Go to bed, Leesie."

"I think I will."

Mandy went back out to the kitchen and made some toast and hot cocoa. Then she put on a sweater and sat on the darkened deck to eat it, listening to the night sounds as she thought about the day.

When she finally came inside, she opened the small pantry next to the washroom and searched among the few commodities she had bought on her one trip downriver, for something she could feed to company the next night.

Mandy served enchiladas Monday evening. All day, as her frustration with Grange increased, she looked forward to dinner. She soothed herself by picturing the way the cheese would spiral out of the small holes of her grater like Rumplestiltskin's golden threads, and how the sharp aroma of onions and cheese would combine with the spicy, earthy, essence of red chili and masa. She would use the brown tablecloth with a centerpiece of Vince's leftover daffodils, and she imagined the palette of green, red, and yellow the enchiladas would make as she presented them to her guests.

Still, no matter what mental exercises she devised, she wasn't able to keep her mind off the office two doors down from hers. Her frustration with Grange lay not in any verbal fireworks, but in the fact that she didn't get a chance to fire even one salvo. His calendar said he would be at the high school all morning, so she spent that time planning clever, subtly stinging things to say to him. She would point out the fact that it was his salary, not hers, that threw the district's budget out of whack. The district had always operated without an assistant superintendent, and they could do so now. He had been replaced. Hasta la vista, baby.

After noon, as she waited for Grange to arrive, she worked in her office, struggling to package her vision for the district reading program. Each time she heard a car on the gravel in the parking lot, she looked up, and her pulse ratcheted up a notch in expectation. In the end, all her scripting of clever, biting dialog was for nothing. He never showed.

By the time Mandy went home, she was wound up as tight as a banjo string. Determined not to think about Grange again, she changed clothes and put on her running shoes. After scribbling a note for Leesie, she left the front door unlocked, trotted down the steps, and headed up the hill. At Timberlain Road, she turned right and jogged past Fran's house. Tulips marched along her fence line, and a bush by the corner of the house was beginning to break out in yellow blossoms. As a robin hopped across the lawn as if to accompany Mandy on a leg of her journey, she took a deep, cleansing breath and felt the stress begin to ebb.

The woods took over again just beyond Fran's lawn, dense and tangled with dusky undergrowth, though here and there the chartreuse of new green looked like a candle in the darkness. Mandy ran on, noting after a mile that the look of the woods had changed. Instead of short-needled fir, these trees had long needles, and they were lined in a grid, as if planted by design rather than by the random hand of nature. Bushy undergrowth was gone, and the woods had a park-like feel. She stopped and considered for a moment, then made her way carefully down and across the deep barrow pit alongside the road. As she entered the woods, she recognized the smell of pine, and she picked up her pace as she trotted along a straight lane under the bristly canopy. A soft bed of needles muffled the sound of her footfalls.

At length, she came to a bluff over the river. Swiftly moving water thirty feet below reflected the blue sky. It was a steep drop, and as she backed away from the edge to stand for a moment and catch her breath, she noticed a path that paralleled the riverbank. She decided to see if it would take her home. As she trotted along, the trail alternately swallowed her in a sylvan tunnel or opened up to dazzle her with picture-postcard scenes of mountains, river, and eagles. When she finally spied her house off to the right, she had not only shed the frustrations of the day, but a lightbulb had turned on in her mind, and she knew how she wanted to do her presentation on the reading program.

When she got home, the house was empty, so she showered, changed, and began to start food prep for dinner. Leesie arrived with Rael and his family while Mandy was chopping onions, and she wiped her streaming eyes as she met Jake for the first time. He had the same gaunt wiriness about him as his father and the same honey curls, but he was taller by a good six inches.

Jake carried a guitar, and Rael chased him and the girls outside so his strumming wouldn't interfere with the piano tuning. Rael opened up a satchel and took out his tools.

"How long will you be?" Mandy asked.

"I don't think it will take longer than half, three-quarters of an hour. It seems to be just the lower register. The rest of the keys are pretty much in tune."

While he worked, she sat at her desk and outlined what she wanted to do on Thursday at the staff meeting. Then she went to the kitchen and quietly assembled New-Mexico-style enchiladas, layering onions and cheese between flat corn tortillas, fried and stacked three high.

As she worked, she watched Rael. The last rays of sunlight coming in the window made a halo of his sandy curls, accentuating the hollow in his cheek as he cocked his head to listen and defining the muscles in his arm each time he put pressure on the tuning lever.

Mandy popped the last plate in the oven and announced, "We're just about ready to eat. Can you leave that and finish after supper?"

"Sure can. Want me to call the kids in?"

Mandy cracked an egg on the rim of a cast-iron skillet. "That would be great."

Rael put down his tool, poked his head out the door, and hollered. "I think they heard me," he said. "Jake wouldn't go so far that he'd miss the call to supper."

"He seems like a nice boy."

Rael smiled. "He is. I don't know where he came by that. Not through the Timberlains, certainly."

Mandy looked up from the eggs she was frying and grinned. "Oh, I don't know." She was interrupted by her sister's boisterous entrance.

Leesie had her head turned, talking to the boy behind her. "And I couldn't believe it when I saw you in Contemporary Problems! Can you believe it that we have four periods together? What are the odds?"

"Pretty good when you've got a school as small as Inches." Jake set the guitar in the corner. "I imagine you're used to a bigger school."

"Where's Willow?" Mandy asked.

Jake and Leesie looked at each other, and he shrugged. "She was with us for a while, but then she wandered off." He went to the door and bellowed her name.

"He's got good lungs," Mandy said as she carefully lifted eggs out of the skillet and onto a plate.

Jake shouted again and came in to report. "She's just coming down the road. I don't know where she's been."

Mandy opened the oven door. "Well, never mind. Sit. Rael, you be at the head. Jake and Leesie on this side. Willow can sit on the other when she gets here."

As they took their places around the table, Mandy slipped an egg on top of each enchilada, ladled chili sauce over the whole, and arranged chopped lettuce around each circumference. Using a dishcloth, she carried the plates to the table. "Watch out. It's hot," she warned.

Willow entered and slid into her seat, then frowned and sniffled at the dish set before her. "What is this?"

Mandy was determined to look beyond appearance and manners. "Enchiladas. Leesie and I were raised on them."

"Is this an egg on top?"

"Willow," Jake said in a warning undervoice.

"Yes," Mandy said brightly. "Are you allergic to eggs?"

"You might say so. I'm allergic to anything that takes advantage of animals. I'm a vegan."

Leesie bent down and peeked under the table. Then she bobbed back up and said, "Just checking your shoes, making sure there's no leather."

Mandy frowned and shook her head at Leesie. "Well, take the egg off, Willow. Though, is catching an egg that surely would be laid whether someone was there to exploit the chicken or not—is that really taking advantage?"

Willow dragged her knife across the top of her enchilada with a look of distaste on her face. "Is that cheese?"

Mandy looked across the table at Rael. His eyes were twinkling, and he winked at her so quickly she wondered if it really had happened, but the humorous set to his mouth gave her a lead to follow.

"Yes, it is cheese, but you can scrape that off, too. What you'll have left is onions, tortillas and lettuce. Why don't you enjoy that, and if you would like a second helping, I'll be glad to make it for you."

"But how do we know the onion wasn't exploited?" Leesie asked earnestly.

Jake snickered, and Mandy said, "That's enough on that subject. Leesie, tell me about your first day of school."

"Well, it took all of first period to get registered, and then, when I got to my second period class, who should be there but Jake!"

"And third period," Jake said. "And fourth and fifth."

"What do you have first period, Jake?" Mandy asked. She was surprised to see the young man color up, and he seemed reluctant to answer the question.

"Go ahead," Leesie urged. "Tell us what you've got. Maybe I can get the same thing."

"Mmm. Norfice."

"Norfice?" Leesie's brows knit. "What's that?"

"He says he's in the office," Willow said.

Leesie went into a peal of laughter. "You arranged it! You arranged for us to have classes together. Why didn't you tell me?"

Jake looked down at his plate and shook his head. "I don't know."

"Well, I'll be eternally grateful," Leesie said. "I've never been to a school where I didn't know lots of kids. It was totally awesome, walking into that room and seeing you there."

"Are you going to play for us tonight, Leesie?" Rael asked.

She didn't answer but frowned, her gaze fixed on the front deck. "What's that?"

Everyone turned at once. It was getting dark outside, and all Mandy could see was the hump of a back, as if someone was scurrying across the deck, bent over to escape detection.

Jake jumped up. "What's going on?"

"I don't know." Mandy rose as well. She walked to the door and opened it. "There's no one . . ." Her voice trailed off.

Rael was right behind her. "What is it?"

"There's a shoebox on the deck."

"Let me get it. I have an idea it's a schoolboy prank." He stepped out and looked around, then picked up the box. He lifted the lid and bent his head to peer inside. Suddenly his head snapped back and he shouted, "Ugh!"

"What is it?" Mandy asked in alarm.

Leesie and Jake crowded onto the deck, wanting to see, but Willow hung back in the doorway with the ghost of a smile on her face.

"Pee yew!" Leesie wrinkled her nose. "What is that smell?"

"What is it?" Mandy repeated, looking inside. "What are they? Hold the box to the light."

As Rael held the carton under the porch lamp, they could see it was teeming with lime green bugs, each no bigger than a nickel.

"They're called shield bugs," Rael said. "See how they're shaped like a shield? It's early for them to be out, but sometimes they winter in a warm shed or outbuilding."

"Another name for them is stinkbug," Jake said. He looked from Leesie to his dad, both of whom were glaring at him, and added, "Except that usually they're called shield bugs." He cleared his throat. "Usually, that's what they're called."

"It doesn't matter what they're called. Why would anyone leave a box of bugs on my deck?"

Rael laughed. "It's spring. Do teenage boys need a reason?" He replaced the lid. "Jake, you go dump these way far away. I'm going to go in and finish the piano. Then we'll listen to Leesie play for us."

"I'll go with you, Jake," Leesie said. "Want to come, Willow?"

Willow blinked. "Um, I guess. Sure, I'll come."

"I'll get a flashlight from the truck," Jake said. He disappeared into the darkness beyond the deck, and the girls followed.

Rael and Mandy went in. She did the dishes while he finished his job. When he was through, he sat down at the piano and picked out a simple melody. "I can tune it, but I can't play it," he said. "Will you?"

She dried her hands on a dish towel. As she slung it over her shoulder and approached the piano, she asked, "What is that sound outside? It's a little bit like crickets, but not really."

"It's frogs. Sure sign of spring."

"Frogs! Really?" She slid onto the bench. "Listen to the way it pulses. Hear it? *Ching chink-a, um, chink-a. Ching chink-a, um, chinka.*" She picked up the slow cadence in the left hand. "This is one of my favorites."

Mandy began to play a song by an obscure jazz musician, a haunting tune in a languid, Latin rhythm. She closed her eyes and let the music flow through her fingers, not from the memory of a printed page, but from somewhere deep inside. She played night sounds and loneliness, leaden skies and dark-haired strangers; she played faraway, starry, desert nights and someone whispering "chérie" in her ear.

As she played, just after the bridge, something under the muted rhythm began to swell, and she was suddenly swept along in a breathless cascade of tones that became an elegant, soaring counterpoint to the melody. She dropped back to a soft, under-texture of rhythm and chord change and glanced for the first time at Rael. He sat in the dim corner with Jake's guitar in his lap, and as the melody sprang from his fingers, all moody passion and smoldering intensity, it ripped the scab off Mandy's heart. Tears beaded up on her lashes as they played through another chorus, and she felt inexplicably tied to this surprising man, because she could hear through his music that love was a raggedly painful subject for him, too.

He let her take the lead again, and when the song was over, she sat with her hands lax on the keys, letting the chorus of frogs and the calls of the teenagers on their way home from disposal duty bring her back to here and now.

When Rael stood to put the guitar back in the corner, Mandy sighed and turned around on the piano bench. "I think I'm in love," she said. "Where on earth did you learn to play like that? And how do you know about Carlos Rosa? I thought I was his only American fan."

Rael shrugged. "Oh, you pick things up here and there. How about you? You're really good."

She laughed. "As long as you stay in the key of C, I do okay."

"C is good." Rael looked out the window. "Looks like the kids are back."

Leesie and Jake came clattering up the steps, laughing about a raccoon that had been caught in the flashlight's beam down by the river and had stood up and bared his fangs at them.

"I won't have warm, fuzzy feelings about raccoons anymore," Leesie declared. "He looked totally pit bullish."

Rael looked outside. "Where's Willow?"

"Isn't she here?" Jake looked around in surprise. "She said she was going back to the house."

Leesie took off her sweater. "Last I saw her she was sitting in the chair on the deck. I saw her silhouette in front of the window."

Rael frowned. "Jake, go check the truck. See if she's there."

Jake saluted with the flashlight. "I'm on it."

"We probably better go," Rael said. "The kids need to be up early, and I think Jake has some homework to do. Can we come another time and listen to Leesie play?"

"Yes, but only if it's soon. Thank you so much for tuning the piano. It felt as if everything was out of kilter until that was done."

Rael laughed. "I know the feeling." He held out his hand. "Thank you for supper. Most enjoyable."

Jake stepped in from outside. "She's there, in one of her black moods. I left her be."

"That's fine. We'll go on home now."

"Aw, Dad! Leesie was going to play for us."

"Another night."

"But Dad!"

"You've got homework."

Jake's shoulders slumped. "All right." He turned to Leesie. "I'll pick you up tomorrow?"

"You better."

He smiled and turned to Mandy. "Thank you, Dr. Steenburg. Dinner was great."

She walked them to the door. "You're welcome, Jake. Come anytime. Thanks again, Rael."

Standing behind her, Leslie called out, "'Night, Jake. 'Night, Rael." Just as Mandy was about to shut the door, she added an afterthought. "Tell Willow good night, too."

Jake, standing on the running board of the truck with the door open, waved to show he got the message. Then he was in and the lights came on, and they drove off into the night.

Leesie threw herself down on the couch. "What a day!" She leaned her head back against the cushions and grinned.

"For someone who just parted from someone who—how did you put it? makes you weak in the knees?—you seem to have got over him in a hurry."

"Don't you believe it," Leesie said. "Jake is sweet, and I love him already, but like a brother."

"I don't know that he wants to be your brother," Mandy replied dryly.

"He will as he gets to know me better. Right now I'm someone new and different. Pretty soon I'll be an old shoe, and we'll be great friends, I know."

"He forgot his guitar."

"He meant to leave it." Leesie popped up from the couch and picked it up. "He's loaning it to me. I'm going to learn to play it. Listen." Leesie played a C scale and looked up for approval.

"Very nice," Mandy said. "Did you just learn that today? I'm impressed."

"That's what we were doing while Jake's dad was tuning the piano. At least, that's what Jake and I were doing."

Mandy rubbed her arms. "So, what's with Willow?"

Leesie set the guitar back in the corner. "I don't know. She dresses all Gothic, all in black and with those high-heeled boots—they're manmade materials, mind you, but hardly easy on the feet. I imagine if someone tried to force those on some dumb animal, she'd haul them in for cruelty."

"You mustn't tease her," Mandy admonished. "It's a cause she believes in, and she's brave about standing up for it. Are you cold?"

"A bit. But what about the shield bugs?" Leesie sat down. "Aren't they animals? Well, I guess they're really not, so it's okay to sacrifice them."

Mandy looked up from lighting the stove. "What are you talking about?"

"I can't believe she wasn't involved in that little trick. It's the only time she smiled all evening."

"I didn't notice that. What I did notice was how you and Rael tried to shush Jake when he said they were called stinkbugs. What was that all about?"

"Well . . ." Leesie looked at the floor and grimaced.

"Go on."

"You're not going to like it."

"Try me."

Leesie flopped back again. "Ooh, this is just too painful!

So, I get to school and I register, right? And my name is Leesie Wheeler, and at first no one knows I'm your sister. But I don't make a secret of it, and it isn't too long before people start to know who I am and how I'm related to you. And I find out that they've started calling you Dr. Stinkbug. Oh, I knew I shouldn't tell you! No, don't cry, Mandy."

"I'm not crying," she said, but she sat with shoulders hunched and elbows on her thighs and couldn't keep the tears from running down her face. "I don't care what they call me."

Leesie moved over and put an arm around her sister. "Well, I care! You're not a stinkbug! You're a sweetiebug. Dr. Sweetiebug—that's what I'll call you."

Somehow that ridiculous epithet loosed the floodgates. Mandy leaned her head against her sister's shoulder and sobbed.

Leesie pressed her cheek against Mandy's dark curls. "I've never seen you cry, Sweetiebug. You've always been so capable and self-assured. Never mind. You go ahead and cry." Leesie held her close and rocked her gently, and presently Mandy stopped crying.

"I've got to blow my nose," she said and went to get a napkin off the table. "I feel so ridiculous."

"Don't," Leesie said. "I'll tell you what. Let's play. The only thing that will make you feel better than a good cry is a good song." She opened her cello case and took out her instrument. "We haven't played together in a long time."

"Oh, I don't know, Leesie." Mandy wiped her eyes.

Leesie dragged a straight-back chair to the piano and sat down. "Let's tune."

Mandy sighed and drifted over, then obediently played the tones for her sister. "I don't think I have any music," she said apathetically. "There's nothing in the piano bench."

"I have music for both of us. Here."

Mandy spread the pages out and studied them as Leesie unfolded her music stand. "This is one of my favorite pieces."

"Mine too. Ready?"

Mandy took a deep breath and began to play the opening bars of Schubert's "Serenade." The cello came in at measure five, full-throated and rich as melted butter and honey. As muscle memory carried Mandy's fingers over the familiar phrases, her spirits rose with the sound, and the sour humiliation of being the butt of a teenage prank was forgotten in the sweetness of the melody. When the last full measure had been played, she smiled, leaned over, and gave her sister an awkward hug.

"Thank you, Leesie. I'm so glad you're here."

"I am too, Dr. Sweetiebug." Leesie kissed her sister on the cheek. "What an adventure this is going to be!"

"Yeah, this is an adventure, all right." Mandy stirred the pot of oatmeal the next morning and looked out at a gray, drizzly day. "Welcome to Washington," she greeted as Leesie came out of her room with her school things.

"Isn't this beautiful?" Leesie set her backpack down by the door and stood gazing out the front window.

"You're kidding, right?"

"No. I think it's totally gorgeous. Look at the way the mist is lying low on the trees across the river. And the colors are all muted, like an English impressionist painting. Is there such a thing as an English impressionist painter?"

"I have no idea." Mandy spooned oatmeal into a bowl and handed it to her.

"Me neither. Do we have any raisins?"

Mandy joined her sister at the table. "Uh-uh. We'd better get a shopping list started. It's a forty-minute drive to the market, so we don't want to forget anything. Eat fast because your ride will be here in about five minutes."

Leesie obliged and they ate in silence, looking out over the pastel landscape. Leesie finished first and carried her dishes to the sink. "What are you doing today?"

"I'm going on a tour of all the elementary schools in the district."

"Oh? How many are there?"

"Four. One is in Trillium, one in Cedar Springs, one in Birch Falls, and the one here in town."

"It's not a very big district, is it?"

"Not in numbers, but some of the kids ride thirty miles one way to come in to high school."

"Wow!"

Mandy sighed. "I'm wrestling with next year's budget, and the cost of transportation is a huge slice of that pie."

Leesie slipped a book inside her backpack and zipped it shut. "I believe it. You should see the number of busses lined up at the high school."

"Which reminds me, Leesie. You mentioned maybe trying to be a student helper first period?"

"Jake wanted me to, and I thought I might."

"Would you be willing to work at the bus garage? I need someone to plow through about ten years of filing."

"There's my ride." Leesie gathered her things. "I'll think about it. Maybe I can talk Jake into doing it with me. That would be fun."

Before Mandy could remind her to wear a coat, she was out the door, running down the steps and piling into the waiting pickup.

Mandy sighed and finished her breakfast. Then she put on her suit jacket and looked at herself in the downstairs mirror. Forcing an artificial smile and a hearty manner, she said, "It's an adventure, Dr. Stinkbug. Chin up!"

She picked up her purse, and as she dashed out the door and over to her car through the rain, she was grateful she wouldn't have to face Grange Timberlain today. If he had spent the previous morning at the high school, he probably knew what the kids were calling the new superintendent.

There was no light in his window as she drove around the district office, but taking no chances, she had arranged for Mo to wait for her on the porch. He was there, looking ineffectual with his rounded shoulders barely filling out his blue nylon rain jacket, the few damp strands of hair combed over his bald spot, and his skinny moustache following the drooping curve of his mouth. He held a briefcase in front of him with both hands and looked nervously over his shoulder. When he spied Mandy, he scuttled down the stairs and climbed into the car, then perched the satchel on his knees.

"Buckle up," she instructed as she pulled away.

She had just pulled onto the road when Mo obediently pulled out the shoulder strap and turned to fasten the seatbelt. At that moment, the case slid off his knees and knocked the car out of gear. Mo dove for the satchel, but in the cramped cockpit of the Miata, as he hauled it back on his lap, he inadvertently grabbed Mandy's jacket, too, and jerked her sideways. Surprised, she looked over to see what was going on, and while she tussled with Mo, trying to get him to let go her jacket, the car veered into the other lane. It was only when an opposing driver sounded his horn that she realized their peril and corrected course.

"That was Grange," Mo said, turning around to look behind.

"I know who it was," she said between clenched teeth. "If you'll let go of my jacket, I may be able to keep from hitting anyone else." She pulled over and slowed enough so that Mo could disentangle himself. "Are you buckled?"

"Oh. No." He pulled out the shoulder harness again.

"I'll stop until you're strapped in."

While he fiddled with the latch, she looked in her rearview mirror and noticed that Grange had stopped in the parking lot driveway and was apparently watching them. When she saw his backup lights go on, she threw the car into first and let out the clutch, causing Mo to scramble yet again with his briefcase.

"I wasn't buckled yet." He pulled the strap away from his Adam's apple.

"Give me the latch," she commanded, holding out her hand but keeping one eye on the rearview mirror. When she saw Grange drive into the parking lot, she finally looked down and clicked the buckle home.

"Thanks." Mo's voice was subdued.

"Sorry to be so brusque," Mandy said. "I was afraid Grange was going to come back to see if something was wrong. I just wanted to get out of there."

"No problem."

Silence.

Finally she said, "So, we'll go up to Trillium first. On the way I want to know all about their budget. I want to know what we're spending money on, and I want to know what we're getting for that money. How much is federal money, and how much is from the state? I want to know about the demographics of the community and what the test scores are. Anything that can be measured, I want to know."

Mo nodded and unlatched his case. Pulling out a file folder, he said, "I've come prepared. I think I can address all the issues." He began to speak, and all the clumsiness and awkwardness disappeared as he entered his comfort zone of numbers and statistics. Mandy listened intently, nodding as he made statements and substantiated them with figures. If she didn't understand or didn't agree with his conclusions, she asked questions until his logic was clear.

As she toured the school, she decided it had been a good political move to have Mo accompany her, for the staff at Trillium Elementary School was politely, though guardedly, welcoming. She spent half an hour talking to the resource-room teacher, and then she and Mo sat down with the principal for the better part of an hour before they returned to the Miata.

Before they got in, Mandy opened the trunk. "Get your folder for Cedar Springs Elementary. We'll stow your case here."

Mo laughed and agreed, and soon he was briefing her as they headed down the road. They visited the school, talked to the resource-room teacher and principal, and then went on to the next school, repeating each procedure until the afternoon was spent and they were done.

When they left the last school, Mo said, "That was really something. I can't believe how you got those principals to open up. They told you about problems I've never heard of, and some great solutions, too."

"I've got a lot better idea what I'm dealing with now," Mandy said. "Thanks for all your hard work, Mr. Smith."

"Call me Mo. Was it really a help?"

"Certainly it was. You have a gift for making numbers mean something. The district is lucky to have you."

"Oh, uh . . . really?"

"Yes, really." She pulled into the parking lot and stopped by his car. "Let me ask you something. Do you remember that first night, when I slept on the couch in the waiting room?"

He looked down at the folder in his hands. He nodded and cleared his throat.

"You came in to get something—a briefcase."

He nodded again.

"What was in the briefcase? I saw you give it to Vince."

Mo looked out the window. "It was his."

"What was his?"

"The briefcase."

"But what was in it?" Mandy persisted. "You said Vince wanted it, and I wasn't to tell Grange that you had come and got it."

Mo cleared his throat again. His mouth opened, but no sound came out. He tried again. "Vince wanted me to check some figures. He thought someone might be cooking the books, and he wanted me to check."

"And was someone cooking the books? And why not tell Grange you'd been there?"

Mo finally looked at Mandy. The color had drained out of his face, making his moustache a dark pencil line. "I don't want to . . . It's not worth . . . You don't understand. Grange brings lots of money to the district. Lots of money. He practically funds the whole music program."

She frowned. "But what's that got to do with Vince and cooking the books?"

Mo opened the door. "I'm not going to be the one to explain it to you." He scrambled out. "I need to get going. Will you open the trunk?"

She pulled the lever to pop it open and waited for him to retrieve his briefcase. She rolled down the window and called. "Thank you for coming, Mo. It was a most educational day."

He closed the trunk and bent down to look in. A light, misty rain beaded up on his bare scalp. "You're welcome, Dr. Steenburg."

"Call me Mandy, please."

He stepped away. "I don't know if I can." He waved his free arm in farewell and turned to go.

She paused before putting the car in gear and pulling away.

As she drove, she took her planner out of her purse and laid it on the passenger seat, open to the list she had made before she went to bed last night, but her mind wouldn't focus on the tasks she had set for herself. It kept returning to Mo's cryptic comments: *Grange brings lots of money to the district. Lots of money. . . . I'm not going to be the one to explain it you.*

"Explain what?" she asked aloud. She pictured Grange in her mind, with that sinister, frozen half of his face distorting every expression. "Where would he get that much money? And is that why the school board is so anxious to hold on to him? Is it really his sterling leadership abilities?"

Mandy had an uncomfortable ride home. She squirmed in her seat, trying to get rid of the crawly feeling up her back. Something wasn't right, and she was afraid she was going to end up in the middle of it and perhaps be tarred by association.

When she pulled up in front of her house, she turned off the key and made herself focus on the list in her planner. She had marked everything off except three tasks: *Call Granny Timberlain. Talk to Tammy Wilcox. Make appointment to rotate tires.* She looked at her watch and decided she could probably still do them all, so she stuffed her planner back in her purse and got out of the car.

As Mandy got to the top of the steps, she noticed a shoebox sitting in front of the door. She stopped mid-stride and looked at it. "Oh no," she said, picking it up. "You're not going to catch me twice."

She set her purse by the door, descended the steps, and walked purposefully around to the back deck where the garbage can was sitting. Opening the lid, she set the unopened box on top of the stack of plastic-bagged refuse and slammed the lid down with a satisfactory bang. She dusted off her hands and went back around to unlock the front door.

Leesie had said she was staying after school for some sort of practice, so Mandy didn't expect her for at least another hour. She climbed the stairs to her bedroom and hung up her jacket, then sat on the bed to make her phone calls. Granny Timberlain didn't answer, but Tammy sounded glad to get the call and said tomorrow afternoon would be a good time to talk.

Stevie Joe at Limestone Garage said he could rotate Mandy's tires if she would come by after work the coming Monday. She got directions to the garage and wrote them down on Monday's page, then closed her planner with a snap and carried it down to put in her purse.

She was halfway down the stairs when she saw Fran pull up in her pickup. Mandy waved at her through the window and went to open the door. "Hi, Fran," she called as her friend got out with a can of paint in one hand and a paintbrush in the other. "I've been meaning to thank you for helping my sister get settled."

Fran came in and took her shoes off, setting them neatly by the door. "She said you didn't know she was coming. Were you surprised?"

"Was I ever!"

"I didn't have any idea you were Conroy Wheeler's daughter," Fran said, looking around.

"Stepdaughter, actually. Isn't that something that your sister worked for him? What are you looking for?"

"Something to set this paint can on that will protect the countertop—a piece of cardboard or something."

"Out on the back deck." The phone rang, and as Mandy ran up the stairs, she called, "Go ahead and look around out there. I'm sure there's something." She caught the phone on the third ring. It was Tammy calling with directions to her house. Mandy thanked her for remembering she was new in town, then hung up and hurried down the stairs to write the directions in her planner before she forgot them.

She was just putting it away when Fran walked in with the shoebox. "Are you feeling all right?"

Mandy frowned. "What do you mean?"

"I found this in the garbage. I thought you loved cream-filled goodies."

Mandy held out her hand. "What are you talking about? What's in the box?"

"You mean you don't know? What's it doing in the garbage then?" Fran handed her the box but kept the lid. "To put under my paint can," she explained.

Mandy looked inside. The box was lined with crumpled-up tissue upon which sat a single homemade éclair, frosted with chocolate icing and chock-full of cream filling. A small envelope sat by it, with "Welcome" written in a quivery hand across the front. Mandy set the box on the table, picked up the envelope, and drew out a small card with a picture of a hummingbird on the front. "Join us at church this Sunday," it said.

Mandy turned the card over, but there was nothing else to indicate who had brought it.

"Who is it from?" called Fran from the kitchen.

"I'm not sure. Sounds like someone from church."

"What's it doing in the garbage, then?"

Mandy laughed. "It's a long story." She carried the box to the kitchen. "Here, I'll share this with you while I tell you about it. You don't mind that it's been in the garbage, do you?"

Fran shook her head. "Too many carbs for me. But you go ahead. I'll listen while I paint."

"What are you painting?"

"The insides of these cupboard doors. I only got one coat on them."

"Nonsense. They look great."

"Now they do, but they won't stand up to lots of scrubbing. If I spend the time now to do a second coat, I won't have to strip and repaint later. Now, why was the box in the garbage?"

Mandy took a bite of the éclair, and as she explained about the contents of the first shoebox that had been left on the deck, she found that she could speak of the stinkbugs with ease and humor.

"Kids," Fran said when Mandy had finished. "What a rude thing to do."

"Well, it really was high spirits, I'm sure. I'm an authority figure, which makes me fair game to a teenage mind. It was a harmless prank." She held up the goodie. "Are you sure you don't want some of this? It's really excellent. The filling is almond flavored and has something in it that's got some texture. Maybe it's coconut."

Fran jiggled the can to mix the paint. "Sounds entirely too rich for me. So, how are things going at school?"

Mandy shook her head and sighed. "I don't know, Fran. If I hadn't signed a year's lease, I might not stick it out even to the end of the year."

Fran paused in the act of opening the can. "You're not serious. What's wrong?"

Mandy licked some cream off her fingers. "Well, for starters, Grange Timberlain seems to think he's still in charge, and he's not the only one who thinks so. Two-thirds of the school board support him."

"How do you know?"

"They told me. Said I should listen to Grange. He's a leader."

"Be fair," Fran said. "He's done a pretty good job so far."

"Well, math scores are up, but reading scores are below state average. Way below, and as far as I can see there's no plan to address that." Mandy took a bite of éclair and added thickly, "Yet."

Fran sat on the floor and opened a cupboard door. "So what I'm hearing is, you see this district as a challenge. You're not really thinking about leaving, are you?"

"Who wants to stay where they're not wanted? There's a school up in the bush in Alaska that wanted me. The money is great, they provide housing and a trip out each summer, and I could really do some good there. I could make a difference."

"Is the position still open?"

"I don't know. I haven't inquired because I signed the lease. I feel that, if only for that reason, I'm committed here."

Fran sat back on her heels. "I don't want to be the reason you stay if you're going to be miserable. If you've got someplace else you can make a difference, then let's see if we can work something out."

"Don't tempt me." Mandy took the last bite and took a pot from the cupboard. "Leesie gets soup tonight. I've had my supper."

Fran didn't look up from her painting. "Carb city."

"So, tell me," Mandy said, "where does Grange's money come from? Was it a settlement for his face?"

Fran paused with brush in midair and frowned. "What do you mean?"

"I mean—" Mandy suddenly clutched her belly.

"What's the matter? You're as white as a sheet!"

"Ugh," Mandy groaned. "I don't know. I had a cramp all of a sud—" She didn't finish the sentence, for saliva poured into her mouth as a tsunami of nausea swept over her, and she made a lunge for the sink.

Fran got rid of the paint can and scrambled to her feet. She stood by as Mandy's body convulsed, giving up the éclair and the tuna sandwich she had for lunch at the grade school cafeteria. Fran wet a rag and wiped Mandy's forehead and cheeks and turned on the tap to flush the vomit down the drain.

Mandy tried to say thanks, but the room began to spin, and it took all her conscious effort to stay upright. She clung to the sink, but an ebony ring haloing the outer edge of her vision began to close in. A buzzing sound grew louder and louder until the darkness was complete, and then, from far away, she heard Fran saying, "I can't hold you."

After that, she floated through obscurity punctuated by sensory islands, sometimes sight, sometimes sound, sometimes both, but all with a surreal, dreamlike skew. Leesie's voice calling her Dr. Sweetiebug hailed her in from the flow, but as she opened her eyes, she was hit by another wave of nausea, and she struggled to get up on her elbow. A strong hand supported her head, and someone said, "Use the basin," and held it for her as she retched again.

"Thank you," she whispered as she was gently laid back down, but her benefactor had turned into Grange Timberlain, only his face wasn't contorted, and as he smiled encouragement, both sides of his mouth turned up. When she opened her eyes again, Rael was beside her, calling her by name.

"Yes," she answered, but the darkness swallowed him up, and she never heard what he had to say to her.

It was almost noon before Mandy made it to work the next day. Leesie, who had driven her home from a night spent in the emergency room at Hiesel Valley Hospital, tried to insist that she stay home, but Mandy overruled her. After a trip to the A-frame so both could shower and change, she dropped Leesie off at the high school.

"You're sure?" Leesie furrowed her brow as she looked at Mandy's pale face and hollow eyes.

"I'll be fine. As good as you, anyway. You were the one that was up all night."

Leesie grinned. "Just half the night. You finally settled down around two. So, what do they think it was? Food poisoning?"

"Probably. That's why I'm so determined to get in to work. If it was the tuna sandwich, we may have other cases we have to deal with. So out you go."

Leesie leaned over and kissed her sister. "Bye, Sweetiebug."

"Bye." Mandy leaned back against the headrest and watched her bounce up the stairs. Then she drove to the district offices.

Willow Timberlain was out at the reception desk talking to Elizabeth when Mandy stepped through the door. Both girls fell silent and stared as Mandy walked past with a nod in their direction. She felt their eyes following her as she leaned on the railing for support and plodded up the stairs.

Mo came to his doorway as she rested on the landing. "Can I help?"

She shook her head and turned to cross the mezzanine above the entryway, pausing again opposite Grange's door because her legs were turning to rubber.

Grange, standing at his file cabinet, dropped the papers in his hand as he looked up at her face, which she knew must be ashen. He wrenched open his door, but got no farther than his doorway, because at that moment Vince burst in downstairs shouting, "Mandy!" He ran across the reception area, leaving the high school girls gaping as he took the stairs two at a time.

When he gained the landing, he hurried over to Mandy, then turned his back on Grange and put a supporting arm around her waist. "What are you doing here?" he asked fiercely. "I just came from the hospital. I can't believe they released you."

"Oh, Vince, don't make more of it than it is," she said. "Will you help me to my office? My knees seem to have gone south on me." As he bent to scoop her up, she wrenched away. "No, Vince. You're not going to carry me. I will walk. Just support me."

His hand stayed on her waist, and his face was still close to hers as she held his gaze and clenched her jaw. His mouth compressed in a straight line, and they engaged in a brief skirmish of wills.

Suddenly, he smiled and said, "Yes, ma'am." Suiting his pace to hers, he walked with her to her office and held her chair. As soon as she was seated, he stepped away.

Mandy leaned her head back and closed her eyes. "Thank you."

"You shouldn't be here," Vince said.

Her eyes flew open, and he held up his hands in defense. "No, don't fire up. I won't say it again, but did they find out what happened? Was it food poisoning?"

"Nothing showed up in the tests. They're not sure."

Vince looked at her intently. "May I come and take you home when you're finished here?"

"I have my car. I'll be fine."

At that moment, Mandy's secretary swept into the room with a steaming mug, which she set on Mandy's desk. "Drink this. It'll cure what ails you."

"Thank you, Mrs. Berman. I just realized I didn't have anything to eat today. I think I'm suffering more from that than anything else. Will you ask Grange to come in and talk to me?"

"I guess that's my cue," Vince took a card out of his pocket and handed it to Mandy. "I've got a satellite phone. Call me if you need me. Any time, night or day."

She took the card and smiled up at him. "You are very kind, but don't worry. I'll drink Mrs. Berman's tea, and it will fix me right up."

"See that you do. I'll come by and see you tonight."

Mandy shook her head. "I don't think I'll be fit company tonight. Come by tomorrow night. Come for dinner."

There was a tapping on the doorframe, and they both looked up to see Grange standing in the hallway, a grim expression on his face.

Vince flashed his brilliant smile at her and sketched a salute. "Tomorrow for dinner it is," he said and strode out the door.

Grange stepped back to let Vince pass, meeting his eyes in stony silence. Then he walked to Mandy's desk. "Edith said you wanted to see me."

Mandy took a tentative sip of the steaming brew in front of her. "Yes. Thank you. Will you please close the door and have a seat?"

He did as she asked, sitting quietly while she took another drink from her mug.

It took a moment for it to register with Mandy that both of his eyes were blinking as he regarded her.

"Is anything wrong?" he asked.

She realized she had been staring and dropped her eyes. "No. I'm sorry. I'm not really with it today. You'll have to forgive me. I had a spot of trouble last night."

"I know."

"You do?"

"I rode with you in the back of the ambulance to the hospital."

She stared blankly.

Grange shifted in his seat. "I'm an EMT. We have an all-volunteer community response team, and I was on call."

As the memory returned, Mandy put her hands to her cheeks and said faintly, "You were the one holding the basin?"

He smiled slightly. "Part of the job."

She could feel the color rising in her cheeks. "I'll never live that down."

"Don't give it another thought. What did you want to see me about?"

Mandy put her hand to her forehead as she tried to remember. "Oh, yes—the school lunch. Did you have any other emergency calls? Anyone else have to go to the hospital?"

"What are you thinking?"

"Maybe I got a touch of food poisoning from the tuna sandwich I ate at Birch Falls Elementary yesterday. I was afraid if that were the case, we might have a food poisoning incident on our hands."

"May I?" Grange asked, pointing to her phone. She motioned for him to go ahead, and he asked Edith to check on the number of absentees in the district for today.

While they were waiting to hear back, he asked, "What else did you have to eat yesterday?"

"I had a chocolate éclair, but I had only just eaten it. There wasn't time for it to make me sick."

"Where did you get it?"

"The éclair?" Mandy felt her cheeks flushing again as she remembered that it had come out of her garbage can. "It was on my doorstep when I got home. I think someone from the church left it."

"How do you know that?"

"The card had an invitation to come out next Sunday. Surely—"

The phone rang and Grange picked up. He listened for a moment, said thank you, and hung up. "Absenteeism is down today. I don't think it was the tuna fish."

"Well, it may have been just a vicious, short-term bug. Whatever it was, Mrs. Berman's yarbs have done their thing, and I'm feeling better already."

"I'm glad to hear it." He stood. "If I can do anything to help, just let me know."

"Thank you. If you have anything you want on the agenda for the meeting tomorrow morning, will you please let Mrs. Berman know? She's going to be sending it out to everyone this afternoon. I'm having all the resource-room teachers join us for the second half of the meeting to discuss the district reading program."

"All right." Grange turned to go.

"Oh, and one more thing," Mandy said. "You were logged out on your calendar all yesterday morning but showed yourself in the office in the afternoon."

"Did I?" There was just a hint of a challenge in his question. "Did you have something urgent to discuss with me?"

"Yes, I did."

"We can do it right now." He grabbed the chair, ready to sit back down.

"Not right now," she said, raising her hand to forestall him. "I would request, however, that your calendar reflect where you are going to be."

He leaned on the chair and looked down at the floor for a moment. "And your calendar for this morning?" he asked pleasantly. "Was it a true reflection of where you were?"

"That's different. That was an emergency. It couldn't be helped."

Grange chuckled. "Next time, I'll tell Mr. Ruggles he'll have to call in and calendar his heart attack ahead of time."

She frowned. "What's that got to do with it?"

"You're not the only one who got a ride downriver. I was in the back giving him oxygen yesterday afternoon."

"Oh."

The silence stretched out as Mandy and Grange looked at one another, she with a frown and he with a bland, unreadable expression.

"I'm sorry," she said. "Of course that was unavoidable. Forgive me."

"Nothing to forgive," he said. Then he walked out the door and down to his office.

He didn't turn around and look back, so he didn't see the tear rolling down her cheek, and Mandy was grateful. "Pull up your socks, Dr. Stinkbug," she muttered. With a trembling hand she reached for her cup and drank half the contents. Then she searched in her purse for a peppermint, which she popped in her mouth and chewed. Determined not to let the weakness get the best of her, she turned on her computer and began composing an email to Mrs. Berman.

That capable lady sailed in moments later with a steaming Styrofoam cup. She handed it to Mandy and commanded, "Eat."

Mandy took the cup and sniffed at the contents. "What is it?"

"Chicken soup with some added yarbs. Go ahead. We need to get some color in those cheeks." Mrs. Berman sat on the side chair and watched expectantly.

Mandy took a sip. "Not bad," she said. "I'm not even going to ask what's in it."

"Never mind that. Tell me what you had to eat yesterday."

"Nothing that I can think would have poisoned me. I had oatmeal for breakfast, a tuna sandwich for lunch, and just minutes before I got sick, I ate a chocolate éclair." Mandy hastened to explain, "The cream filling was still cold. I don't think we have to worry about salmonella."

"I don't suppose there's any of that éclair left, is there?"

Mandy shook her head. "I ate it all. I'm a sucker for cream-filled things."

"What did it taste like?"

"Why are you asking me this, Mrs. Berman? The cramping and nausea set in shortly after I ate the éclair. There wasn't time for it to poison me."

"That's just the thing. It's a little early, but we've been having warm days . . ."

"What are you talking about?"

"Mushrooms. We have one that grows in the meadows on this side of the mountains—looks like a normal mushroom, but the gills are tinged with pink. It's fast-acting and extremely poisonous. Not enough to kill you, but enough to make you wish you were dead. That's why I was asking about the filling. This mushroom has a distinctive taste."

"Like what?"

"I asked you first. I don't want to plant an idea in your head."

"The filling tasted of almonds."

Mrs. Berman sprang from her chair. "I'm going to get Grange."

Mandy watched her stride out the door. A few minutes later, Mrs. Berman returned, followed by the tall assistant superintendent.

He looked at his watch. "I'm due over at the high school, Edith." Then he added, with a twinkle in his eye, "You must not have checked my calendar."

"Never mind your calendar. I think somebody fed Dr. Steenburg some rosy-gill mushrooms."

Grange cocked his head. "And you base that accusation on what?"

Edith Berman counted off on her fingers: "First, it was fast-acting. That's the way rosy-gill does. Secondly, it tasted of almonds. That's like rosy-gill, too."

"I've seen rosy-gill poisoning," he said. "It wasn't this severe."

"If you're thinking of Pooky Lefflinger, he weighs over two hundred pounds. I'd be surprised if Dr. Steenburg weighs ninety. Makes a difference, you know."

"It's too early in the year for rosy-gills." Grange stood. "Don't say this to another person, Edith. You know how rumors fly, and there's not a shred of evidence to support this." He looked at his watch again. "I've got to go. Goodbye."

Edith watched him leave and muttered something under her breath. Frowning, she stood and admonished Mandy to finish her soup. Then she stalked back to her desk.

Mandy was grateful to be left alone. She ate her soup, and as strength gradually returned, she worked on preparations for the staff meeting the following morning. When she finished she leaned back and closed her eyes.

A timid knock at the door brought her back to attention. Mo smoothed the hair over the top of his head and stepped into the room. "I just wanted to ask how you are."

"Thank you, Mo. Much better than this morning. Mrs. Berman has been dosing me with her yarbs."

"You still look a little peaked. I'd be glad to drive you home, if you wish."

"That is very kind. I'll be fine."

He continued to stand with his hands clasped in front of him and a worried expression on his face.

Mandy forced animation that she didn't feel into her smile. "Truly, Mo. I'm fine. Go on home."

"All right." He reluctantly retreated, and she heard him saying to someone downstairs, "She wouldn't let me drive her home. I think she does look a little better than she did this morning. She looked like death warmed over."

Mandy heard the door close, and soon Mo and Midge emerged from under the porch roof and separated to go to their cars.

"It's four o'clock, Dr. Steenburg. Can I do anything for you before I go?"

She swiveled around. "No. Thank you, Mrs. Berman. I appreciate all you've done for me today. I'm feeling much better."

The secretary nodded, swung her purse up on her shoulder, and left, calling "Good night" over her shoulder.

Moments later Mandy heard the sound of the front door closing and the ensuing backwash of silence. She sighed, took her planner out of her purse, and opened it to today's date.

There it was in black and white, the appointment to meet with Tammy and talk about reading lessons. As Mandy looked at the directions to the woman's house, a dozen excuses leapfrogged through her mind, most of them involving the phrase "death's door." She had almost decided to call and cancel when she remembered Millie Barlow. Mandy had already failed in her promise to go to church last Sunday. She didn't want to fail again. Summoning the last of her reserves, she stiffened her spine, gathered her things, and headed for the stairs.

Mandy pulled up at Tammy's house and sat for a minute, surveying the neat cottage with its high-pitched, blue metal roof and cedar shake siding painted white. Masses of shiny-leafed bushes ringed the perimeter of the lawn, and well-tended beds of tulips and daffodils framed the sidewalk all the way to the front porch.

Just as Mandy opened the door to get out, Rael pulled up beside her in his postal-service jeep and hopped out. "How are you doing?" he called. "I didn't expect to see you out and about already. Last time I saw you, I thought you were ready to stick your spoon in the wall."

"I worked half a day," Mandy said, holding out her hand. "Thank you, by the way, for everything last night. Leesie said you took charge of getting the ambulance and drove down with her so we'd have a way home."

Rael clasped her hand in both of his. "Don't mention it. Jake dropped Leesie off about the time you passed out. Fran looked like she was about ready to go down too, so he got on the horn to me. What was the matter, by the way?"

Mandy shrugged. "Several theories. No smoking gun for any of them."

Rael walked to the back of his Jeep, opened the hatch, and took out two black, bulging garbage bags. As walked to Tammy's door, Mandy accompanied him, looking curiously at his burden.

"Tammy runs a black-market garbage collection service." He held up the bags. "I patronize her because she's my cousin and she's a single mom."

Mandy laughed and reached for the bell, but the door opened before she could ring. They were greeted by a slender, smiling woman with dark hair plaited into a single braid that hung halfway down her back. Dressed in jeans, a blue flannel shirt, and clogs, she wore no makeup, and her delight at seeing Rael and Mandy was unforced and natural.

"Come in, come in. Hello, Rael." She kissed her cousin on the cheek and then turned to Mandy.

"And you're Mandy? Goodness, you're about knee high to a slug. And so young. Not at all what I expected."

Rael asked the question that was on the tip of Mandy's tongue. "What did you expect?"

"I thought she'd be larger than life—at least seven feet tall, forty years old, and able to go bear hunting with a switch." Tammy laughed. "Come in and sit down. Did you bring me more needles, Rael? Thank you! I could have come and got them, but I've been pushing to get this order done." She looked around. "I'll make a place for you to sit."

"I can't stay," Rael said, his hand on the doorknob. "I just wanted to bring those to you." He spoke to his cousin, but his eyes rested on Mandy.

Tammy took the bags and carried them into another room, and Mandy was left alone with Rael. "Thanks again for last night. You're my good angel."

He smiled, winked, and closed the door behind him. She turned to find Tammy moving a stack of boxes off the couch.

"Sit down," the woman invited.

Mandy sat and looked around. The tiny living room contained a couch with two end tables, a TV, a folding worktable at right angles to the couch, and a straight-back chair. All other wall spaces were occupied by stacks of cardboard boxes. Directly opposite the couch, a bank of old-fashioned, double-hung windows looked out on a large back yard complete with orchard. Two of the trees were covered in white blossoms.

"I work at home," Tammy explained, sitting in the chair. "I make pine-needle baskets." She handed one to Mandy. It was an exquisite filigree bowl with an intricate, secondary pattern created by the way the long pine needles were tied together.

Mandy examined the basket. "This is beautiful! I've never seen anything like it. You make these, you say?"

"Yes. I supply them to a catalog store. I feel very lucky to be able to do this. There aren't many jobs in Limestone that pay very well, and though I don't make a lot of money making baskets, I get by, and I don't have to worry about child care."

"You have children?"

"Two boys, nine and eleven. They're at Granny's house right now. She's got them helping her with her garden."

"Granny Timberlain? That's right. She's your grandmother, too. I'd like to meet her."

"I'll take you over and introduce you, if you like."

"Thank you." Mandy handed the basket back to Tammy. As she did so, her arm brushed against a carved figure on the end table and knocked it over. "I'm so sorry!" She picked up the little stone orca.

"Don't worry about that," Tammy said. "That's one of my earlier tries."

"You did this?" Mandy inspected the statue, running her thumb over the crosshatching on top and noting how the contrasting colors had been represented by texture.

"Yes. I'm trying to branch out. The gift shops out on the islands are a good market for sea creatures, and there's lots of soapstone around here. There's an outcropping on Rael's property that he gives me for free. The boys and I go out and mine it and bring a trunkload home at a time."

"This is very clever," Mandy said, setting the carving down.

Tammy looked at her earnestly. "Millie Barlow said you had agreed to try to teach me to read. I'm determined to learn. I feel I could make better money if I could market on the internet, but if I can't read . . ." The words trailed off, and she shrugged.

"I don't know why Millie asked me to do this. I'm not a reading teacher."

"My sister-in-law's a teacher. She tried, but it didn't do no good."

Mandy pulled out her planner. "I might not do any good, either, but I'm willing to try. How about I come and teach you right after school, about this time of day, three days a week, Monday, Wednesday, and Friday. Will that work for you?"

"Yes." Tears shone in Tammy's eyes. "I've got the shivers all of a sudden. Excuse me." She left the room and returned moments later, blowing her nose. "I never cry," she said. "I haven't cried since . . . oh, for four years. Not once." She sat in the chair, dabbed at her eyes, and cleared her throat. "I've got a good feeling about this. Millie Barlow said that good would come out of you coming to Limestone, even if—"

"Even if what?"

Tammy compressed her lips. "I was speaking out of turn. What I meant to say was that I'd like to do something for you in return. Can I come and do housecleaning for you?"

Mandy shook her head. "That isn't necessary."

"But I want to do something. There must be something I can do for you."

"Well . . ." Mandy paused, considering.

"What? Go on, say it."

"I want to know about Grange. He is your cousin, isn't he?"

"Grange? Yes. Me 'n' him are the same age. Rael's five years older." Tammy frowned. "What do you want to know?"

"Someone said something about him rising above adversity. I thought at the time they were talking about his face being paralyzed, but today it seemed that his face was better."

"Yes, I heard that he could finally blink both eyes." Tammy smiled. "We've been so worried about that one eye, afraid it wouldn't stay moist enough and the lens would dry out. If it did, he'd be blind in that eye."

"I don't understand," Mandy said. "What was wrong?"

"He's had Bell's palsy. You know, where one side of the face is paralyzed. It comes on all of a sudden, usually as a result of stress. Sometimes it lasts just a few weeks, sometimes months."

"How long has he had it?"

"About a month, I think." Tammy sat with her eyes turned up to the ceiling, counting. "Maybe six weeks."

"About the time I got hired. Was that the stress that caused it?"

"Possibly." Tammy reached over and touched Mandy's arm. "Not you, of course. But the situation."

"So the facial paralysis is something recent. It's not the 'overcoming adversity' that was spoken of."

"Who told you about that?"

"Wesley Gallant. He really didn't tell me anything. That's why I'm asking you. I'm in a situation where I'm running blind. There are some deep undercurrents that I don't understand." Mandy spread her upturned palms. "Like, what's going on between Vince and Grange? It poisons the whole atmosphere. I have an idea that's Mrs. Barlow's 'even if' that you mentioned."

Tammy took a deep breath. "Okay. I'll tell you." She stowed her tissue in a pocket and picked up a pair of scissors and a pine-needle cluster. Methodically, she began snipping off the end that held them together. "This starts a long time ago, back in high school. Grange was dating my best friend, Lori Wilcox."

Mandy raised her brows in question.

"Yes. I married her brother. But that's another story." She continued snipping as she talked, making a little pile of single needles on her right. "Grange and Lori was made for each other. She was an outdoors girl, not afraid of anything. Loved to hike and hunt and go adventuring. It was in our senior year, about this time, when there come a rain like you wouldn't believe. The river come up, and there was lots of flooding. Kids got out of school to sandbag and move people out of houses that was in the flood plain."

Tammy grabbed another handful of needles. "Then the flood was over and the river went down some, and things got back to normal. We had a marvelous sunny day—it was a Saturday—and Lori talked Grange into taking his boat out on the river. I was there when it happened. He didn't want to—said he didn't know what'd been carried down in the flood. He knew about the danger of logjams when the river is running high, but she kept on and kept on till he give in."

Mandy thought of the girl in the picture on Grange's desk. "What did she look like?"

"A little like you. She had brown, curly hair and dark eyes, like you. Taller, though. Very outgoing. Loved to laugh." Tammy paused and looked beyond Mandy. "She and Grange was very much in love and planned to marry as soon as school was out."

"What happened?"

"They put in above Rael's place, where the bank is lower. Grange had a fifteen-foot skiff with a little outboard on it. They hadn't gone very far when they rounded a bend and there was a logjam right in front of them. He tried to get out of the sweep, but the outboard wasn't strong enough, and they was pulled into it.

The boat capsized and swept them against the trees. Grange hung on to a limb and tried to hang on to Lori, but the water was so cold he lost his grip."

There was a moment of silence and then Mandy whispered, "She was pulled under?"

Tammy nodded. Her hands, still holding pine needles and scissors, were still.

"So what happened? How did Grange get out of the logjam?"

"Vince found them. He worked for a man who had a real powerful riverboat, and he was working upriver and saw them take off. He—he was in love with Lori. She didn't give him the time of day, but he hung around as much as he could. As soon as he finished what he was doing, he decided he'd take a run downriver, and he found Grange hanging on, just about to go under himself."

Tammy cleared her throat. "Rescuing him was a real dangerous piece of work, because Vince had to keep his boat going fast enough upriver to just hang there in front of the logjam while he threw a line. Grange's hands was in such bad shape that he couldn't hold on, and so Vince tossed him a loop to put around his shoulders and under his arms. Grange had to manage that himself, because Vince was at the controls, trying to keep the boat in the right place. It was a real sticky situation. He saved Grange's life, that's for sure."

"What about Lori?"

"Vince hauled Grange into his boat, and they went looking for her downriver. They found her about two miles down, caught on a snag on the riverbank."

Mandy leaned forward. "Alive? Was she alive?"

Tammy pulled the tissue from her pocket. "No. She was dead. I should have said they found her body."

Mandy leaned back against the cushions. Some things were falling into place, but not all. "So, Vince blamed Grange for Lori's death?"

Tammy blew her nose. Then she picked up her scissors and continued snipping the ends off pine needles. "No more than Grange blamed himself. He's worked for years to try to—to atone. Just as Vince has worked for years to try to . . ."

"Make him pay?"

"Maybe. I don't know. Maybe he's been trying to prove to a woman who's been dead for over fifteen years that he's a better man than Grange."

Mandy shook her head. "I don't understand it."

"I think it's a guy thing." Tammy put her scissors down and scraped all the tops she had cut off into a garbage can sitting under the table. "Are you ready to go over to Granny Timberlains?"

"Yes. Except, would you answer one more question?"

"If I can."

"Where did Grange come by all his money?"

Tammy's jaw actually dropped. Then she laughed. "Who told you Grange had money?"

"Someone who should know. You mean he doesn't . . . hasn't . . . isn't wealthy?"

"He works for the public schools in Podunkville. Not many people getting rich doing that. Or maybe you know different?"

"Maybe his father left him something?"

"Uncle Fred was a gyppo logger, wouldn't work for the big companies. He left Grange some wore-out machinery and not much else. The only Timberlain that ever made any money was Uncle Buck, and I don't think any of it was made honest."

"I see. Well, thank you, Tammy. You've answered a lot of questions." Mandy stood. "I've got one more, though. It's not about Grange. It's about Vince."

"What's that?"

"Do you know who his father is?"

Tammy shook her head. "I often wondered about that and had my suspicions. I'll tell you something that I never told anyone before. Granny Timberlain always made sure he had something nice for Christmas under his tree. She never put her name on it, but she always made sure."

"What did that say to you?"

"It said that Vince must be—" Tammy stopped and put a finger to her lips. "I'd better not even say it out loud. It's like gossip. Never mind."

Mandy didn't press her to say what she had been thinking, but followed her out the front door and down the walk. "Shall we take my car?"

"No need," Tammy said. "Granny's house is right next door."

Mandy looked at the neighboring cottage, a twin to the one Tammy lived in. "These are cute little houses."

"They were company houses for the people who worked for the cement plant way back when. Granny bought both of these with the insurance money when my grandpa died in a logging accident. I rent from her."

Mandy didn't know why, but she felt nervous as she approached the front door. She was glad for Tammy's down-to-earth presence as she prepared to meet the matriarch of the Timberlain clan.

"I met Granny Timberlain yesterday," Mandy announced.

Leesie looked up from her oatmeal. "You did? What did you think?"

"She wasn't anything like what I expected."

"Really? What did you expect?"

Mandy stirred milk into her cereal and considered. "I think I expected someone round and soft. Big bosom. White hair. Dowager's hump. Maybe even with a cane. She's eighty years old, you know."

Leesie grinned broadly. "Boy, were you in for a surprise! Do you know who I think she looks like? That movie star in those old-fashioned movies Grandma Steenburg used to make us watch. The one with the black hair and lavender eyes?"

Mandy frowned. "I haven't a clue who you mean."

"Oh, you know, she was in the one about the Southern girl who goes to Texas with the big, buff, rich guy who is determined to keep her under his thumb, and the studly cowboy is in love with her. *Giant.* That was the name of the movie."

"Elizabeth Taylor? You think that Granny Timberlain looks like Elizabeth Taylor?"

"Yes. Look at the cheekbones and the eyebrows. And the black hair all done up on top of her head. She's still beautiful, I think."

"She's had a lot of sorrow in her life. Her husband and two sons were killed in a logging accident, her son Benjamin was murdered, and her only daughter died five years ago of breast cancer."

"Wow. That visit must have been a real downer."

Mandy shook her head. "It wasn't. She's quite the lady. Indomitable."

"What does that mean?"

"Unconquerable, unable to be subdued."

Leesie nodded. "And it rubs off, you know? That's the way I feel when I'm there in her house."

"Yeah. I'm gaining new respect for Mrs. Barlow."

"The preacher's wife?"

"Yes. When she asked me to visit Granny Timberlain, I thought it was because Granny was needy. I see now that Mrs. Barlow knew it was the other way around."

Leesie laughed. "You, needy? I don't think so." After glancing at the clock, she said, "I've got to get my things together. Jake will be here in a minute."

Mandy picked up the breakfast dishes and carried them to the sink. "Will you do something for me today?" she asked. "I need some modeling clay. Can you go by the art room and borrow some? I'll return it next week."

"Clay? What do you need that for?"

"It's for a project I'm working on. Can you do that for me?"

"I suppose." Leesie put on a jacket, picked up her backpack, and stood at the window to watch for her ride. "Oh, I forgot to tell you that Fran came by last night to see how you were doing. She was amazed when I told her you worked all afternoon. Heathcliff came by, too."

Mandy closed the dishwasher and straightened up. "Heathcliff?"

"That dark guy. The one you were with the day I came."

"Vince Lafitte. He came by last night?" Mandy picked up the spray bottle and a dishcloth and began to clean the stove.

"I told him you were in bed. By the way, what time did you give it up? I got home at seven and you were dead to the world."

"Probably about six. What did Vince want?"

"He said he had to go out of town. Something about he couldn't keep his date with you. Did you have a date?"

"He was going to come for dinner tonight. I had forgotten all about it."

"There's my ride. See you tonight. I'll be home late. Got practice."

Leesie slipped out the front door and was running down the steps by the time Mandy thought to ask, "Practice for what?"

As Mandy watched her sister climb into the pickup, Jake waved and Mandy returned the greeting. Then she hung the dishcloth on a peg at the end of the counter and went to search in the bookcase, finding what she needed in a corner of the bottom shelf. She put on her jacket and grabbed her purse, and just before leaving, she checked her reflection in the downstairs mirror. She still had dark circles under her eyes, but other than that, she was none the worse for her ordeal.

Arriving at the district office, Mandy saw a black Escalade parked in back. Vince sat inside, engrossed in something he was reading, and on a whim, she pulled up beside him. As she parked on the passenger side, he didn't seem to notice her. She gathered up purse and book, hopped out, and went around to tap on his window. Surprised, he looked up, and immediately his face broke into that attractive smile.

He rolled down his window. "Mandy! I've been waiting for you."

"You have? What for?"

"I wanted to see how you are. You were asleep when I came by last night."

"I told you I wasn't going to be fit for company. Want to come up to my office?"

He shook his head. "I've got to go." He looked at his watch. "Right now, in fact. I just wanted to see you, say goodbye."

"Where are you going?"

"Miami."

"Miami! What in the world for?"

"I've got a job going sideways."

Mandy shot him a puzzled look. "I thought they were supposed to come straight down. The buildings. Sideways would be a problem."

Vince laughed. "It is a problem. I've got a superintendent that can't—well, it would take too long to explain. The bottom line is I've got to go rescue the situation." His eyes flicked to the side and back, and she turned to see what he was looking at. Grange's old pickup had just pulled into the parking lot.

Turning back to Vince, she asked. "How long will you be gone?"

He shrugged. "Three, four days. As long as it takes to get the job done."

"Well, have a good trip," she said, backing away. "Give me a ring when you get home, and we'll have you over to dinner."

He flashed a grin and gave a thumbs up, and Mandy waved before turning to climb the porch stairs.

Grange, looking like a thundercloud, held the door for her.

Determined to be pleasant, Mandy smiled. "Thank you." She went directly to her office and spent the first part of the morning getting prepared for the staff meeting, and when nine o'clock rolled around, she was ready.

She began by saying they would consider a section of the district policies each staff meeting and passed out a pre-test about policies for various communicable diseases and conditions ranging from impetigo through lice to TB. Then she used the pre-test to go over the policies in a teaching situation and warned that she would give the same test the next staff meeting as a post-test.

Midge, Mrs. Berman, and Mo all worked diligently on the pre-test, but Grange was obviously put off by the exercise. He seemed to answer randomly, then threw his pencil down, leaned back in his chair, and crossed his arms. As they went through the questions point by point, his brows grew lower, and his body language fairly shouted his discontent.

After that, Mandy asked Mo to make a presentation about the four elementary schools, detailing for the staff the things he had told her as they rode around the district. He passed around folders he had prepared, but as he stood in front of everyone, Grange's scowl seemed to make him shrivel. Mo stumbled over sentences, left out conclusions he had drawn, skipped over important data, and generally made a hash of things.

Grange was no more cooperative during the portion where the resource-room teachers from the four elementary schools joined them. As Mandy outlined her vision for the district, everyone seemed to take a cue from Grange. No one looked at her. They either doodled on the handout she had given, looked out the window, or in the case of Mrs. Reilly, sat with her eyes closed. The enthusiasm that had swept Mandy along ran out long before she had finished, and all she could do was grit her teeth and persevere. When she finally made her closing statements, there seemed to be a general feeling of relief, and people silently picked up their things and left. Only one teacher took the handout Mandy had prepared.

Mandy erased the chalkboard and threw away the clever poster she had made about banning cracks for reading students to fall through. Then she picked up the handouts and carried them upstairs. As she passed Grange's office, she poked her head in the open door and tried to keep her voice even as she said, "May I see you for a moment, please?"

He was still scowling. "I'm on my way to the high school."

"It won't take long." She walked to her office without listening to his protestations and laid the stack of handouts on the corner of her desk. She didn't sit down but stood by her desk, with her hand resting on the papers.

A long moment later, Grange followed her, stopping in the doorway.

"Step in, please, and close the door."

He hesitated then did as she bid, but he stayed in front of the door, feet planted slightly apart, hands behind him.

Mandy let the silence lengthen. At last she said, "I went to see Granny Timberlain yesterday. I can't believe that she would approve of the manners you just displayed in the staff meeting."

"You're going to lecture me on manners? What about professional courtesy?"

Mandy blinked. "What are you talking about?"

"This meeting. You're off on your own personal little crusade without a word to me about it."

"Not so. I said last staff meeting that we'd be talking about a vision for a new reading program. I sent out the agenda for this meeting and asked if you wanted to add to it. I doubt if you even did me the courtesy of looking at it. If you wanted input, you could have had it. The signal I got from you was that you wanted nothing to do with anything I might be doing as far as the district was concerned."

"You pretty much made it clear that this was your own little kingdom, and we lesser mortals weren't welcome, except as peasants," Grange said. "You didn't ask me for input. You told me *you* were going to be explaining *your* program to the rest of us. If you had asked, I would have advised that you get the principals in here and get them on board if you want this to succeed. You'll not do it without them."

"My plan was to get the resource-room people conversant with the program before presenting it to the principals, so they could advocate for it. Thanks to your example, they closed their minds before I even began talking."

"I doubt that."

"Oh? Let me ask you this: Did you carry away the handout that I gave you? Is it on your desk?"

He didn't answer.

"I thought not." She picked up the stack of papers and tossed them to the middle of the desk. "I handed out eight. There are six here. Mo took one, and Mrs. Reilly took one. Everyone else followed your lead."

Grange changed his tactics. "And what was that about the lice and TB? How is that going to help educate the district if we cover those things in our staff meetings? It's the people out in the field that need to go over that information."

She picked up the meeting agenda. "If you'll see number 5 on the agenda I sent you, it's 'Brainstorm ways to convey this information to the district.'"

"So, why didn't we do that?"

"You had the meeting shut down. No one was going to offer an opinion on anything because they perceived you didn't want it discussed."

"That's ridiculous!"

"Oh, is it? Do you know what you did to Mo? He prepared a superb presentation on the four elementary schools from a standpoint of budget and value received." Mandy's hands clenched into fists. "When he rode around with me on Monday, he was eloquent. But today, because you were so against everything,

everything I had planned for the meeting, he was afraid to venture an idea in the face of your wrath." Her voice began to quiver with indignation. "He's a thinker, that man. He's a district treasure, and I can see he's not valued as he should be."

Grange's lip curled down in something very close to a sneer. "And upon what do you base that wild assumption?"

"Did you carry his excellently prepared folder back to your office to study? No? I thought not. Here it is." She picked up the folder and held it out to Grange.

The moments dragged by as she stood with arm extended and chin up, her brown eyes locked with his blue ones. Finally, he stepped forward, took Mo's handout, and turned to leave.

When he had his hand on the doorknob, Mandy asked in a neutral tone, "Will you be at the high school all afternoon? Does your calendar reflect that?"

Grange muttered something under his breath and wrenched open the door, walked out, and closed it sharply behind him.

She tried not to smile as she sat at her computer and clicked first on district calendar and then on his blank page. "Oh, Mandy," she said under her breath, "you really shouldn't tease the man." Just then, on the computer screen, all the afternoon hours were blocked out with the words "High School." Immediately afterward, she saw Grange through the windows of her door as he stalked out of his office and across the mezzanine, pulling on his jacket as he went. She heard his tread down the stairs, and without conscious thought, she rose and stood at the window, waiting for him to appear from beneath the porch roof. When he emerged, she watched him stride across the parking lot. He stopped halfway and turned to look fiercely up at her window, impaling her with his gaze.

His jacket collar was turned up, and a breeze lifted the hair that hung over his forehead. He had a day's growth of beard on his face that shadowed his jaw and accented the blue of his eyes. For a moment neither of them moved, but this time it was Mandy who turned away first. She walked to her desk and sat with her hands clasped between her knees as she stared at the calendar on her computer screen and waited for her heart to quit thundering in her chest.

Mandy unclenched her hands when she heard Grange's pickup leaving the parking lot. With two firm keystrokes, she got rid of his calendar page. Then, noticing the stack of folders, she was reminded of the failed staff meeting. She opened the empty file drawer in her desk and dropped them in. "Take that, Mr. Timberlain."

"Dr. Steenburg?"

She looked up to see Elizabeth peeking through her partially opened door. "Yes?"

"Um, could you come down to the reception desk for just a moment? There's something . . . I've got a couple . . . I'd like to, like, talk to you about something."

Mandy closed the file drawer. "Right now?"

"If you could. I'll be leaving in a few minutes, and I kinda wanted to, you know, see about some stuff."

Mandy leaned back in her chair. "What kind of stuff?"

Elizabeth cleared her throat. "Lots of stuff. Will you come down so I can, like, show you?"

Intrigued, Mandy said, "Certainly." She followed the young woman across the mezzanine, and as they descended the stairs, she said, "I remember the first night I saw you at the Qwik-E Market. I thought your smile lit up the room."

Elizabeth stopped at the bottom of the stairs and looked up at Mandy. "You did?"

"Yes. It was a dark and rainy night, and I was a stranger. Your smile was particularly comforting to me. I haven't seen it much lately. Is everything all right in your world?"

The young woman paused for just a moment as if she would say something, and then she turned to go around the reception counter. "Everything's fine," she said as she opened the lower cupboard doors. "Here's what I wanted you to see."

Mandy bent down so she could see the stacks of T-shirts and sweatshirts. "Yes?"

"We need a cabinet at the high school where we can put these on display. We'd sell a lot more and have a lot more school spirit if they were out where everyone could see them."

"I agree." Mandy straightened up. "That's an excellent notion. Do you have an idea of where this cabinet should be?"

"No. But I thought maybe I could look around the high school to see if there's a place we could put one."

"If you will do that and draw up a sketch with measurements of what you envision, we'll talk about the next step in getting one."

"I figured that, at first, the profits could pay for the case, if the district would put up the money to build it."

Mandy nodded. "Good thinking."

"And we might be able to get someone from the shop class to take it on as a senior project."

"Even better thinking! I'll look forward to seeing your design. Are you here on Monday? Good. Can you be ready to meet with me about this time?"

Elizabeth nodded.

"I'll put it on my calendar."

At that moment, Willow Timberlain put her head in the door. "I'm going to be late for class, Elizabeth. Come on!"

Elizabeth got a stricken look on her face. "All right, Willow," she called. She closed the cabinet doors and grabbed her books.

"I'm sorry, Dr. Steenburg," she said, brushing past her. "I've got to go."

Puzzled, Mandy watched Elizabeth hurry to the door. The teenager paused there, turned, and almost said something, but must have thought better of it.

It wasn't until Mandy left work that afternoon that she understood Elizabeth's odd behavior. She understood, too, the bursts of laughter that had periodically come floating up from downstairs as people came and went. As she walked around the corner to where she parked her car that morning, she stopped in her tracks when she saw what someone had done to it.

Cleverly attached to the top of the Miata were wings made of lime green fabric stretched tightly over kite-stick frames. They were held in place by Velcro straps that went through the windows and fastened inside. On the front, between the headlights, were two huge antennae, fastened with suction cups. "I'll learn to lock my doors," Mandy muttered.

She walked around the car, examining it from every angle. It really did look like one of the stinkbugs in the box left on her doorstep. All of a sudden, she understood that Elizabeth's conversation about a cabinet for clothing with the Tarheel logo was a ruse to get her out of her office while Willow dressed her car in a bug's costume. Mandy didn't know whether to be angry or admire the inventiveness and audacity of the deed. Admiration won out, and she smiled as she broke the seal on the suction cups and stowed the antennae in the front seat. The wings were a more complicated situation, but she figured how they came apart and folded up. As she put them in with the antennae, she said to herself, "That girl needs to be channeled."

The smile stayed with Mandy all the way home. She looked forward to Leesie's return so she could laugh with her sister about it. But Leesie was so late that, by the time she got home, the smile had faded and Mandy had passed through anger to worry. She had the phone book out and was looking up Rael's number when she heard the familiar sound of Jake's pickup outside.

When Leesie came in the door, she took one look at Mandy's fierce countenance and said, "What's wrong?"

"Do you know what time it is?"

Leesie's eyes moved to the clock and back. "It's ten o'clock? Is that the right answer? What's wrong?"

"What were you doing out until ten?"

"I told you this morning. I had practice." Leesie went to the kitchen, opened the refrigerator door, and poured a glass of milk.

"What kind of practice?"

Leesie took a drink. "Band practice," she said, raising her glass. "We were making moosic."

Mandy didn't smile at the pun. All of a sudden, she was out of gas. The staff meeting, her reading program presentation, the round of sparring with Grange, even the stinkbug incident, had all taken a toll, and now she was done. She closed the phone book and put it away in the kitchen cupboard. "I'm going to bed," she said wearily.

"I've got some homework to do," Leesie said. "See you in the morning."

Mandy climbed the stairs and got ready for bed. She brushed her teeth and read a few pages from the book on her nightstand, but her eyes grew heavy and she turned out the light. Floating up from below she heard the muted sound of Leesie playing scales on Jake's guitar, and her last thought before she drifted off to sleep was, *This is homework?*

Mandy came downstairs the next morning to find the kitchen table transformed into a stinkbug. She had dumped the wings and antennae by the door, and apparently Leesie had found and reassembled them.

Leesie looked up from the pot of oatmeal she was stirring. "What did you think of your car?"

"I thought it was terribly clever. In fact, I looked forward to sharing it with you all the way home, but you weren't here."

"Oh, Sweetiebug, I'm sorry. It's awful to have something to share and not be able to, isn't it? Well, move a wing and sit down. I've got breakfast fixed."

Mandy undid the apparatus and put it back in the corner before sitting at the table. "That Willow is really talented, isn't she? Did you see how ingeniously this was put together?"

Leesie set a bowl of steaming cereal in front of Mandy. "So you know it was Willow?"

"Yes. I wish you could have seen it on the car. It actually looked like one of those shield bugs."

"I did see it—or a picture of it, anyway. There was one hanging in the hallway on the bulletin board." Leesie paused, clearly wondering how her sister would take the news.

Mandy was quiet for a moment. She spooned some sugar in her bowl, added some milk, and stirred. "Leesie—" she began.

Her sister waited for her to go on.

Mandy didn't look up. "What if I gave up my contract here? What if I didn't stay?"

"You mean what if you didn't stay next year? That wouldn't make any difference to me, because I'll be off to college anyway. Although . . ."

"Although what?"

"Jake's going to do his first two years at the community college downriver, and I've been thinking of that, too, rather than New Mexico State. If I did that, I'd want to stay here with you. If I could, that is."

"But what if I decided not even to stay the rest of this academic year?"

Leesie frowned. "What are you saying? You mean just give up? Because someone dresses up your car like a stinkbug?"

"It's not that. There are lots of things going on in the district that you don't know about." She sighed. "Everything is a battle. I can't think of a day when I haven't had to go toe-to-toe with someone over something."

"Like who? Who's battling you?"

"Principally Grange Timberlain."

"Mr. Timberlain? You fight with him?"

"Is that so unbelievable?"

"Well, yeah." Leesie laughed. "All the girls are just a little bit in love with him. He's such a hunk."

"Leesie!"

"Or at least since his face got back to normal, he is. It was a little like Halloween at first—weird and creepy. But he's been good humored about the whole thing. He's really a crack-up."

"I hadn't noticed," Mandy said.

Leesie stirred her oatmeal. "I do see what you mean, though. You're not the most popular person at the bus garage. And by the way, I don't know that I want to go back there for just that reason."

"You went to the bus garage?"

"Hello? You asked me to. I showed up to organize Mr. Berman's office yesterday morning, and he was so grouchy and ungrateful."

Mandy's brows shot up. "What did he say to you?"

"I can't remember all the things he said." Leesie chewed thoughtfully. "It was, like, everything was fine before you came to town. One of the lady bus drivers told me not to worry, that he was just mad because someone came and repossessed his boat, and he's blaming that on you. But how could that be your fault?"

"It can't," Mandy said. "Let me find someone—an adult—to go with you. I promised him some help, so I have to deliver, but I don't want him using you as a scapegoat for his frustrations."

"I had already decided not to go back." Leesie cleared the dishes and put them in the sink. "Oh, I brought your clay."

"You did? Good girl. I forgot I asked you to get me some."

"Willow got it for me." Leesie grinned, taking a plastic grocery bag out of her backpack. "You'd better check to make sure it's clay and not a bag full of snakes."

Mandy looked inside. "Did Willow know the clay was for me?"

"Sure. Why?" Leesie went into a peal of laughter as Mandy pulled a long, venomous-looking clay snake out of the bag. "I assure you, I didn't know what she had done when I said that about snakes. That's too funny!"

"Pardon me if I don't laugh." Mandy coiled the snake up and put it back into the bag. "You didn't answer my question. What if I don't stay?"

Leesie paused in the act of zipping up her backpack and set it on the table. "It's not that I can't go back home. I can do that now, and I'd be all right. But I don't want to. If you don't stay, I think I'd see if Granny Timberlain would let me stay with her. Maybe I could work for my board and room. Or maybe Fran would give me a job so I could pay Granny."

Mandy frowned. "You've only been here five days. In five days you've decided you want to stay?"

Leesie grinned. "Crazy, isn't it? There's my ride. I'll be home late again. Practice tonight." She opened the door, stepped out on the deck, and put her head back through the doorway. "Oh, and I told Rael that we'd go trang with him and Jake and Willow tomorrow. I said you make a mean pot of chili, so you need to make one to take with us. Okay?"

"What's trang?" But Mandy spoke to empty air. She watched Leesie bound down the stairs and saw Willow smile as she opened the door for her. "Well, what do you know," Mandy muttered. "She does know how to smile."

After picking up the bag of clay and finding her purse, Mandy looked out the window. The sky was its usual gray, but the clouds were high, so she didn't wear another coat over her suit jacket. She drove to work, getting there ahead of everyone else, and spent some time on the Internet looking for possible grants to fund part of her reading program. "Just in case I decide to stay," she murmured. She found one site that had something almost tailor-made for what she wanted to do, and she was so intent on reading about the application process that she didn't hear Grange until he stood in her doorway and rapped on the doorframe.

"May I come in?" He had a file folder in his hand.

She eyed him warily. "Yes, of course. I thought you were at the high school all day today."

"Checking on my whereabouts?" he asked lightly.

She tried to match his tone. "I had a question. I looked to see if you were to be in today. Your calendar said not."

"What was the question?" He sat down in one of the chairs in front of her desk, leaned back, and crossed his legs. His jaw was dark with a two-day's growth of beard.

"I wondered if the district had someone on staff who is good at writing grants. Or perhaps a parent?"

"Midge has taken a shot at it a time or two, but she's never had much success." Grange tossed the file folder on her desk. "This is more of a sure thing."

"What is it?"

"Levy."

"I don't understand." Mandy took the folder and opened it.

"It's the way a school district in Washington raises money for things the state doesn't fund. New school busses, special programs."

She eyed Grange. "Like music?"

He shook his head. "We've got that covered elsewhere." He nodded toward the folder. "We need to get on this right away. Form a parent committee, submit a budget to them—a compromise between what you'd like to have and what you think the voters will approve."

"So it's like a bond election?"

"Yes, without the bonds. It's to levy a tax to support schools. An election where people vote to tax themselves."

"Who has done this in the past? Who knows how to do it and could do a good job of pulling it all together?"

Grange smiled wickedly, and there was a twinkle in his eye as he stood. "Nettie Maypole has headed up the levy for the last fifteen years."

"Nettie Maypole? The Yum Yum Potatoes lady?"

He nodded and paused as Mandy absorbed all the implications of the situation. Then he said, "Well, I'm off to the high school now, unless you have something else you want to discuss."

She gritted her teeth as she saw how much Grange enjoyed her discomfort. "No thanks. That's all." Ignoring him, she began to read the contents of the folder he had brought. When she was sure he was out of the room, she slammed the folder closed and dug her planner out of her purse. Looking through the notes she had made in the calendar at the job fair in Las Vegas, she found the phone number of the man who had acted as agent for North Cascades School District. She used her phone card to make the call.

"Hello? Mr. Skinner? This is Mandy Steenburg. I met you at the job fair in Las Vegas last February. You hired me for the North Cascade School District. Yes, I was the tiny one. Yes, the young one, too. Well, it's a bit of a difficult situation, actually, because it seems they just wanted a figurehead. The former superintendent is my assistant, only he's not. I was wondering if the job in Chevak is still open?"

Mandy listened for a moment and said, "No, I'm not applying for the position. I just wanted to know if it was still a possibility. I realize it looks bad for me to be leaving this situation so soon, but . . . No, I think I can be released from my contract. Two members of the school board don't want me here anyway. Yes, thank you, Mr. Skinner. I'll let you know."

She sighed and hung up. Turning back to her computer, she tried to rekindle her enthusiasm for finding a grant for her reading program, but it was heavy going. Finally, she picked up the yellow phone card, found Midge's number, and invited her up.

At first, the woman was cool to the idea of being put in charge of securing a grant, since she'd had no training and didn't completely understand the process, but as Mandy talked with her and promised to support her, Midge grew willing, even excited, to try again. She went back to her desk with the name of the website, a list of preliminary instructions, and an appointment to meet with Mandy on Monday afternoon to look over what she had done to that point.

Mandy spent several hours immersed in the book she had brought from home the day before. Her studies were interrupted by Mo, who tapped at her door.

He poked his head in. "Do you have a minute?"

She looked up and smiled. "For you, always. Come in." She closed her book and pushed it to the corner of the desk. "Sit down. What can I do for you?"

He sat on the edge of the chair and clasped a folder in his lap. "First, I want to say I'm sorry about my awful presentation yesterday."

She waved away his apology. "Don't give it another thought."

"I was prepared. I practiced, but I've never been good at public speaking."

"Well, Grange wasn't the most appreciative of audiences. He certainly put a damper on my reading program proposal."

Mo rubbed his cheek. "He scared me silly, but he came and apologized."

"Oh?" Mandy's brows went up. "When did he do that?"

"First thing this morning. He said he read my paper—which is funny, because I didn't think he took a copy with him. I know he read it, though, because he asked a couple of pertinent questions."

"He did?" Her cheeks grew a shade rosier. "Well, I'm glad, Mo. You had some really good information to share, even if he didn't seem to listen yesterday."

Mo shrugged. "That's all right."

"So, what did you come in to talk to me about?"

He cleared his throat. "Um, I think I've found a way so we don't have to let any teachers go, and perhaps still help fund your reading program."

Mandy leaned forward. "Is it legal?" Confronted by Mo's blank stare, she said, "I was kidding. Tell me where you found all this money."

He eagerly dragged his chair around to sit beside her desk and then spread the contents of the folder in front of her. They spent the next hour and a half discussing each of the pages and doing more research online. At the end of that time, she sat back in her chair. "I'm convinced," she said. "Now we just have to convince other people."

"By 'other people,' you mean Grange." Mo rubbed his cheek again, and Mandy noticed a fuzz of whiskers along his jawline.

"I nominate you to be the one to approach him," he said.

She smiled. "I accept the nomination. Let's set the appointment right now." She opened the calendar page on her computer and looked at Grange's Monday appointments. "I'll catch him first thing in the morning. He's at the high school in the afternoon. Can I have copies of everything in this folder?"

"That's yours. I made it for you."

"Thanks." Mandy laid the folder aside. "So what's the thing about the whiskers? I thought at first that Grange was just not shaving out of pure obstinacy, but I see you're sprouting a beard, too. There must be some significance."

"It's for Opening Festival. The beard-growing contest."

"What's Opening Festival?"

Mo smiled. "I imagine it's pretty frantic at your house with Leesie playing catch-up."

Mandy frowned. "What are you talking about?"

"You mean you really don't know? I thought you were— when you said, 'What's Opening Festival,' I thought, you know, you were being funny."

"No. I know nothing about it, and nothing about Leesie playing catch-up, whatever that is."

Mo cleared his throat. "Well, uh, Opening Festival is a town celebration we have each year to celebrate the opening of the road over the mountains. It's a huge fundraiser for music in the schools, and the kids have a big part in it, both in planning and putting it on and performing. It's mostly a bluegrass festival, and we have visiting bands from all over the country."

"Bluegrass," Mandy said faintly.

"Yes. Leesie's playing in one of the bands the school sponsors. I thought you knew."

"I knew she was going to practice, but I never thought to ask what she was practicing. How do you know this?"

"I've heard her."

"What is she playing?" Mandy searched her memory for things she might know about bluegrass and came up with very little.

"All the old standards. 'Wabash Cannonball,' 'Will the Circle Be Unbroken,' 'Wildwood Flower'—you know."

"No, I mean, what instrument?"

"Bass fiddle. She's good, too, for having just picked it up."

Mandy shook her curls. "She's a cellist—it must transfer. But how do you know this, Mo? How did you happen to hear her, while I don't know anything about it?"

"I go to the high school after school and help. I play bluegrass, too. Mandolin. Sometimes I go to Granny Timberlain's before school to coach them a bit."

When Mandy looked mystified, Mo explained, "The Timberlains have been playing bluegrass forever. Jake's group practices there so Granny can teach them all the old songs she knows."

Mandy paused a moment to digest that information and then asked, "So, is this Opening Festival something that I need to be involved in?"

"No. It's Grange's baby. That's why he's spending so much time at the high school right now."

"Well, that's a load off my mind." She picked up the folder Grange had brought. "But here's something I just discovered I have to do, and I don't know anything about it. I want you to educate me about the levy."

"What do you want to know?"

"Everything. We don't have that process in New Mexico. The state funds everything there."

"All right." Mo began to instruct Mandy about the levy system, taking her through the part the district played in the process and, particularly, her role. As he spoke, he drew diagrams on the inside leaf of the file folder.

"I see," she said when he was finished. She pointed to the triangle that represented the chairman of the citizens' committee. "Whom do you suggest we choose for this position?"

"Nettie Maypole."

"Why?"

He held up his index finger. "First, because she knows the ropes. Second, because we're late getting going on this. We should have been up and running last January."

Mandy interrupted. "And why weren't we?"

"Because the administration was in flux. Grange didn't think he was even going to be here. And then, after Wesley and Mrs. Foley convinced him to stay, you arrived, and it's been a mess."

"Okay, so we're at number two, we're late getting going."

"Three, Nettie can deliver. She's related to half the people in the district, and Mutt is related to the other half. Every levy she's chaired has passed overwhelmingly."

"I see," Mandy said. "Is there a number four?"

"Four is the most important one. She's done it so long, it's tradition. There's an old saying: tradition is more binding than the law. That's especially true in a small town."

Mandy leaned forward. "Do you think Nettie would do it if I asked her? She doesn't have warm fuzzies toward me, you know."

"I know. Hmm." Mo leaned his elbow on Mandy's desk and cradled his chin in his palm. "I don't know. You may have to get Grange to go with you, but I think it's critical that you are the one that does the asking."

"I'd rather die than take Grange with me." She spoke more vehemently than she intended.

"The district needs the levy," Mo reminded her.

"I'll think about it. When do I need to talk to her?"

"Yesterday." His lips curled in a tight little smile. "Kidding. Realistically, if you could get her on board next week, it's still doable. She won't have to reinvent the wheel. In fact, if I know Nettie, she's already got her committees formed, and she's just waiting for an official invitation." He considered a moment. "Which makes it twice as imperative that you move quickly. You don't want to wait so long that she gets her back up and decides she won't do it just to spite you, since you took so long to ask her."

Mandy buried her face in her hands. "I hate the politics! Can't we just focus on the kids?"

Mo stood. "I think that's what you're doing, Dr. Steenburg."

She looked at him over the tips of her fingers.

He nodded. "If you decide to go ahead and ask Nettie, it's because the kids are your focus, and you're not letting personal animosity—on her side or yours—get in the way."

Mandy dropped her hands and leaned back in her chair. "Did anyone ever tell you that you're wise?"

He looked at his feet and shook his head.

She stood. "Well, you are. Thank you for all you've done for me today." She extended her hand.

Mo clasped it. "You're welcome, Dr. Steenburg." Beneath his sparse whiskers, his cheeks had a rosy tinge.

"Mandy," she insisted.

He shook his head, smiling. "Let me know how your talk with Grange comes out." He pointed to the folder on her desk.

"I will." She remained standing until he was out of the room. Then, looking at her watch, she opened the book she was reading earlier and bent over it in deep study until it was time to go to Tammy's.

21

Mandy sat in Tammy's living room at her basket-making table as the young mother beside her struggled through an oral reading test.

"I know this is really hard," Mandy said as they paused between passages, "but I need you to do the best you can. This will give me an idea of where we can begin."

"Don't worry about it," Tammy said grimly. "This is what I go through all the time."

It was an intense half hour for Mandy as she watched Tammy try under her breath before speaking aloud each halting attempt. "Okay," she said finally, closing the book. "We'll stop there. We've got a benchmark now, and we'll be able to measure your progress with this same test."

She set the plastic bag of clay on the table. "I hope you'll understand that I'm not a reading teacher. My mother is, but I didn't learn anything from her. She did give me a book to read, though I didn't read it. I've had it on my shelf and never opened it until today."

Tammy didn't say anything. She sat with her eyes on Mandy and her hands in her lap.

Mandy picked up one of the baskets. "I was interested when I found that you made baskets and carved little statues, because it made me remember what my mother said about the man who wrote the book she gave me. This may sound a little off-the-wall, but hear me out." She took a deep breath. "This man is dyslexic. He's also a sculptor. He says he thinks that a gift that dyslexic people have is their ability to see things in three dimensions, and that's one of the things that causes problems in reading. Causes the reversals, you know? It's like, when you see the word "was," if you see it in three dimensions, your mind may flip it around so you're seeing the backside, and what you're reading is "saw" instead of "was." That's the first problem."

"Just the first one?" Tammy asked.

"Well, it's actually more of a situation than a problem. It can be dealt with. In fact, he says that your mind can learn to keep all the words flat and two dimensional, but what can happen is, as you're reading along with everything flat and well behaved, you may suddenly come to a word that makes everything on the page misbehave, and all of a sudden things spring into three dimensions all over the place, and it's a mess, and you just want to give up."

"Who is this man?" Tammy breathed. "He's talking about my life."

"What he says is that people with this gift tend to think in pictures, and they learn to read by picturing words. That's why, as we were just reading a passage in the test" —Mandy patted the book— "you read the word 'elephant,' but stumbled over the word 'of.' He says that's because you associate the word with the picture, and there's no picture for the word 'of.'"

"If that's right, what can I do?" Tammy sounded anxious.

"We're going to make a picture for it. He's given us a list of words that invariably make things spring into three dimensions, and we'll work through them. Or I'll show you how, and you'll have to work through each one. This will test your willingness to learn, Tammy. It's very time intensive."

Mandy took the clay out of the bag. "We'll start with 'was.'"

"My goodness! What is that?"

Mandy dangled the snake. "I borrowed clay from the school. Willow worked with it before she put it in the bag. Clever, isn't it?"

"She's a very talented girl no matter what she's doing. She even helps with the fireworks for Opening Festival, and the things she comes up with there are amazing. I'm glad she has that outlet. I think it will be her salvation."

"Fireworks?"

Tammy laughed. "No. Art—creating things."

"Probably so." Mandy broke off the snake's tail and rolled it between her hands to make a long worm. "We're going to make letters and spell the word out. Will you make the three letters that spell out 'was' and set them on the table?"

Tammy took the worm and quickly formed the word in clay.

"Now," Mandy said. "You're going to trace over the letters with your finger, and as you trace over each letter, you're going to say it.

Tammy did as Mandy instructed.

"Now, do it backwards."

"Backwards?"

"I said it might sound off-the-wall," Mandy said.

Tammy traced and repeated, "S–a–w."

"Now you're going to use the word in a sentence."

"Something like, 'I couldn't answer the phone because I was in the bathtub?'"

"Excellent!" Mandy gave her a lump of clay. "Now, I want you to illustrate that sentence."

"Illustrate it?"

"Make a little statue or something so that when you see it, you'll remember that sentence."

"Okay." Tammy took a piece of clay and made a tiny telephone and set it on a miniature table she fashioned. Then she made a bathtub and a small figure to sit in the bath. Her fingers were so nimble and quick that it took only a few minutes.

"And what was the sentence again?" Mandy asked.

"I couldn't answer the phone because I was in the bathtub."

"Now trace the letters forward and back."

Tammy did as Mandy asked.

"Now, close your eyes and spell the word 'was' forward and backward."

Tammy closed her eyes and spelled "was," then "saw."

Mandy laid a three-by-five card in front of her with the word on it. "Here is the word you just did. That's the first one. Here is a stack of words you need to get through with that same process."

"Holy cow. That will take years!"

"There are about two hundred words here. If you did four each week, that would take you—" Mandy paused to do the figures in her mind.

"—fifty weeks," Tammy said. "One year."

"I'll be honest with you. I don't know if this will work or not. But it looks to me like you have all the parts of reading. You know the letters and what sounds they make. You know the different vowel sounds. You just have to get where you can put all of it together. Maybe this will help."

"I've tried just about everything else. I have nothing to lose."

"Let's do another one. How about the word 'of.'"

Tammy quickly went through the drill, illustrating the sentence "May I borrow a cup of sugar?"

When they were finished, Mandy pulled out a reading text. "You need lots of easy practice. This is a reader from beginning second grade. I think you'll be comfortable there, because you have lots of coping mechanisms. Let's try it.

Tammy read through a page and looked up at Mandy, smiling broadly. "Did you notice anything? I didn't trip up on a single 'was' or 'of.'"

"I noticed," Mandy said. "Remember, Tammy, this isn't magic. This is an opportunity to put in lots of hard work. Reading takes practice. You're not going to spend a little time making clay figures and all of a sudden be a reading whiz."

"I know. But for the first time, I've got hope. Leave me the stack of cards. I'll get the boys to help me with them."

"I'll leave you two more. You've got to give your brain time to process before you dump more information on it. If you want to spend more time, you can always practice reading out of the book." Mandy peeled off the next two cards and set them by the clay. Then she picked up her purse. "That's enough for today. Monday at the same time, okay?"

"Yes." Tammy walked Mandy to the door and hugged her. "Thank you. I don't know if you know it, but I prayed you here."

"Does that mean I have to stay for fifty weeks?"

Tammy laughed. "Unless you let me learn more than four words a week."

Mandy walked briskly to her car, but before she got in, she turned and waved at Tammy, who still stood in the doorway. Mandy smiled all the way home, thinking, *Maybe this is how I can make a difference. It would be worth battling Grange Timberlain for a year if I helped Tammy learn to read.*

When she arrived home, Mandy unlocked the door and was disappointed to find that Leesie wasn't there to talk to. Full of energy that needed to be spent, she put on sweats and her running shoes and jogged up the hill.

Fran was out in her front yard mowing, and Mandy waved as she trotted past. Her neighbor killed the motor and walked toward the road, so Mandy stopped and waited. "Hi, Fran."

"Hi, yourself. How are things going? Is life any smoother?"

Mandy grimaced. "Some parts are smoother, some are rougher."

Fran brushed some grass clippings from her shoes. "Any more thoughts about leaving the district?"

"I actually called the headhunter that hired me to see if that job in Chevak was still open," Mandy admitted.

"And?"

"It is."

"And?"

"And . . . that's all. I just called. I was mad at Grange again and wanted out. But then, I talked to Mo and got excited about making a difference. By the way, I just found out about Opening Festival."

"Oh, yeah. Grange has me doing fireworks again. I've got a committee of students and parents. It's going to be great this year."

"I thought I'd call my mother tonight and let her know that Leesie is going to be playing in it."

"What if you leave before then?"

"Leesie would probably kill me. But that would be better than me killing Grange, wouldn't it?"

Rael drove by in his white postal-service jeep and honked the horn. Both women waved.

"Another thing found out today," Mandy said, turning to Fran. "I have to set up a committee to oversee the levy. Grange told me that Nettie Maypole has been doing it for years, but I seem to be her sworn enemy. Do you think I should ask her to chair the committee?"

"What does Grange think?"

Mandy sniffed. "That is the standard reaction. Grange thinks it's right, so it can't be wrong. I've a good mind to ask someone else just to prove otherwise." She stepped away. "I'd better get running. Talking about Grange has made me grouchy, and I was in such a good mood." She waved and jogged back to the road and turned toward Rael's place.

By the time she had run the loop up to the pine woods and back down the riverbank trail, her good humor was restored. She showered, and as she opened a can of soup for supper, she remembered that Leesie had volunteered her to make chili for their outing the next day. After setting a pot of beans to soak, Mandy held her breath as she opened the freezer door, hoping to find a package of hamburger. One was there, so she put it out to thaw. She carried her mug of soup to the piano, then sat down and doodled around, trying to think of something to play. As she did, a bubbly tune appeared, full blown, complete with chord structure, and worked its way from her heart through her fingers. She set it to a bouncy ragtime bass and played it through a couple of times, smiling at nothing in particular.

Perhaps it was a feeling evoked by the tune, perhaps it was the need to share an accomplishment, but all of a sudden she had the desire to talk to her mother. Glancing at her watch, she wondered if it was too late to call. Then she remembered she needed to tell her mother about Opening Festival, so she picked up the phone and punched in the numbers.

Mandy's mother sounded sleepy, but she claimed she was not in bed yet. She became animated when Mandy told her about the festival, and she began planning immediately for a trip in mid-April. When she asked how work was going, Mandy, careful to talk only about the positive parts of the job, was surprised at how much she had to tell.

Just as she hung up, she heard Leesie come in. She came to the balustrade and called down, "How was practice?"

"Super!"

"Are you hungry? Want supper?" Mandy padded down the circular stairs.

"There were leftover sandwiches in the cafeteria that Mrs. Schonefeld left out for us. I'm good."

Mandy sat on the couch and tucked her feet under her as she watched Leesie take a textbook from her backpack. "How come you didn't tell me you were in a band, Leesie?"

Her sister took a piece of notebook paper out of the book and unfolded it. "You mean the practice I was at tonight? I thought you knew. You never asked about it."

"I guess I didn't. I've been pretty wrapped up in my own problems, haven't I?"

Leesie smiled. "Well, I would say that being poisoned and dubbed Dr. Stinkbug, not to mention having Heathcliff panting after your bod, classify as problems. What do you know about Spinoza?"

"He's not panting after my bod," Mandy said, laughing. "And I don't know anything about Spinoza. Want to play, or do you have too much homework?"

"No. I'd much rather play than think about some philosopher that's probably drier than dirt. And I found that Schumann piece in my case—the one we used to play for Mother. Want to try it?"

Mandy crossed to the piano bench. "Aren't you afraid you'll get homesick?"

"Are you kidding? Why would I want to be anywhere else?"

As she took the music, Mandy looked at her sister. "Is there something you're not telling me?"

Leesie unzipped her cello case without looking up. "Like what?"

"Are you in love with Jake?"

Leesie laughed. "Jake and I are both in love, but not with each other. Oh, come on, Sweetiebug, don't look so serious. I'm talking about bluegrass."

"You've lost me."

"What's to lose? I love bluegrass. That's why I want to stay here. I want to be able to continue playing with the band."

"Oh, Leesie," Mandy moaned. "You're a wonderful cellist. You have such talent. To let that beautiful instrument languish for—for hillbilly music! I can't believe it."

"I seem to remember Poppy supporting you when you would rather play jazz than classical. Give me a C so I can tune."

Mandy obliged. "Well, yes, but jazz is an intelligent form of music. It's full of gifted musicians who can improvise, who can play something totally spontaneous without straying from the framework of the melody."

Leesie smiled. "We're playing for a dance next weekend. I want you to come listen to us, and after that, we'll have this discussion again. Ready?"

She drew her bow across the strings, and the house was again full of melody. It pressed against the windows, resonated in the rafters, and lay over the house like a benediction. When they had finished and Leesie was putting her instrument away, Mandy launched into the tune she had composed earlier.

"That's cute," Leesie said. "What's the name of it?"

"I've been trying to think of a name. I felt so good tonight that it just fell out my fingers."

"You wrote it? How about 'Stinkbug Boogie'?"

Mandy laughed. "'Stinkbug Boogie' it is."

"Wow!" Mandy could think of nothing else to say. It was Saturday afternoon, and she sat in the hard passenger seat of Rael's postal-service jeep, face to face with a sheer wall of snow that had avalanched across Highway 20 sometime during the winter. "Does this slide come down every year?"

Rael nodded. "You can depend on it."

"Do they wait for it to melt before they open the highway?" Leesie asked from the back bench where she, Jake, and Willow were squished together.

"No," Jake said. "They'll be up here next month with big front-end loaders and dig a path through. The snow stays until late spring."

"I thought this was late spring," Leesie said.

"Our late spring is first of June."

Rael turned the Jeep around, drove back down the road a mile, and veered off on a logging road that headed uphill. "Hang on," he warned as he switched to four-wheel drive.

"Hanging," Mandy said. "Where are we going?"

"Up there."

She looked where he pointed and saw a white clearing halfway up the mountain. "Oh." She clutched the seat.

After a steep, bone-jarring ride, Rael parked and cut the motor. When Mandy climbed out and turned around, the panorama spread out before her took her breath away. The sky had cleared after a cloudy morning, and a mid-afternoon sun studded the snowy landscape with diamonds. The craggy, glacier-frosted mountains on the opposite side of the valley stood out in stark relief against a cobalt sky, and the river, twining through the valley far below, looked like blue braid adorning a woolly skirt of hunter green.

Leesie climbed out the back, took one look, and hollered, "Yee-haw! Have you ever seen anything like that, Mandy?"

"I never have. It's like a Christmas card."

Jake took a stack of plastic cafeteria trays out of the back of the Jeep and handed one to each person.

"Oh!" Mandy laughed. "I understand now. It's 'tray-ing.' I thought Leesie said 'trang,' and I had made up my mind that it was a place, not an action."

"I did say 'trang,'" Leesie said. "It's one syllable, not two. At least if you speak Tarheel—which I don't, though I'm trying to learn."

"Let's hear some," Jake prompted.

Leesie thought a moment. "If brains was lard, he couldn't grease up a good-size skillet, bless his heart."

Jake grinned. "You say that so good, it'ud make a rabbit hug a hound."

Leesie topped him with, "I'm busy as a farmer with one hoe and two rattlesnakes."

Willow's eyes slid sideways to Mandy as she added her mite. "She has a face like a blind cobbler's thumb."

"Are we trang, or are we flapping our gums?" Rael asked.

Jake took off up the hill. "We're trang! Come on, Leesie."

Leesie grabbed Willow's hand and followed.

"So, what do we do?" Mandy asked, looking doubtfully at the tray in her hands.

Rael's angular face broke into a grin. "Go up and come down." He took her hand and began the ascent. "Come on."

Mandy followed, trying to keep in his footsteps. About halfway up, they stopped to watch the teenagers. Jake slid by, folded up like a pretzel and perched on the tray. He was followed by Willow, riding serenely with her hair blowing behind her, and Leesie, squealing at every bump.

"They're not going very fast," Mandy said.

"Not yet. It gets faster as the snow gets packed down."

That proved to be the case. By the time Mandy descended for the first time, sitting cross-legged and hanging onto the narrow tray sides with her fingertips, the speed was enough to take her breath away. The trays were surprisingly versatile sleds, allowing the friends to go in tandem or as a five-person chain, which invariably broke at the weakest link halfway down and scattered them, laughing, willy-nilly along the way.

Before the sun set, Rael built a fire. They sat around it as Mandy's chili heated, and Leesie, Jake, Willow, and Rael sang old songs like "My Dear Companion" and "Farther Along"—songs that had been passed down among country folk for a hundred years or more.

It was dark by the time supper was over, but a full moon rose and reflected off the snow, creating an iridescent, blue-tinged world. The teenagers set off up the hill with their trays again, while Rael and Mandy sat talking.

"Thank you for inviting us," she said. "It has been such a fun day."

"We try to come up every spring. Each year I think the young 'uns will have outgrown it, but they haven't yet."

"They're good kids," she said.

He nodded. "I didn't hear about the stinkbug thing with your car until today. Willow will be by to apologize, for sure."

"It was really quite clever," Mandy said. "Very inventive."

"She's irrepressible." He smiled. "Like her mother. That was one of the things I loved about her."

There was a silence as they both stared into the fire. Rael stood and pushed a half-burned log back into the flames with his boot.

Mandy, sitting with her arms around her knees, looked up at him. "When did she die?"

He paused with a piece of wood in his hand and stared at Mandy. "She isn't dead."

"But Willow told Leesie—" Mandy was silent for a moment while she worked it out. "Oh, I see. Willow must be very angry at her mother."

"She probably feels she has a reason." He threw the wood on the fire. "Mind if I tell you about it?" He sat on the log beside Mandy, looking intently at the flames. "I promise not to cry on your shoulder. I'd just like you to know the lay of the land."

"No, I don't mind." She laid her cheek on her knees, facing Rael so she could watch him as he told the story.

"I left Limestone when I was seventeen. Never finished high school. I took my guitar and went first to Seattle, then to Los Angeles, then to Nashville. I worked as a carpenter to keep a roof over my head, but I spent every waking minute on my music."

"You were a musician?"

Rael nodded.

"Of course," Mandy whispered.

"I met Lovey in Nashville. She was the singer for the band I was playing in."

"Lovey? Was—is—that her name?"

"Her name is Maggie Loveday, but everyone calls her Lovey."

"What was she like?"

The glow of the fire accentuated the hollows in Rael's cheeks and highlighted his unruly hair. He considered a moment before answering. "She was all that is bright and good in the world—all that is warm, all that is comfort. For me, she was breathing. I thought I could not survive without her."

Mandy nodded. The silence stretched out, but she didn't say anything, waiting instead for him to continue.

"We married, had children, toured with our own band. We were successful. We worked with some very talented people and made a lot of money. But it's no life for a family, no life for children, you know?"

Again Mandy nodded.

"I wanted to give my children what I was given by my parents. I wanted them to have roots—freedom to roam in a safe, rural environment. I wanted them to have old friends and family around them. I wanted Granny Timberlain to be part of their lives." He brushed back a curl that had fallen over his brow. "I felt that the music would be with me wherever I went, that I wasn't defined by how famous I was or how much money I made. More than that, I felt that I would be defined by how good a father I was and how much good I did with my music."

Rael picked up a stick and poked the fire. "Ten years ago I made the decision to move back here. Lovey didn't want to come. The job of postman was open, and I took it to have a steady income and health insurance. Very mundane considerations, but important ones if you've got a family. The hours are good. I start early in the morning, and I'm done by early afternoon. Plenty of time to devote to other things."

"Did she come with you, then? Back to Limestone?"

He nodded. "She stuck it out for five, six years."

"And then what happened?"

"She left. She just wasn't able to leave the performing life behind. She said she felt suffocated here in Limestone. The first year we did the Opening Festival, we had some out-of-town musicians come to play. She sang for one of the bands." He paused and cleared his throat. "Actually, she fell in love with one of the musicians, and when he left, so did she."

"Oh, Rael. I'm so sorry," Mandy said softly.

He shrugged. "I've found that I can breathe on my own." He chuckled. "It's kind of a cross between asthma and emphysema, but I am breathing." He took a deep breath and exhaled.

Mandy smiled. "Was that a demonstration?"

He laughed out loud. "No, that was a great big sigh, like a load off my shoulders. I haven't talked to anyone about Lovey for a long time. It's not as hard as I thought it would be."

"So, are you able to move on?"

"Glacially. I'm still married. That's—that's what this conversation is all about."

"The lay of the land," Mandy said. "I see."

Rael stood and put another log on the fire. "I know I've got to face . . . well, you know. But I haven't been able to yet. I'm still finding my way as a man alone."

Mandy fished in her pocket for a tissue to dab her eyes. Then she stood and embraced him. "Thank you for telling me," she whispered.

Just as he tightened his arms around her, a coal popped out of the fire. He lifted her and swung her out of the way, and she laughed as she stood in the circle of his arms and looked up at him. She put a hand on his cheek. "Are you growing a beard, too? Your chin is scratchy."

"Yes, ma'am."

In the distance they could hear Leesie and Jake whooping as they rode down the slope.

Mandy hugged him once more. "You're a good man, Rael."

He laid his cheek against her hair. "Thanks for listening."

They parted, and as they sat down on the log again, she saw movement in the shadows beyond the firelight.

"Come and sit by the fire, Willow," Mandy called, but nobody answered.

23

The campfire crackled and popped, and the scent of burning wood filled the air. Mandy felt the encircling arm of the man next to her, and she nestled in, resting her head on his shoulder. "I'm worried about Willow," she said. "She stays out there in the dark."

"Don't worry about her. She's working on an apology."

It wasn't Rael who spoke, and as Mandy straightened up to look at her companion, she heard Leesie in the distance calling her name.

Rael had turned into Grange, and as he bent his half-frozen face down to kiss her, Leesie called again, from closer this time.

"Mandy, wake up! The house is on fire!"

She sat up in bed, her senses scrambling for formation as sound and smell mounted a dawn assault. "What's happening?"

Leesie stood at the foot of her bed in an oversized New Mexico State T-shirt with her hair all awry. "Get up! The house is on fire!"

"Where? How?"

"I don't know. Out on the back deck. Oh, hurry, Mandy."

Adrenalin propelled her out of the bed ahead of her wits. She grabbed a pair of shoes and sped barefoot down the stairs. Rounding the corner by the kitchen, she coughed as she inhaled the smoky air that piled up against the low ceiling under her sleeping loft.

Narrowing her eyes, she rushed to the sliding glass door and tugged on it. "I can't open it," she said frantically.

Leesie was right behind her. "Unlock it."

Mandy undid the catch and pushed the door open. Stepping out on the deck, she was hit by the heat that radiated from a column of fire licking the cedar siding beside the bathroom window. She looked up and saw that the shake roof over the deck was beginning to burn, too. "Go call 9-1-1," she said to her sister.

Just then someone shouted, "Mandy! Leesie!" A moment later, a breathless Fran emerged from the woods behind the house. She sprinted the last hundred feet and motioned to the end of the deck. "There's a hose there," she managed to say between shallow breaths. "Get it."

"We're calling 9-1-1," Mandy said. "Go and do it, Leesie."

"It'll take twenty minutes for them to get here. Get the hose!"

Leesie brushed past Mandy and ran to the end of the deck. She jumped to the ground, grabbed the coil, threw it on the deck, and turned on the faucet. After she climbed back up, she grabbed the nozzle gun and pulled the trigger, pointing the end up in the air so the water would reach while she dragged the hose closer.

Fran shoved a bucket into Mandy's hands. "Get upstairs and fill this with water," she commanded. "Go out on the balcony and pour it on the deck roof there by your bathroom. Do it!"

"Where did you get the bucket?" Mandy asked.

"It was under the deck. Now go!"

Mandy cast an apprehensive glance at the fire, smaller now since Leesie was training a vigorous spray on it. When Fran pushed her gently but firmly, she dropped her shoes and hurried back into the house and upstairs. While the pail was filling in the bathroom, Mandy turned on the exhaust fan to try to get rid of the smoke that had seeped into the room. Then, with her right arm extended to balance the load, she carried the heavy bucket out and hefted it up to sit it on the railing. She took a deep breath and flung the contents as far as she could. The water hissed as it hit the roof, and a cloud of steam rose.

Mandy headed back to the bathroom with her bucket, heedless of the fact that she had splashed almost as much water on herself as she had the roof. She repeated the process a second time, and the third time she dumped it, the water rolled down the cedar shakes and off the roof. No hissing. No steam.

She set the bucket down and leaned on the railing. "How's it coming down there?" she called.

Fran answered. "I think it's out."

Mandy's knees suddenly felt weak. "Hallelujah," she whispered through chattering teeth. She leaned on the balcony railing for a moment and then called, "Are my shoes down there?"

"Yes, but they're all wet," Fran answered. "Are you coming down?"

"Let me get something on my feet." Mandy noticed her hand was shaking as she opened a drawer to grab a pair of socks. Once she had her hiking boots on, she pulled on a jacket over her flannel pajamas. She clenched her teeth to stop the chattering as she headed down the circular staircase, leaning on the banister for support.

Out on the deck, Leesie and Fran stood staring at the charred swath on the wall. A tiny wisp of smoke curled up from the crack between two cedar planks. "You'd better hit that again, Leesie," Fran advised.

Leesie put the nozzle right up to the crack and pulled the trigger. Water shot out in all directions.

"Go put some clothes on," Mandy admonished her sister. "You're soaked. Get something on your feet, too."

"Since the crisis is over, I think I'll go get a shower," Leesie said. "I'm going to church with Jake." She eyed Mandy in her boots and pajamas and smiled. "You look totally stylish."

"Thank you. Why are you going so early?"

Leesie had the door open and answered over her shoulder. "The Timberlains are singing, and they want me to sing with them. We're going early to practice."

Mandy nodded and then turned to Fran, who was kneeling on the deck, examining the charred wood at the base of the wall.

"What did you put here?" Fran asked.

"Nothing."

"No oily rags? No ashes?"

"Where would I get ashes? The fireplace is gas."

"I'm just searching for a reason for this." Fran stood. "There's no way it could be an electrical problem."

"What else could it be?"

"I don't know, unless it was deliberately set."

Mandy's eyes widened. "Who would do that? A box of stinkbugs on my porch is one thing, but to set my house on fire? There's got to be another explanation."

Fran picked up the hose and shot another jet of water into the crack between boards. "I need to get this siding off." She looked at her watch. "I've got to get to the store up in Trillium. I was just on my way when I saw the smoke. Here." She handed the hose to Mandy. "I've got to take time to do this. You watch that crack while I go get my tools. If you see smoke coming out of it, shoot it with water again."

"All right." Mandy held the nozzle and fingered the trigger. As she stared at the crack, she gritted her teeth to keep them from chattering, but she couldn't stop the shivering.

It seemed like forever before Fran returned. She parked around back, jumped out, and grabbed some tools from the pickup bed.

Mandy stood aside as Fran went to work, expertly hammering the wedged end of a pry bar under the siding and levering it out. She pulled the nails and tore off four planks, which she threw on the ground behind the deck.

The sheeting under the siding was charred and creviced like alligator skin in several large, oval areas. Each oval was edged with ashy lace and studded with tiny orange jewels that glowed as the breeze blew by.

"Hit that again with water," Fran said.

Mandy pulled the trigger and watched the steam rise.

"That's okay now, I think." Fran threw her tools into the pickup bed. "I've got to go. You keep an eye on this until I get back."

"I was going to go to church this morning."

Fran shook her head. "I've got to be in Trillium until eleven. I'll come right back, but I need you here checking for wisps of smoke. If you see anything, douse it."

"I'm going to call Doc MacDonald," Mandy said.

"Why?"

"If it was deliberately set, he needs to know about it. That's arson."

"I know what it is," Fran said grimly. She looked at her watch. "But don't do anything until I get back, okay? Except check out here every fifteen minutes or so." She went down the stairs and pitched the four blackened planks into her pickup bed.

"Okay." Mandy's teeth were chattering again.

Fran stood with her hand on the pickup door. "Are you all right?"

"I'm fine. When Leesie gets out of the shower, I'll get in. I think I'm just cold."

"I'll see you a little after eleven." Fran got in and drove away.

As Mandy watched her round the corner of the house and disappear, a breeze tickled the back of her neck and made her shiver again. She turned up her jacket collar and, still clutching the nozzle, folded her arms for warmth. She stared at the blackened sheathing on the house, but no smoky threads arose from the charred places. She blasted each with water just in case and then, unclenching her hand with difficulty, she laid the nozzle on the deck and went back in the house.

The smell of smoke was still strong, so Mandy left the sliding glass door wide and opened the front door and all the downstairs windows. When she heard the whine of Leesie's hair dryer, she judged that it was safe to shower without robbing her sister of hot water, so she crept upstairs. Each step was an effort, for her joints felt rusty and on the verge of seizing up. She dropped her clothes in a heap at the bathroom door, turned on the hot water, and leaned into the shower to feel the warmth of the steam as it billowed up. Almost reluctantly, she adjusted the temperature of the water to something less than scalding, stepped inside, and closed the shower door.

There was something comforting about standing in a square, tile-and-glass cocoon, swathed in clouds of warm, ethereal mist, with water washing over her shoulders and sliding down her back. The shivering stopped; her joints became supple again as she lifted her arms to wash her hair, and she felt the warmth creeping back into her core.

Over the sound of splashing water, Mandy heard Leesie calling through the bathroom door. "I'm going. I've checked out back. Everything's fine. The living room has aired out, but it's colder than a well digger's shovel down there, so I've closed the doors and turned on the fire."

Mandy didn't open her eyes because she had water running down her face. "Thank you," she called.

"See you later. I'm gone."

Mandy stood under the shower, willing her mind away from the memory of orange flames and cedar smoke and the panic that made her limbs work like rusty hinges. She thought about her mother and what she would think of Leesie's newfound interest in bluegrass. From there, Mandy's thoughts turned to Opening Festival just weeks away, and she wondered if she should tough it out or if she should look for another situation.

She didn't leave the shower until all the hot water was gone. Reluctantly, she turned off the tap, reached for her towel, and stepped out. The mirror was fogged clear to the bottom, and a cloud of steam hung in the air. She toweled off, dressed, and went downstairs to sit by the fire, allowing her dark, springy curls to air dry.

She braved the chilly, gray morning for just a moment to go out on the deck and check the siding. No smoke. She laid her hand on one of the black spots, but it was cool to the touch. Brushing the soot from her hand, she went back in. As she washed at the kitchen sink, she eyed the clock. Two hours until Fran was to show up.

It was a long two hours. Minutes stretched to eighty or ninety seconds at least, and the little hand on the clock seemed frozen in place. Mandy prowled around the house, unable to be still, unable to read, unable to think about anything except a fire deliberately set. She looked up Doc MacDonald's phone number, and twice she had the handset to her ear and her finger on the first button before deciding to wait until Fran got back. Finally, she sat at the piano and began playing hymns. As her fingers found the chords and melodies that were as familiar to her as her grandmother's face, she became calmer, and the nervous restlessness that had kept her in constant motion began to leave. When Fran returned, she had to hammer on the door to be heard over Mandy's rollicking version of "Count Your Blessings."

She let her neighbor in and assured her that she had checked the burn site frequently. The fire was definitely out.

"Thank heavens!" Fran sank into a chair. "You have no idea how worried I've been. I hated to leave, but I'm shorthanded right now. It's hard to keep good help when Vince won't pay anything more than minimum wage."

"I was a little worried, myself," Mandy said. "But everything's fine. Now, why didn't you want me to call Doc MacDonald?"

Fran grimaced. "Insurance. My premiums are sky high as it is. I had a devil of a time finding someone to insure me because of where the house is situated. I have to have insurance because of the mortgage. But if there was a police report about a fire, I might be cancelled, and I don't know who I could get to insure me then."

"Surely if somebody set the fire it wouldn't affect your insurance!"

"Well, that's just the thing. I've been thinking about it. I don't know if you've noticed a faint musty smell?"

Mandy nodded. "Just when I moved in. Not lately."

"It's left over from the flood," Fran said. "Maybe there's a bit of mold somewhere under the house."

"Mold? What does that have to do with fire?"

"Do you know anything about spontaneous combustion?"

Mandy frowned. "What do you mean?"

Fran laughed, a short, nervous bark. "I forgot. You're from the Southwest. They never have that problem there. Do you know the expression 'Make hay while the sun shines'?"

Mandy's frown deepened. "Fran, what are you talking about?"

"You need five good, dry, sunny days to put up hay—mow it, dry it, and bale it. That's hard to come by up here sometimes. If you get pushed by rainy weather coming in and the hay isn't completely dry, you run the risk of having the hay bales spontaneously combust and burn down your barn."

"I've never heard of such a thing. Are you making this up?"

Fran laughed again, less nervously this time. "No, truly. It's something about the compression of the hay, and being stacked densely in the barn that causes internal heat from bacterial growth in the wet hay to build up until it gets so hot that the hay actually ignites. Every year we lose at least one barn in the county that way."

"So, what does that have to do with anything?"

"I wonder if that may not be what happened here. Maybe there was some bacterial action that started the fire."

Mandy wrinkled her nose. "It sounds a little far-fetched.

"Any more than hay bales spontaneously combusting?"

"Well, no."

"Let me do a little investigating, see if that ever has happened. Don't call Doc until after that, okay?"

Mandy wrinkled her brow as she considered.

"I'm going to go down under the house and check around, see if I can feel any areas that are hotter than they should be," Fran continued.

"That might make me breathe easier," Mandy drew her hand across her brow. "I don't know, Fran. I'm real uneasy about this."

Her landlady was quiet for a moment, staring at the ceiling. "What I'm uneasy about is, why didn't the smoke alarm go off? Or wasn't there any smoke in the house?" She got up and dragged a chair to the passageway beside the kitchen.

"I never thought about that! There was lots of smoke in the house." Mandy followed her and watched as she stood on the chair and took the cover off the alarm.

"There's no battery." Fran looked down at Mandy. "Did you take it out?"

"Why would I do that?"

"I don't know. I know that when I rented the house to you, there were batteries in all the smoke alarms."

"This isn't making me feel any better." Mandy folded her arms and hunched her shoulders. "Spontaneous combustion I might be able to believe, but spontaneous battery disappearance? I don't think so."

Fran replaced the cover. "Well, call Doc if that will make you feel any better." She jumped down and pushed the chair back up to the table. "But what will he say, besides advising you to get out while the getting is good?"

"What do you mean?"

"Like you said, Mandy, a box of stinkbugs is one thing. Poison and fire are completely different."

"Poison?"

"I was there when you got sick, remember? Word is going around that it was likely mushroom poisoning."

"But Grange said it was too early for mushrooms."

"Mutt Maypole had morels a week ago. Oh, Mandy!" Fran flung herself back in the chair. "I don't want to sound so selfish and money hungry! Go ahead and call Doc. Tell him everything. I don't want something to happen to you and it be my fault because I was afraid of losing my house."

"Losing your house? Surely you wouldn't lose it!" Mandy sat opposite and looked earnestly at her friend.

"If the insurance rates doubled or tripled, it would really tap me out. I don't know if I could make the mortgage payments."

"But you said you'd let me out of the lease. Wouldn't the same thing apply if I left you holding the bag for the rent?"

"No, because it's coming on to summer, and I can easily find a renter then. In fact, I can rent it as a vacation cabin and make three times what I get from you."

Mandy leaned back in her chair and sighed. "Leaving seems so cowardly."

"It seems practical to me. I mean, what do you owe these people?" Fran seemed to think for a moment. "Not to get all spiritual on you, but do you ever think God may have a purpose for you somewhere?"

"Yes. Certainly."

"Well, what if that purpose isn't here? What if God's trying to get you somewhere else, only you're resisting pretty hard?"

"I've thought of that myself. It's so hard to know." Mandy ran her fingers through her curls. "Okay, here's the thing. I won't call Doc—yet. But the next suspicious thing that happens, I'm on the phone immediately."

"If you decide to leave, the news will be all over town in a minute. Mission accomplished. There won't be a next suspicious thing."

"There is that. But it's so hard to let 'them' win."

Fran stood. "There you go again," she said with a laugh, "fighting God."

Mandy smiled and stood to walk her to the door. "Maybe so. But if I do decide to leave, the trip up here has been worth it to have you as a friend."

Fran gave her a hug. "I think so too. I'm going to run up and grab some batteries and come down and make sure all your smoke alarms are working. Then I'll get under the house and have a look."

"Thanks."

Mandy followed Fran out the door and watched from the porch as she got in her pickup and drove up the hill. Mandy went back in and glanced at the clock, noting that Leesie would be home before too long. Though nothing had been resolved and she knew no more than before, when she went into the kitchen to make lunch, she was humming a tune.

"Your eyes look like two burnt holes in a blanket!" Leesie paused in the act of scrubbing out the oatmeal pot and regarded her sister as she came down the stairs. "And you're late. I thought you wanted to get to work early today."

"Thanks for that positive start to my day." Mandy took a spoon and tasted the oatmeal congealing in a bowl on the counter. "I had a bad night." She put the cereal in the microwave and pushed some buttons.

"How come?" Leesie crouched to put the pot under the counter.

"I thought I had to stay awake to listen, in case someone was coming to set the house on fire again."

Leesie stood. "Really?" Her eyes were wide. "You think someone set the fire deliberately?"

After the microwave dinged, Mandy carried her breakfast to the table. "What other explanation is there?"

"I don't know. I'm pretty clueless about how a fire gets started—my tent mates at summer camp will swear to that. But isn't it a stretch to think someone was going to try to burn the house down? I mean, we talked about the fire all the way to church, and Jake was wondering if there couldn't be some corrosion in the wiring from the flood. He thought maybe something shorted out and started the fire in a wall."

Mandy shook her head. "Fran said it couldn't be electrical. There isn't any wiring in that wall."

"You don't think so? I know there aren't any outlets right opposite where the fire was, but I'll bet you anything there are some wires that go across that wall. I mean, the electrical panel is in the laundry room, and there are all kinds of outlets in the bathroom. How do the wires get there?"

"Why would Fran say something like that, then?"

"I don't know why she'd say it to you, but I can see why she'd say it to her insurance agent. I'll bet she's afraid her premiums will go up or afraid she'll have to rewire or something."

Mandy leaned her chin on her hand and stared at the steady drizzle outside as she considered. "Fran did say something about that. She didn't want me to call the deputy sheriff for just that reason."

"Well, there you go!" Leesie looked at her watch. "Jake will be here any minute." She grabbed her coat and backpack and went to stand by the window.

Mandy sighed. "Now I'll stay awake worrying about corrosion in the wires and another short somewhere else."

"We've got smoke detectors."

Mandy grimaced. "That's another thing. There weren't any batteries in the smoke detectors, and Fran swears she made sure they were there when she rented the house to us."

Leesie snorted. "Or she meant to make sure they were working and forgot but doesn't want to admit it, since we almost ended up as toast. Oh, there's that pickup again."

"What pickup?"

Leesie pointed as a shiny red, 80's vintage pickup drove slowly by. A fellow with a sandy, Butch Cassidy moustache and a baseball cap pulled low over his eyes turned his head to look at the house as he passed.

"Who's that?" Mandy asked.

"I don't know, but he was pulling onto the highway as we turned off onto our road yesterday. There's Jake and Willow. Bye."

Mandy took a bite of her oatmeal and chewed thoughtfully as she watched her sister dash out to catch her ride. Shortly after they disappeared up the hill, the red pickup cruised slowly by again. The hair on the back of Mandy's neck prickled, and she stared at the road long after the bright red tailgate had disappeared behind the screen of blackberry bushes that clawed their thorny way out of the barrow pit where the road turned.

Her mind worked for a while on the puzzle of the red pickup but returned to the conversation she had with Leesie about the cause of the fire. "But wouldn't a short have blown a breaker?" she murmured, turning an inquisitive gaze on the door to the laundry room.

She put her dish in the sink. Then she rose and went to the hall, where she peered through the half-open door at the gray box on the wall above the washing machine. "You're on your own, Mandy," she chided herself. "Suck it up! There's no one to take care of you."

Taking a deep breath, she pushed the door open and approached the corner occupied by the washer. She leaned over its solid bulk and gingerly touched the metal door of the electrical panel, half expecting to be zapped. When nothing happened, she exhaled, pulled it open, and examined each of the switches. Not knowing if she should feel relieved that all the switches were in the "on" position, she closed the panel door and frowned all the way to the kitchen.

She put her dishes in the dishwasher and checked her planner, realizing with a sinking heart that she had an appointment with Grange first thing. She couldn't muster the same enthusiasm this morning that she had felt last Friday when she promised Mo she'd speak to Grange about their plan. Sighing again, she stowed her planner in her purse. She put on her jacket and checked her image in the mirror. Leesie was right—her eyes had smudgy half-moons underneath.

"I look like a hag," Mandy muttered in disgust, then wondered why she should care how she looked when she met with Grange.

She opened the door, ducked her head, and leaned against the stiff breeze that made needles of the chilly rain as she ran to her car.

She was halfway to her office before the heater started blowing warm air. "My kingdom for a sunny day," she said aloud. As she slowed to turn into the district office parking lot, she passed a yellow mini-van emblazoned with the words "Short Hauling" in purple.

She parked in the superintendent's space and dashed for the porch, glancing around to see if Grange's pickup was there. She spied it, and the hour she had pledged to spend with him stretched out ahead of her as bleak and chilly as the weather.

No one was at the reception desk, but Mo came out of his office to greet Mandy as she went up the stairs. "He's not in the best of moods this morning," he warned, glancing at Grange's office.

"Perfect," she whispered, leaning against the newel post and closing her eyes. When Mo nervously cleared his throat, she opened her eyes, and the sight of his anxious face made her straighten up and make a show of taking heart. "Don't worry, Mo. The worst he can do is say no."

"I know," Mo said in an earnest half voice. "He's not really like that. He's really supportive and fair and great to work with. It's just that when . . . since . . . whenever . . . ." He looked at the floor. "Today just isn't a good day, I think."

"Tell me about it," Mandy murmured as she turned to traverse the mezzanine. She had just rounded the corner by Grange's office when she was startled by a sudden *thunk,* and a large, rectangular box bounced off his open door and landed in his doorway. She kept her eyes on her own office and marched on, resolving to be pleasant and unflappable in the approaching conference, no matter what.

She felt enthusiasm begin to creep back as she studied the folder Mo had left on her desk on Friday. She had forgotten, in the excitement and trauma of the weekend, how well he had laid out his case and how solidly he had buttressed it. She glanced at the clock and saw it was time to present the idea, so she took the folder and rose. Checking herself in the mirror, she forced herself to smile at the solemn face that looked back at her. She took a deep breath.

Mandy had deliberately set the meeting in Grange's office because she didn't want him to feel she was dictating to him from a position of power in the larger, superintendent's domain. As she slipped out of her office, she paused a moment to say good morning to Mrs. Berman and then knocked gently on Grange's doorframe.

He sat with his back to her, elbows on the desk, head in his hands, and fingers rumpling his dusky locks. She knocked again.

As he turned and saw her, his eyes widened. He sprang from his chair, scooped up the box that still lay in the doorway, and set it on top of a filing cabinet. "Yes?"

"We had an appointment, I believe?" *Remember, pleasant and unflappable,* she inwardly coached.

His eyes narrowed.

Pleasantly and unflappably, she waited.

Grange looked at his watch. "Did we?" He frowned.

She forced a smile. "It's on your calendar."

"I can give you five minutes," he said. He unloaded a stack of books off a chair and piled them on the box he had just set on the cabinet. "Sit down."

A vein started beating in Mandy's temple. She sat and consciously relaxed the grip she had on the folder in her hand. *Pleasant and unflappable.* "Actually," she said in an even tone, "what we have to accomplish will take more than five minutes. If you will check your calendar, you will see that I blocked out an hour."

His brows came down. "You what?"

"Really, Grange," she began in a light, conversational tone, "you cannot complain one day that I don't include you in planning, and then the next, refuse to sit down with me and discuss issues at hand. I needed to talk something over with you. Your calendar was free. I made an appointment. If you had something planned for this morning, your calendar should have shown it."

He looked at his watch again. "What do you want to talk about?"

"It's a plan to balance the district's budget without letting any teachers go, and at the same time, pay for the new reading program."

There was a long pause, and then it was his turn to speak lightly. "Planning on robbing a bank?"

Mandy drew a chair up beside his desk and opened her folder. "No. I am proposing that we go to a four-day school week."

Grange didn't look at the folder. He stared at her, his face set in lines of incredulity.

She returned his gaze calmly, determined not to be the first to speak.

"What turnip truck did that idea fall off of?"

She raised a brow. "Is this a sterling example of—how did you phrase it—professional courtesy? I am indebted to you, sir."

Their eyes were locked for a full half minute. The pulse in her temple beat more rapidly, but she kept a firm grip on her temper. Grange was the first to look away.

"All right," he said. "Explain."

"This is not a revolutionary idea. I found at least twenty school districts in the Northwest that have gone to this model. They are all very like our district: small, spread out, and strangled by operating and transport costs. They immediately save almost twenty percent on those costs alone by going to a four-day week."

"How do we meet the mandated instructional time?"

"We extend each day by an hour and fifteen minutes. That's all. The kids start at seven forty-five instead of eight. Instead of going home at three, they'll go home at four."

Grange's eyes scanned the page Mandy had opened in front of him.

She forged on. "You can see that studies have been done in schools that have gone to this schedule, that dropout rates have declined, and student disciplinary referrals have decreased. Achievement doesn't seem to have been affected either way."

"What about the child-care issue?"

Her voice took on an edge. "What about it? We're not in the child-care business. We're in the education business, and we need to find a way to do it with the money we have." She paused, and then said more gently, "Older students will be free to tend younger students. I'm sure parents can work out something."

"And what about the kindergarten? That's too long a day for the little ones."

"We can find out what other schools have found successful. One district schedules more academics in the morning and more play learning in the afternoon. It's something that can be worked out."

Grange closed the folder and pushed it away. "It will never work. The people would never go for it."

Mandy rose. "Not even if the great Grange Timberlain spoke in favor of it?"

"Grange Timberlain isn't going to speak for it." His eyes flashed and his consonants were clipped. "I don't know what you mean, coming in here without any investment, without knowing the people, trotting out some simplistic, harebrained idea and think it's going to solve all the district's problems."

"As to that," she said, "it wasn't my idea at all. It was Mo's."

Grange clenched his teeth and turned his head away.

"It seems to me," she said, forcing herself back into patient, unflappable mode, "that he has an investment, that he knows the people. And more than that, I think he has vision. He's not afraid to think outside of the box to solve problems. I've said before that he's a treasure and underappreciated."

All of a sudden, Mandy's throat tightened. "But that's often the way." She opened the door, but turned back with her hand on the knob. "I'll leave his folder with you. If you have second thoughts, you may want to study the information he's gathered. It's pretty impressive."

Realizing her eyes were welling, she quickly stepped into the hall. She walked to her own office and managed to get the door closed before the frustration and disappointment she had been suppressing boiled over. Hating herself for the tears that were coursing down her cheeks, Mandy strode past her desk to the filing cabinet in the far corner, away from sight of the door, and leaned against it, biting the knuckle where her thumb joined her hand in a vain effort to stem the flood.

Her office door opened. She didn't turn around but stood quietly, face to the wall, chin up, and waited.

"Uh . . ." It was Grange.

She didn't answer, didn't turn.

He cleared his throat. "This box came this morning. Ben Short brought it from downriver. It was addressed to the superintendent, and he brought it to me, but I think it's yours."

Silence.

Grange cleared his throat. "I'll just set it here on your desk, then."

Mandy had just about worn the paint off a spot on the wall by staring at it, but she wasn't going to turn around and give Grange Timberlain the satisfaction of seeing her in tears.

"I'm just off to the high school, then," he said. "I've put it in my calendar."

She stood ramrod straight until she heard the door close. She counted to ten and dove for the tissues on her desk. After wiping her eyes and blowing her nose, she noticed the box on her desk was the one that Grange had picked up off his floor. One flap was half open, and she saw something yellow inside. Curious, she pulled it back and then unfolded the others. There, nestled in a bed of tissue, was a bouquet of yellow roses and a card slantwise in the envelope, as if it had been hastily stuffed in. She pulled it out and read:

I saw on the weather map that you're having rain today. Here's some sunshine for you. I've got to stay here longer than I thought I would. Funny, I used to love jobs like this. Now all I want is to get back to Limestone. I'll try to make it back on Saturday. If I do, save me the last dance.

She smiled as she read the note, then buried her face in the flowers and let the familiar perfume soothe away the ragged edges her meeting with Grange had left on her composure. Noticing the flowers were a little wilted, she decided she'd better get them in water, and she took a step toward her door. She stopped, for

Grange was on the other side of the glass, as still as a statue, staring at her with flinty eyes.

Mandy's chin came up. Holding the bouquet at her waist like a bride, she met his gaze. When he turned on his heel and strode around the mezzanine, her eyes followed the tall, erect figure until the bright blue of his plaid wool shirt disappeared down the stairs. Moments later, she heard the front door close with more force than necessary.

All of a sudden, her chin began to quiver. She bit her lip, but the tears were flowing again, and a high-pitched, closed-mouth wail fought its way through every barrier she put up and escaped out into the room.

Mrs. Berman entered moments later with a mug in her hand. She took one look at Mandy and set the cup down on the desk. Putting her arm around Mandy's shoulders, she murmured, "There, there. Don't take on so. There, there." She guided Mandy to her chair, offered a tissue, and waited. When the tears showed signs of abating, the older lady said gently, "You mustn't mind him, dearie. He has a hard time being second best. Just bad luck that Ben Short mistakenly delivered—but never mind."

Mandy blew her nose. "I don't mind him," she said damply. "At least not usually. I think the fire must have got to me."

Mrs. Berman handed her the cup. "Drink this. What fire?"

Mandy took the steaming mug in both hands. "Thank you," she murmured and took a sip.

"A fire?" the secretary pressed. "Where was it?"

Mandy looked at her over the rim. "On the outside wall beside the sliding glass door."

"Of your house? What caused it?" Mrs. Berman was out of nurture mode. She peered inquisitively over her glasses.

Mandy sighed. "I don't know what caused it. It may have started in the wall, though there's no indication of that."

"You could find out quick enough by cutting a hole in the wall."

"I'll leave that to Fran." Mandy took another sip of the herb tea. "Thank you for this."

Mrs. Berman wouldn't leave it. "Did you hear anybody? See anybody?"

"I was in bed asleep. It happened early in the morning."

The older lady's eyes widened and she paled. "In bed? Why, you could have been killed! That house is built of cedar, which means it's built of kindling."

"We were lucky. Leesie woke up and Fran showed up, and we put the fire out ourselves."

Mrs. Berman nodded. "Lucky, indeed." She walked toward the door and paused to say, "Drink that whole cup, now."

"I will."

Perhaps it was the comfrey, or perhaps it was Mrs. Berman's attentions, but Mandy soon felt better. She dried her eyes and repaired her makeup, and when Midge knocked at her door, she was able to greet her normally. They had a long, productive meeting, and when Mandy saw the woman's progress in preparing a grant proposal, her spirits rose a notch.

Mandy was able to smile at Mo when he knocked tentatively at her door after lunch and asked about the meeting with Grange. "I didn't think it went well," he said, eyeing the flowers on her desk. "It was certainly a short meeting."

"To be fair, he had the same reaction I had when you presented the idea to me," she said. "He kept the folder. We're not done yet." She sent Mo off in a hopeful frame of mind and prepared for her appointment with Elizabeth.

Mandy's eyes twinkled as the student aide edged through the doorway and sidled to the chair. "Sit down," Mandy invited. "Let's talk about your idea."

Elizabeth couldn't talk about anything until she had unburdened herself. She confessed her part in Willow's car decorating scheme and begged forgiveness.

Mandy assured her she already knew the whole and drew her into a discussion of a way to market school-spirit items in the school. When Elizabeth left, her characteristic, incandescent smile was back, and Mandy had fully recovered her own buoyant composure. She was able to spend the rest of the afternoon focused on district matters and was surprised when Mrs. Berman poked her head in to say she was going home.

Mandy glanced at the clock. "Is it that time already?"

The older woman nodded. "Are you leaving soon? Shall I lock up? Everyone else is gone."

"No, I'll do it. I'm leaving pretty soon, too." Mandy turned off her computer. "I'll see you tomorrow. Thanks, Mrs. Berman, for your concern this morning."

She smiled. "Call me Edith. I'll see you tomorrow."

Mandy got her jacket and purse and picked up the levy folder Grange had given her. Carrying it with her, she descended the stairs, locked the door, and sprinted to her car. She drove through the steady drizzle to Stevie Joe Hawes's garage, where she was to leave her car to have her tires rotated while she taught Tammy's reading lesson. She turned up her wipers and wished she'd brought an umbrella for the walk.

Mandy was delighted to see that the garage was just down the street from Tammy's. She pulled in beside the familiar 80's vintage pickup painted a shiny candy-apple red. As she got out of the Miata, she looked inside the pickup and noted the gun rack over the rear window, empty except for a pair of binoculars hanging from one of the arms. She grabbed the file folder and her purse and hurried in to leave her keys with Stevie Joe. Then she headed down the street to Tammy's.

Mandy found that her pupil had been diligent in her studies. She had locked in the two words that Mandy left with her and two others besides.

"I find if I work on one and then sleep on it, something happens that keeps it in my brain," Tammy said, laughing as she pulled a chair up to her work table. "Come over here. Listen to me read."

With such an eager pupil, the hour flew by. When the lesson was over, Tammy begged for something she could do to repay Mandy. She thought a minute and said she really needed someone to help Leesie organize Harvey Berman's office at the bus garage.

"But if I can't read, what help would I be?"

"Leesie can help you get started. It's really just a matter of reading numbers and putting things in the right folders. I think you'll do fine."

"What do you know!" Tammy grinned. "Me working in an office. Who'd a thunk it? I'm not going to tell him you sent me, though. You're not Harvey's favorite right now."

"I know," Mandy said, picking up her purse and folder. "I'll see you on Wednesday."

Tammy walked her to the door. "Where's your car?"

Mandy pointed down the street. "I left it at the garage to have the tires rotated."

"Stevie Joe's my little brother, did you know?"

"No, I didn't. My goodness, there are lots of relatives in this small town."

"He's married to one of your teachers. Vonda Hawes?"

"Oh." Mandy looked down the street toward the garage. "Is that his red pickup?" When Tammy nodded, Mandy said, "I've seen him driving by my house a couple of times." She let the question hang unasked.

"Do you live by the river?"

Mandy nodded.

"He was probably watching for nesting eagles. This is the time they lay their eggs, and he's got a couple of pair he's documenting for Fish and Game."

Mandy looked next door. "Is Granny Timberlain home, do you know? I need to talk to her about something."

"I think she is. Try the door. She'd be glad to see you."

Mandy thanked Tammy for saying she'd help Leesie and headed toward Granny Timberlain's with her levy folder in her hand. She intended to ask that venerable lady for help when she went to eat humble pie—probably called Tarheel Humble Pie—served up by Nettie Maypole.

Granny Timberlain asked Mandy in, listened serenely as her guest recounted her history with Nettie Maypole, and nodded a sage approval as the younger woman framed her request. Since the Maypoles lived right behind Tammy, they walked through the lot and stood in a small portico out of the rain as they waited for an answer to their knock.

Nettie led them through a narrow hall into a tiny living room and invited them to sit on a couch covered with an afghan. Mandy, with sweaty palms and a mouth so dry she had a hard time pronouncing *T*'s, asked Nettie to head up the levy committee. She was so relieved to hear her say, "I thought you weren't going to ask," that she willingly listened to a recital of minute campaign details. When Mandy and Granny Timberlain left half an hour later, Nettie was dialing the first number on her telephone tree.

As they walked through the gathering dusk, Mandy heaved a sigh of relief. "Thank you for going with me to talk to her, Mrs. Timberlain. I could never have done that alone."

"Oh, I don't know. You did fine. You made her feel needed. That's all anybody wants."

"Well, I do need her, and that's the truth." Looking past the Maypoles' house to the street, Mandy asked, "Is that Vince Laffitte's car parked out in front?"

"Probably. When Vince goes out of town, Mutt takes him to the airport and then just keeps his car here."

"I guess the whole town knows when Vince is away."

Granny smiled. "I don't know if everyone does, but I like to keep track of him."

"Why is that?" Mandy opened a gate at the back of the Maypoles' yard and held it for her companion.

Granny paused halfway through and smiled at Mandy. "He has very fine eyes."

Mandy laughed. "I guess he does." She closed the gate and followed the older lady to her back door, at first declining the invitation to come in.

"You'd better let me give you an umbrella," Granny said. "It's starting to rain hard, and you'll be soaked by the time you get down to your car."

Mandy agreed and stepped inside while Granny opened the hall closet and rummaged inside. Looking around idly, Mandy noticed a family portrait on the end table.

"I didn't see this picture last time I was here," she said, picking it up and turning it to the light.

"It's been put away in a box. I just got a new frame for it." Granny emerged with a black umbrella.

"You haven't aged a bit," Mandy said.

The woman in the photograph had the same dark hair piled high, the same luminous eyes, the same high cheekbones. That woman's cheeks were smoother, and the hand that she had around her youngest son had no age spots on it, but there was no doubt it was the same person.

"This is Jacob," Granny said, pointing to a sandy-haired man who looked to be about twenty-five. He's Rael's father. This is Fred. He's Grange's father. There's been a Frederick Granger in my family for six generations. This is Lucinda. She's Tammy and

Stevie Joe's mother, and this is Benjamin. Everyone called him Buck."

"He has very fine eyes," Mandy murmured.

"Yes, he did." Granny said softly.

Mandy set the picture down. "I think you need to tell Vince."

"Tell him what, my dear?"

"Tell him that he has fine eyes."

"When the time is right."

Mandy picked up her purse. "Actually, he already knows. I just think he needs to hear it from you."

"When the time is right," Granny repeated. She put her arm around Mandy as she walked her to the door. "Here's the umbrella. Drive carefully."

"I will," Mandy promised. She was grateful for the protection as she hurried to her car. She got in, found the keys under the front seat as Stevie Joe had promised, and started the car. It was pitch dark, and the rain streamed down so hard the wipers had a hard time keeping up. She drove slowly, peering through the windshield to track the fog line on the side of the road. It seemed to take forever, but finally she saw the lights of Fran's house ahead and looked for the turnoff to her gravel road. When she found it and veered gently to the right, she was conscious that now there was no white line to show her where the edge dropped steeply off into blackberry bushes.

Carefully negotiating the curve, Mandy saw that her sister was home and had every light in the house on. Grateful for that beacon shining in the night and pointing the way, grateful for the soup and toasted cheese sandwiches that Leesie fixed for dinner, grateful for a good bed, Mandy retired at eight and didn't wake until Leesie roused her just before leaving the next morning.

Liz Adair

Her eyes fluttered briefly when she heard Leesie call, but it wasn't until the slamming of the door broke through her sleepy fog that Mandy looked at the clock and realized she needed to be up. She threw back the covers, bolted out of bed, and headed for the shower. Dressing with an eye on the clock, she decided there was no time for breakfast. She stuffed two granola bars in her purse, ran to her car, threw it in reverse, and backed out of the drive.

Halfway up the hill and still accelerating, she heard a sudden, sharp *click click click click,* and the front of the car began to shimmy violently. Before she even had a chance to wonder what was happening, there was a loud *whang,* and the Miata lurched to the right. Mandy yanked the steering wheel to the left, but the car had already sailed off the road. The brambles cushioned the landing, but she slammed against the seat restraint so hard that it knocked the wind out of her. Try as she might, it seemed an eternity before she could loosen the invisible bands cinched tightly around her chest and draw in that first, blessed breath. She took another, less painful than the first, and then another. When her breathing returned to normal, she took stock. Everything had happened so quickly, it was hard to go back and replay the experience.

What she did know was that right now, the car stood on its nose with the motor running, and she hung in her harness like an unused puppet, with a tangle of wicked-looking blackberry canes pressed against the windows. Feeling ridiculous, she put the Miata in park and turned off the key. Next, she unlatched the door and pushed on it, but she was in an awkward position and couldn't exert enough force to open it more than an inch. The passenger door didn't look any more promising.

Mandy twisted around and looked up through the back window. She could see gray sky beyond the vines that crisscrossed her field of vision. "It's like a vertical prison," she muttered.

Her eye fell on the steel teeth of the zipper that encircled the window, and the idea of a jailbreak began to stir. Still hanging in her shoulder restraint and seat belt, she stretched her arm until it pulled painfully against the socket, but she couldn't reach the zipper handle. She needed to get free of her seat belt. She drew up her knees and knelt on the steering wheel for support so she wouldn't drop when she undid the latch. Even so, when she pressed the release, she fell sideways and had to catch hold of one of the struts that held up the top to keep from ending up down by the foot pedals. As Mandy fell, her knee hit the horn, and the sudden blast made her jump. She paused for a moment to get her balance and let her pulse quiet.

After a deep breath, she held onto the passenger's headrest, grabbed the zipper tab, and pulled. In two seconds she had the window down and tentatively poked her head between two lethal-looking blackberry canes. There wasn't enough room to get her shoulders through without lacerating her jugular, and with a sinking heart, she eyed the sheer embankment and wondered if a car driving by could even see her. She doubted it.

She turned around and considered. Even if she could get the door open far enough to get out, she would be flayed alive by the time she made it out of the thicket.

Her legs began to cramp, and as she held onto one of the crossbars supporting the soft top in order to shift her weight, she suddenly realized she was hanging on to her escape route. It took ten seconds to undo the latches at the top of the windshield, another ten to get the top halfway folded down. She met resistance from the two canes that crossed over the back window, but they finally gave way, and she sat in the open air.

"Hallelujah," she said aloud. "It's even stopped raining."

Just then she heard a car going by on the gravel road above. She called out, but it kept on going, rounded the bend, and the sound died away. Moments later, it returned, and Mandy heard Fran calling her name.

"I'm down here," Mandy hollered. "I ran off the road."

"Where?"

"Down here."

Fran stood at the top of the embankment with her hands on her hips. "What happened? I was washing dishes and saw you go by down at the bottom of the hill, and then you never came out on top. It was like the Bermuda Triangle."

Mandy crouched on the folded-up top and looked up. "I don't know what happened. There was a sound like a machine gun and then a sound like a shotgun—or maybe a cannon. And then I was sailing off the road."

Fran looked around. "First thing to do is get you out of there. Wait and I'll run back to the house and get a ladder. I think we can get you up without too much blood. While I'm there, I'll call Stevie Joe to send the tow truck."

"Don't be long." Mandy thought that the sound of Fran's truck driving away was the lonesomest thing she had ever heard. She pulled the keys out of the ignition and then fished her purse off the floor. After that, she crawled up to where she could sit on the upended trunk and bumper and folded her arms to try to stay warm. The minutes crawled by. Eventually she heard the sound of Fran's approaching truck, and soon her friend was standing at the top with a ladder in one hand and a rope in the other.

"I hope the ladder is long enough," Fran said. She tied the rope to one end. "I'm going to throw this to you, so you can keep the end up out of the blackberries. Set it on the bumper, and I think it'll bridge the worst of it."

She threw the rope, but it went wide and fell in the thicket. She tried again, and Mandy almost tumbled off her perch trying to catch it.

The third time, the rope landed in Mandy's lap. "I've got it," she called. "Send down the ladder."

As Fran obliged, Mandy stood on her little green island and used the rope to keep the long extension ladder out of the blackberries. When she finally set it on the back bumper of the Miata, it made a bridge to the top of the embankment.

"Wow!" Mandy breathed.

"Okay," Fran said. "This is a fiberglass ladder, so it's going to be springy. Don't get scared if it bounces a bit. You'll be fine."

Mandy slung her purse over her head and one shoulder, crouched down, and grabbed the fourth rung. Tentatively, she placed a foot on the bottom rung and then started climbing.

"Look at me," Fran urged. "Look up here. You're doing fine."

The ladder flexed with every movement.

"It's a bit scary," Mandy admitted. "It doesn't feel secure."

"You're doing fine. Keep coming. Now, give me your hand."

Mandy stepped off the ladder onto the road. The first thing she did was hug Fran and tell her thanks. Then she turned around and looked at her car. "What could have happened?"

"Maybe something in the steering went out. Wait. What is that?" Fran trotted down the road, calling over her shoulder, "Pull up the ladder, will you?"

Mandy did as she was asked, casting frequent looks at Fran, who was scrambling down the slope at a place where there were no blackberries and gingerly retrieving something from the prickly bushes at the bottom. She came back up on all fours and returned, out of breath, with her prize.

"What is it?" Mandy set the ladder down on the road.

"Wheel cover," Fran said, panting. "You lost a wheel." She handed the aluminum disc to Mandy. "Wait, what's this?" Taking it back, she examined the inside surface. "There's something written on it."

"Something written on it? What do you mean?"

"Here. See for yourself."

Mandy looked at the block letters painted there. "GET OUT OF TOWN." She looked up at Fran. "Did you call the tow truck?"

"Nobody answered. I left a message."

"Well, before we get the tow truck, we need Doc MacDonald here. Someone sabotaged my car, and I know just who it was."

Fran asked who, but Mandy wouldn't say anything more. Grimly, she helped stow the ladder in the back of Fran's pickup. Then she asked to be taken home so she could call the deputy sheriff and the district office. Fran drove her down and wanted to stay with her, but Mandy wouldn't even let her get out of the pickup, insisting that she go on to work.

"If you're sure, I will," Fran said. "I just got word I've got auditors coming. It's no problem. Vince's accountants like to do spot audits, but I've got some prep work to do in the office."

She rolled down her window as Mandy got out and walked around the pickup. "You're sure you're all right?"

Mandy approached the window. "I'm fine. Not to add to your worries, but I'm giving notice. I'll take you up on the offer to break the lease. I'm not going to stay where I keep having to look over my shoulder. Life is too short." She laughed nervously. "Or it may become too short."

"When are you leaving?"

"As soon as I can."

"I hate to think of you leaving, but I don't blame you." Fran waved, turned around, and drove off with the ladder rattling in the back.

Mandy watched her go, then unlocked the door and headed for the phone. She found the deputy's number, dialed it, and held her breath as she counted the rings. He answered on the fourth, and after hearing her story promised to be there in twenty minutes. He made it in fifteen.

"How do?" he said when Mandy answered the door. "You sure 'nuff put that little car in the briar patch. Now, what's this story about sabotage?"

Mandy invited him in and had him sit. "This will take a while." She told the story, beginning with the chocolate éclair and ending with the fire.

"So, why'nt you call about the far?"

"I really couldn't believe that someone would set my house on fire while I was sleeping. I could have been killed."

"So, who do you think did it?"

"Stevie Joe."

"Stevie Joe! If that isn't a pea-brained idea! Where'd you come across that 'un?"

"Okay, here's the thing. Stevie Joe is married to Vonda Hawes, one of the schoolteachers that I've had to let go. He's been driving down here back and forth in front of my house, looking at me."

Doc MacDonald shook his head.

"No, wait," Mandy said. "Listen. I had my car in to him last night to rotate the tires. It was a perfect time to sabotage my car—to make it so I could drive a ways, but for sure I'd have an accident somewhere. What if it had been on the way home last night in the rain? No one would have found me. I'd have been out in the rain all night. Or worse, in the river."

"Let me see that wheel cover," Doc said. "You said there was some writing in it?"

"Yes. It was a warning to leave town."

Doc took the aluminum disk from her and examined it. "There's no way Stevie Joe did this."

"What makes you so sure?"

"Stevie Joe never learnt to read and write. He can't hardly even write his name."

26

Mandy spent almost two hours with Doc MacDonald. He listened intently to her recital and then asked her to tell it again, but this time, to include the part about the stinkbugs. At her surprised look, he assured her the whole county knew about it. She insisted it wasn't connected with the fire and the car accident—that the parcel on her doorstep and the decoration of her car were teenage pranks. Doc said, "Maybe so, but I want to hear it all." He pulled a small spiral notebook and a pen out of his shirt pocket and took notes in block letters as she spoke. Afterward, he prowled around the back deck and got down on his knees to examine the area around the charred siding. He crawled under the deck and even shimmied his girth through the hole into the crawl space under the house.

Mandy paced back and forth as she waited for him to reappear. When he finally crawled out from under the deck, she peppered him with questions, but he only shook his head as he dusted himself off. "It wasn't wiring," he said, though it sounded more like 'warring.' "You can sleep sound and not worry 'bout that."

Yeah, sure, she thought. *That's real comforting to know.*

Doc told her he would supervise the rescue of her car and then gave her a ride to the district office. "I wouldn't spread around any accusations about who did that to your car, if I was you," he warned as he drove. "Now, I've got some revenue agents comin' up, want to crash around in the woods a bit lookin' for a still they think is operatin' upriver." He chuckled as he looked at his watch. "But they won't be here 'til five. I'll have time to talk to Stevie Joe. Shucks, I'll sit with him as he fixes it and find out what he has to say. Don't worry, if it was him as did it, I'll know, and I'll be all over him like a rat on a Cheeto."

He pulled up in front of the district office. "Next time somethin' happens, call me. You shouldn't ought to have taken off that burnt siding without me seein' it."

Mandy sighed. "No, I know. But don't worry. There isn't going to be a next time." She opened the door and got out.

"You got a ride home if your car ain't done in time?"

"I'll manage."

"Well, give me your keys. Stevie Joe'll leave them under the seat."

She took the Miata key off her ring and gave it to the deputy. "Thanks again," she said and closed the door. She walked in front of the deputy's cruiser to the porch steps, and as she mounted them, she saw the whole staff standing at the window. She forced a smile as Grange solemnly held the door open.

"Hello, all," she greeted. "Don't look so concerned. I had a small accident—I took a curve too fast and tangled with a blackberry bush. No harm, no foul. Have I missed anything exciting here?"

Mo wanted details, but she assured him there weren't any except for her own stupidity. She asked Mrs. Berman to come to her office and led the way upstairs. As Mandy crossed the mezzanine, she looked down and caught Grange staring at her. He was frowning, and he looked so fierce that she dropped her eyes to the carpet and kept them there all the way to her office. Once there, she threw herself into her chair and clenched her hands in her lap to stop them from trembling.

Mrs. Berman closed the door and stood in front of it. "What happened?" Her voice was kindly and held a note of concern.

Mandy cleared her throat. "I hope I'm not going to act like a baby now," she said, tears brimming in her eyes. "It's all over, and though it could have been bad, I wasn't hurt at all, except—"

"Except what?"

Mandy rubbed her chest. "I'm a bit sore where the seat belt was. I wondered if you had anything that would help. I don't want it to be worse tomorrow."

"I'll fix you some comfrey. But tell me, what happened?"

"I ran off the road at a place where it was pretty steep. My landlady rescued me. I reported the accident, and Doc MacDonald gave me a ride. He's going to see that my car is fixed, too."

"That's it?"

"That's it."

"All right, then." Mrs. Berman opened the door. "While I fix that comfrey, you need to look at that note on your desk. Nettie Maypole has your whole afternoon planned. Remember, I warned you she was a bulldozer."

Mandy smiled at that moment, but throughout the afternoon, as she watched Nettie lay the groundwork for a successful election, she reflected that the description was apt. Mandy sat as figurehead through meetings with Mrs. Foley and Wesley Gallant, and nodded in support as Nettie primed a reporter from the *Hiesel Valley Herald* with facts and figures. In another meeting with committees from each of the towns in the district, Mandy endorsed Nettie's plans and realized that, as hard as it had been to swallow her pride, she could not have asked for a more capable person to head up the levy campaign.

At the end of the day, as Mandy sat at her desk examining her list of assignments from Nettie for the next week, Mrs. Berman tapped at her door.

"I'm going now. Doc McDonald called while you were with Nettie. He said don't worry about your car. Everything's fine. I see it's in the parking lot. Do you need anything else?"

"No, thank you, Mrs.—Edith. I'll see you tomorrow."

Mandy cleared off her desk, gathered her things, and went down to check out her car. The front bumper had a small dimple, and the right front fender had an ugly bulge on the top. Mandy ran her hand over it.

"You didn't tell us you lost a wheel."

She whirled. Grange stood just behind her. "How did you know?" she asked.

"It's pretty obvious. The lug nuts get sheared off, the wheel comes off, and when the car drops on the wheel, it bends the fender." He stepped closer and traced the misshapen place. "I lost one once. It's a pretty scary thing. I didn't run off the road, but the wheel chased me and ran over me."

"Not really!"

He grinned. "Well, it didn't run over me personally, but it ran over my pickup. It went up over the fender and hood and continued on down the road. I went sliding along after it on three wheels and a hub."

She smiled back. "I'm glad to know it's happened to someone else."

Grange didn't reply. He looked at his feet for a moment and cleared his throat, and when Mandy stepped away, he stuffed his hands in his pockets and said, "I've got to run downriver to buy some groceries. Do you have any shopping to do? Would you like to come with me?"

She considered. "Why, yes. As a matter of fact, the cupboard is bare. I was just wondering what we were going to have for dinner, since Leesie opened the last can of soup last night."

He held out his hand in an "after you" gesture. As she started walking toward his truck, he walked beside her. "A can of soup? I heard you make a great pot of chili."

She laughed. "I know who told you that. But I would say that a hungry man is no fair judge." She climbed in the cab as Grange held the door for her, and then she watched as he walked around to the driver's door. His mouth was set in happy lines, and his blue eyes had a merry look about them as he got in.

"It will be nice to have company on the way down," he said as he started the truck.

Mandy replied suitably, and they continued on in silence for a while. Grange was the one who spoke first. "I noticed you were marching to Nettie's tune all afternoon."

"I'm glad to do it. She seems to know what she's doing."

He agreed and went on to talk about other levy elections Nettie had presided over. Mandy asked questions, trying to understand the process, and before they knew it, they were at the market in Stallo. They shopped separately and met again after checking out. Grange had large plastic bins with locking tops in the back of the pickup that they stowed their groceries in, and as they drove home, he told the story of how he lost a pickup load of food to a flock of crows one summer when he was a teenager and working at a logging camp upriver. "I had come to town to do the shopping for all the workers," he explained. "There was a pretty girl that worked at a drive-in, so I stopped for lunch and stayed too long. By the time I got out, there wasn't much left of the meat or cheese or eggs. They didn't care much for the salad."

"So what did you do?"

"I went shopping again, but I paid for it myself. It cost me almost a month's wages."

Mandy countered with a story about how she had gone out with her grandfather on fall roundup as camp cook, and how a grizzled old cowboy taught her to make biscuits in a Dutch oven after her first attempt turned out to be hockey pucks.

They shared other stories of monstrous failures. Mandy told about her first paying gig, playing the organ for a wedding at a huge cathedral, and how she lost the key to the organ just before the service. Grange told about trying to set the brake on a flatcar full of logs but turning it the wrong way so that it rolled down the hill and coasted a mile before he got it stopped. "It was a spur line," he said, "so there was no danger of a collision. But my boss was really torqued because he had to send someone out to haul it back up the hill."

Night came on as they drove. Mandy asked about working in the woods and watched Grange in the dim light cast by dashboard dials as he talked. He had a nice profile with a straight nose and high brow. A week's worth of beard fringed his strong chin, and his dark hair fell over his forehead. Every now and then, he'd turn to her as he talked, and though she knew his eyes were blue, in the dim light they looked dark. She could see the curve of his mouth and thought how much better he looked when he was laughing.

He smiled a lot when he talked about logging, even when he said his mother made him promise he'd get an education and find another way to earn a living. "It's one of the most dangerous jobs there is. My grandfather, my father, and my uncle Jacob were all killed in logging accidents. I know that, and yet there's nothing like being out there in the woods, working with an experienced crew, making it happen. I got my degree, like my mother asked, but I still work in the woods during the summers. Or I did, anyway."

"That's past tense?"

Grange turned off the highway onto Shingle Mill Road. "Yeah." He didn't offer any more, so Mandy didn't pry, and they rode in silence to the district office.

He pulled up beside the Miata and got her groceries out of the back of the truck while she popped her trunk. "This will hold a couple loaves of bread," he said. "Where do I put the rest?"

"In the front seat. Just stack it in." She opened the passenger-side door.

When all the groceries were stowed, she closed the door and extended her hand. "Thanks a lot, Grange," she said. "I enjoyed the ride."

"You're welcome, Dr. Steenburg." He clasped her hand briefly and then walked around to open her door.

She followed him, and just before she got in, she said, "Call me Mandy."

There was the briefest of pauses before he said, "All right, Mandy."

She looked at him narrowly, but his face was in shadow, and she couldn't see his expression. She found the key on the floor under the seat, and as she started the car, Grange closed the door and stepped away. She waved at him, backed out of the parking space, and headed for home. Looking in the rearview mirror as she turned onto Shingle Mill Road, she saw he was standing where she left him, watching her drive away.

Even though Doc McDonald said not to, Mandy had intended to worry about her car all the way home. She intended to drive slowly in case another wheel should happen to fall off. But she forgot about that, and instead played back in her mind her conversation with Grange. The corners of her mouth lifted as she remembered him telling about riding on the front of the railroad car, holding on to the brake, too scared to turn it. She smiled, too, at the story about him slicing his leg open when he worked out in the woods, and how the cook had sewn him up with quilting thread. It wasn't a funny story, but the way Grange told it had made her laugh out loud. She didn't know what made him extend the invitation to go downriver, but she definitely preferred Grange Friend to Grange Foe.

She reached the turnoff from Timberlain Road before she remembered to worry about the car. Shaking her head at her fears, she shifted down, made the turn, and accelerated around the curve.

Mandy saw that Leesie was home, and someone else was there, too. It wasn't Jake. They had decided Leesie wouldn't have friends over when Mandy wasn't home, and besides, this was a sedan she had never seen before. She parked, got the grocery bags out of the front seat, and climbed the stairs, looking at the car as she passed for some clue as to who the visitor could be.

Leesie met her at the door and took the bags. "I'll take care of the groceries. Christmas has come, so you must greet your company."

Mandy's brow creased as she relinquished her burden. "What are you talking about, Leesie?"

"A fellow named Guy Noel. Says he knows you?"

"Guy? Is he here?" Mandy grabbed for the doorframe as she stepped in.

At her appearance, a man rose from the couch. Of medium height, he had broad shoulders, a lean face with a well-tended Van Dyke, brown eyes, and brown hair cut short.

"Hello, chérie," he said.

27

Mandy waited for the earth to tip back to a horizontal plane before she spoke. "Hello, Guy." It came out sounding a little breathless. "What on earth are you doing clear up here?" She didn't offer to shake hands.

"I'm going to an international conference in Vancouver. Canada is right next door, almost, so I took an extra day and thought I'd drop by and see you."

Mandy sat in the chair opposite the couch. "Oh? Is the district sending you?"

Guy cleared his throat. "No. There wasn't any money in the budget, but it was something I wanted to attend."

"That's right, you're French-Canadian, aren't you? Old stomping grounds?"

Guy brushed the suggestion aside with a wave of his hand. "No, I'm from Quebec. I'm here to do research on an article I want to write."

Mandy took a deep breath and exhaled. She smiled for the first time since greeting her guest. "Well, it's nice to see you. We can offer you supper. Would you prefer chicken noodle or vegetable soup?"

"I picked up some chicken noodle at the Qwik-E Market," Leesie announced. "It's in the pot. Not that I'm listening to your conversation or anything."

"That's all right, Leesie," Mandy said, standing. "We won't exclude you. Come into the kitchen, Guy, and talk to me while I set the table. Then we'll eat, and afterward, Leesie will play for you."

"Um, I was going to go study with Jake," Leesie said.

"Not tonight. We have a guest." Mandy gave her sister a meaningful look before turning to Guy. "Where are you staying?"

"I hadn't made any plans. I suppose there's someplace in town, unless you'll let me stay on your couch."

"You wouldn't get a wink of sleep on that couch." Mandy picked up the phone and dialed a number. "Elizabeth? This is Dr. Steenburg. Does your grandmother have a room for tonight? Good. How late do you work? Okay. I'll make sure he's there before then so you can show him where to go. Call your grandmother and reserve the room for him, okay? Thanks."

Mandy hung up and began to set place mats, silverware, and glasses on the table. "You're in luck. There are two beds for hire in this town, and one of them is available. You'll have to be at the Qwik-E Market by eight thirty, though, to find your way."

Guy looked at his watch. "That's in less than an hour."

Mandy grinned. "We'll have to eat fast, and then Leesie can play. You can come and see the district offices tomorrow before you head out to Vancouver."

Leesie dished up the soup, and as they ate, Mandy and Guy talked about what was going on in the Albuquerque schools. After dinner, they worked together to get the kitchen clean. Then Mandy asked Guy to sit on the couch again, and she told Leesie to get her instrument.

They played the Schubert number and were halfway through the other when Leesie mentioned that Guy needed to get on his way if he was going to meet Elizabeth before she went off shift.

"Oh my goodness, yes," Mandy said. "I was so into the music that I forgot the time. Here." She grabbed a napkin off the table and drew a map to the Qwik-E Market and another from there to the district office.

"Come in the morning about nine," Mandy said, smiling as she gave the napkin to Guy. "I've got an hour free then, and I can tell you all about the challenges of a small district."

"Yeah. Sure." Guy took the napkin and stuck it in his shirt pocket. "Walk me to the car, chérie?"

Mandy laughed as she opened the door. "You're in Washington, Guy. Walking is not a social exercise up here—at least not for people bred in the desert. It's raining." She kissed him lightly on the cheek. "Come see me tomorrow."

He patted his breast pocket. "I have the map. I'll be there."

"Good." She waved to him as he descended the porch steps, and then she closed the door and leaned against it.

"I'm getting the feeling," Leesie said as she put her cello in the case, "that I'm not the only one who left Albuquerque because of a man."

"What makes you think that?"

"Oh, puh-leeze! Do you think I didn't see how you kept either the width of the room or the kitchen table between you?"

"I kissed him on the cheek."

"Yeah, with me standing right beside you. I notice you wouldn't go out in the dark with him."

"Not on your life."

Leesie set her case in the corner. She didn't turn around as she said, "I also noticed there was a wedding ring on his left hand."

"There always has been." Mandy walked over and hugged her sister. "I'm so glad you're here."

"So am I, Sweetiebug. But who's going to chaperone you tomorrow?"

"I'll get Mo, or Mrs. Berman." Mandy grinned. "Or better still, I'll get Grange."

Then, without sparing another thought for the man who was driving through the rain and the dark, following a sketchy map drawn on a napkin, Mandy picked up a book she had begun and settled down to read.

The next morning at work, the first thing Mandy did as soon as she checked her calendar was sort through the papers Edith had put in her inbox. When she spied the familiar round penmanship on wide-ruled notebook paper that heralded another list of commandments from Nettie, Mandy stood and saluted.

"What was that about?"

She looked up to see Grange standing in the doorway. "Oh, hi," she said, eyes twinkling as she sat down. "I just got another set of marching orders from Nettie."

He smiled and entered. "You catch on fast." He held out a red and white can. "I found this in my truck. Your groceries must have been fraternizing with mine on the way home last night."

Mandy took the can and read the label. "You're sure it's not yours?"

He shook his head as he sank into the side chair and stretched out his long legs. "I haven't eaten tomato soup since I got out of grade school. We used to have it every Friday. Tomato soup and toasted cheese sandwiches."

"Oh, me too," Mandy said, holding the can to her chest. "Didn't you just love it?"

Grange rubbed his bearded chin as he considered. "No."

"Oh." She set the can down on her desk. "I thought you were at the high school all morning."

"I am. We're a little more than a week away from Opening Festival, and it's getting to be crunch time. I just came back to give you your soup."

She grinned. "You lie through your teeth. You didn't drive over here just to give me a can of soup."

"Well, I needed to get a stack of posters. Oscar is taking a crew and going downriver to plaster the area."

"What can I do to help?"

Grange stood. "You're doing it. You've got Nettie minding the levy, Mo minding the budget, Midge writing a grant, and Harvey Berman's office getting organized."

Mandy cocked her head. "I can't tell if you're serious or sarcastic."

"I'm serious, though Harvey is the only one who doesn't seem to be getting with the program."

She laughed. "He will. I'm going to have Mo sit down with him and teach him about budgeting, and I'm going to send him to a couple of other districts to observe their methods. Before we're through, we'll make a manager out of him."

"If I were a betting man . . ." Grange's voice trailed off as something outside caught his eye. "Now, who would that be?"

She stood and walked to the window. "Oh, that's a friend of mine from Albuquerque," she said. "His name is Guy Noel."

Grange lifted an eyebrow. "He's a little far afield, isn't he?"

"Not too far. He's on his way to a seminar in Vancouver." As Mandy waved at Guy, she said, "Stay for a moment, and I'll introduce you."

"He looks very natty," Grange commented.

Her eyes crinkled at the corners. "Natty? Where did you get that expression?"

"From Granny Timberlain. Gramps would say he looks fine as frog's hair."

Mandy wrinkled her nose at Grange as she walked past him and out to the mezzanine.

"Uncle Buck would say he's done up like a dog's dinner," he called out to her.

She shook her head. "I don't understand that at all." She leaned over the railing and called, "Hello, Guy! Come on up." She watched him mount the steps and smiled as she waited for him to walk around to her office. "I see you found the place all right."

He touched his breast pocket and smiled down at Mandy. "I have your map."

"Let me introduce you to the assistant superintendent, Grange Timberlain." Mandy held out her hand in Grange's direction.

Guy's eyes flicked away from her face momentarily, but he barely acknowledged the other man's presence.

"Well, then, I'll be off," Grange said. "Pleased to make your acquaintance, Mr. . . . uh . . ."

"Noel," Mandy supplied.

Guy nodded absently in Grange's direction and turned to face Mandy. "Is an hour all you can give me?" he said in an undervoice.

Mandy looked up at Grange as he passed in front of her and out the door. The corners of his mouth lifted as he sketched a wave, and she felt her cheeks get warm. She turned to Guy. "I've never known you to be rude before."

"What? Oh, you wanted me to make nice to that hayseed?" He closed the door. "I didn't come here to make small talk with rustics. I came to see you, Mandy." He took her by the hand and led her to the far corner of the room, out of the line of sight of anyone on the mezzanine.

Mandy didn't say anything. Guy's nearness, the smell of his aftershave, the crispness of his pale green shirt, the way his hair fell artfully over his forehead, accentuating his eyes—all flooded her with memories of a different time, a warmer place, almost a different Mandy Steenburg.

"Listen, chérie," he said with quiet urgency. "I've come with Dr. Brenner's blessing. He wants you to come back. He hasn't filled your position. We all want you back."

Mandy tore her eyes away from his face. Looking at the floor, she shook her head. "I can't," she whispered.

"I want you back. Do you understand, chérie? I want you back, and I'll make it happen. I'll leave Mary. I—I've left her, actually. I don't love her anymore. I love you."

Mandy felt as if she were caught in one of the eddies in the Hiesel River, being whirled around and sucked under. She closed her eyes to block out the feeling of the room turning and felt her right hand being lifted, felt Guy pressing his lips against her fingers. She could almost hear the water pulsing and surging in her ears as it dragged her down.

"Come back, chérie. Leave this backwater and come back with me right now."

He kissed her hand once more. His left hand held her right, and as she opened her eyes, she had an up-close, full-screen view of his wedding band. She felt his arm slip around her waist, and as he pulled her to him and bent his head to kiss her lips, she tried to push him away.

She leaned back. "Stop it, Guy."

"Don't tell me you haven't been thinking the same thing I have, chérie," he said urgently. "I've seen it in your eyes, felt the heat of your glance. You want me as much as I want you."

"Don't, Guy." She twisted, trying to escape from his embrace.

From the doorway, someone spoke in a conversational tone. "Do you know—" Mandy and Guy both turned and looked at the speaker, and she felt the blood rising to her cheeks again as she realized how she looked, bent backward with Guy leaning over her.

Grange stood with one hand on the doorknob, a packet of posters in the other hand. Though his voice was restrained, his eyes were hard as he spoke to Guy. "—I don't believe you've got that right, or she wouldn't be trying to get free."

Guy released her and stepped away, breathing heavily as he turned his back on Grange.

"Can I do anything for you, Dr. Steenburg?" Grange asked neutrally.

"No. Thanks, Grange." Mandy ran her hands through her hair as if that would gather her scattered wits. "Thanks, no."

"I'll be off, then. I've calendared myself at the high school all day for the rest of the week."

"Yes, I saw that. Thanks."

Grange raised the packet of posters in salute, then turned and walked away, leaving the door open behind him.

"Sit down, Guy." Mandy pointed to the side chair Grange had recently vacated.

"Mandy," he said pleadingly.

"Sit down and listen," she commanded, eyes blazing. Balling her hands into fists, she strode to her desk and sat opposite him.

"How dare you presume that I would be unprincipled enough to break up a home. No, you don't get to talk right now. Listen to me!"

Guy closed his mouth and sat back in his chair, eyes wide.

Her voice had an edge like flint. "Yes, I had feelings for you. That's why I left my job and left Albuquerque. And I was" —she searched for the word— "naive enough, starry-eyed enough to imagine that you were going to try as hard as I to work through this."

"Can I close the door?" Guy asked as Mrs. Berman passed from her office across to Mo's.

"Don't waste the energy. I've only got a couple more things to say." Mandy paused a moment, and her eye fell on the can of tomato soup. She picked it up and rolled it between her hands, frowning as she chose her words. "Do you think that I would want someone so weak, such a moral wet noodle, that he would leave his family because of an infatuation? You've got two children, Guy. How can you even think to betray that trust? How can you betray Mary? She loves you!"

Guy leaned forward with his elbows on his knees and his face in his hands. "Don't, Mandy," he moaned.

"Did you tell Mary why you were coming up here?"

He didn't answer.

"Guy? Did you?"

"I left her a note."

"Why am I not surprised you would leave a note instead of telling her to her face?" She sat back in her chair, still holding the soup can. "You know, I really have to thank you. You certainly cured me of my infatuation." She smiled. "And thank you for telling me that my job is still open. I just might take them up on that."

Guy finally looked up. "You're kidding!"

"I'm not. I've a tough decision to make here, and this just might be the answer."

The color drained from his face. "Mandy—"

She sighed. "Go home, Guy. Go see if you can make it up with Mary. If she takes you back, it's more than you deserve."

He slumped in his chair for a moment, looking at her with a hangdog expression. Then he slowly stood.

"And give me back my map. I don't want you hanging on to any mementos."

Silently, he pulled the napkin from his breast pocket and dropped it on her desk. Then, without a backward glance, he walked through the door and out of her life.

Mandy sighed again as she watched him go, realizing after a moment that she was holding the soup can against her cheek. She set it down, picked up a corner of the napkin, and dropped it in the wastebasket.

At that moment, Elizabeth called up to Mrs. Berman, who was on the landing outside her office. "Mr. Farley is on the phone about the cellos. Is Mr. Timberlain in?"

"He's on his way down to the high school," the secretary called back. "He should be there in five minutes."

Mandy blinked twice and pursed her mouth as the seed of an idea wafted into her head. She opened her desk drawer and pulled out the yellow directory card. Running her finger down the list, she found Glen Farley's name at the bottom of the page, only he wasn't the music teacher. His room number was listed as the metal shop.

Metal shop? She checked again to make sure she was tracking across the page correctly. What would that have to do with cellos? Maybe she'd heard wrong. Maybe Elizabeth said bellows. That would make more sense.

Mandy put the directory away, but the idea was taking root and sending out tendrils, growing like Jack's beanstalk in the fertile soil of her mind. She spent the rest of the afternoon either on the phone or on the internet, and just before quitting time, she called Mo and made an appointment to talk to him the next day about the music budget.

It was only later that evening, when Leesie asked her about Guy, that Mandy realized she hadn't given him another thought.

Leesie giggled. "I wish you could have seen the expression on your face! It's funny how quickly you can get over a guy, isn't it?"

"Yes, and then you wonder what you ever saw in him. Ugh." Mandy shivered.

As Leesie laid her homework out on the kitchen table, Mandy said, "I've been thinking about an orchestra."

Leesie looked up. "Is this a game? Am I supposed to guess which orchestra you're thinking about?"

"No, silly! I'm thinking about a North Cascades High School orchestra."

Leesie grimaced and shook her head. "It would never fly."

"Why not? You sell these kids short. I want to give them a taste of something beyond 'upriver.' I think, if we can give them something fine, a way of expressing themselves as an ensemble, it will really do lots for them as they go out in the world."

"Believe, me, Sweetiebug, I don't sell them short. In fact . . ." Leesie didn't finish her sentence.

"What? You were going to say something. In fact, what?"

Leesie grinned. "Never mind. Say, can you help me here? Define 'paradigm.'"

It took Mandy a moment to shift gears. "Paradigm? It's a framework, or model, that is accepted and that everyone works—and even thinks—within."

Leesie furrowed her brow. "So a paradigm shift would be . . . "

"You know when you hear people talk about thinking outside the box? Maybe that's what it means—seeing the world in a whole different way. It's like moving from base ten to base five in math. All of a sudden, ones and zeros and place value means something completely different."

"Thanks, Mandy. That makes sense. I think I can answer this question now."

Leesie bent her head over her homework, and Mandy sat down with her book. Though her eyes traveled over the words, her mind was working on the steps necessary to introduce a string program into a resistant school district.

The subject occupied her focus so much over the next few days that she forgot to worry about the next "accident" that was to befall her. Twice she passed Stevie Joe Hawes's red pickup pulling onto Timberlain Road from her gravel road without having the hair on the back of her neck prickle. And when Doc MacDonald called to check on her, it took a moment for Mandy realize what he was talking about.

She read everything she could get her hands on about the benefits of a school orchestra. She talked to administrators in other rural districts that boasted a string program and even traveled the hundred miles to a small district outside of Seattle. They were eager to talk about their string program but unwilling to cheer for Mandy's crusade. They even seemed to try to discourage her. At the end of the day, she sat across from Mrs. Wilson, a spare, gray-haired music teacher who looked over the glasses perched on the end of her nose and asked Mandy, "Have you heard the expression 'If it ain't broke, don't fix it'?"

Mystified, she nodded.

"Why on earth do you want to change the music program at North Cascade?"

"Oh, well, bluegrass," Mandy said. "I would hope to expand the horizons of the students beyond the confines of that valley."

Mrs. Wilson stared at her for a moment. "How long have you been there?"

She did the math. "Um, a little over a month."

"Do you know anything at all about North Cascades' music program? Oh, I don't mean the bluegrass bands. I mean the complete program."

Mandy opened her mouth to reply and then shut it again. "I guess I don't."

Mrs. Wilson stood and went to her bookshelf. "F. Granger Timberlain wrote the book on an integrated music program," she said over her shoulder. "Well, not the book—the pamphlet, really." She pulled a spiral-bound booklet from her shelf and dropped it in front of Mandy. "I can't believe you haven't read this."

"There's been lots to do," Mandy said in a subdued voice. "We've got a levy to get ready for, and we want to revamp the reading program."

"But not the math program?"

"No. The math scores are excellent, actually."

"And do you know why?"

Mandy shook her head, and Mrs. Wilson amazed her by breaking out in song. In a distinctly Caribbean accent and rhythm, she sang the seven times tables, all the while dancing around with her arms above her head, clapping as she swayed forward and back. Mandy watched, round eyed, and when the older lady stopped and indicated with raised brows and upturned palms that she was waiting for an opinion, Mandy could only stare. "I'm sorry. That's clever, but . . ."

"Page 7. Open the book."

Mandy obeyed and saw a half-page picture of a small steel band playing on a stage, with a gym full of elementary children dancing, their arms above their heads much as Mrs. Wilson's had been.

"All of the math facts—and I'm talking about addition, subtraction, multiplication, and division—have been put to music and dance. There are any number of small, steel-band ensembles that go several times a week to help the grade school kids learn math songs and dances. These kids know their facts. They learn the patterns and can work complex problems in their heads. They don't use calculators in school until they hit algebra."

Mandy studied the picture and read the narrative underneath.

Mrs. Wilson went on. "Add to that the fact that the shop classes build the instruments, and they have to use math to figure out depth and temper and frequencies and metallurgy and any number of things. Math begins to mean something. And it all begins with music."

"Yes, but a steel band playing 'The Banana Boat Song'?"

"Last year I attended a concert where they played the first movement of Beethoven's Fifth and brought down the house. I never miss Opening Festival. April is a pretty gloomy time in the Pacific Northwest, but listening to that steel band is like standing in the sunshine."

Mandy paged through the book. "I didn't realize," she said lamely.

"Well, I don't imagine anyone welcomed you with open arms. When we heard that Grange Timberlain had been replaced, we couldn't believe it. Last December he helped me write a grant to the Bill and Melinda Gates Foundation for money to duplicate his program."

Mandy stood. "Thank you, Mrs. Wilson, for telling me this. I feel so stupid."

The older woman put her arm around Mandy and walked her to the door. "Don't. I've just given you a little education. Education is a good thing."

Mandy nodded and turned to make her way through the corridor to the parking lot. As she pushed through the door at the end, she heard someone call her name.

Turning with the door half open, she saw Mrs. Wilson standing in her doorway. "It ain't broke," she called. "Don't try to fix it. Embrace it."

Mandy waved to show she had heard, but she couldn't muster a smile. She let the door swing closed behind her, and as she walked through the drizzle back to her car, she reflected that she could use a little sunshine.

30

Saturday evening, Mandy stood in the hallway in front of the door to the high school gym and took a deep breath. She had promised Leesie she would come, but she would much rather have hibernated in her loft so she wouldn't have to face F. Granger Timberlain until Monday. She didn't know which made her more reluctant to face him—the fact that he'd caught Guy trying to kiss her or that she had been just about to propose a district orchestra to the man who wrote the book on music programs.

She put her hand up to smooth her curls and felt the flower pinned there. Somehow the feel of Vince's gift gave her courage. A single, fragrant gardenia had arrived that afternoon with a note that said, *Save the last dance for me.* The ribbon gracing the blossom was claret red, and though Mandy had intended to wear one of her tailored pant suits, when she saw the color of the ribbon, she pulled a dress of soft burgundy crepe out of her closet, one with a fitted bodice and a flowing skirt.

She hung up her coat. Hearing a band inside the gym playing a lilting tune, she pushed the door open a fraction and peeked inside. The setting was so familiar, so normal, that she took heart. She had seen this scene so many times before: high ceilings with cages over the lights, basketball backboards pulled up out of the way, brown walls, and brown bleachers. Even the gymnasium smell signaled familiar territory.

A young man suddenly pulled the door open and surprised both Mandy and himself. He stepped back out of the way to let her enter; she murmured thanks and wandered in. Staying close to the wall, she circled around to find a seat on the bottom row of bleachers opposite the bandstand.

People of all ages thronged the floor, grooving in the styles of several different decades, but all seemed carried away in the joy of music and dance.

Mandy's toe tapped in time as she watched the band. There were three girls, one on mandolin, one on guitar, and one on fiddle, while a boy played the standup bass and another played the banjo. None of them looked older than thirteen, but their playing was energetic and assured, and their rhythm was dead on. Mandy inclined her head and closed her eyes as she listened to the riffs the fiddle played counter to the mandolin's melody, and she smiled at how fresh and inventive it was.

Suddenly a voice spoke into her ear from behind. "So how did you get on with the Dog's Dinner after I left?"

She jumped and turned around in her seat. "Oh, you startled me!" she said to Grange. "I didn't hear you come up."

"Actually, I came down. I was sitting up there and saw you come in."

Her eyes flicked up to the top of the bleachers, where several people were obviously interested in her conversation with Grange. "I see," she said, turning back around.

He sat beside her. "So, what do you think of those kids?"

"They're marvelous. How old are they?"

"Middle school. They'll be playing at Opening Festival for the first time this year."

Mandy looked around. "I haven't seen Leesie," she said.

"She's back in the music room. Want to go wish her well?"

"Yes." Mandy stood. "Just tell me how to get there."

"I'll take you." Grange rose as well. Putting his hand on her elbow, he guided her through the crowd to a corridor on the far side of the gym.

Nervous at finding herself alone with him in a dimly lit hallway, she searched for something to say. "How many bands do you have playing tonight?"

"You mean bluegrass? Three—this one, Leesie's, and one other. They'll all play at Opening Festival. And then the school band is going to play." He grinned. "I guess this is what would pass for a spring concert at some other schools. Ours is more of a structured jam session and dress rehearsal for the festival."

Just then Leesie, Jake, and four other students came out of a room, carrying their instruments. Mandy hugged her sister awkwardly around her bass fiddle and told her to break a leg. She wished Jake well and then noticed that their mandolin player was her computer tech. "Hello, Oscar," she said. "I didn't know you played, too."

"You've got to play bluegrass if you go to Inches," he said.

Leesie blew a kiss over her shoulder and headed toward the gym. When Mandy started to follow, Grange touched her arm. "They won't be on for a bit," he said. "Would you like to see the music room?"

"Why, yes. I would." She followed as he continued to the end of the hall. "I'd be glad for the chance to talk to you, too."

"Uh-oh. Those words usually mean I'm in your black books."

Mandy shook her head. "Nothing like that."

"I've been expecting you to come visit the high school. The principal, Fred Wimmer, said you invited him to your office."

She felt her cheeks getting warm. "That sounds a little black bookish. Are you offended?"

He stopped in front of a set of double doors. "Not at all. I was hoping you didn't stay away because of me."

"Coming here was on my to-do list, but I will admit I was a little hesitant. I didn't want to invade what seemed to be your domain."

She passed through the door Grange held open for her and stepped into a huge room with terraced platforms around three sides of the room. She took in the array of shiny, cylindrical instruments of all sizes that stood on each of the tiers. There were huge, oil-drum-size pans set in groups of three and four, and half-barrel-size pans, and smaller ones set on tripods at waist height.

Mandy had never seen anything like it. "I can't believe this," she said. "I just—it's almost too much to take in. When you talk about the school band, you're talking—"

"About a steel band."

"But why?"

Just then a student came in. Mandy recognized the young man who worked with Willow in Midge's office.

"Hi, Randy," Grange said. "Did you come to practice your solo?"

The young man grinned. "Just one last time."

"We'll get out of your way." Grange turned to Mandy. "Come into my office? That way we can talk without bothering Randy."

She followed Grange through the music library room to a closet beyond that had been turned into a tiny office. He dragged a chair from the library and wedged it into a place behind the door so Mandy could sit.

She looked around at the crowded bookcases lining the walls. "So this is where you are when you're not. . . "

He sat at his desk. "I call it my hidey hole. Trouble is, there's not room to stretch out, so I have to nap sitting up." He smiled.

Mandy picked up a catalog and looked at the cover. "You're not the music teacher, are you? I thought I saw someone else. Mrs. Plumbley?"

Grange nodded. "I take care of all the extra stuff—the logistics of getting kids to schools to help do math facts, and I'm the organizing force behind Opening Festival." His teeth flashed against the darkness of his beard and moustache, and he looked at her sideways. "Would this qualify as beating around the bush? What did you want to say to me?"

Mandy put the book back down on the desk and carefully squared it up with the corner. "I, um, just wanted to—" She shook her head. "This is really hard."

"You wanted to tell me that the Dog's Dinner is the reason you left Albuquerque. He's a married man that has the hots for you, and maybe you felt the same. It was an untenable situation, so you left. He followed you here and tried to rekindle the fire. You doused it. The end."

Mandy looked up and smiled wryly. "That's pretty much it. How did you know?"

"Why else would someone with credentials and references like you have come upriver?"

"Oh, I don't know. Don't sell your district short."

"Believe me, I'm trying not to."

They sat in silence for a moment, neither looking at the other. She riffled the pages of the catalog. "I spoke with Agnes Wilson yesterday," she began tentatively. "She told me about all the things you're doing with music and math."

Grange frowned. "How did you happen to talk to her? She's way down by Seattle."

"Yeah. I was blown away by all the things you're doing. Why didn't you tell me?"

He shrugged. "You never asked."

Mandy sat back in her chair and regarded him. "Why a steel band?" she asked. "I understand the bluegrass, but why the other?" She gestured toward the music room.

He looked at his watch. "It's a bit of a story, and I really have to go back to the beginning, back to when I got out of high school and didn't have any ambition to get an education. I just wanted to work in the woods, marry, have a family. But something happened, something quite final, to make it so that dream wouldn't come true."

Grange paused for a moment, and she looked up to find his eyes resting on her. She looked down again and placed her hand over her heart, conscious that it was beating faster than normal.

He continued with his story. "I lived in a black place for a long time. One day my Uncle Buck told me I needed to get myself squared around with God, and I needed find a way to serve my fellow man."

Grange picked up a pencil and rolled it between his thumb and forefinger. "This was advice that came from way beyond left field," he said wryly. "If you knew my Uncle Buck, you would know he wouldn't even have been in the ballpark. But he talked about choices and how the ones you make early mark you for what you'll be. He talked about how hard it was to change what you had become and said he wanted me to do something good with my life."

Mandy ventured another look. Grange's gaze had been on the pencil, but he raised it to her face, and she noticed how the darkness of his hair and beard accentuated the blue of his eyes.

"I don't think I would have listened to anyone else, but I began to wonder if I'd made that decision—the decision to serve—earlier, maybe I wouldn't have lost . . ." His voice trailed away, and his eyes dropped to the pencil again.

"I talked to Pastor Barlow, and he handed me off to his wife. She's a lady that knows the meaning of the word 'outreach.'"

Mandy nodded. "I know."

"Yeah. I heard about you and Tammy. Well, Millie Barlow sent me to Jamaica, and I ended up working in an orphanage that was run by a group of nuns." Grange set the pencil down on the desk and leaned back in his chair. "This is where I confess that every part of Inches' integrated music program was lifted from what those nuns were doing."

"What do you mean, every part?"

He ticked them off on his fingers. "The steel band, students learning to build and tune the pans, the math-facts songs, the dances that go with them. I didn't write the melodies—Sister Ethelberta did. Steel bands didn't originate in Jamaica. They come from Trinidad, but they spread to Jamaica, and the nuns saw how they could be a tool for their mission." He leaned forward. "These amazing ladies created a joyous, industrious, educational environment and gave these cast-off children the tools to go out into the world and thrive."

"But why a steel band? Couldn't you have reproduced the whole thing with stringed instruments. You've got lots of talented kids playing bluegrass. Couldn't they do the math stuff?"

Grange shook his head. "Two reasons." He picked up the pencil again and drummed on the desk with it. "It's something about the physical process of beating on something. That appeals to everyone. Everyone can do it, and there's a place—a voice—for everyone, from the most talented to the least. We don't have a lot of discipline problems at Inches. I think that's because so many kids are involved in this common cause. But I also think it's because they are able to channel aggression into whacking on a steel drum."

"So did that count as two reasons?" Mandy asked.

"Nope. The second reason is the sound. It's like sunshine, and where is a better place to play sunshine than in rainy Hiesel Valley? It draws the kids in. They want to be involved. You don't get that with stringed instruments, or with brass, either."

"So tell me," Mandy said. "I've seen the music budget. I know it doesn't come from the state or from the local levies. Where does it come from? Mo won't tell me."

Grange grinned. "That's because he knows what's good for him. He's been sworn to secrecy." He looked at his watch. "It's almost time to go back in. Let me ask you something—no, two things."

He spoke so earnestly that her reply was tentative. "Okay."

"Fran told me you intend to leave, right away. Is that true?"

"Why would she say—" Mandy broke off as she remembered the morning she ended up in the blackberry bushes. "Oh. I think I did say that."

"And is it true?"

"Um, I don't know. Guy—the Dog's Dinner—told me they're holding my old spot open, and I could go back now without, you know. But . . ."

"But?"

"Every now and then I get to thinking that I could make a difference here. But there's the budget thing—my salary, as you pointed out. And the district doesn't need me." She took a deep breath. "They need you. There, I've said it."

"Don't worry about the budget. I think I know a way around that. The thing is, Mrs. Reilly came to see me yesterday. She wanted to talk to me about your reading program."

"Oh?"

"She said something about me being the north end of a southbound mule and told me the plan was worth more consideration than I gave it. She wants to hear more."

Mandy grinned. "I like that part about the mule."

"So, what do you say? Will you stay? At least through the end of this year?"

"I think I can do that," she said. "That was easy. Now, what was the second question?"

"Your perfume. What is it? It reminds me of Jamaica. Calls up lots of memories."

"My perfume? Oh" —she touched the flower— "you must be smelling my gardenia. It's very fragrant, isn't it?"

"It's real? I thought it was—"

Mandy watched as Grange's brain processed the information, and she saw in his eyes the moment he realized she was wearing a flower from Vince Laffitte.

Just then the door to the office opened, and Fran stuck her head in.

"I thought I'd find you here. Mandy, Leesie's on stage, and they're calling for you."

She jumped up. "Oh! Thank you, Fran. I'll get right in there."

As she left, she heard Fran say, "Stay a minute, Grangie."

She didn't have time to puzzle on Fran's playful tone or the pet name she used, for she met Rael at the music room door.

He smiled a greeting. "They're calling for you. Come on."

"For me?" Mandy followed him through the crowded hallway leading into the gym. When they emerged, a cheer went up, and people began to chant, "Dr. Steenburg, Dr. Steenburg."

As Leesie beckoned from the bandstand, Rael took Mandy's hand and led her across the floor and up the stairs. She stood uncertainly, looking out into the sea of upturned faces as Leesie took the microphone.

"Ladies and gentlemen, may I present Mandy Steenburg playing her own composition, the 'Stinkbug Boogie'!"

A wave of laughter swept over the crowd, followed by a burst of applause.

"Leesie!" Mandy protested. "What are you doing?"

Rael led her to the piano and signaled Jake to give him his guitar. As Rael fastened the shoulder strap, Mandy gave him one last, beseeching look. He winked at her and said, "One, two, one-two-three-four."

The old warhorse musician surfaced, and she began to play, picking up the beat laid down by Rael. Maybe it was her pledge to Grange that she would stay, or maybe it was the infatuation she had shed; maybe it was the welcoming applause, or perhaps it was the memory of those blue eyes resting on her as Grange told her his story. Whatever the reason, her happiness bounced out and onto the keyboard.

She heard Rael come in on rhythm guitar and then felt Leesie's bass walking up and down underneath both of them. They played through two more choruses, and Mandy ended with a flourish, then stood and faced the exuberant audience with shining eyes. Leesie gave her a one-armed squeeze, and Jake pumped her hand. Rael, divested of his guitar, stepped up, wrapped his arms around her, swept her off her feet, and kissed her full on the mouth. The crowd roared and clapped, and when Rael released her, Mandy stood in the circle of his arm with rosy cheeks and a wide smile as she looked around the room.

"Way to go, Sweetiebug." Rael's beard brushed against her cheek as he whispered in her ear.

Willow stared daggers from the front row. Mo applauded and whistled from a few rows back. Mandy's eyes sought Grange, but he stood by Fran with his hands in his pockets, leaning his head down to catch what she was saying. Suddenly, he threw back his head and laughed, and Fran reached up to ruffle the hair curling at the nape of his neck.

Mandy looked away and caught sight of Vince just entering the hall. She cast a quick glance back at Grange, but he was still smiling down at Fran. Turning, Mandy again found Vince in the crowd, and when he saw her, she touched the flower in her hair. He raised his hand in reply and started toward her.

She made her way to the bandstand stairs, acknowledging congratulations shouted up to her as she went. At the steps, she paused, and as she did so, she met Grange's eyes. He looked from her to Vince and back, then turned and, it seemed, made some sort of joke to Fran.

Mandy hurried down the stairs and walked through the friendly crowd to where Vince stood. His clean-shaven face creased into a welcoming smile, and he extended both hands. She gave him hers and smiled up at him when he complimented her on her playing.

She didn't spend the rest of the evening exclusively with Vince, but she was constantly aware of him and of the way he watched her. He stood beside her and cheered enthusiastically as Leesie's group played. He listened with a warm expression in his eyes as Mandy laughingly told him how she'd had no idea her sister was in a bluegrass band until a few days before. He followed Mandy to the bandstand with his hand just touching the small of her back as she pressed through the crowd to congratulate the band and hug her sister. And later, Vince was beside her, moving with the beat, as the steel band filled the gym with metallic sunshine.

She was aware of Grange, too, as he moved around the room, talking with students and citizens. Several times she caught him watching her, but each time his eyes slid away and he turned to speak to someone else.

Another bluegrass group played the last set. They began with lively tunes but ended with a slow, mellow song in three-quarter time. "Last dance," Vince said as he turned to Mandy. She drifted into his arms and closed her eyes as they moved in unison across the floor. Just as the last strains of the music faded away, he whispered, "I missed you."

She nodded but somehow couldn't bring herself to echo the sentiment.

Vince didn't seem to notice. "I'll walk you to your car."

Again Mandy nodded and was conscious of his presence close behind as she made her way through the crowd to the corridor. She let him help her on with her coat, and as she preceded him out the door, she saw Grange. Head and shoulders above the surrounding people, he walked beside Fran, looking down at her and smiling as he talked. She laughed and took his arm, and they walked out into the night side by side.

Mandy's throat tightened, and she suddenly felt lonely and a little weepy. Stepping to the side, she let Vince come beside her, and she reached for his hand.

When they got to her car, he opened the door for her but stood in the way, prolonging the moment by talking about inconsequential things. An evening mist diffused and dimmed the parking lot lights, and she leaned back against the Miata's soft top as she asked about his trip. He answered lightly, turning the problems he faced into an amusing narrative. As she listened and laughed, she watched a pulse beating at his throat and was conscious that his nearness, the smell of his gardenia, the feel of his body heat in the cool night air left her deliciously breathless.

It began to drizzle, and Mandy, pulled back to her surroundings, realized they were almost the last ones in the parking lot. "I've got to go."

Vince moved so she could get in the car, but he took her hand. "Come to Seattle with me tomorrow."

She shook her head. "It's raining. I've got to go."

But she let him kiss her. She stood in the corner between the open door and the car, and as he leaned down and she turned her face up to his, she felt the roughness of his palm on her cheek. Their lips touched, and his hand moved to the nape of her neck and buried itself in her curls. His other arm slid around to the small of her back and pulled her close. The coolness of the night air mixed with the feel of his strength and gave her a sense of shelter as she tasted his mouth on hers. It didn't help that when they came up for air, she found herself looking into those eyes.

"You tip me off balance," Mandy said. "I've got to go."

Just then the shower turned into a downpour. Vince kissed her once more and said, "Get in." He closed the door for her and stayed as she started her car and pulled away.

Driving out of the parking lot, Mandy saw a familiar figure, shoulders hunched against the rain, locking the front door to the school. It was only as she recognized Grange's pickup as one of the last cars in the lot that she began to wonder if he had seen her kissing Vince. "Well, what if he did?" she muttered. "It wouldn't matter to him."

Somehow that thought brought back the weepy feeling. As she drove through the pelting rain toward the Timberlain Road turnoff, a tear spilled over and ran down her cheek.

"I don't think you'll have any more problems with pranks," Leesie said to Mandy as they drove through a driving rain to church Sunday morning.

"What do you mean, pranks?"

"Oh, you know—people trying to get you to leave town."

Mandy's brow creased. "Do you call car wrecks a prank? I call it a threat on my life. Why do you think they are now magically going to cease?"

"Because you played the 'Stinkbug Boogie.' People got to see what you're like. It didn't hurt that Rael kissed you, either."

Mandy turned the wipers to high. "That's faulty logic, for sure. By the way, who told him to call me Sweetiebug?"

Leesie grinned. "I told Jake, and Jake must have told him. How was it, by the way? The kiss?"

Mandy tried to keep from smiling. "It was, um, surprising. Very surprising. But nice."

"Feel any twinges? Any quickening pulse?"

"I'd be foolish to do that. He's no freer than . . . well, never mind."

"He isn't? I thought he was a widower."

Mandy shook her head. "Not only is Jake's mom still alive, but Rael and she have never divorced."

"No! Really?" Leesie was silent a moment, obviously digesting that information. "Still, it was a great kiss," she said finally.

Mandy tried to suppress a smile. "It wasn't the only kiss I got last night."

"I knew it! I've seen the way Mr. Timberlain looks at you. Where did he make his move? In his office? It's nice and private."

"No, silly! Vince."

"You let Heathcliff kiss you? Not very choosy, are you?"

Mandy frowned over at her sister. "Aren't you being judgmental? I don't think you've spoken two words to him. You don't know anything about what kind of man he is."

"You're right," Leesie said as they pulled into the church parking lot. "If he's at church today, I'll make a point of asking him afterwards what he thought about the sermon."

Mandy found a parking space close to the back door. She dashed through the rain behind her sister and followed her into the church, catching sight of Grange across the foyer in a navy suit and a blue tie that made his eyes brilliant. It was the first time she had seen him dressed up, and something fluttered in her chest. She couldn't seem to keep from glancing at him when he wasn't looking, but she didn't want to have to face him. Once they entered the chapel, she pulled Leesie into a pew on the other side of the aisle from the Timberlains, and as soon as the service was over, she bolted.

Leesie followed her out the door. "What's the hurry? Aren't you going to stay and visit?"

"Not today. I've got things to do at home." Mandy unlocked the car, and they got in.

Her sister turned in her seat and continued to press. "What is so important at home?"

Not willing to confess that she was embarrassed to meet Grange Timberlain, Mandy tried a diversion. "I didn't see Rael."

"No. He had to go back east for something. I don't know if it was the business or a tour."

Mandy drove slowly out of the parking lot. "Business? What business? He's a mailman."

Leesie stared at her sister. "You mean you don't know that he's a luthier?"

"A what? A Lutheran?"

Leesie giggled. "A luthier. He builds guitars. Really, really good ones. People pay thousands and thousands of dollars for his guitars. He built the one I have in my bedroom."

"Thousands of dollars? And you have it just leaning up against the wall in your bedroom?"

"It's okay, Mandy. That's what Jake said to do."

"You mentioned a tour. Rael told me he had quit performing."

"It's something for the National Endowment for the Arts." Leesie thought a moment. "Do I have that right? It's a concert about different guitar-playing styles. Roots music, I think. Very PBS."

"When will he be home?" Mandy asked. "He won't miss the festival, will he?"

"He'll be here for the opening ceremony on Friday, I know. There's going to be some big announcement that concerns him."

"Leesie, how do you know all this?"

She shrugged. "I listen, I guess. You know, this is going to be such an exciting week. I'm so glad Mom is coming."

"Oh my gosh! I forgot! Where are we going to bed people down?"

"Mom's coming alone, so I'll give her my room and sleep on the couch. You'll be on your own to shop and get ready," Leesie warned. "I'm going to be buried in festival prep."

Monday morning, as Mandy sat in her office, she reflected that, besides Nettie Maypole, she must be the only person in Limestone not involved in getting ready for the festival. Everyone seemed to have a mission. Somehow, Mandy had hoped for a change after Saturday night—a sign that she was accepted, like being asked to help with the festival. Forgetting that she had pointedly ignored Grange the day before, she frowned when she saw he was calendared out of his office all week long.

Her dark mood disappeared with Mrs. Reilly's appearance Monday afternoon. The reading teacher announced she had arranged for a sub for the next three days and that she wanted to spend however long it took working out details of Mandy's proposal for revamping the reading program.

"It's all well and good for Grange and half the district to take off two weeks for Opening Festival, but some of us have to make sure that education happens," Mrs. Reilly declared. She also mentioned that Grange had given the meeting his blessing.

Mandy agreed with Mrs. Reilly's stand on the festival and gave her all the time not already commandeered by Nettie. As they worked together, Mandy found the reading teacher knowledgeable, pragmatic, and not the least bit hesitant to say what would not work and why. The result was that, after a three-day marathon, they ended up with a workable plan, a schedule, and ideas for funding.

In the meantime, Mandy accepted an invitation to go to dinner with Vince on Monday evening. In the cold, gray, light of a very rainy Sunday, she had realized that the night before she might have given Vince a signal that their relationship had taken a step toward physical intimacy, and she was determined to flash an amber light. As they sat in a corner booth at Bobo's Burgers in Stallo, and Vince reached over to take her hand, Mandy took a deep breath and plunged in. "Vince, I need to talk to you."

He looked a little startled, but said, "Okay, go ahead." He didn't release her hand.

"How much time have we actually spent together?"

He smiled. "Not nearly enough."

"Be serious. We've talked at the district offices a couple of times, once in my office, and once through your car window. We spent a part of a day together, and Saturday night we spent an hour or so at the concert."

"And a half hour in the parking lot. Don't forget that."

Mandy gently pulled her hand away. "That's what I'm talking about. I can't blame it on the moonlight, since there wasn't any, but I was carried away by . . . something, and I acted completely out of character."

Vince sat back and regarded her. "You looked glad to see me. Was that out of character?"

"No. I *was* glad to see you. But I don't really know you. You don't know me or what I expect in a relationship, and I don't know what you expect when we get to the end of what we began in the parking lot. I don't want either of us to be surprised or hurt."

His white teeth flashed. "I like the sound of that—that we began something in the parking lot."

"What I'm trying to say is that I don't want to complicate the 'getting to know' process by a physical entanglement. What I want is more than a lover, more than monogamous till death, and until you can understand all that entails, I don't want to muddy the water."

"Is there 'more than monogamous till death'?" he asked.

"To me there is. I think a couple needs to have a common goal. They need to be willing to work together for things they're passionate about." Mandy was going to continue, but she was interrupted by the sound of Vince's phone ringing.

"Sorry," he said. He checked the caller's number and swore under his breath. The phone rang twice more before he said, "I'm expecting a call. Do you mind?"

She shook her head, and he rose. As he walked away, she heard him say, "Hi, Doc."

While she waited, she finished her burger. Vince returned and asked if she minded if they left right then. "I've got a ton of stuff to do, and something has come up. We can work on getting better acquainted on the ride home." He held out his hand to help her out of the booth, and as she stood, he looked down at her with warm, expressive eyes. "I've learned that good things, like good wine, often take time to happen. I'll wait."

"Interesting analogy," Mandy said dryly.

They talked about lots of things on the way home, but Vince carried the burden of the conversation, obviously trying to shepherd the acquaintance process. When they got to her house, he put his arm around her shoulders as they ran through the pelting rain to the door. Then he kissed her on the cheek and said, "I'm crazy about you, Mandy, though it may not seem like it this next week."

"What do you mean?"

"My schedule and yours will make it so we won't have any time to work on our 'getting to know you' project. But next week should see everything taken care of. Dinner next Monday for sure?"

"For sure," she said.

As he turned to go, he said, "The river is coming up pretty fast with all this rain, but it shouldn't overtop the dike they put in after your house got flooded last time. Keep an eye on it. Even if the dike should break, it wouldn't do anything more than inconvenience you and wet your rugs. Call me if you see it leaking water. You've got my phone number?"

"Yes. You gave it to me—oh, it seems so long ago, but it was just weeks. Thank you, Vince. Good night."

"Good night." He sprinted through the downpour to his car, and Mandy went inside, trying to decide whether she was happy or sad about the fact that she didn't have to face the complications of her relationship with Vince for a week.

She may not have to face it, but that didn't mean it wasn't on her mind. She was glad for meetings with Nettie and Mrs. Reilly that tore her attention away from Vince's plans for her future. And from Grange's empty office.

During this time, Mandy tried to get in touch with Fran to let her know she wasn't leaving, that she didn't want out of her lease. She tried Fran's house and her office, but the phone rang and rang without the answering machine picking up. Mandy called the Qwik-E Market on Wednesday afternoon, and when Elizabeth answered, she asked if she knew what Fran's schedule was.

"I haven't seen her, actually," the young woman said. "Mr. Laffitte has been managing the stores this week because Fran is getting ready for an audit next week. She's been really grouchy, so I'm not sorry she's not here, but Mr. Laffitte is a bit of a slave driver."

"If you see Fran, please tell her I need to talk to her," Mandy said. Elizabeth said she would, but it wasn't until Thursday that Mandy was able to talk to Fran. The driving, soaking deluge that had poured down since Saturday night finally stopped, but Mandy was aware that the river would continue rising for a while, and she wanted to check on the dike above her house. When her work session with Mrs. Reilly ended at noon, she headed home.

Mandy was slowing down to turn off onto the gravel road when she saw that Fran was home. She drove there instead, catching her friend as she was getting in her car. Mandy pulled into the driveway, turned off the key, and jumped out. "Fran,

I'm so glad I caught you. I've been trying to reach you by phone."

At her greeting, Fran turned. Her hair was pulled back into a ponytail, and she wore no makeup on her flat, round face. Dark circles under her eyes accentuated an unusual pallor, and Mandy exclaimed, "Oh, Fran! Are you all right?"

"I'm just tired. Vince isn't paying me enough for all the responsibility I shoulder. When this audit is over, I'm going to hit him up for a raise."

"Well, here's one less thing for you to worry about. I'm not leaving."

Fran's reaction was almost a snarl. "What?"

For a moment Mandy could only stand with her mouth open. "I'm staying," she repeated. "At least through the end of the school year."

Fran's face twisted into an ugly sneer. "So you caved. I thought you were built of stronger stuff."

"What are you talking about, Fran?"

"Do you know what Grange says about you? He doesn't want you here. He says he wants to find whoever made your wheel fall off and give him a medal. He says some of the things you do are so wrongheaded it curls his hair, and the happiest day of his life will be when he sees your shirttail hitting your backside as you leave town."

Mandy felt tears welling. "Fran, why are you saying this?"

"To help you. Wise up! You think that because Grange invited you into his office for a cozy little chat that he's fallen for you, but I'm here to tell you that ain't so. He and I have an understanding. He's mine, Mandy."

Fran got in her pickup, slammed the door, and started the engine, but seconds later she rolled down her window. "And here's another thing. Those incidents stopped when I put out word you were leaving. Don't be surprised when they start up again. People want you gone. I won't be responsible for what happens because you're so stubborn."

Mandy felt as if someone had hit her in the chest with a sledgehammer. Hugging her arms close, she bent over and turned away as Fran spun gravel driving away. Long after the sound of the pickup had faded in the distance, Mandy stayed, leaning against her car for support because her knees had gone weak. "You and Grange?" she asked the silent, empty air. "You and Grange?

Mandy was so debilitated by her meeting with Fran that she almost forgot what she had driven home for. After she finally got in her car and drove down the gravel road, she saw the river in the distance and remembered the dike.

She parked and trudged upstairs to put on her sweats and running shoes. Though she didn't feel like it, she forced herself to head out on a trail through the woods to a place where she could look down on the barrier thrown up to protect the house. From where she stood, everything looked fine. The water still had a foot to go to reach the top, and the downstream side of the dike was dry.

Mandy was grateful for that assurance, but it didn't displace the hollow feeling in her chest. She recognized a return of the dark emptiness she'd felt as she watched the lights of Albuquerque in her rearview mirror. "So, is that it, Dr. Stinkbug?" Her voice sounded loud in the stillness of the woods. "You're in love with Grange Timberlain?"

Sighing, she looked back toward her house, not quite ready to face a long afternoon alone shadowed by the memory of Fran reaching up to ruffle the hair at the nape of Grange's neck. Instead, she turned upriver and began to trot along a path that, she suspected, would bring her to the familiar one that followed the riverbank.

She found the trail presently and quickened her pace, trying to outrun the memory of Fran's words. *He wants you gone. The things you do are so wrongheaded, it curls his hair. He's mine.* When she came to the place in the pine plantation that led out to Timberlain Road, Mandy didn't even pause but continued at a punishing pace alongside the river. She was in new territory now, and in places the trail ran perilously close to the edge. She slowed her pace in those areas because the path was ribbed by the roots of trees and bushes that grew beside the trail and sprang from the steep sides of the riverbank.

Mandy had run almost to the limit of her endurance when she finally stopped to rest. Standing with her hands on her hips, she looked down at the dark, swirling water below as she inhaled air heavily laden with the scent of pine. The only sound she could hear above her own breathing was the river, but as respiration grew easier, she heard voices.

Thinking that she might be able to beg a drink of water, she walked toward the sound, making her way through the trees and sparse undergrowth. The voice she heard was deep and booming with a strange accent. The man was complaining about the cold, and as she stepped into a clearing, she saw him. Dressed in a blue jacket and black watch cap, he bent over a large metal apparatus and stuffed wood into a firebox. It took her only a moment to process the meaning of the circular vat and the loops of metal tubing and realize this must be the still Doc MacDonald had talked about.

Instinctively, she stepped back into the cover of the bushes, but at that moment, the man in the watch cap shut the firebox door, turned around, and spied her. He looked African American and loomed taller than she expected, with muscular arms and a neck as thick as a small tree. He raised a ham-like hand to his mouth and hollered, "Hey, Grange! You got a visitor."

"Grange?" Mandy whispered. As he stepped out from behind the steaming still, she remembered Mo saying, "Grange brings a lot of money to the district." Mo wouldn't tell her how Grange got the money, but right here, right now, the means was graphically evident, and it was criminal. She had fallen in love with a crook.

She felt her diaphragm tighten, and saliva streamed into her mouth as she turned and began to run back the way she had come, afraid that at any moment she was going to be sick to her stomach.

She heard Grange call her name, but that only propelled her faster. Crashing through the bushes, she finally came to the trail. As she paused to catch her breath, she tried to will the nausea away.

"Mandy, wait!"

She could see glimpses of Grange's blue shirt through the branches that were just now beginning to leaf out. Panicked by the thought that he might catch her, she sprinted down the trail, her mouth open as she gasped for air. A bothersome black edge appeared around her field of vision, and she shook her head to clear her sight as she plowed on. She could hear the pounding of his footsteps behind her, and when she looked over her shoulder to see where he was, her toe struck a root. She stumbled forward out of control, arms windmilling as she tried to stay upright. She almost managed it, but the last step she took was only half on the trail. The end of her foot hung in thin air, and when the ground under her heel crumbled away, she felt herself pitching head first over the edge. Frantically, she grabbed at the bushes growing on the vertical bank, snared a slender willow, and hung suspended in midair.

"Mandy!" Grange bellowed. "Mandy!" He sounded frantic.

"Here," she croaked, but she knew he couldn't hear her.

"Mandy!" He was right above her.

She looked up and saw him sliding on his belly over the edge, reaching out his hands to her. He seemed to be hanging by his toes, and he stretched his fingers out to touch her hand.

"Can you climb up the branch?" he asked.

She shook her head. "I don't have the strength."

"Yes, you do. Look at me! Mandy, look at me. You can. Six inches higher, and I can reach you."

She looked into his eyes, but just then the willow tore away from the bank, and she dropped another foot. Held only by two cord-like roots, she was a few scant feet above the murky floodwater.

"Mandy, listen. Moses is going to pull me up, and I'm going to send him for a rope. Hang on tight, and we'll get you out of there soon. Don't be afraid. Hang on tight."

As she dangled from the willow branch and watched Grange disappear over the edge, she suddenly felt the full weight of her peril.

"Grange!" she shouted.

His head appeared over the bank. "I'm here. I've sent Moses back for a rope."

"I don't know how long I can hang on."

"You can do it, Mandy. You've got strong hands. You'll manage."

"Grange!" she screamed as the roots tore farther away from the bank and dropped her knee-deep into the water.

He reached his hand out in a futile gesture. "Hang on, Mandy. I hear Moses coming. Hang on, darling. He's almost here."

Grange disappeared for only a moment, but in that instant, the bank gave away around the roots, and Mandy and the willow slipped into the icy waters of the Hiesel and began to drift downstream.

There was a surreal, slow-motion quality about the whole

experience. She sank up to her chin and then bobbed and twirled around in the water, facing upstream where she had a good view of Grange standing on the bank, making sweeping gestures with his arms as he spoke to his companion. Then he sat on the bank and slid over the edge, dropping feet first in the river. He disappeared from view in the foliage at the bottom, but soon Mandy saw his head sticking up above the muddy flow.

Her teeth began to chatter as chilling reality set in, and she examined the nearest bank. It rose steeply and offered no way out of the floodwaters for as far as she could see, but she knew that around the bend the bank wasn't so high. In her mind's eye, she saw the dike that protected her house and decided she would put all her energies into staying afloat until she could make her way to the side of the river, where she could climb out at the levee.

Mandy turned around to look for Grange, but all she could see was the dark bulk of a tree trunk bearing down on her, sideways. Stroking as hard as she could and coming up with a mouthful of dirty water in the process, she tried to get to the end of the log before it bumped into her. She just made it, and as it passed, she kicked and lunged, reaching to grasp a crooked limb. Her hands were so cold she couldn't feel the branch, but she immediately felt the drag of the river lessen. She pulled herself close to the log, draped her arms over it, and was just about to murmur a thankful prayer when she heard Grange.

"Mandy!"

He sounded quite close. She twisted around to mark where he was.

"Mandy!" He was upriver and farther out. "You've got to let go," he hollered. "Get out in the middle."

She was so cold she could hardly unclench her jaw, but she shouted, "No! We're just about to the bend. After that the bank drops off. Come here."

He began swimming toward her. When he got nearer, he shouted urgently, "The logjam, Mandy! You've got to get away from it! Come out here!"

Grange didn't have to say it twice. Mandy's adrenal glands kicked in the afterburners as she remembered the story of how his fiancée had died. She pushed away from temporary safety and began furiously swimming toward the middle. He continued to stroke toward her, calling encouragement.

"Come on, Mandy. A little farther. We've got to be past the middle."

"I don't think—" she began, but she got another mouthful of water and came up coughing and sputtering.

Grange's voice was louder. "Come on, Mandy. You can do it."

She saw that they were sweeping around the bend, and she lost heart. "I can't. I can't go any farther."

Then he was there beside her. She heard his voice in her ear and felt the warmth of his breath on the nape of her neck. "Yes, you can," he said. "Grab onto me and I'll pull you."

She turned and looked into his eyes. "My hands won't work. I can't hold on."

"It doesn't matter," he said, looking downriver. "We'd never make it now. We're too close. Listen, Mandy, I'm going to try to steer us to the best place, and at the last minute, I'm going to get us as far out of the water as possible, so when I say kick, you kick like a mule. I'll get the best handhold I can, and I'm going to hold onto you while I do it. I'll pin you to the log. It won't be comfortable, but it will keep you from going under, I think. If we can hang on until help arrives, we'll be all right."

She felt him put his arm around her as they drifted toward the jumble of logs that didn't look anything like they had the day she sat there in the sunshine. They were partially submerged and the water boiled around them, but there was no great sucking sound, no evidence of danger.

"Ready?" The logs loomed closer, and they were being swept laterally. "Now! Kick!"

Mandy did her best, but she couldn't feel her legs to know if they had obeyed the message. Grange had his arm firmly around her waist, and as his efforts lifted them out of the water, he grabbed onto a limb on the opposite side of the log. The current pinned him against her and held her fast.

"Can you grab on to that knob sticking up?" he asked.

"I don't know. I don't know if I can work my hand." She reached out and saw that her hand did close over the stubby limb, though she couldn't feel it against her palm.

"That's my girl. Now grab that other one with your other hand."

Mandy did so, and they clung in silence to their tenuous handholds as the inexorable pressure of the Hiesel tried to scrape them off of the log and swallow them whole.

"Grange?"

"Yeah?"

"It feels like it's pulling me down. It feels like I've slipped down."

"I've got you," he murmured. His mouth was by her temple. "We're going to be all right. We just have to hang on."

"I don't know if I can."

"Then I'll hang on for both of us. Don't give up, Mandy. I've got you."

"I'm slipping, Grange. I can feel it."

"It's an illusion. The water fools you into thinking you're going down, but you're not. Listen!"

She strained to hear, but could detect nothing over the sound of the water. "What is it?"

"I thought I heard—there it is. It's a boat. Do you hear it?"

She shook her head. "Don't tell me lies just to give me hope, Grange Timberlain."

"I'm not. We're going to be all right."

"How do you know?"

"I told Moses to go to the Qwik-E Market and get Vince."

Just then Mandy heard the roaring engine of a riverboat that swept in an arc until it was just above them, and then it drifted down under power, stopping to hang just feet away from the logjam. Moses stood in the back with a rope, and between him and Grange, they got it fastened around the two in jeopardy. Moses said something to Vince, and as he slowly eased the throttle forward, Mandy felt the rope tighten around them, cutting off her wind.

"Oh, Grange!" she gasped.

"It's all right. It won't be long," he promised through gritted teeth.

He was right. The next moment, she heard a deep voice say, "Slack the rope," and she felt herself being lifted into the boat by the strong hands and arms of Grange's friend. Shivering violently, she looked anxiously over the gunwale as Moses grabbed Grange under the arms and hauled him in.

Immediately, Vince pushed the throttle forward, and the boat leapt into the current, leaving the logjam behind as it circled around and headed downstream to the boat landing at Limestone. It was only then that he turned and looked at Mandy. He didn't say anything, but his eyes were stern and his face ashen.

Her teeth began to chatter again, and Moses silently handed her a fleece jacket. She pulled it on and turned to look at Grange, slumped on the bench seat beside her with his head tilted back and his eyes closed. He held his left arm with his right hand, and blood trickled between his fingers.

"What happened?" Mandy asked. "Let me see." She tried to pull his hand away.

"Leave it," he said without opening his eyes. "I'm putting pressure on it."

"What happened?" she repeated.

"There was a branch sticking out. Puncture wound." His dark beard accentuated the pallor of his skin.

She sucked in her breath as she remembered his arm around her and how the current had pressed them against the massive tree trunk. She had been frightened and whining, and he had held her, even though doing so had driven a wooden spike into his flesh. "Oh, Grange, I'm so sorry." She covered his hand with hers.

"Not to worry." His fingers lifted just slightly and curled around hers.

Moses peeled his jacket off, wrapped it around Grange, and then stripped his watch cap off and pulled it over Grange's head.

"You're a true friend, Moses," he murmured.

Vince piloted the boat slowly through submerged shrubbery to the floats that had risen in the flood well above the regular docking area. As he tied up the boat, he spoke to Moses. "You'd better get him down to Stallo and have someone look at his arm. If there's some of his shirt inside the wound, it could turn ugly. He'd better have a tetanus shot, too."

"Yes, sir." Moses put his arm around Grange and helped him up.

Grange turned to Vince, who had climbed back in the boat and was standing by Mandy. "Thanks for coming, Vince."

"I came because of Mandy," he said curtly as he scooped her up in his arms.

Grange met his eyes. "I know."

Moses nodded to Mandy. "Ma'am." Pulling on Grange's good arm, he supported him as he stepped over the gunwale and made his way up the walkway to the pickup.

"You don't need to carry me. I can walk," Mandy said as Vince stepped out onto the dock. "Oh, look. It sucked the shoes and socks off my feet."

He carried her up the hill to his SUV. "Whatever possessed you to be running along the side of the river?" he asked grimly.

"Oh, Vince, don't scold," she said tiredly.

"I'm not scolding," he said, tightening his hold on her. "I was afraid I wasn't going to make it in time, that's all."

"Well, you did." She smiled for the first time all day. "And I was sure glad to see you."

He put her on the seat, got in, started the car, and turned the heater on high. He didn't speak as he drove, but more than once his eyes rested on her as she sat with her knees pulled up under her chin, the jacket tucked under her feet, and her hands buried in the sleeves.

When they pulled into her driveway, there was a car with Tennessee license plates parked by the Miata. "Who is that?" Vince asked as he opened the door and lifted her out.

"I don't know." Mandy put her arm around his neck.

He carried her up the front steps. "Is the door locked?"

"No. I didn't intend to be gone long." She looked up as the door opened and a tall, raven-haired woman stood on the threshold. Mandy stared. She knew she had never seen this stranger, yet there was something familiar about the high cheekbones, slender frame, and hair that fell straight and loose down her back.

Vince paused briefly. "Hello, Lovey," he said as he passed through into the living room. "What brings you into this part of the country?"

Mandy opened her eyes and looked at the digital readout on her bedside clock. It said eight, but it was full dark, and as she tried to remember what day it was and why it should be dark at eight in the morning, the sound of a rich contralto voice singing "on the wings of a pure, white dove . . ." floated up to her loft from the room below. It was then that she remembered.

She remembered Vince carrying her upstairs with the black-haired stranger following, asking questions about what happened. Vince had answered in clipped sentences, but as he set Mandy down by the bathroom door, his tone had changed. "Take a hot shower," he advised tenderly. "I'll go fix a warm drink."

"I'll do that," Lovey had said. "I can take over from here. I'll put her to bed with a hot water bottle and stay with her while she rests. I know you've got things you've got to do."

Vince's voice had showed more than a hint of irritation. "How do you know that, Lovey?"

"I would imagine you'd like to get your boat out of the water. And when I was at the Qwik-E Market a while ago, people were standing in line four deep because there was only one clerk. She looked pretty frazzled."

Lovey walked past Mandy into the bathroom and turned on the shower. "I thought you'd be glad to know I'm going to stay with her," she said over the sound of running water. "Ease your mind."

"Yeah. Okay." Vince turned to Mandy. "I hate to leave."

"Don't worry!" She kissed his cheek. "Thank you so much for dropping everything to come to my rescue. I know you saved my life."

His eyes filled with tears, and he cleared his throat. He laughed a small, rueful laugh. "It was pretty tense there for a few minutes. I was worried about, um . . . our project. Uh, I'm glad it turned out all right."

Lovey came and stood with her hand on the bathroom door. "I'm going to put her in the shower now."

Vince dropped a quick kiss on Mandy's lips and smiled for the first time. "I'm outta here. Call you later?"

"Call her tomorrow," Lovey said. "I'm hoping she'll sleep."

Mandy did sleep. Sometime in the late afternoon she warmed up and surfaced enough to pull off the wool socks that were making her feet sweat. Then she rolled over and disappeared again into a deep, restoring slumber.

Awake now and with her memory returning, questions she had been too cold and tired to ask earlier came tumbling one after another. She threw off the covers and padded over in her red sweats to stand at the balustrade. Below her, haloed by the light of a single lamp, sat Lovey Timberlain, playing Jake's guitar and singing.

"Hello," Mandy called down to her.

Lovey looked up and smiled. "Feeling better?"

"Yes. I finally got warm."

"I'm Lovey Timberlain—Willow and Jake's mother."

"I know. Even if Vince hadn't said your name, I'd know who you are because Willow looks so much like you."

"Does she?" Lovey set the guitar in the corner. "Do you want to know why I'm here?"

"In the worst way!" Mandy came downstairs and sat in a chair opposite her guest.

Lovey watched her descend but didn't look at her as she began to speak, tracing the pattern on the upholstery with her finger. "I came back to see Rael, to see the kids, to see if maybe there was a place for me in the family again. I called Granny Timberlain and told her I wanted to stay in neutral territory, and she said I should come to your house. She was going to call and let you know, but I think you must have been out."

Mandy laughed. "I was otherwise engaged this afternoon. But tell me, what made you decide to come back?"

"It's a bit of a story, and one that begins badly. I was such a fool." Lovey shook her head at the memory. "Have you ever done something that you knew you shouldn't, but you couldn't help yourself? No, that's silly. Of course you haven't."

Mandy tucked her feet under her and leaned back against the chair. "Like falling for three men in quick succession? The first is married, the second owns a winery, and the third runs a still."

"Oh, no! Really?" Lovey thought a minute. "Is Vince the second one? Then who is the third? Is he from around here? Do I know him?"

Mandy covered her face with her hands and wailed, "It's Rael's cousin, Grange, and I'm just sick about it."

"Grange has a still? No! That's not possible!"

"I saw it with my own eyes this afternoon."

Just then there was a knock at the door. "What if that's Grange?" Mandy whispered.

"Do you want it to be?"

Mandy stood. "He was hurt, you know, saving my life."

"I thought you said Vince saved your life."

"He did. But Grange saved it first. It's all so complicated." Mandy walked to the door, opened it, and stood gaping at the man who stood on the porch holding out a package.

"Hello, Mandy," Rael said. "I brought you something."

With her hand on the doorknob, Mandy looked at Lovey and back at Rael. "You're not going to kiss me again, are you?"

"Well, now that you mention it—" He strode in and chucked the package onto a small table by the door. Eyes twinkling, he put one arm around Mandy's shoulders and another around her waist, bending her back in a vintage Hollywood pose as he brought his lips down to hers.

"Mmm," she said, pointing awkwardly to the corner where Lovey sat. When she could speak, she whispered, "We're not alone."

Rael looked up, did a classic double-take and would have dropped Mandy if she hadn't had her arms around his neck. As he straightened suddenly, she regained her feet, laughing at his discomposure.

"Breathe, Rael, breathe," she whispered in his ear. Stepping away, she smiled at him and said cheerfully, "I see you already know my guest." Turning to Lovey, Mandy was surprised to see a tear running down her cheek.

"It's not like it appears," Mandy assured her. "It's a bit of a joke, really. You see, he kissed me the other night in front of the whole town . . ." Her voice trailed off as she realized she wasn't helping the situation.

Lovey's face lost color as she watched Rael move to stand by Mandy, and her voice was husky. "You didn't tell me the name of the married man."

"His name is Guy Noel," Mandy said briskly and added, grinning, "Grange calls him the Dog's Dinner." Looking sideways at Rael, she was glad to see a tiny smile crease his grim face.

"I want to see what you got me," Mandy said, trying to ease the tension. She picked up the package, and after tearing off the paper, she looked up, mystified. "You got me a box of printer labels?"

Rael had been staring at Lovey. "What? No. I used that because it fit."

Mandy opened the box and frowned. She flipped a switch to illuminate the room so she could read and examined the sheet of paper lying in the bottom. "It's music," she said. "By Carlos Rosa? Manuscript? And signed 'To Mandy'? Rael! Where did you get this?"

"From Carlos. He was on the tour with me. Playing one of my guitars, I might add. I told him how big a fan you are, and he sent that to you."

"Oh, thank you, dear friend!" Mandy danced over and hugged him. "We'll play it together later, but you interrupted a story Lovey was telling me. Finish the story, Lovey."

Lovey shook her head. "I'd rather find out about Grange's still. I think you're wrong, you know."

Rael looked from one to the other. "Grange's still what? What do you mean?"

Mandy grimaced. "I found out today that the way Grange supports his music program is by making moonshine."

Rael stared openmouthed at Mandy.

She nodded in the face of his unbelief. "I saw him. There was no mistake."

Rael cleared his throat. "You're right. The still supports Grange's music program, but not—"

It was Mandy's turn to stare as Rael turned his back to her, hunched his shoulders, and began to make a coughing sound.

She put a hand on his shoulder. "Rael? Are you all right?"

He turned to face her, and her concern turned to dismay when she saw he was laughing. Tears streamed down his face as he opened his mouth and let the sound roll out, great, deep guffaws that made him stumble over and collapse on the couch. "Oh, Mandy," he said when he could finally talk. "You *are* a wonder."

"Well, you've made it all perfectly clear," she said. "What is there to laugh about?"

"That's my still. Grange was tending it for me."

"Your still! Hold the phone, Ramon!" She plopped down on a chair. "You mean you're the one that—that—"

"Stop jumping to conclusions, Mandy." Rael sat up and wiped his eyes. "I use the still to make the finish I put on my guitars. It's an old family recipe made of pine pitch. My grandpappy planted that grove of pines up the road just so he could harvest the sap to make his own shellac, and he taught me how to make it before he died."

Mandy frowned. "I don't understand. What does that have to do with the school's music program?"

Rael spread his hands. "My guitars have become, um, popular, and when musicians know that by buying one of my guitars, they're directly supporting music in the schools, they generally pay two, three times what I ask. It's crazy. That's what I meant when I said that the still supports Grange's music program."

"Oh. Then you mean Grange isn't . . . doesn't?"

"Nope."

"But why wouldn't he tell me? What's the big secret?"

"That's my fault. I wouldn't let him tell anyone but Mo that the money came from me."

"Oh, Rael! I'm so relieved! I've got to go see how he is." Mandy jumped to her feet and got her jacket out of the coat closet. "He was hurt, you know. Where does he live? I don't even know where he lives."

"Just past me. It's Timberlain Road, after all."

Mandy looked around for her purse and car keys. "Lovey, while I'm gone you're to tell Rael your story." When he put up his hand in a defensive gesture, Mandy shook her finger at him. "You are to listen. That's not an order—it's an earnest request. Please, Rael, listen with your—"

Mandy never got a chance to finish the sentence, for a huge explosion ripped through the silence of the night, rattling windows and echoing down the valley.

Mandy and Lovey spoke together. "What was that?"

Rael sprang off the couch and opened the door. "It came from upriver," he said grimly. "I can't imagine Grange left the still unattended."

Mandy sucked in her breath. "He had an emergency this afternoon. He may—"

"Listen!" Rael hissed.

All three stood motionless and silent on the deck. "Hear it?" Rael whispered.

Mandy shook her head.

"Someone running?" Lovey ventured, but she spoke to empty space, for Rael suddenly sprinted down the steps and rounded the corner of the house at a dead run.

Mandy walked to the side of the porch and looked into the blackness beyond the pool of light that fell through the windows onto the ground below. She could hear the sound of someone crashing through the brush, but she couldn't see a thing. "Where's he going? And why am I whispering?" She looked around. "Lovey?"

"I'm over here. I'm so weak-kneed I thought I'd better sit down."

"Was it the explosion? I don't think we're in any danger."

"No. It was being that close to Rael again." Lovey took a deep breath and exhaled slowly.

Mandy walked over and sat on the railing opposite her. "Was it hard, seeing him again? How does he look?"

"He looks wonderful, but my heart sank when he kissed you. Tell me, Mandy, do you feel anything for him?"

"Certainly. I love him. Who wouldn't? But I'm not in love with him. I think I could have been, but he let me know early on that his heart was taken. Or was it his lungs? He said he didn't think he could go on breathing when you left."

"He said that?"

"Yes. Of course that was when Grange and I were crossing swords. And Grange was ugly then, too. I forgot all about Rael when Grange handsomed up and got civil."

Lovey laughed. "You're not making sense, but you make me feel better. So, you truly like Grange? How does he feel about you?"

"Well, yesterday I was ready to believe that he and my neighbor . . . at least that's what she said. But then, when he was trying to save me, he called me 'darling.'" She paused a moment and then spoke more softly. "And he asked Vince to come out on the river and save us. I know what that cost him. He did it for me."

"So you know about how Lori Wilcox died?"

Mandy nodded.

"And Vince? Where does he figure into all this?"

Mandy grinned. "Ah, Vince. Well, he has money." She counted on her fingers. "He's handsome, he's mysterious, and he knows how to blow up buildings. What more could a woman ask for?"

"Be serious. He's obviously in love with you. I don't think he's the kind of man you play fast and loose with."

"I will be serious. Everyone seems to think he's a little sinister. I think he's a good man. It's just that his idea of success is colored by his childhood. He's driven by a need to . . . to . . ."

"To outshine the Timberlains?"

Mandy laughed. "I think so. And speaking of Timberlains, I think I hear Rael coming." She moved back to the edge of the deck, and Lovey came with her.

Presently, Rael stepped into the circle of light. He was breathing hard and walking with his hands on his hips.

"Who were you chasing?" Lovey asked.

He shook his head. "I don't know, but whoever it was ran up the hill on the path to Fran's house. I was too far behind to see who it was, but—"

"But what?" Mandy asked.

He looked back into the darkness, then down at the patch of light at his feet, and finally at Mandy. "When I got to the top of the hill, a car was just leaving Fran's driveway."

Mandy said nothing, but she didn't take her eyes off Rael.

"It looked like Vince's car. I couldn't be sure, but it looked like he was in it."

Lovey turned to Mandy. "You did say he knows how to blow up things."

She shook her head and made a dismissive gesture. "Was Fran there? Did you talk to her?"

"The house was dark. I didn't see her pickup. It looked like no one was home."

Lovey walked to the railing and looked out into the darkness. "But what was the explosion?"

Rael let his eyes rest on his wife for a moment and then turned to Mandy. "Do you have a flashlight? I want to check on something."

She got one out of the kitchen cupboard and watched him descend the stairs and walk out of the circle of light, heading upriver.

"Where's he going?" Lovey asked.

Mandy stood by her with her arms folded for warmth. "I don't know."

"Have you thought about the possibility that Vince came to see you and got here just as Rael kissed you? You were standing right in front of the window."

Mandy shook her head. "He saw Rael kiss me the other night. He never said anything about it."

"That was in front of the whole town. This was private, at home, and the room was pretty dark."

Mandy shook her head again. "I can't see him parking up there and sneaking down."

"There's Rael," Lovey said. They both stood, waiting for him to get within speaking distance.

"The dike's breached," he reported. "That's what the explosion was. Someone blew a hole in it and water's pouring over it."

"Who would do that?" Mandy gripped the porch railing and peered into the darkness. "Do we evacuate?"

Rael shook his head. "I don't think the river's going to rise much more. Why don't you move your cars to higher ground? You might have to wade to get out in the morning, but I don't think it'll be deeper than a foot or two. It won't come in the house."

Mandy walked to the phone and dialed a number she had taped to the fridge. "I'm calling Doc," she announced to the room in general. It was the answering machine that picked up, so she reported the vandalism and hung up. "You don't think there's any danger in staying here?" she asked, digging her car keys out of her pocket.

"I don't think so," Rael said. "Is Leesie sleeping over at Granny's house with Willow and Jake?"

Mandy didn't answer. The feel of the keys in her hand reminded her she had been on her way to see Grange. The sudden explosion, the adrenalin rush and ebb, had swept away the urgency of the moment and made her see that it made more sense to wait until morning.

"Is Leesie staying at Granny's tonight?" Rael repeated.

Mandy looked up. "Oh. Yes. Sorry. I forgot about that. Tomorrow is Opening Festival." She went down the porch steps and headed toward her car.

"Would it make you feel better if I stayed here tonight?"

"Oh, Rael, would you?" She spoke from the shadows. "I've already been in the river once today. I'd feel better if you were here."

Later, as they ate tomato soup and toasted cheese sandwiches, Rael made Mandy tell about her afternoon's adventure. He laughed again at her mistaken assumptions about Grange and the still, but he became solemn and quiet as she talked about falling in the river and how first Grange and then Vince and Moses rescued her. "You were lucky," he said. "Not many people escape the Hiesel."

Lovey cleared the dishes and asked Mandy to play her Carlos Rosa song. She said she would, but only if Lovey would sing afterward. An hour spent with Lovey and Rael singing old harmonies went a long way toward breaking down constraints, and when Mandy said she was going upstairs to bed, they said they would stay up and talk a while longer.

"Don't mind me, I'm putting in earplugs," she called as she turned down the covers. Since she didn't hear a reply, she figured the devices must work. She knelt at her bedside and whispered gratitude for delivery from her fall in the river, and gave thanks for Lovey's return and for what it would mean to all the Timberlains. When her mind wandered to the picture of Grange hanging over the edge, calling out 'Darling,' she decided that wasn't really something she could be thankful for—yet. First she needed to make sure he was calling to her and not to the memory of a woman who died in the river years ago. She said amen, crawled into bed, and made a mental to-do list for tomorrow that had as number 1 a talk with Grange.

Mandy was up before her alarm rang. She dressed quietly in jeans and an NCHS Tarheels sweatshirt and stepped out on the deck. The morning was fresh and windless, and overhead the clouds parted to reveal a small patch of blue. A chorus of birds warbled unseen behind a lacy curtain of white blossoms that had suddenly appeared in the stand of trees at the edge of Mandy's back yard. She took a deep breath and smiled for no reason and then remembered she had come out to check on the flood status.

She looked down and saw the water was still a good twenty feet from the house. Looking like chocolate soup, it spilled diagonally across the road and disappeared in the woods on the other side. Grateful she wouldn't appear on Grange's doorstep in soggy shoes, she checked her image once more in the mirror and then softly descended the stairs.

Rael was asleep on the couch, his hair tousled, an arm hanging over the side, and the blanket pulled up to his ear. Mandy looked at him fondly, whispered, "Cousin," and noiselessly pulled the phone book out of a kitchen drawer. In her planner, she wrote first Fran's address, then Rael's, and finally, Grange's, learning from this exercise the relative location of his house on Timberlain Road.

She picked up her purse and car keys, let herself quietly out of the house, and walked briskly to where the Miata was parked. As she drove up the gravel road, she looked out at the river and shivered, remembering the sapping cold and the drag of the current as she clung to her handholds on the logjam. At the stop sign, as she turned right, lingering impressions of the warmth of Grange's body, the arm that encircled her, and the sound of his voice comforting her, crowded out scarier images. But when she remembered the blood that ran from between his fingers, she pressed harder on the accelerator.

She soon passed the place where the pine plantation began. She had never driven down the road beyond this point, but she recognized the number on the mailbox at Rael's driveway. Grange's would be next.

Mandy's heart began to pound, and she gripped the steering wheel so tightly that each knuckle was topped with white. Fearful of missing the mailbox, she slowed, and it seemed forever before she saw the gap in the trees signaling a driveway. She shifted down and turned onto the lane that led straight through the woods to a clearing on a bluff over the river. As she braked to a stop, she exhaled a great sigh and said, "Well, look at you, Grange Timberlain!"

He lived in a two-story log house facing the river. Topped by a blue metal roof with three dormers and circled by a wide porch covered in the same blue, it had huge, arched windows that let in light and gave a contemporary look to the rustic design. His pickup wasn't in the yard, and though there was another building behind the house, it wasn't a garage. He obviously wasn't home.

Mandy sat a moment surveying the scene, then put the Miata in gear and drove back to the highway, trying to figure out plan B. She was reluctant to see Grange in a public place because of the private nature of what she had to say to him. Which was what? She frowned as she sped along the road. What did she intend to say—*I think I love you?* A little too bold. *So, how are things between you and Fran?* Too snarky. *Thanks for saving my life, and by the way, what did you call me when you were hanging upside down?* Much better.

She almost passed Fran's house before she noticed Grange's pickup sitting in the driveway. As she hit the brakes, did a U-turn, and pulled in beside the truck, Mandy's heart thudded in her chest again. She sat for a moment wondering whether it would be better to wait but decided her courage was waning fast; she'd better talk to Grange while she still had the nerve.

As she got out of the car, she noticed Stevie Joe's red pickup approach the gravel turnoff to her place. It slowed then continued on, and as it rolled by, he turned to stare at Mandy.

Ignoring his rudeness, she went to knock on the back door, which opened into a small breezeway between the house and the garage. No one answered, so she opened the door and called, "Grange? Fran?"

Still no answer. Mandy stepped inside and called, "Grange?" The door that led to the garage was open and the light was on, so she stepped in and looked around. Fran's pickup was stacked with cardboard boxes and the driver's door stood open, but no one was there.

Against the wall by the door sat a stack of boxes labeled "Fireworks. Store away from heat source." A flap on the top box hung open. Mandy looked inside and noticed half the contents were gone. What was left looked like green plastic golf balls, each with three knobs on top and a long fuse.

She thought she heard a sound, so she turned and looked around. "Grange? Fran?" She felt the hair on the back of her neck stand on end, and she quickly stepped out of the garage and back into the breezeway. She opened the other door and called again, then cautiously made her way to the kitchen. No one was there, but as she stood at the window over the sink, she saw Jake's pickup turn off to drive down to her house. Mandy smiled to see that

Willow was in the truck with him and imagined the reunion about to take place. She watched them disappear behind some bushes and waited for the pickup to come into view at the bottom.

Moments passed, and they didn't reappear. Mandy leaned closer to the window to get a wider view, certain she remembered Fran saying she saw Mandy leave her house on the day she lost a wheel. As she stared at the line of vegetation that cut off her view, she sensed, rather than heard, a movement behind her. Just as she began to turn around, something struck her on the side of the head, and all the fireworks in the garage exploded in her brain.

The next thing Mandy was aware of was the discomfort of something pressing into her cheek. She opened her eyes to find a mossy stone six inches away from her nose. When she turned her head, a sharp pain stabbed through it, and a strobe light flashed behind her eyes. As she lay quietly again, the situation eased, and she was able to look around.

A large cedar tree towered above her to the right, and alders sporting new green crowded in on three sides. She held her breath and listened intently, but the only sound she could hear was the chirping of birds in the branches above her.

As she tried to sit up, she found that her hands and feet were bound with bungee cords. The effort to sit cost her a return of the light-and-stab show, but she decided that curling up in a ball because it hurt wasn't going to get her out of there, wherever "there" was. She made another try. This time she was successful.

She drew her knees up between her arms and set to work at the cords on her ankles. Soon, she had her feet unfettered. The bungees wrapped around her wrists weren't so easily undone, but Mandy found if she held her hands together under her right ear, she could grab one of the hooks with her teeth. Heedless of the pain in her head from the pressure, she managed to pull one hook far enough that it slipped off the other, and she was free.

Slowly, she stood and looked around. She was on a primitive road, little more than two tracks through the woods. She could see no farther than the trees that surrounded her, so she had no way of getting her bearings.

"So, Mandy," she muttered. "You have two puzzles. First, who did this to you? Second, which way do you walk to get out of here?"

As she looked one way and another, trying to solve puzzle number two, she became aware of the sound of an approaching vehicle. "Wouldn't it be something if I was right beside the highway?" she said aloud as she started walking in the direction of the sound. She stopped when she saw, flashing through the trees ahead, the red of Stevie Joe's pickup coming down the lane toward her.

Mandy's mouth went dry and she froze, trying to decide what to do. The moment the pickup broke into full view, her feet made up her mind, and she bolted into the woods. Running was difficult because of the downed and rotting trees and thick underbrush, so she hadn't made much progress when she heard a door slam and someone call her name.

"Mandy! Wait!"

The sound of that call was so familiar that she hesitated.

"Mandy! Come back!"

She turned around and saw Grange making his way toward her. Stevie Joe and Moses stood behind him. Grange looked so fierce that she almost ran again, but he stopped her with one word.

"Darling."

Mandy leaned against a tree and waited, watching him walk toward her, noticing how his eyes softened and the corners of his lips lifted as he got closer. A few feet away, he opened his arms. She stumbled forward and felt them close around her.

He pressed his cheek against her hair. "I was afraid we wouldn't find you."

After a moment, she pulled away. "How did you know to look for me? Were you at Fran's?"

"No. Not when you were, anyway. It's all a bit complicated, and I don't understand some of it."

Mandy glanced at the pickup. "What does Stevie Joe have to do with it? He's always driving by and staring at me. He did it again today, just a while ago. I've got a bad feeling about him."

"Don't. He's the one who discovered that Fran kidnapped you."

"Fran? Kidnapped?"

Grange began walking back to the pickup with his arm around Mandy. "Stevie Joe is Tammy's brother, you know. My cousin. He knows you've been teaching Tammy to read, and he's been trying to get up the nerve to ask you to teach him, too."

"But he's married to a teacher! Can't she work with him?"

"Apparently he thinks you can work miracles. Anyway, he was on his way to try again today, and he saw you go into Fran's house. When he came back a few minutes later, Fran was driving off alone in her pickup, your car was still there, and you were no place to be found. I drove up a few moments later—"

"But your truck was there already."

They had reached the red pickup. Mandy greeted Moses, who smiled and extended his hand. She thanked Stevie Joe for coming to get her, and he looked at the ground and mumbled something inaudible in reply.

"We'll ride in the back, Stevie Joe," Grange said. "Moses takes up too much room." He lifted Mandy into the pickup bed and climbed in behind her. "Let us use your coat, Moses. There's a good heater in the pickup. You won't freeze without it."

"This is getting to be a habit," Moses grumbled, but he handed over his jacket and climbed in the cab.

"Who is Moses?" Mandy asked as Grange wrapped her in the huge jacket and then sat beside her.

"He's from Jamaica and comes for every Opening Festival. I first met him in the orphanage when I was there. He teaches here at the high school for the week before, making sure the students in charge of tuning the pans are doing a good job of it. It's a highlight of the year, and the students love to have him come."

"Okay. Let's get back to what happened. You and Moses showed up at Fran's. But wait—your truck was already there. I don't understand."

"Arrgh!" Grange hit his forehead with his fist. "This is so embarrassing. Fran came to my house last night after we got home from the hospital."

"Oh!" Mandy exclaimed in a stricken voice. "How is your arm?"

"It's okay. Fran was all upset and said she wanted to clarify things about us. When I finally understood she was talking about us being a couple—you know, romantically—I'm afraid I was a little blunt. I told her—" Grange stopped and cleared his throat.

"What did you tell her?"

"I said that my heart belonged to someone else."

Breathing seemed to be a problem for Mandy. "Did you mean—were you talking about someone you lost a long time ago?"

He picked up her hand and laced his fingers through hers. "No, I was talking about someone else. Someone I just found."

Mandy took a deep breath. "And who is that someone else?"

"It's you, Sweetiebug." He smiled and leaned down to kiss her.

As Grange's mouth met hers, she put her hand on his cheek and felt the pulse under her fingers. It seemed to be beating in concert with her own.

She sighed and leaned back in the crook of his arm. "So when did you first feel that your heart was taken?"

"The moment I saw you."

Mandy frowned. "But you looked so forbidding, and you couldn't say anything nice to me!"

He laughed. "I had that dang Bell's palsy, and it made me look so strange that I knew you'd never give me a second glance. And then every time I turned around, Vince was there in his brand new Cadillac, bringing you flowers, giving you presents, being suave and polished— all the things I'm not. I'm afraid I didn't handle it very well."

"Oh, yes. Vince." Mandy was quiet for a moment.

"Do you care for him?" Grange asked.

She nodded and felt him stiffen. "I care for him like I care for Rael, I think. You look at him and see someone with money who owns half the town and who travels all over doing something dangerous and dashing. But I see someone who just wants to be a Timberlain."

"I don't understand," Grange said, but he had relaxed.

"Talk to Granny Timberlain about it—she'll explain. I'll tell you what I don't understand. If Fran talked to you last night at your house, what was your pickup doing at her house this morning?" Mandy nestled in and pulled the coat tighter around her as Stevie Joe turned onto the highway and picked up speed.

Grange leaned down to speak in her ear. "She called me first thing and asked me to give her a ride to the school, so I did. I figured that since Moses was with us, I'd be safe from any more moves she was trying to put on me. I was wrong. She's a resourceful lady—I'll say that for her."

"Oh? That sounds interesting." Mandy thought a moment. "But that still doesn't explain your truck being at her house."

"We were busy getting set up at the school, and Doc MacDonald showed up, asking people where she was. She got wind of it and asked me for the keys to the truck. I didn't know at the time why she wanted them. I just gave them to her and went ahead setting up the sound system. When Doc found me and said he was looking to arrest her—"

"Arrest her!" Mandy pulled away to look up at Grange. "What for?"

"Embezzlement. She's stolen about a hundred thousand dollars from Vince in the time she's been working for him."

"Really? Fran? How did he find out?"

"He had Mo go through the books. He found how she'd done it."

Mandy combed Grange's hair away from his brow, but the wind blew it back. "I remember. Mo didn't want me to tell you about it," she said. "Why?"

"He must have felt it would be disloyal because of the bad blood that's always been between Vince and me."

"Okay. So, Doc tells you he's going to arrest her, and you do what?"

"Moses and I rode with him to Fran's, and that's when we met Stevie Joe with his story. He didn't know for certain, but he was pretty sure that when Fran left, you were with her. Doc turned on the siren and took off, and we followed in the pickup. We came upon Fran pulling out of the woods onto the highway. She took one look at Doc's cruiser and made a dash for it. He followed her, and we figured we'd look down the road where she'd been to see if you were there."

"I'm so glad you did." Mandy sighed. "You're making a habit of showing up at bad times. It's a nice habit."

"So, why did you run away yesterday?" Grange asked.

She covered her face with her hands. "Oh, it's so embarrassing."

"I told you my embarrassing story," he reminded her.

She told him how she thought he was selling moonshine to support the music program, and when she finished, Grange threw back his head and laughed.

"That cracks me up," he said, "but it doesn't explain why you ran."

"I had just discovered that—that my heart was taken, too. By you. And there you were, making yourself totally ineligible. I think that's what I was running away from. I was heartsick."

Grange chuckled and pulled her closer as they turned into the high school parking lot.

When they pulled into the parking lot, Leesie hollered, ran over, and hopped up on the running board. "Oh, Mandy! I've been worried sick! And Mom's having heart flutters."

"Mother? Is she here?"

"You didn't forget!"

"I've had a lot on my mind," Mandy said.

"I see." Leesie looked at Grange and grinned. "But imagine, Mandy. It was Fran that was doing all those things to you!"

"All what things? I know she just conked me on the head. What else?"

"The fire. The wheel that fell off. The poison. All of it."

"Fran? Our Fran? Oh, I don't—" All of a sudden Mandy remembered looking out Fran's kitchen window and wondering at the discrepancy in her story. "How do you know this, Leesie?"

"Doc MacDonald brought her in. You weren't here, so he told Mom and me all about it. Oh, Mandy, it's such a mystery! She used to work for Poppy!"

"No. That was her sister."

"That's what Fran said, but it wasn't true. Fran worked for Poppy, and she embezzled a bunch of money and went to prison for it. Mom remembers her. Apparently she was one of Poppy's favorite people until she was caught."

Mandy blinked. As she tried to process the alien information, she heard a familiar voice calling her name.

"Mother?" She sat up and looked around.

"Over here," Leesie called to their mother.

Clara Wheeler made her way through the crowd. Tall and slender, with dark brown eyes, and prematurely gray hair piled on top of her head, she was an eye-catching figure. "Oh, Mandy," she said. "What have you got yourself mixed up in?" Her eyes shifted to Grange's bearded face and back to her daughter.

Mandy rose to her knees and hugged her mother over the side of the pickup bed. "This is Grange, Mother. He's my—"

Grange broke in. "Fiancé, ma'am."

"Not yet," Mandy said, but no one paid attention to her protestations.

Leesie clapped her hands. "That's such good news! Oh, Mom, isn't that the coolest?"

"This is all too much!" Mrs. Wheeler said. "First that awful woman, and now this!"

"Fran? Have you seen her, Mother?" Mandy asked.

"Yes, and she doesn't look a thing like the Fran Porter I knew. She used to be fat and had thick glasses and buck teeth. I never would have recognized her."

"I guess that could be changed with braces, contacts, and a diet," Mandy mused. "She was always counting carbs."

Leesie explained. "When she rented the house to Mandy Steenburg, she didn't know it was Poppy Wheeler's daughter. It wasn't until I came up that she found out. When she knew you were coming up, Mom, she did everything she could to convince Mandy to leave, so there would be no chance that you would see and recognize her."

"You didn't help," Mandy said to Leesie. "She thought Poppy was coming, too, since you insist on talking as if he is still alive."

"I heard she blew a hole in the dike last night," Leesie said.

"Was that her? Lovey thought it might be Vince."

"Who's Lovey?" Leesie asked.

"Who's Vince?" Mrs. Wheeler asked.

Grange rose to kneel by Mandy and put his arm around her. "I think I may be the reason Fran blew the dike. When she left my house, she said something about making things uncomfortable for you. It was pure spite, the same reason she knocked you out and dumped you in the woods."

"Speaking of Vince," Grange went on, nodding toward the parking lot entrance where the Escalade was just pulling in, "you need to talk to him, you know."

"That's Vince?" Mrs. Wheeler eyed the SUV speculatively.

Mandy turned and looked into Grange's eyes. "I love you, Grange Timberlain. What a generous thing to say." Then she kissed him on the mouth, a long, lingering, expressive kiss in a most public place.

"Mandy!" Clara Wheeler protested.

Mandy kept her arms around his neck, but turned to look at her mother and grinned. "He looks a little rough and rustic right now, Mother, but he cleans up real good."

"Really, Mandy! What's become of you?"

She laughed. "Wait until you see what's become of our Leesie."

Mandy stood and pulled Grange up beside her. Patting his cheek, she said, "I'm going to go talk to him right now." She looked around until she spotted Vince, standing by his car, staring grimly at her. She waved, climbed out of the pickup bed, and made her way toward him.

He met her halfway. She held out both her hands, and he took them, looking intently down at her. "Doc told me what happened. Are you all right?"

"Yes, I am." When Vince continued staring, she repeated, "I'm fine. Come and walk with me." She tugged on his hand, and he followed her to the edge of the parking lot.

"Where are we going?"

"We're just walking. I want to talk to you, and I need more privacy."

"That doesn't sound good. You'll kiss Grange in front of everyone, but you need privacy to talk to me?"

Mandy didn't answer at first. They walked past Mutt Maypole's house, and she guided their progress around the corner before she spoke. "It isn't good, Vince. I won't say I wasn't attracted to you. I was. You're very . . . very, very attractive. I was flattered and very attracted to you." She glanced up at him.

He stared straight ahead, and a muscle in his jaw stood out. "You've said you were attracted three times. Was it nothing more than that?"

"Yes, it was. I admire you. I think you're an outstanding individual. I—"

Vince stopped and turned her to face him. "But not love? You've said nothing about love."

"Love, yes," Mandy said gently. "But not in the way you want, Vince."

He turned his face away.

"Let's take this road," she said. Tucking her arm in his, she drew him around another corner so they were heading back in the direction of the high school.

They walked silently. Once, Vince cleared his throat, and another time he wiped something from his eye. It wasn't until she stopped that he spoke. "Don't say anything, Mandy. I couldn't take the 'Let's just be friends' speech right now."

"I wasn't going to do that. I want you to talk to someone."

"Not right now. I couldn't—"

"I think this is just the time," Mandy insisted, leading him up a walkway.

He hung back. "I know whose house this is."

"But you don't know what she's going to say." Mandy led him to the porch and knocked on the door.

Granny Timberlain answered so promptly that Mandy knew she must have seen their approach. "Good morning, Granny," she began. "I think this is the time for you to talk to Vince."

"It's too little, too late," he said bitterly.

Granny looked at him affectionately. "My dear, we have all suffered because Buck made bad choices. I kept my distance because your mother chose not to acknowledge the Timberlain connection. That doesn't mean I didn't love you from afar."

Vince's lip curled. "How could you do that?"

"Would you like to see? I have a scrapbook full of things about you." She reached out and took him by the hand. "Come in."

As Granny drew him into her living room, Mandy stepped back. "I'll leave you two to have some private time together."

Just before the door closed, Vince sent her one last, beseeching look. That look shadowed her all the way back to the high school. But the sun broke through the clouds—the steel band was in full swing, and Mandy caught a glimpse of her mother with her hands in the air, grooving to the beat in the parking lot, along with half the county. Mandy laughed out loud and went to join her.

The afternoon was a busy, joyous affair. Mandy watched as students managed everything from parking to tech support, and Grange was the hub around which all the organization revolved. Often during the day, she caught sight of him listening intently to something a student was saying or giving directions for something that needed to be done, and invariably he would sense her gaze, look up, and their eyes would meet. It never failed to send her pulse racing.

As she and her mother wandered from one venue to another, Mandy introduced her to Millie Barlow and Edith Berman, as well as Midge Cooley, Nettie Maypole, Tammy, Mrs. Reilly, and a host of other people in the district. When it came time for Leesie's group to play, Mrs. Wheeler leaned over and said, "Enchanting. What kind of grass did you say this is?"

At seven in the evening, Mandy and her mother found seats in the gym to watch a group called the Dusty Millers. Mandy was surprised to see Rael tuning up and even more so when Mo walked onstage with his mandolin. When Lovey appeared, there was a ripple of applause and conversation, and Mandy clapped enthusiastically with the rest of the crowd, explaining to her mother the story of Lovey and Rael. There was polite applause when the fiddler and the fellow playing standup bass appeared, but when Grange walked out with his banjo, everyone stomped and cheered.

Wesley Gallant walked out onto the stage and held up his hands. When the audience quieted, he took the microphone. "As a member of the school board, I have an announcement to make. Grange Timberlain is leaving North Cascade School District."

Mandy's jaw dropped, and a babble of consternation swept around the auditorium. Wesley held up his hands again. "But—" he waited for the talking to cease "—but he's not leaving Limestone. He is to be the first director of the Sister Ethelberta Educational Foundation, which has been set up to foster academics through music."

"Who's Sister Ethelberta?" Mrs. Wheeler asked, leaning close to Mandy.

"She's a nun. I'll tell you about it later."

"The school board is in hopes that Dr. Steenburg will stay on with us and work in tandem with Grange to make sure North Cascade stays on the cutting edge of this process."

Mandy felt her cheeks grow warm as the crowd roared its approval. Grange caught her eye and winked.

"And now," Wesley continued. "Let's celebrate this occasion with music. Ladies and gentlemen, the Dusty Millers!"

Grange set the pace with the banjo, picking furiously on a swinging, uptempo song that set Clara Wheeler's toe tapping. "I didn't know he played the banjo," she said to Mandy.

Mandy's "I didn't either" made her mother raise her eyebrows.

Leesie slipped into a chair by her mother and leaned over to Mandy. "Have you seen Willow?" When Mandy shook her head, Leesie pointed to where her friend stood against the wall, smiling, clapping in rhythm, and wearing a red shirt.

The piece ended with a flourish, and Grange stepped to the microphone. "Here's a song I wrote a week or so ago, and I'd like to dedicate it to a particular lady. She knows who she is." He played eight bars of introduction to get the rest of the band on board and then began to sing in a full baritone, looking directly at Mandy.

I met a little gal on the way to school.
Her hair was curly and her eyes was brown.
She made me feel like a clumsy fool.
You know I ain't never been to town.

But I love her like a mule a-kickin'.
Love her more than banjo pickin'.
More than Granny's Sunday chicken,
You know I love that Sweetiebug.

I know she'd never look at me,
Though she flirts with all the other guys.
I'm just a Tarheel, don't you see?
But when I see her, my heart cries:

I love her like a mule a-kickin'.
Love her more than banjo pickin'.
More than Granny's Sunday chicken,
You know I love that Sweetiebug.

Sweetiebug is the one for me,
Though she's far above me.
Sweetiebug is the one I see.
I just want her to love me.

I love her like a mule a-kickin'.
Love her more than banjo pickin'.

More than Granny's Sunday chicken,
You know I love that Sweetiebug.

When the last chord died away, the room erupted in applause. Strangers around Mandy smiled at her and reached out to shake her hand and pat her on the shoulder.

"I don't get it," Mrs. Wheeler said. "Who's this Sweetiebug?"

"She's somebody who came to Limestone with an attitude," Mandy said. "But she found a new way of looking at things."

Leesie leaned over and asked, "Would that be a new paradigm?"

"That would be a Tarheel paradigm." As Mandy stood to applaud, she made a mental note to tell Grange that his song was infinitely better than flowers.

A native of New Mexico and mother of seven, Liz Adair lives in northwest Washington with Derrill, her husband of 47 years. A late bloomer, Liz published her first Spider Latham Mystery just as AARP started sending invitations to join. After writing three books in the Spider Latham series, Liz moved into romantic suspense with *The Mist of Quarry Harbor.*

Liz took a break from suspense to write *Counting the Cost,* a novel based on family history. The book won the 2009 Whitney Award and was a finalist for the Willa Award and the Arizona Publisher Association's Glyph Award.

Liz is back writing romantic suspense with *Cold River* and feels that's where she belongs. "I remember when I was a young mother with all those kids and a slender budget," she says. "I was so grateful for books that let me go places and meet people who carried on adult conversations. That's what I want to write—cheap vacations."

Heeding advice given to writers not to quit their day jobs, Liz works as a forensic scheduler on schedule delay analyses. She also serves on LDStorymakers' board of directors, is a member of American Night Writers Association, and chairs the annual Northwest Writers Retreat. Visit her blog at www. sezlizadair.blogspot.com.